THE GIRL FROM KRAKOW

THE GIRL FROM KRAKOW

Alex Rosenberg

Published by Lake Union Publishing, Seattle

www.apub.com

Amazon, the Amazon logo, and Lake Union Publishing are trademarks of Amazon.com, Inc., or its affiliates.

ISBN-13: 9781477830819
ISBN-10: 1477830812

Cover design by Shasti O'Leary-Soudant / SOS CREATIVE LLC

Library of Congress Control Number: 2015900140

Printed in the United States of America

IN MEDIAS RES

O*ctober 24, 1942.* Margarita Trushenko, *Volks-Deutsche*—ethnic German, from the east, almost an Aryan, and with papers to prove it—was on the quay, waiting for the 21:00 express to Warsaw. No, it wasn't her. It was Rita Feuerstahl, trying hard to become Margarita Trushenko. It wasn't going to be easy, Rita knew. In six years she'd never even been able to think herself into her married name. Inside she had always been Rita Feuerstahl.

How was she going to do this?

The German soldier checking documents at the platform barrier actually said *Danke* when she handed him the *Ausweis*, and again *Danke* after she had opened her case for inspection.

If you knew the truth, you'd sooner shoot me down than be korrekt.

A vacuum of fear was sucking at her intestines, the sort of cramps she had lived with through the first weeks of the occupation sixteen months before. Now it had started again—the dread, the feeling someone was playing Russian roulette with your life. She knew it would be constant for days or weeks. She decided to sit as near to the soldier on the quay as possible. A soldier offered protection. Rita . . . or rather Margarita Trushenko, *Volks-Deutsche,* needed it, waiting alone for the Lemberg train in a vast and empty train station at night. She took out the catechism booklet that had come with the forged baptismal certificate and tried to study it. Perhaps she'd be able to distract herself from the raging *angst*.

A few minutes later, an express came in from the west—from Berlin, Warsaw, Lemberg—full of officers and men on their way to join the victorious Wehrmacht divisions in the Donbas, still cutting through whole Soviet army groups. Pretending to be fixed on her catechism, Rita didn't notice the two Germans in civilian dress descending from the first-class carriage.

The German sentry did. He came to completely respectful attention as he examined their papers: one was an *Oberst*—a captain. The other was Friedrich von Richter, major general, *SS-RSHA*—Reich Security Main Headquarters, evidently traveling out of uniform. Of course, neither the sentry nor anyone else in Karpatyn that night could know that Richter wasn't SS at all, but *Abwehr*, military intelligence and an officer in the first section, responsible for code security.

She could hear them clearly.

"Herr *Generalmajor*, there is no car awaiting you here," said the sentry.

"We were not expected. Get on the telephone to Leideritz. Tell him to send a car immediately." Evidently this man already knew the name of the SS *Obersturmführer* in charge of the town of Karpatyn. What he couldn't know was that one reason he had come was sitting there on the platform waiting for a train in the opposite direction, Rita Feuerstahl. And she didn't know she was the reason either.

Once the general's car had left, the sentry came back onto the platform. Rita decided she should smile at him. He returned it with a look of complicity and a shoulder shrug, as if to say they were both better off beyond the penumbra of high-ranking officers. Rita's eyes moved from him to the dark shape of the large station, then across the switching yards to the town beyond.

She knew that even if she survived, she would never come back. Nothing to return for—not her child, certainly not her husband, Urs. Her son was less likely to survive than she was. Urs's odds in the Red Army medical corps were better, but it hardly mattered anymore. She had let him escape east, knowing he wouldn't be strong enough to survive the Germans. Then she had tried to save their son, Stefan, by sending him out of the ghetto. But he was almost certainly already dead. The child had been the only bond cementing a marriage broken early by her adultery. Now, even if she and Urs both survived the endless war, there was nothing left between them.

She could have loved Erich, whom the occupation had brought into her life, if only he had let her. Yet he must have loved her in a way, for he left her with a secret so enormous that only love could have made him disclose it. She would not have believed what he told her except for his refusal to even try to save himself. Erich could have provided himself identity papers when he secured hers. Instead, he had allowed himself to be shipped with the last few hundred from Karpatyn to the extermination camp at Belzec.

Sitting there, under the dim lights of the quay, Rita still couldn't decide if Erich had told her the truth or just a clever story to make her survive.

That night a week before, the final *Aktionen* had begun. After the news about her boy, Rita had been ready to end things. She still had the vial of potassium cyanide her husband had left behind. The Germans were going to win. The Reich would last a thousand years. She had no will to live. "Leave me to it, Erich."

They were alone in the dark.

"No, Rita. The Germans will lose. It's a matter of a few years—two or three, no more. And you will be alive to see it. I know something. But if I tell you, it could put Germany's defeat at risk."

"Well, then, keep it to yourself."

"Listen, Rita. And then try to forget . . . End of September '39, the Polish government came through Karpatyn—the commander in chief in his shiny boots, the prime minister, everyone—on the way to Romania. Well, one of the war ministry staff looked me up. We'd been close in Warsaw at the math faculty. He was carrying a typewriter case handcuffed to his wrist. And he told me why. The general staff had brought the case to the math faculty with a 'typewriter' inside it, in 1938. Only it wasn't a typewriter; it was a German code machine. Some of the research students had been put to the task of figuring out how the machine worked and to crack the code. Well, they did it. They broke the code. We started to read German signals. Too late to help against their blitzkrieg in Poland, but with the ability to read the most secret German radio messages, the Allies can't lose. Once they are fully mobilized, they have the key to winning the war. And you'll be alive when they do."

"But if they have the code, why has the German army cut through Russia like a scythe? What use has the code been to the Soviets?"

"The Reds don't have it. The general staff wasn't going to tell them when the Russians were Hitler's allies in '39. The secret is with the Brits, and they don't trust Stalin any more than the Polish government did." Rita nodded. "So, Rita, stay alive! Do anything to still be there at the end. Because it's coming, and coming sooner than anyone realizes."

"But if what you say is true, it would be crazy for me to know. The first time a policeman starts checking my documents, I could give it all away. It's a story you've invented to save me, maybe to make up for my losing Stefan. You wouldn't risk the whole outcome of the war—that would be madness . . . even if I believed you for a moment."

"Believe me, Rita. What I have said is true. As to whether it's crazy to tell you, well, there's a line about that in your favorite philosopher, Hume."

Now, looking down the tracks at the approaching train, Rita recalled the words again: "'Tis not contrary to reason to prefer the destruction of the whole world to the scratching of my finger." They had remained with her, puzzled her, amused her, disturbed her, ever since she'd first come across them.

PART I

BEFORE

CHAPTER ONE

Civil procedure was the first-year lecture course in the law faculty in Krakow. By November it had become as boring as it sounded. The only excitement Rita could still muster up for it was the frisson she felt three times a week as she edged through the narrow aisle to find her place in the lecture theater.

The nationalist students in the law faculty had taken to forcing the Jewish students to sit along one row of desks—the ghetto benches. When Rita chose to sit among the men in the ghetto benches, there were glares. The Green Ribbon bullyboys were taken aback to see the tall blonde girl sitting among the Jewish students. Some would lean back in their seats to call her a traitor, a Yid-lover, or worse, whispering that she was one of their gentile whores. Sitting there made her feel a bit heroic. It made student life a little more adventurous.

Still, after an hour, it was hard to keep awake in a hard seat high up in the unheated, ill-lit amphitheater. The sudden sound of the bell ending the lecture made Rita realize she had been dozing off. *An expensive nap*, she thought. She screwed the cap on her fountain pen, closed her notebook, and stretched. The last time she had looked up at the windows that ran around the room level with her seat high up the rear wall, the sky had been a uniform gray. But the sullen afternoon gloom had since turned a minatory black. Rita belted her trench coat. It was already too thin for the autumn weather, but cheaper than an overcoat and more fashionable.

What she needed was an hour in a warm café with her hands cupped around a large glass of tea. An espresso wouldn't last long enough to warm her.

Never mind; both were luxuries Rita had become accustomed to denying herself. It wasn't just the expense. Cafés were places to waste time arguing about politics. Each cult had its own table, a few even their own cafés. The only things the groups shared were a commitment to "free love" and a favorable ratio of young men to the few women students.

Moving slowly with the tide of bodies down the wide marble staircase, she suddenly felt herself being pulled down the steps by the loose end of her knotted trench-coat belt.

"Let go!" Loud and indignant, her voice turned several heads toward her, though not the one belonging to the elongated figure heedlessly drawing her down the steps. "What do you think you're doing?" Rita yanked back on the belt hard enough that the hand at last released it, sending its owner stumbling down the last few steps.

Catching himself on the balustrade, the man turned toward her. "I'm so sorry. I was just reaching back to grab the end of my coat belt." He looked down his frame at his open trench coat and then back up at her. "So crowded! Must have felt yours and just grabbed at it."

"Well, you might look where you put your hands." With that, Rita started down the stairs again. The man was still mumbling his excuses.

Rita passed through the broad lobby of the law faculty building. As she approached the doors, she glanced back. There he was again, right behind her—very tall, very thin, very young, she thought. His coat was now belted against the expected cold, and he was carrying a very heavy volume. He caught her eye and tried on a smile. Rita frowned back, turned, and strode toward the door.

Her pursuer was not discouraged. In the thinning crowd, he moved faster and was again finally beside Rita. "I'm so embarrassed, *Panna*—Miss . . . ?"

Rita did not supply her name. She was not in the mood to encourage him.

"Really," he protested, "it was an innocent mistake. Could have happened to anyone. How can I apologize?"

"You already have. The matter is forgotten. Good night."

Steps from the doors, the young man's hand reached out to prevent her from moving on. Rita looked down at the hand on her arm, then slowly up at its owner. "This is getting to be a habit. Another apology coming?"

He immediately released her. "I'm rather stupid about these things. Look, I'm really sorry. Can I offer you a coffee to show my contrition?" He nodded toward the cafés across the street, crowded as the night fell. Now Rita noticed the heavy book under his arm, leather with gold lettering. *Pathology.* A medical text. *So,* she thought, *a Pole.* There were few Jews at the medical school.

The chill wind coming in through the open doors got the better of Rita. "A coffee?" She shrugged. "Why not?"

They came out of the faculty into the dark, accentuated by the wan glow of the streetlamps. It was cold, and they walked quickly to the largest of the cafés in the square. As they entered from the gloom, it was almost blindingly bright. On the walls Art Deco tracery framed mirrors that went from the wainscoting to the ceiling. Beneath the mirrors spread a sea of small round tables and bentwood chairs, filled by animated talkers. It was warm and suffused by a cirrus of aromatic Virginia tobacco smoke.

They moved toward the large white and blue porcelain stove at the rear, put their books on the table, and said, simultaneously, "What's your name?" Laughing, they interrupted each other again, each answering over the other: "Urs, Urs Guildenstern." "Rita Feuerstahl." Then, for the third time, they spoke over one another's words: "Nice to meet you, Rita" and "Funny, you don't look like one—a bear, that is." They fell silent for a moment, smiling as a waiter approached.

Urs looked from the waiter to Rita, who immediately said, "A large café au lait." He was paying, and the breakfast-style coffee might just as well provide supper. Urs followed with, "Tea, please."

As they waited, there was a chance to look each other over. He was still very tall sitting across from her. His lean cheeks were marked out by a tracery of small, dark points. Dark curly hair was already thinning back from a widow's peak, despite his age, which she guessed at early twenties. But it was the long and narrow nose that dominated his features.

Looking at Rita, Urs saw a woman tall enough for him. Her blonde hair loose to the shoulders, straight, not bobbed. A lank of it curved down and across her rather broad forehead. Blue eyes and high cheekbones beneath fair skin made Rita look altogether more German or Ukrainian than anything else.

The drinks arrived. Rita began, "So, you are a medical student," gesturing toward the volume on the table. He nodded, and she went on, "From Warsaw?"

"No, I'm from a town in the east." Only now as Urs spoke could she detect a slight trace of eastern, in fact, Yiddish-inflected, Polish.

"But you're Jewish," she blurted. "How did you get into Polish medical school?"

"Hard work, and some luck, I guess. They do hold ten percent of the places for Jews." He paused. "You're actually the first Christian who's twigged to my background before asking."

"Well, that's because I am the first Christian you've met who's just another Yid."

"No! I figured you for the complete *BDM* girl. Blonde, blue-eyed . . ." Rita looked at him quizzically. Before she could ask, Urs explained. "*BDM, Bund Deutscher Mädel—League of German Girls.* It's the female side of the Hitler Youth. So we're both mistaking each other for what we are not. Shall we start again?"

"Actually, I'm relieved," Rita confessed. "There are limits to my interest in assimilation, and I was sure you were Polish nobility."

"Both our families can rest easy, I guess."

By now Rita had warmed up. "So, what were you doing in the law faculty today? Trolling for Aryan-looking women law students?"

"No, I'm final year. We have to write a research paper. Mine's on forensic medicine, and I needed to look up a case. What about you? Pretty pointless, a woman studying law, especially a Jew. No government posts: 'No Jews, no women need apply.' Politics interest you?"

"Not much," she lied. "How about you? Interested in politics?"

"Just medicine, thank you."

Rita smiled. "Smart. Seems to me men here get interested in politics mainly to meet girls. Anyway, I'm studying law because it's the only faculty I could get into."

"So, what will you do with the law?"

Rita shrugged. "I don't know. Maybe nothing. Probably I'll just go home when I've finished. But there's always a chance . . . first-class marks on the examinations, catch the interest of a professor . . . There's a chance." Rita finished her coffee and then looked at her watch for an excuse to end the conversation and get away. "It's late, and I have some work to do."

Without thinking, Urs reached for her hand. "Can I see you again?"

"You can usually find me in the philosophy faculty library." And she was gone.

∾

Why did she tell him where she could be found? *Better stay away from there the next few days if you don't want to see this guy again soon.*

Maybe she wouldn't mind seeing him again. In any case, it would be hard to steer clear of the philosophy library. Even the glare of the other students, all men, could not keep her out. She enjoyed their looks of discomfort when they found a woman opposite them at the table reading Kant or Plato. It wasn't so different from the looks of the law school bullyboys when she sat down among the men in the ghetto benches.

All too often, sitting there under the lamps breaking the gloom of the reading room, she'd lose the thread of what she was reading and begin to ask herself for the thousandth time the questions Urs had asked. *What exactly are you doing here, Rita? What did you really come for?* It wasn't the law, not really.

She wanted a life. She wanted what any twenty-year-old did who knew she was very smart, almost beautiful, willing to take a chance, put her optimism to the test. She wasn't going to find those tests in her father's town or anywhere near it. Sometimes Rita wondered whether it was emancipation she yearned for or apostasy. At fourteen she had forced her parents to send her to the only girl's gymnasium in town, operated by the Dominican sisters. By that time, in a school uniform, Rita was already tall, angular, looking out of place in her mother's kitchen.

The required Catholic catechism class quickly confirmed her as an unbeliever. And atheism made it easy to reject her own culture's patriarchy. But wasn't it really just an excuse for doing something she wanted to do anyway: go her own way in life, not the one prescribed for her? Was it apostasy just to want to be yourself?

Be yourself? Who exactly was she, anyway? *Who is it, really, peering out at the world from inside my body, and why did it turn out to be me?* She had felt she needed to answer this question as far back as she could remember. She wasn't going to in a small town in Silesia.

So she had announced an attachment to the law and come to Krakow.

Three days after their first meeting, there was Urs, at the bottom of the marble staircase of the fac', waiting for the end of civil procedure. "I've been looking for you in the philosophy faculty library the last couple of days. That's where you said you'd be."

Rita was not really surprised. "I was indisposed. Studied in my rooms." *Rooms? As if I have more than one*, she laughed to herself.

"May I take you out for supper?"

Why not, was her first thought, but she replied, "It's a bit early . . ."

"I'll come for you at seven o'clock. Just give me your address."

"No. I'll meet you. Tell me where." She was not about to reveal where she lived. That would be much too forward, and the address was not nearly chic enough. For Rita, lodgings were a fifth-floor walk-up bedsit across the Vistula, in the only tenements poorer students could afford. The wallpaper was peeling, and the threadbare stair carpet covered treads that had been sagging since the nineteenth century. They groaned, even under her light step. Her room was no worse than most. A bed, a deal table and chair, a standing cupboard, a bureau on which sat a chipped but serviceable ewer and bowl, all illuminated by a bare electric bulb hanging from where a gas lamp used to shed a dimmer light. Plumbing had been installed on the floors below Rita's, but the remains of an outhouse could still be seen at the back of what passed for a garden. Under the bed there was a chamber pot, nothing even the better-off weren't used to. There was a gas ring for warming meals. The only real problem was the cold. Rita was always cold. Staying warm—enough coal in the grate—was dearer than life, and Rita could never afford it.

"How about Wierzynek?" he suggested. It was the best restaurant in Krakow, and it was warm.

~

Rita was in Market Square by six thirty, walking slowly along the arcades. She watched the town hall clock tower's angle change as she moved along the vast quadrangle. It had rained briefly, and the paving stones still glistened, reflecting the streetlights up onto the Bohemian spires of St. Mary's Basilica, looming in shafts of moonlight that broke through the clouds.

She should have declined this invitation. Urs seemed too serious. But when would she get another chance to dine in near splendor, at a table covered by starched linen, set with heavy silver, laden with china and crystal, beneath the mullioned windows and heavy beams of a formal dining room?

Rita stopped under a portico from where she could watch the restaurant's entry door. Let Urs get there first. What if he didn't come? Wouldn't she look the fool, asking the *maître d'* for his table? And if he did come, well, let him be seated and wait, stewing awhile before she made an entrance.

It was 6:55 when she saw him walking across the square. Rita was getting cold. She waited only a brief moment and caught up with him at the entry. "Shall we go in?" she said brightly. He smiled, relief spreading across his face. Evidently each had had doubts about whether the other would turn up.

She took his arm as they strode past the heavy velvet door curtains. Urs gave his name, and they were led to a table.

Men preferred talking to listening, Rita reflected. "So, tell me about yourself."

He was from Karpatyn, a large town five hundred kilometers southeast of Krakow, beyond Lvov, on the Dnieper, just north of the Romanian border. A few Poles, but mainly Ukrainians and Jews. "My father is a doctor. I'll go back to join his practice next year." He fell silent.

"Anything else?"

"I'm not interested in much besides medicine. And you . . .?"

"I'm from a little town in Silesia you never heard of, Gorlice." It was one hundred kilometers south of Krakow, near the Czechoslovak border. "My grandfather is in lumber, sawmills in Nowy Sacz. He's the one paying for me to be here." Urs nodded in recognition of the name. "But there were too many children—twins run in on my grandmother's side—so he sent one son to start a lumberyard in Gorlice. That's my father. No head for business. He and my mother never had twins. Just me. I don't look forward to going back."

A silence descended between them.

Urs broke it. "So, what are you going to do?" There was that question again. Rita had no more of an answer than the first time he'd asked. A grave look came over his face. Rita turned to the menu.

Urs's thoughts were indeed solemn. Rita was the first woman that had ever seriously interested him. In three days he had become very serious about her. He needed an answer to his question. Everyone always said Urs Guildenstern was too serious. He was certainly cautious, methodical. Not exactly calculating, but he weighed things up carefully before acting. It went along with the anxiety that drove him. There was always something to worry about. Now he took on Rita's problem.

Finally Rita replied, "What am I going to do? I think I'll order."

She couldn't know it then, but that evening was the beginning of the end of the law faculty for Rita. By the spring she was already planning her life as a doctor's wife. At Easter they visited his family. In the summer they married at her grandfather's home in Nowy Sacz. At the end of September, after a wedding trip to Warsaw and the Baltic, Rita and Urs made the long journey three hundred kilometers east to Lvov, and then another two hundred south to Karpatyn.

౿

Months later, sitting alone in her warm flat, she asked herself how it had happened. Had she grown tired of always being cold and mostly alone in the Krakow bedsit? Had she been too easily daunted by the likelihood of a bleak future with a useless law degree? Worn down by the boredom of contracts and torts? Or had she simply surrendered to her family's insistence that nothing could come of her studies?

Why had she given in and stopped swimming against the tide? The answer that felt most convincing was a calculation that the world would not let her have the outward life she sought. Marrying Urs, being comfortable, would at least allow her the inner life she really wanted. She'd be able to scratch the itch of the questions that had driven her into the philosophy library; Urs had happily bought her book after book that first spring together. Then there was the unspoken anticipation of sex.

Rita had looked forward to the intimacy of marriage. Her brushes with sex had been pleasurable enough. Twice she had found herself with a fellow student in the last row of a Krakow cinema, kissing instead of watching, tasting each other's tongues. Both times, when they turned back to the screen, Rita would begin to feel the boy's arm moving across her back. The hand would casually drape itself down her shoulder, then the fingers would slowly crawl along her breast till they were moving over the nipple beneath her blouse and camisole. The pleasurable warmth and moistness it produced told her she could gladly anticipate the carnal dimension of marriage. But she stopped the boy whenever he tried to move his hand toward her lap. In bed alone, she didn't stop herself, enjoying the driving throb that would finally crest into . . . what did the French call it? *La petite mort.* Now she hoped making love with her husband might be all the love she would need.

In Krakow, spending time with Urs had been easy. Once he began to pay court, she didn't need to stint on the small things—a coffee, a pair of gloves, a nicer fountain pen, all those philosophy books. First, she became accustomed to little indulgences, and then to expect them. But she knew well enough that it wasn't love that had seduced her.

She had declined Urs's first few proposals. She tried to convince him that his feelings were not enough to build a marriage on. But instead she concluded that not feeling much of anything was not an insurmountable obstacle. There was enough of everything else: they were of the same religion, and he was of the right class. Neither of them was going to do any better. Eventually, with a little help from her parents, she accepted the match as fated. When he raised marriage for the third time, she accepted.

Well after they arrived in Karpatyn, Pan Doctor Guildenstern, Urs's father, remained formal. The Polish *Pan* had all the hoary honorific overtones of its German equivalent, *Herr*—not just Monsieur or Mr., but something that put the taste of obsequiousness in your mouth. The whole family was a bit wooden, even with each other, and the more so with this exotic girl who spoke "Warsaw" Polish and carried herself like a Krakow university student.

Even after months the slight but persistent chill remained in her in-laws' very correct demeanor. A trace of formality would cling to Urs when he came back to the flat from the office he shared with his father, often stopping halfway at his parents' house. An only child, Urs was right to be attentive to his mother. But did he need to carry his respectful demeanor home every night?

Really, though, Rita had nothing to complain of but a certain ennui, lassitude, routine. She was warm now, always. There was plenty to eat, and as much coffee as she wanted. She had declined a maid to begin with and learned housework by trial and error. Cooking came naturally, and it gave her a reason to do the marketing, to get out of the flat, to explore the town.

Rita's first impressions of Karpatyn had not been so bad. It was a town of forty thousand rising up on the flat Galician plain. That first time, most of the way from Lvov, the train had rattled alongside country lanes rutted by a fresh rain, under looming clouds. The rutted lanes between the fields began to broaden. They turned into hard-packed roads, flat and broad enough for the farm wagons that trundled into town behind large workhorses. The first houses she saw were attached to barns, rough-hewn, with plaster between the logs. Closer in, the buildings were mainly brick. Some with smokestacks had to be factories. Now the streets crossing the tracks began to be paved, lined by wispy plain trees with whitewashed trunks, but too spindly to be pruned in the French manner. Nearer the town square, the houses were stuccoed and painted white and pastel colors. A few were dressed in stone.

The train finally came to a halt beside a vast railway station, a pile built in Viennese style to assert Austro-Hungarian imperial authority. Through the entrance hall, Rita and Urs emerged onto the main square.

Rita looked around and smiled. She could live here. The trapezoidal square enclosed a stand of mature trees and was lined with shops, cafés, even a cinema. And there were what looked like streetcar tracks leading away from the square. Was this town large enough for a tramway? Down the track there were some multistory buildings that would not have looked out of place in Warsaw. A motorbus was moving slowly down this broad street toward the square. Yes, she could live here.

The flat Urs had found them was in one of the newer buildings, close enough to the main square to see the warm glow of electric lights, which had only recently replaced the gas lamps.

Thursdays there was a farmers' market in the square. Twice a week elderly men and flat-faced women in kerchiefs presided over root vegetables in winter, orchard fruit in the summer, and bigbulbed green onions, long leeks, and potatoes all round the year. There were scrawny, half-plucked chickens, sows' knuckles, and too frequently for Rita, a baby pig's ear. Sometimes when one of the older men made change and handed it to her, she thought she could detect a suppressed tug at the forelock, as though the rituals of serfdom had not yet been entirely shed.

Rita persisted in shopping at the open market, though her mother-in-law frowned on the practice. It was a sore point Pani Doctor picked at whenever she stopped at Rita's flat, and she did not disappoint on this day, well into Rita's new, married life in Karpatyn.

"Give your trade to the Jewish shops, not those anti-Semites."

"The produce is fresher, and the prices are lower. Besides, they are perfectly nice to me."

"Nice to your money. Or maybe nice to your blonde hair. Besides, what if you get something that isn't kosher?"

Rita blurted out, "I'm not keeping particularly kosher."

"Not keeping particularly kosher?" Her mockery turned to anger. "Why don't you get slightly pregnant while you're not keeping particularly kosher?" With that, Mother Guildenstern strode out the door.

Willing herself to be unperturbed, Rita sat down again. She picked up the book she had hidden under a cushion when her mother-in-law had turned up. It was Freud's *Civilization and Its Discontents*, an easy read in the original German. The aroma of a cigarette, the slight sting in her nostrils as smoke emerged in two dissipating clouds, might help transport her back to her bedsit in Krakow. Putting down the book, she lit one.

After a few minutes, she realized it wasn't going to work this time. Pani Doctor's words kept intruding. But it wasn't Rita's fault. Urs seemed to have little more interest in sex after they married than before. That last year in Krakow, she had been ready enough to fend him off when he brought her back to the bedsit or collected her for a walk, a film, or dinner, but it hadn't been necessary. He never advanced beyond holding her hand in the movies, a chaste kiss on the cheek when they met, and squeezing her when she had agreed to marry him. He wasn't anything like the students who argued politics and advocated free love.

She thought it was just his strict upbringing—saving himself. He was certainly no prude. Once they decided to marry, Urs demonstrated a thorough (if clinical) enough understanding of sex. He owned a *Marriage Manual* translated from the French that advocated foreplay to ensure the woman was prepared and satisfied. Urs put it at her disposal a few weeks before the ceremony with no evident sign of discomfort. She made a point of returning it dog-eared at the page on the subject of the woman's pleasure.

On their wedding night, both parties' homework with the *Marriage Manual* had paid off, at least to the extent of provoking no embarrassment. But thereafter Urs was not inclined to importune his new wife for sex. He seemed satisfied with no more of it than once a week, typically Friday evenings. On other nights Rita sent out signals that she would not repel advances—parading through the flat in nightgowns of low décolletage—yet Urs rarely even loosened a tie much before bedtime.

He was prepared to leave pregnancy to the coincidence between Friday nights and the peak of her cycle of fertility. But now it had been almost a year since their marriage.

∾

Beyond the farmers' market lay the other main attraction of Karpatyn, Jastrob's bookstore. Rita was there at least twice a week, once to change her book at the lending library Jastrob's operated, and again to look at the latest magazines and newspapers from Warsaw and Krakow that were available nowhere else in town. *Mr.* Jastrob was nowhere to be seen, but Mrs. Jastrob didn't seem to mind her browsing.

One afternoon in June 1937, almost a year after her arrival in town, Rita was just leaving the bookshop when her glance directed at the magazine rack. Distracted, she ran right into a rather short, dapper young man. His smile raised a pencil mustache above his upper lip. It was black, like his pomaded hair, and he was rather fashionably dressed for a Polish market town on a weekday afternoon: two-tone Italian summer shoes, a houndstooth coat over tan trousers, and no tie and the shirt collar spreading over the jacket lapels, like the American crooners you could see in the movies. Or maybe he looked like one of those French film stars—Pierre Fresnay? A thinner Marcel Dalio?

"Excuse me." He grinned. But he didn't move on.

"My fault. I was not looking where I was going." She smiled back.

"Where were you going?"

Rather forward, she thought. "Out. Good-bye." She was already a few meters down the footpath when he caught up with her. This was really rather cheeky. "I am a married woman." She waved her left hand at him.

"My interests are literary, not romantic. I just noticed you were carrying my favorite novel out of the shop."

"What's that?

He looked down at the book in her hand. "It's Remarque, *Three Comrades*."

"But it just arrived." Rita held it toward him. "As you can see, it's so new the pages haven't been cut. I'm the first one in town to read it. So it can hardly be your favorite already." Having put him in his place, she started to walk away. The book was due back in a week, and she wanted to make a start on it.

The young man replied to her back. "I didn't get it from my mother's bookstore. I read the French translation in Barcelona last year." Rita turned back. "Permit me to introduce myself. Tadeusz Sommermann. Jastrob was my mother's maiden name. Her parents started the bookshop." He offered his hand. She took it. He held it just slightly too long.

"What were you doing in Barcelona?" Not every day she met someone who had been in Spain.

"I am a medical officer in one of the International Brigades."

Rita let out a slight gasp. Here was someone worth talking to.

"I go back soon," he said. "May I buy you a coffee?" Somehow his imminent departure made the invitation a little less brash.

"No, but you may call on my husband, Dr. Guildenstern, and me for tea, and tell us about Spain. We would be very interested."

"Your husband is Urs! I have been gone a long time! He gave me this once playing soccer." Tadeusz pointed at the break across his nose. "I'll be only too glad to come."

They fixed a date, and he turned back to the store. Instantly Rita noticed how much more alive she felt, part of Europe again.

৵

The phone rang. Urs rose, carefully placed his cup of tea on the sideboard, and went to the hall. After a moment he returned and said, "I'm on call, and it's a burst appendix. I'll probably be the night at the clinic. So sorry." He turned to Tadeusz. "No reason for you to go. I am so sorry you leave tomorrow. How long before you will be back again from Spain?" Urs asked the question as he pulled a woolen scarf around his neck and headed for the door.

"No idea. It depends on how well the Loyalists can fight. Everyone expects an offensive on the Ebro this summer. The better they fight, the longer I'll be able to stay."

Urs nodded, mulling over this bit of analysis. Then he left. But Rita was interested.

"I will worry about you." She did look concerned. The news from Spain had been bad for the Republic steadily now for months.

Tadeusz realized he was going to have to tell her something approximating the truth at some point. He liked her far too much to keep lying. "Don't concern yourself about me. I am leaving the brigades soon. I have an offer to work in a women's hospital in Barcelona." This he thought of as more a transformation into truth than another lie. He had never gone near the front and had been at the hospital for more than a year.

"I'm so glad. Will you take the offer?"

"Should I?"

"Yes, you must," she replied a little too eagerly, surprised that she would already care.

"I'll tell you about it if you will allow me to write to you . . ."

Rita felt she should frown at this suggestion, but she didn't.

Tadeusz had spent the afternoon answering their questions about six years in Paris, then the south of France, now Cataluña at war, while trying to learn what he could about her. The past year living in the predominantly women's world of a maternity hospital had taught him how to listen to women. He waited for Rita to say something.

She sat opposite him, drawing a long breath on her cigarette. The afternoon had transported Rita back to days in Krakow, sitting, slouching, sometimes sprawled across a bed, among other students in someone's rooms, feeling languid and lazy after a week's lectures, knowing one could sleep in, contemplating—but only contemplating—temptation. Why had she ever given up Krakow?

Suddenly, in the silence, there was a slightly electric atmosphere in the room. Both were asking themselves the same question: when would they ever be alone like this again? Knowing the answer they began mutually to explore the possibility before them, trying to measure it without risking a rebuff. Together they began a little pas de deux, dancing in what would turn out to be the same direction, but neither taking an irrevocable step.

"Well, you've told us your adventures." She paused. "What are you looking forward to?"

He thought for a moment and began, "Working in a women's clinic will be very different. Of course, the Spanish Republic is rather like the Soviet Union. Women have all the same rights as men. They reach high in politics, even serve in the army. Contraception and abortion are allowed in Barcelona. Doctors are expected to discuss marital relations with their patients. These are

things I will have to do at the women's clinic—providing contra-
ceptives, performing abortions."

Contraception was one thing, abortion another. Rita wanted to
signal she had no trouble with the former. "It's hard to see how you
can agree to carry out abortions. It's against all the teachings of all
the religions—ours, the Catholic church, the reformed denomina-
tions, everyone. It must be wrong."

"I agree, it's difficult to reconcile oneself to it. But so far as the
scruples of religion go, they won't stop me."

"So, you are an atheist?" Rita's observation was obvious, but it
was also another test of the possibilities.

"Yes, but even if I wasn't, religion wouldn't help me with this
problem."

"Why not?" Suddenly she was focused on what he was saying,
not what he might be signaling.

"Here's an argument I heard in Paris that I can't shake. Take
the prohibition of abortion. God forbids it, right? So, is that why
it's wrong, just because he forbids it? Or did God forbid abortion
because it's wrong? Which is it?"

Rita thought she knew what was coming. Should she cut him
short? No, he wouldn't like that. At least he was talking about
something interesting. It made a change from Urs. She replied, "So,
wrong because forbidden by God, or forbidden by God because
wrong? It's obvious. Forbidden by God because it's wrong."

Tadeusz nodded. "Right. Now, if abortion is really wrong, there
must be something about it that makes it wrong, something besides
the fact that God forbids it. What could that be?"

"Well. It's wrong. It's killing; it's murdering innocent lives."

"Rita, you haven't answered the question. Why is it wrong? It
can't be just because God forbids it. We've ruled that answer out.
It must be something about killing itself that makes it wrong, bad,

evil." He stopped to secure her assent. Then he continued, "That's presumably what God has figured out about killing—what makes it wrong. That's why he imposed the rule against it. But what is it about abortion that he's figured out? Something about abortion itself that makes it wrong, not just God's rule against it."

It was a version of a subversive argument Rita remembered from Plato, but she wasn't going to mention it now. "So, what is the answer—what is it about abortion that makes it wrong?"

"I don't know. But the point is, God's saying it's wrong can't be what makes it wrong. When it comes to right and wrong, we have to think for ourselves." Tadeusz thought, *Will she see the argument works just as well for "Thou shalt not commit adultery"?*

Rita rose. "Somewhere Dostoyevsky writes, 'If God doesn't exist, everything is permitted.'" She walked out of the sitting room and turned down the darkened hallway to the bedroom.

When she came back, four or five minutes later, she was wearing a dark blue silk dressing gown, the white tassel inscribing a soft curve as she walked past Tadeusz, went to the front door, locked it, and threw the bolt. Slowly Rita turned around and walked through the apartment, methodically turning off every light in the house. In the twilight she stood, looked down at him, still in a chair, while their eyes adjusted. Crooking a finger, she led him back down the corridor to the darkened bedroom.

He found himself sitting back on the bed, with Rita looming above him astride his legs. He could hear the rustle of the slightly stiff dressing gown as it moved over her stockings. At thigh height, the rising hem revealed garters holding stockings, then a belt, but no panties. A tuft of fur no darker than the blonde above made a triangle between the belts. She had obviously left all but the panties to be removed. Slowly he did so, unclipping each fastener from its form-fitted holder, and rolling down the hose, as she continued to hold up the gown. Now she opened the robe to reveal the belt floating loosely at her waist, the ribboned fasteners no longer moored to the stockings but black against her white thighs. He decided on an approach Rita would remember. It was one of several things he had learned in Paris years before.

CHAPTER TWO

Not everything Tadeusz Sommermann said that afternoon was a complete lie. He had been in Barcelona, and he was going back. He had treated a few combat casualties from the International Brigades. Remember that Englishman with the look-alike pencil mustache and the bullet wound in his throat? What a waste to be maimed like that. It was the Spaniards' Civil War, not his. Of course, he knew what side he was on. The "Nationalists"—that's what they called themselves—were just fascists, openly armed by Hitler and Mussolini. Their *caudillo*, their *Führer*, Franco, didn't have any qualms about using Moroccan shock troops. Surely there was more useful work Tadeusz could do than stop a Moorish bullet while pumping morphine into some illiterate Republican foot soldier's thigh. He would support the Spanish Republic. That it was supported by several different communist parties in Spain and by Stalin's Soviet Union didn't trouble Tadeusz at all. But he was neither a Stalinist party hack nor a supporter of POUM, the Trotskyite party. Paris had made him "a plague on both your houses" leftist. He needed to preserve his freedom of action, even on the barricades of the Popular Front.

The idea of going to Spain had come to him when he first heard about the International Brigades, after his final year of medical lectures in Marseille. Tadeusz had begun his medical degree in Paris. For two years he had allowed its distractions to seduce him. He needed to get away if he was ever to complete his medical qualification. Moving to Marseille, he enrolled in the faculty of tropical medicine. It was open to foreigners, and afterward posts in a French colony—Senegal or Guyana—were not hard to secure. Few French medical students really wanted to spend a half dozen years in Dakar or Cayenne. But the closer he came to climbing up the gangplank of some colonial *paquebot*, the more distasteful grew the prospect of serving as a colonial health officer. There had to be an alternative.

There always had been. He had always found the intelligent alternative before—a way around obstacles, hardships, challenges—as far back as his childhood.

From the time he was a small boy, Tadeusz knew that his mother's bookshop was not for him. He loved reading: first the endless stream of Karl May westerns shelved behind the counter to reduce pilfering, then the histories—especially Napoleon, and finally the Marxian scholars who made sense of Napoleon and everything that came after him. History was intoxicating. But reading books was not the same as selling them. He couldn't be tethered to Jastrob's Bookshop.

Tadeusz had been good at school, and better at chess, which was fortunate since he had neither the physique for heavy labor nor the temperament for poker. At fourteen or so, it was clear. The way out was a profession. That meant university abroad. He could never bring himself to study as hard as he'd need to for a chance in Poland.

Tadeusz would have liked to study history. But there were problems. First, by the time he finished gymnasium, Tadeusz had already acquired a pretty tolerable understanding of the course of human events over the previous several centuries. There wasn't much more to learn once he had discovered scientific socialism. Plekhanov's *Materialist Conception of History* was really all you needed. At twenty, he'd read enough to see that history was an open book. He understood everything now.

But even if there had been more to learn about history, there was no living in it. If he were to escape Jastrob's Bookshop, Karpatyn, or Galicia, for that matter, it would have to be medicine, six years of it, and in another country.

Italy would have been the best bet for medical school. With an Italian qualification, one could work in the British Empire. Entry was not difficult, the fees were manageable, and living was cheap. He'd have to learn Italian. No problem. Tadeusz was good at languages. But Italy was a fascist state, operated by a dictator who made Pilsudski seem like a democrat. France was a better choice. And besides, French was so much more useful a language than Italian. Most of all there was the allure of Paris. The *Faculté de Médecine* was on the Left Bank, a stone's throw from the Latin Quarter.

He had only to convince his mother. She held the purse strings.

∾

Paris didn't make it easy to be a medical student. There was just too much to distract a young man with a world historical understanding.

Tadeusz arrived in the early summer of 1932. Three months would be enough to learn the French he needed before the lectures began in the fall. He found a room on Monsieur le Prince, between the Boulevard St. Michel and the Place Odeon, at the back corner of the medical faculty. The first night he tried to treat himself to a meal at the Crémerie Polidor. The waitresses were famous for surly service to customers seated at communal tables. Frustrated trying to decipher the handwritten menu dropped casually before him at the table, he had to go back outside to study the posted printed one with his Polish-French dictionary in hand.

Even through the language barrier, Paris was exactly what Tadeusz had hoped for. There were a few Polish medical students who eased his entry to the Fac' while playing mild practical jokes on him. Sending him to a haberdashery for a *capot*—a condom—when he wanted a *chapeau*, a hat, for instance. As for the lectures at the Fac', it didn't take very long to see that they were not going to help much anyway. There would be an exam—the *extern*—at the end of two years, filtering those who were capable and serious from the rest. But these lectures wouldn't help.

Two years was a long way off that first fall. Of much more immediate interest were the risqué novels of André Gide and the work of a new author, Louis Aragon. They would help his French, which was just as important as anatomy or physiology. Even more seductive were the politics of the Third French Republic. The Socialist Party was led by Leon Blum; the Communists followed Thorez, who obeyed Stalin; the Trotskyites obeyed Trotsky (or tried to); and the anarchists followed no one at all.

∽

When he looked back on that time, it was smells he remembered most: acrid smoke from the blue cloud of a hundred Galois drifting below the ceiling of a café on a winter's day, the smell of the ground coffee as he stood waiting for a morning *express* at the *zinc*, the ozone draft of a metro leaving the station at Châtelet while the portillon gates opened to a new scrum of passengers, the starch and bleach at a *blanchisseur* in the Rue de Vaugirard, all its windows thrown open on a hot day in May, and all the year round, the early morning aroma of *boulangeries*.

The most permanent of these memories was the scent of Arpège perfume—an ineffable mixture of peach, iris, rose, geranium, and a dozen other hints he couldn't identify. Anywhere, anytime, for the rest of his life, Arpège would instantly bring back the first time he encountered it, that second summer in Paris. It was wafting from the sloping shoulders of a young woman wearing an off-the-shoulder blouse loose enough you were sure it was about to fall below the breasts it clearly silhouetted. Her thick black hair was cut in a plain, almost Chinese style—bangs at the front, falling to a perfectly even length across her neck and shoulders. Her eye makeup suggested the Orient too, accentuating heavy lashes under dark eyebrows. Was it eye shadow she wore, or was it fatigue? He couldn't tell. Below the thin muslin blouse, against which nipples visibly pushed, there was a dark peasant skirt, no stockings, and flat shoes. And the Arpège . . .

She was plastering a poster for the ICL on a wall of the Rue Racine side of the Ecole de Médecine, blotting out the first word of the prominent notice—"*Défense d'Afficher*" (Post No Bills)—in black letters on the gray stone wall. One look from her, and Tadeusz was instantly inducted into her own special cell of the ICL—the Trotskyite International Communist League. He stopped and pretended to read the poster.

Her name was Lena, though he didn't learn it till later. With almost the first words out of her mouth, it was evident that she too was Polish, though much more fluent in French. "Going to report me to a *flic* for defacement?"

Tadeusz smiled. "Only if it's a violation of revolutionary morality. You're Polish, yes?"

"My nationality is proletarian. But I was born in Warsaw."

"I'm from around Stanislava." She didn't seem to care, so he asked her about the bill she was posting.

"It's for a meeting. Read for yourself." She turned and started down Monsieur le Prince, looking for more blank walls. He stayed and read through the hectoring prose until he found the time and place.

෨

The meeting was that very evening, in an amphitheater at the Sorbonne. Tadeusz was early, finding a seat back far enough to scan the room for her. The *amphi* was half full when she came in, and just a little later proceedings began. As the speaker began, Tadeusz realized the subject wasn't French politics, but Germany. The speaker's theme was the complicity of the German Communist Party in the election that had just brought Hitler to power. Following Stalin's orders the German Communists had stood aside and let the Nazis win. Their slogan had been *Nach Hitler Uns*—After Hitler, it's our turn. But the German Communists would never get a turn now, the speaker assured all, and Stalin's Russia would reap the whirlwind. Employing all the tools of dialectic, he predicted an inevitable war between Nazism and Stalin's state fascism that would usher in world revolution.

It all made perfect sense, but Tadeusz was just waiting for the meeting to end. When it did after an hour or so, he managed his exit so that Lena found herself beside him in Place de la Sorbonne. She was fumbling in her purse for matches when he lit her cigarette. "*Merci.*" She looked up at him. "Oh, it's you." She smiled. She was still wearing that thin blouse, and it was still threatening to fall away from her shoulders.

"I didn't report you."

"To the police or Stalin's stooges in the Comintern?"

"Neither. Can I buy you a glass of something?" She nodded, and they moved to the nearest of the four cafés on the Place de Sorbonne. Wordlessly she led him to the inside seats—cheaper and a little more secluded. He liked that.

She lit another cigarette from the stub of her first and offered him one. They ordered two *blondes*, light Alsatian lagers. "So, did you buy all that talk in the meeting?" She exhaled. Her skeptical tone surprised him.

"Didn't you?"

"Not a word."

"But you helped organize the meeting."

"It's the family business. My father is on the political committee of the ICL. You don't have to believe in the lyrics to like the melody."

"I thought the analysis was correct."

She frowned. "The only times dialectical materialism is right about what's going to happen, it's right by accident."

Part of him wanted to argue. But he didn't want to put her off. "It makes a lot of sense," he hedged.

"Yes, *Das Kapital* is a wonderful story. But good stories are easy to make up. Too easy. When it came to predicting the future, Marx got just about everything wrong." When Tadeusz failed to contradict her, she decided to carry on. "The only thing Marxism ever got right was the emptiness of bourgeois morality. But Marxists don't realize their analysis destroyed proletarian values too."

"I don't follow." Tadeusz didn't like admitting it. But he liked listening to her.

"It's all in *The German Ideology*."

Tadeusz looked at Lena blankly.

"That's the title of a book by Marx you haven't read yet." She went on unbidden. "Anyway, Marx was right about bourgeois morality. But he didn't realize his analysis applies to his own values too. When the dictatorship of the proletariat is achieved, it will just be another case of the economic substructure, the new means of production, determining a new set of values. But that won't make them right."

"What are you saying?" She was going much too fast for him.

"Look, five hundred years ago, *le droit du seigneur* was established morality."

"What's that?" Tadeusz was now totally out of his depth. This woman knew more history than he did.

Lena decided to slow down. "The feudal lord had the right to a night with a maiden before her marriage to one of his vassals. Three hundred years later, *le droit du seigneur* is rape, and the French Revolution proclaims the rights of man and of the citizen. *D'accord*—OK? Now people own their labor, and they can sell to the highest bidder. What makes that a moral improvement? It's just a change forced on everyone by the industrial revolution. When the proletariat finally seizes power, will that make communist morality right? Only if feudalism made *le droit du seigneur* right. Get it?" She fell silent.

He thought he understood. "What will make proletarian morality right?"

She glared at him. "Nothing will. There is no right and wrong; there's just what the means of production force on us."

"That's not Marxism. That's nihilism. Where did you get these ideas?"

She shrugged. "Let's just say they're going around."

"I'm confused. You go about pasting up posters in places you could get caught by the *flics*. You go to meetings where students and workers are rallied to the cause of the left. But you don't really share these values?"

"You don't get it. Of course I'm for the revolution. But that doesn't make me right. It's just a matter of taste. I told you I don't believe the lyrics. I just like the tune." Lena lit another cigarette and pulled at a watch pinned to the blouse. Suddenly Tadeusz was afraid she was going to leave. He didn't want the evening to end. "Can I buy another round?"

"I have a better idea. Let's go down to the Latin Quarter, get a bottle of wine, and take it to my place."

As they walked down the Boul' Mich toward the Seine, she casually slipped her arm through his, and he could again smell the trace of Arpège. Her nationality may have been proletarian, but her citizenship was Parisian.

Outwardly stolid, Tadeusz was giddy with expectation. He never expected to lose his virginity so young and so easily. Why had she taken him up? Was it simply that he had been willing to listen?

They drifted down the hill, under the leafy plane trees, past the ruins of the Cluny. Lena's thigh brushing against his, Tadeusz ceased to envy the couples they passed. The avenue opened up at the vast bronze statue of the winged Saint Michel facing the Seine. The *place* was alive with groups and couples and the ubiquitous *clochards*—winos—cadging spare change.

They turned from the broad space to narrow streets of the Quarter. The *épicerie* on the Rue de la Harpe was still doing a lively trade at ten in the evening. They split the price of a bottle of Côtes du Rhône. Then Lena took them back to the Seine, where they passed along the *bouquinistes'* closed book lockers till they reached the Rue Bonaparte. Walking away from the river, she led him past the Ecole des Beaux-Arts. Then they turned right into the Rue Jacob.

At a nondescript door, Lena took out a skeleton key and opened the lock. She dropped her purse in the hall and said in a loud voice to no one in particular, "I'm back." There was a dim light on in the kitchen, but no response. She led Tadeusz up four flights of stairs and opened a door at the end of the hall. He was not going to inquire of this nihilist if her family approved of her taking unknown young men of twenty-two to bed.

Lena didn't ask him if he had done this before. Quietly she took command. "There's no rush. We'll go slowly so we can both enjoy it. No one will disturb us."

She faced him and slowly unbuttoned his shirt, pulled it up from his trousers, and dropped it behind him. There was no undershirt to deal with. He moved both his hands to the sleeves of her off-the-shoulder blouse and slowly pulled. As he had hoped a dozen hours or so before, the blouse finally fell to her forearms. He looked down at two small breasts, which seemed to bud around the darkest areolas he would ever see. She raised her hands to each side of his head, drew him toward her, and kissed him with an open mouth, inviting his tongue with hers, while his hands reached for those breasts and began slowly to brush across the nipples. She smiled, and he seemed to hear the word "*Bien*." Did that mean "Good," or was it an expression of impatience—"*Well?*"

Now Lena dropped her skirt and he his trousers and shorts. With both hands on his shoulders, she pushed him to his knees. "Me first. Then you," she announced. He did not resist but moved down slowly, managing to unroll her drawers as he did so. He had never done any of this, but he knew enough to follow her unspoken cues. There was no rush . . .

CHAPTER THREE

It was in February 1934 that Tadeusz began to realize he'd have to get out of Paris. Either that or give up medicine, his parents' subventions, and any thought of a comfortable life. If he stayed there would be excitement, risk, perhaps even the chance to be a hero, lots of revolutionary solidarity, and penury.

From the summer of '33, Tadeusz had been spending less and less time at the Ecole de Médecine. By then he knew quite well enough that the lectures didn't matter. What mattered was transcribing whole textbooks into your memory. Memorizing was something he could do anytime. Meanwhile, there was too much else he cared about, and nothing much he had to do. There was Lena, her friends, friends of her friends. His fellow medical students, French and foreign, took him drinking. There was an overlapping cinema crowd he fell in with, endlessly fascinated by the intertwined life and art of Jean Renoir. In late spring and early fall, he could always find time for long afternoons playing chess under the centuries-old chestnuts in the sepulchral Place Saint-Sulpice. Saturday mornings he'd be searching for trophies of the 1870 *Commune* in the Marché aux Puces up beyond the Porte de Clignancourt. Somewhere he acquired an inexpensive interest in urban architecture and spent mornings walking from Montparnasse to Montmartre.

And always there was the politics. In the fifth and the sixth arrondissements, everyone was a *militant*, organized into an array of left and far left splinters. One evening a friend sporting a length of black comb under his nose, with a huge cigar in his maw, solemnly and repeatedly announced, "*Je suis Marxiste, tendance Groucho.*" Only the seriously Stalinist could suppress a laugh.

By May Day that spring, Tadeusz had not been in the Ecole de Médecine more than twice in five months. Every time he had opened a medical book, someone had come knocking at his door to attend another meeting, demo, protest. He did not have the willpower to say no. He went. But he was unable to dissemble the skepticism he had learned from Lena and her small group of cynical Marxists over the previous year. He knew that once you got in bed with the Stalinists, you'd be murdered in your sleep. He also knew that Trotskyite dissent was as futile as it was fun. In fact, it was too much fun. He had to leave Paris if he was not to be swallowed up by the Left Bank, if he was ever to become a physician.

When he returned to Karpatyn that summer, he explained to his parents that he wanted to study tropical medicine and needed to move to the medical faculty at Marseille. Besides, he told them, in the south living was cheaper, and his chances of passing into the final years and then securing a post were far better.

Once Tadeusz got to Marseille, it would have been easy to make all the same mistakes he'd made in Paris. But from unknown resources came a steely determination to do nothing but study.

In the late spring of 1936, Monsieur Tadeusz Sommermann presented himself at the national medical examinations, *l'externat*, that would determine his chances to begin clinical medical training, *l'internat*. The evening of the last exam, he took the night train for

Paris. The results would be published. He could just as easily buy a copy of *Journal Officiel* at a kiosk on the Place l'Odéon as he could at Marseille's St. Charles station.

A week later Tadeusz had the good news and the bad. He had passed, but not high enough for clinical training at any hospital in l'Hexagone—metropolitan France. His marks in tropical medicine were just high enough for the health service *outre-mer*, provided he could pass the colonial service *concours* that autumn. He knew it wouldn't wear. He couldn't bear the thought of studying for another examination. He'd never be able to recapture the discipline he'd found in Marseille.

That spring the remittances from home had ceased. He'd saved a certain amount in Marseille. It was a cheap town, and he had been too busy swotting to spend all his allowance. There was enough to spend the summer in Paris, if he was careful.

∾

While Tadeusz had been sequestering himself in the library of the Ecole de Médecine in Marseille, things were happening that would solve his immediate problems rather nicely. It was politics, of course. In February and in May, Popular Front governments opened for the season in Spain and France. The French left, almost all of it, had finally found a way to band together. In Spain another Popular Front had defeated a reactionary government at the polls. In France Leon Blum's Socialist Party carried all before it, at least for a time. But in Spain the triumph of the left almost immediately precipitated a military coup. By July there was a full-fledged civil war in Spain. The next month, talk began in France of forming brigades—International Brigades—to defend the Spanish Republic. In September, recruiting centers opened in Paris.

His money nearly gone and unwilling to continue sponging off his friends, one morning Tadeusz found himself before a non-descript building on the Rue de Turenne, waiting for a Republican recruiting office to open. It was not one of those streets daily hosed down by proprietary shopkeepers. In fact, several store-fronts were shuttered. The gutter was thick with cigarette ends, and loose newsprint skittered down the pavement in the gusts. There were several rather scruffy-looking young men already in line, some with papers in their hands. It was a chilly morning for October, but none was wearing a coat. More than one exuded the strong odor of street living.

When Tadeusz took out his cigarettes, *le gar* in front of him noticed. Offering a cigarette he couldn't really afford to give away, Tadeusz struck up a conversation. "I see you've already got some papers in your hand. What's the drill?"

"It's the usual. They want to see *carte d'identité*, and *permis de conduire* if you say you can drive. Discharge papers from a real army make a big hit."

"How about medical qualifications?"

"No, they give you a physical after they—" Tadeusz interrupted. "I meant do they need doctors?"

"*Sais pas*—Dunno." The man shrugged.

"What are you going to do?"

"Anything. I'm from Lille. There's not much work there. Spain is sunny, and they'll feed me."

"Sounds like you're already signed up," Tadeusz noted. "Why are you in line?"

"I'm back with my clearance. I had to be interviewed by the political office. Which union? *CGT*—the communists, or *CGTU*—the socialist one? How did I vote in the first round of voting last spring? What newspaper do I read? Since the *PCF*—the French

Communist Party—and the Russians are paying, they don't want Trots or other troublemakers."

Now, twenty minutes after the advertised opening, the staff came along, three young women and an older man. They opened the office and sat down behind desks. The woman at reception handed out forms. Tadeusz went to a chair and filled them out, trying hard not to blot the porous oak tag with his fountain pen. He brought the forms back to reception. The woman looked them over and nodded him to the gray-haired man at another desk, who was evidently in charge.

Without looking up the older man took the forms. "Medical graduate, eh? What's in it for you, fighting for the Republic?"

"Don't they need doctors?"

"Badly. But doctors don't particularly need us." Tadeusz noted the pronoun.

"This one does. I can't finish in France. Maybe in Spain I can help fight the fascists and get qualified."

"I see. Well, you'll have to satisfy the political bureau. It's the rule for all university students." The gray-beard handed him another form with an address in the Avenue Jean-Jaurès. There was no point hesitating. He decided to go straight there.

It was in a building that housed the party newspaper—*L'Humanité*—and the Soviet trade delegation. They weren't taking any pains to conceal who was vetting volunteers. A man with close-cropped hair and steel teeth—Tadeusz had never actually seen steel teeth before—took his forms and invited him to sit.

"Ever been a member of the Communist Party of France?"

"No."

"How about the *ICL*?" It was Lena's faction.

"What's that?" Tadeusz tried to sound quizzical, but the party hack was not buying.

"Don't play dumb. They're the Trots, organizing world revolution on the Left Bank."

"Look, I'm from Marseille." He handed over his lecture book, stamped and inscribed.

"*D'accord*—OK." The man examined the papers while he spoke. "Best be straight with us. Eventually we'll get around to checking you out." Finally he looked up, hard, into Tadeusz's eyes. The stare held him in its grip for long seconds. Then the face looked down at the papers again. He stamped Tadeusz's forms.

And so back to the Rue de Turenne. By the time the day was over, Tadeusz had a ticket to Barcelona and instructions about where to present himself for military medical training with the International Brigades.

꒰ ꒱

The Barcelona train left from the Gare d'Austerlitz about eight o'clock in the evening. He had a window seat in second class, nonsmoking, facing a family speaking a language that wasn't Spanish. It must have been Catalan. Next to him was a woman who did speak French and was visibly in the last stages of pregnancy.

They both watched the setting sun paint the wheat fields yellow. Long shadows were cast across them by plane trees guiding the country roads that ran along the tracks. It was almost dark by the time the train rattled past Auxerre, and in the dusk he finally felt he could venture a question.

"Should you be traveling?"

"No choice. My family lives in Tarragona. I was alone in Paris."

There was no ring on her left hand. She noticed his glance. It was already too dark in the compartment to detect a blush, but he thought he felt one. For no reason he could think of, he put his hand over hers on the armrest and said quietly, "Don't worry. I'm a doctor." They fell silent, and when the train stopped at two o'clock in Le Creusot, he awoke to find her head resting on his shoulder. He did not mind.

∾

Awakened by the sunrise, Tadeusz left the compartment for a smoke. He leaned out of the corridor window and let the wind rush past his face. Exactly why did he feel so good about going to Spain? Zeal for the Republic? Revolutionary enthusiasm? It certainly infected Tadeusz, watching the newsreel snips. There was that wonderful Communist woman orator they called *La Passionara* spreading her arms wide, enveloping her audience, promising them *"¡No pasarán!"*—They will not pass! Seeing the anarchist with the funny name, Durruti, leading his column of soldiers into Zaragoza brought tears as Tadeusz sat in the dark of the movie theater. He was glad no one could see. Lena would have laughed at him. The tears also welled up when he sang "The International." What had she said? You don't have to believe the words to enjoy the tune?

But he could admit, if only to himself, it wasn't solidarity driving Tadeusz to Spain. It wasn't romance either. It wasn't even calculation, though he later would pretend to himself and others that it was. It was just the easiest thing to do, the line of least resistance. It turned the page, wiped the slate clean, disembarrassed Tadeusz of all the obligations he had built up in Paris, Marseille, even as far back as Poland—all his covenants with his parents. He wouldn't need to bow to conditions for their continued support, still less come home. He wouldn't even have to excuse or explain his choices to them, or to anyone, for that matter. He wouldn't have to sit any more exams. None of this made him feel heroic, of course, but at least he could look that way. And who knew, perhaps he'd become a hero. He was, after all, going to have to be a soldier, wasn't he?

∾

Well after dawn, somewhere between Avignon and Narbonne, the young woman arose from her seat and left the compartment. An hour later she did the same thing. When she returned for the third time, Tadeusz ventured to ask, "Cramps? Could they be contractions?" The girl nodded with a grimace and dropped into her chair.

By the time they were south of Perpignan, she was holding his hand tightly, and the Catalan woman facing them across the compartment understood as well.

Tadeusz had little trouble retrieving the theoretical details of childbirth and delivery from memory, but he needed more information.

He leaned toward the woman across from them. "Pardon me, do you live in Barcelona?" He hoped the Catalan-speaking woman knew some French.

"Yes."

"Can you tell me whether there is a hospital near the train station?"

"Yes. We come into the Estació de França, in Barceloneta. The closest place is Hospital del Mar, very close."

"Thank you." It was still two hours to Barcelona, and there were the border formalities at Cerbere.

∾

Perhaps because it was a Monday morning, perhaps it was the socialist work ethic of the Republican customs agents, or perhaps they were just lucky. Passport and customs checks that morning were cursory. By nine o'clock the train was perceptibly slowing as the track joined others converging on the station. Tadeusz turned to the pregnant woman. "You won't make it to Tarragona. The contractions are coming every four minutes. We are getting you to a hospital here." She nodded compliance. "Where is your bag?"

"I checked it to Barcelona. I have to change trains for Tarragona." She winced.

"Good. They'll keep it for you at the *Consigne*. By the way," he heard himself say, "I am Dr. Sommermann." He'd never called himself that before. He liked the sound of "doctor." So apparently did she. With a wan smile, she introduced herself, Mms. Borda, Aine Borda.

Slowly they made their way between passengers and valises already crowding the corridor. *"Permisso?"* He had already begun to speak Spanish, or was it Catalan?

On the platform now, she was leaning heavily on his arm, tears of pain running down her cheeks as she controlled the urge to cry out.

At the station entrance, they found a cab. "Hospital del Mar," Tadeusz snapped, pronouncing the 's.' It wasn't in the French word, *hôpital*, and he liked the sound—stronger. In less than three minutes, they were at the *Urgencia*—the casualty ward—where the door was opened by a young man dressed in white, wearing a flat-brimmed cap, also in white. As they entered Tadeusz shouted to no one in particular, "Anyone speak French?" There was a chorus of *"Oui"* from around the waiting room. A nurse, evidently in charge, approached. "Are you the father?"

"No, I am the doctor." Her demeanor changed instantly. She stood back, awaiting orders. So Tadeusz decided to play the part. "Is there a midwife on duty or a physician?"

"Yes, Doctor, I will find her." As she turned to leave, an orderly pushing a gurney turned up.

∾

It was an uncomplicated birth, over within an hour. The midwife did everything, but Tadeusz was surprised that he was able to anticipate and understand almost every move. As a physician he was shown deference—*rather too much*, he thought—and allowed to participate, cutting the umbilical cord and tying it off. The child was a healthy girl, and both mother and daughter were wheeled out of the *Urgencia*.

He found himself wondering what she would name the daughter as he rifled through her purse for the baggage check. Finding it, he walked to the outside door, passing the head nurse, who was in conversation with the midwife. Both looked up. "I am going to get the patient's bag. We just came off the train from Paris."

Coming out of the hospital, he looked around. He was facing the Mediterranean. Between him and the sea was a line of palm trees sinuously curving into the azure. They were the first he had ever seen, and he realized at once that he would love them. Beyond was a broad expanse of sand, already dotted with sunbathers, wearing less clothing than he was used to seeing on a strand anywhere in northern Europe. The beach sloped down so that he couldn't see where it met the water, but the sea was a pointillist pattern of intense purple and phosphorescent white. Without sunglasses he could not stare at it long. He turned right, walked along the beach, and turned right again, into Barceloneta. The quarter was a perfectly regular grid of buildings, some painted in pastel, all about five stories each, close enough across the narrow streets to provide one another with shade even against the late morning sun. There were no balconies, but most of the windows were framed by a grillwork, over which hung tropical plantings and colorful laundry. At each intersection, in at least three directions he could see a fierce blue sky. He realized immediately that this part of Barcelona was a peninsula. Then he began noticing the fishmongers and the fry-up stalls among the bars. Shopkeepers and workers going about their affairs seemed remarkably cheerful and much more gregarious than their French counterparts. He was going to like Spain.

It was an hour before he returned to the hospital, carrying their suitcases. Again he headed for the casualty entrance. As he came in, he saw a middle-aged man in a narrowly cut suit with a chalk pinstripe and a black tie in conversation with the intake nurse. The man abruptly turned from his conversation, walked over to Tadeusz, extended his hand, and addressed him in accented French. "*Bienvenu, M. le médecin*—I am Dr. Marti. We were not expecting you till tomorrow. Still, you obviously came at a moment convenient for one of our patients." He smiled, and before Tadeusz could interrupt, he called over a porter and issued an order, evidently in Catalan. The porter took the bag from Tadeusz while Dr. Marti explained. "He will show you to a room." By this point Tadeusz had decided to allow the misunderstanding to play itself out a little further.

No one bothered him the rest of that day. So he unpacked, went to the hospital canteen for a meal, and took a turn on the beach. Again he was surprised, disturbed, pleased to see women walking along the water's edge with bare midriffs and halter tops, looking like the posters of Josephine Baker he had mooned over in Paris. Well before anyone in Barcelona was even thinking about supper, Tadeusz was sound asleep in a room at the *Hospital del Mar*, overlooking the sea.

The next morning a nurse presented herself at his door, addressing him as Dr. Nadeau. He could not allow the misunderstanding to go much further. He corrected her: "Dr. Sommermann."

"Very well, sir." She spoke French. Off they went on rounds. As they moved to the first bed, she briefly explained the case—symptoms appeared to be simple pleurisy. "But she is not responding to treatment." Then she fell deferentially silent, evidently expecting orders. In no position to give any and in fear that anything he suggested might harm the patient, Tadeusz assumed an air of friendly complicity. "What would you do?" The nurse looked surprised. Evidently she had never been asked for her opinion by a doctor. With a broad smile, she offered two or three observations on the patient's history and made a suggestion.

"Just what I was going to say." He smiled. Fortunately the next patient and the one after that were suffering from the same symptoms. Tadeusz needed to say something intelligent. Looking at the charts surreptitiously, he noticed that all three shared a surname that ended in "ian." They had to be Armenian and perhaps Turkish by nationality. He had it. "Could this be familial Mediterranean fever? It's not uncommon among people from Turkey." This was so rare a disorder only someone fresh from memorizing textbooks of tropical medicine would even have heard of it. Best of all, the prescribed treatment was identical to cases of pleurisy.

The nurse looked at Tadeusz with a little gasp. "How did you know they are Turkish, Doctor? They're sisters, an Armenian family from Anatolia." Tadeusz's omniscience was extended to include his textbook confabulation.

The rounds did not produce any more difficulties, but evidently Tadeusz was treating staff in completely unaccustomed ways. "Please" and "Thank you." "What is your advice, nurse?" Every request he made was met with alacrity. Every question was answered in detail. A surprising number of the staff spoke at least a little French, and the Catalan was not impossible to guess at. Things were going much too well.

At four o'clock that afternoon, Dr. Marti, the director, appeared on the ward, flushed but closemouthed. Sighting Tadeusz, he crooked a finger. "Doctor, follow me!"—the words spoken with a tone of anger. Marti led him to an empty consulting room off the main floor. "I have a telegram from Dr. Nadeau here. He's gotten a better offer and changed his mind about coming. Exactly who are you?" He was fierce but speaking just above a whisper.

"I am Dr. Tadeusz Sommermann. I tried to correct your staff as to my name each time they addressed me. I am a doctor . . . I admit I am not the doctor you were expecting. Give me a moment, and I will explain."

Marti's silence was enough of an invitation to continue.

"I brought in the young woman who was delivered of a child yesterday morning."

"Yes, the midwife and the head nurse told me that you supervised the delivery efficiently. Go on."

"When you said you needed medical staff, I thought there might be something for me here. I came to Barcelona with orders to join the medical units of the International Brigades. But I am much more well suited to a women's lying-in hospital." *Much less suited to a frontline dressing station*, Tadeusz thought to himself.

"So it seems. I have had reports from the ward nurses about your intelligent interventions all day." Marti pressed the tips of a thumb and forefinger to his forehead and drew a deep breath, then released it in a despairing sigh. "What am I to do?" He was looking at Tadeusz, but appeared to be addressing himself or the air. "They've taken away all our experienced men. The only way we were going to keep a doctor was by getting one they couldn't use, a gynecologist who doesn't speak Catalan or Spanish. And now we have been denied even that." Another deep breath, another sigh. Only then did he focus on the man before him. He glared at Tadeusz. "What is your previous experience?"

Here an outright lie was called for, and Tadeusz had no difficulty providing it. "Six months in Sisteron, Haute Provence." He did not offer the name of any hospital, and to his relief none was requested.

"Do you have your medical certificates?" Marti was still glaring. "Bring them to the office immediately." Before Tadeusz could answer, Marti had turned his back and was descending the stairs. Five minutes later, Tadeusz was sitting in the hospital director's office, his medical lecture attendance book and a copy of the *Journal Officiel* of the previous April spread out on the desk between him and Marti. It was the best he could come up with. It did not seem advisable to present his Spanish military medical service orders. After what seemed an eternity of study, the director leaned back in his chair.

"I need OB-GYN staff. You can stay on as long as the International Brigades can spare you. One hundred pesetas a week, meals in the canteen, but I can't give you a place to stay in the hospital. Too dangerous for us."

"I accept." Tadeusz gulped.

A week later Tadeusz was called from the wards to Marti's office.

"You're doing a good job, Sommermann. I want to keep you. But you have to get rid of that name. The authorities have sent warnings around about international recruits for the brigades arriving and disappearing into thin air."

Tadeusz said nothing.

"Here's a death certificate I pulled out of our files." He passed it across the desk. "Memorize the details, go to the registry at the *Ajuntament,* and get a new *carte d'identité.*" He looked down at the form. "Starting today you are Guillermo Romero."

"But the nurses all know me as Sommermann."

"Just tell them. They'll follow orders if you would try giving any, instead of always asking for their advice." The irritation in Marti's voice was tinged with humor. "Besides, the nursing staff turnover is so high that in three months, there will be hardly anyone left who knows you by any other name besides Romero."

CHAPTER FOUR

One night in April 1938, nine months after Tadeusz's last visit to his parents in Karpatyn, Doctor Gil Romero was standing at the counter of a small workers' café in the Barceloneta. It was around the corner from his rooms, on the Carrer Balboa, and close to his favorite restaurant—a workers' seafood grill on Carrer Baluard. The café was not large, the doors were wide open, and he could feel the gentle breeze off the *playa*. Small lamps on the walls and the bar fought vainly against the warm velvet darkness flooding through the open double doorways from the street. Occasionally the aroma of *pulpo*—octopus—being grilled for a *tapas* would overpower the sea smell and tempt him into ordering up a *ración*. Gil had hoped to see an acquaintance or two. But no one had turned up, and after a beer he was ready to leave.

By now he had no trouble thinking of himself as Doctor Gil Romero, a specialist, a *ginecòleg* in the Catalan language, which increasingly expressed his thoughts. He loved working with women and on the medical problems of women. At first he had to listen carefully simply to understand the Catalan. Thus, almost by accident, he acquired a habit of listening. This won the nurses' confidence. He had found a calling, something he was good at, cared about. There was even some money to be made from wealthy women, often officers' wives, who came to him to deal with indiscretions committed while husbands were at the front.

Gil knew that things could not continue this well much longer. The Republic was not going to win. People already knew it, on both sides of the Civil War. In Barcelona the atmosphere was fevered by the knowledge. Military police were combing the bars and bordellos, sending men south toward the Ebro. More and more of those who could get out—the wealthy, freemasons, loyal naval and air force officers—were leaving for France.

Gil picked a newspaper off the bar. The Nationalists—Franco's troops, including Italians and Germans—had finally cut off Cataluña from Madrid. Meanwhile, on Moscow's orders, the Catalan government was rounding up anyone who didn't accept the discipline of the Spanish Communist Party. The last remnant of the POUM leadership—the left opposition—were all put up against a wall and liquidated. It was the sort of reaction to disaster Gil had come to expect. Lose another battle; blame it on the motley conspiracy of Trotskyites, anarchists, utopian socialists, and others who could never take Comintern orders—Stalin's orders. Matters were dealt with by the Spanish Communist Party's version of the Soviet secret police. In fact, they had help from the real one—the NKVD, more efficient in dealing with enemies on the left.

As he was about to leave, Dr. Marti passed along the open front of the café, smiled at him, stopped, and came into the glow of the bar. "May I join you?"

It was a rare occasion. Gil smiled. "What can I buy you?"

"You can get me anything but a sangria." He was using the familiar *tu,* and Gil noticed immediately. It was the first time in a year Marti had been friendly. He decided to take advantage of the moment.

"Dr. Marti—"

"Call me Marti. That's what friends do, Romero." He smiled as he made his point.

"*Molt be.*" He hoped the Catalan carried the same meaning as the Spanish *muy bien.* "I was about to ask if you were a party member. I assume so, since you are director of a city hospital."

"I am indeed. Fully paid up."

"But if you'll excuse me, it's obvious you're not loyal to the party. You hired me instead of sending me to the barracks or even having me arrested. You've helped me cover my tracks."

"You're a good doctor. And I am a poor Stalinist. In fact, I am no communist at all. But I would have lost my post if I hadn't joined. And you?" Marti's frankness was more than disarming. It was dangerous. An admission like that could cost him his position, or much worse.

Gil wondered, *Is he trying to smoke me out? Surely not. He already knows enough to sell me to the NKVD or their Spanish acolytes.* He decided to be cautious.

"I am some kind of Marxist, or at least a dialectical materialist, and that's enough. I won't take sides in parochial disputes on the left."

Marti looked at him. "Dialectical materialism? You are a doctor, a scientist. You can't accept that mumbo jumbo." He drank off half his beer, looked at Gil, and continued. "The only part of dialectical materialism that's right is the materialism part." The thought had a faint echo in Gil's memories of Paris. Gil said nothing. He wasn't going to tip his hand, take sides, give hostages to fortune. The silence hung between them.

"Well, if you are not going to be straight with me, *joven*, I'm off." Marti raised the glass of beer and then finished it off. "Good night." Marti's smile was genuine and left Gil even more perplexed.

ↄ

By September things were falling apart for the Republic. First there was the pointless offensive on the River Ebro by a Republican army that fought well only when defending. Gil recalled its victory in the battle of Madrid. The Fascist general, Mola, besieging the city, claimed to have four columns outside and a fifth column within. But the Republican army had succeeded in resisting encirclement for three years. It was fighting on the offense that seemed to be beyond them. Now, losing on the Ebro front, the Republican government premier, Negrin, unilaterally withdrew his best soldiers, the International Brigades, from the war altogether. And he invited the fascists to send their "volunteers" away. Why? Gil could only laugh out loud. Did Negrin think for a minute Franco would send his German and Italian troops, their tanks, bombers, and transport planes home too? That was the moment Stalin picked to order the Spanish party to complete its liquidation of their allies on the left.

Meanwhile, for most of September, the rest of Europe was preparing for certain war over the Sudetenland in Czechoslovakia. Even in the Spanish papers, British Prime Minister Chamberlain's flights, first to Bad Godesberg, then to Munich, had pushed news of the Ebro front from the headlines.

∾

On September 30, the day after Chamberlain had brought peace with honor, peace in our time, back to London from Germany, Gil was called down from the obstetrical ward. Marti got up as he entered.

"Shut the door, sit, *joven.*"

Gil complied wordlessly.

"It's time for you to leave, my friend. The NKVD has been to see me twice looking for someone named Sommermann who had friends in the Trotskyite ICL in Paris. They said he was supposed to be with the brigades, but they completely lost track of him, till information came in from Paris. Now he's *needed* by his unit. That's what they said anyway. The brigades have to evacuate in good order, no stragglers. That includes the medical services."

"I see."

"You must get a Spanish passport. You won't get out with a Polish one."

❧

It was still hot enough to perspire a few evenings later as Gil carried a single suitcase and a briefcase to the Barceloneta metro stop. The valise packed gynecological instruments among pieces of clothing so they would not rattle. The briefcase held medical certificates for one Guillermo Romero. Sitting in the steaming carriage, sweat pouring down his face, Gil waited out the stops on the metro line to Barcelona Santas, the main railroad station. He'd never get out the way he came in to Barcelona the first time, through the identity checks at Cerbere, on the direct line to France. He might look Catalan now, but he wouldn't sound it to the border police checking for deserters or to the French customs agents who sent back visa-less refugees with a vengeance. His route back to France had to be indirect.

An hour later, no longer sweating, Gil sat on a wooden bench in a third-class compartment, alone but for an elderly lady. She sat beneath a poster from which shone the face of *La Pasionaria*, Dolores Ibárruri, and the hammer and sickle of the Spanish Communist Party. But the woman was no republican stalwart—that was certain. All in black, under a lace mantilla, her eyes moved back and forth across the pages of a missal. Evidently she had nothing to fear from Generalissimo Franco.

With only three cars, the train slowly made its way upland, stopping at a half dozen villages around Montserrat before turning north to the Spanish Pyrenees. The railway line ended at Berga, well south of the French border. There would be no identity checks on this train.

As darkness fell, Gil began to see less of the landscape and more of his face reflected back in the dusty window glass. He liked what he saw: the slightly more defined features that long days had chiseled into his face, the jaded look of world-weary—or was it worldly wise?—sophistication in his eyes, the fashionable mustache, the off-white suit of a man who knew his way round the Ramblas. It only needed a cigarette and some smoke to complete the picture. He lit one.

Gil reflected with a certain amount of satisfaction on how foresighted he had been, making the right choice at each fork in the road. Things had worked out for him. Or at least they would work out if he could escape the net being closed by the military and political police of the Catalan rump state, now almost entirely under Soviet control.

～

In the dim aura of its single streetlamp clamped to the side of a building facing the station—really no more than a platform with shed—Berga was a one-lane town of drab two-story stucco houses and shuttered windows. Coming down from the platform into the dimly lit square, Gil searched for a taxi. There were none—only a grizzled man wearing overalls and cloth cap, leaning back on the fender of a dusty farm truck. He was smoking a Celtas cigarette—a brand too strong for Gil to inhale. He looked at Gil, who looked back, and nodded.

"How much to take me to La Seu d'Urgell?" It was a small town one hundred kilometers to the east. More important, it was as close to Andorra as one could get. *I'm not a smuggler, and I'm not on the run*, thought Gil. *Better haggle.*

"That depends on how many other people off that train want to go there with you," the man replied. They waited in silence, but the handful of passengers all diffused into the night. Finally, the trucker said, "One hundred pesetas. It'll take all night."

"Fifty," was Gil's reply. He was going to pay whatever it cost, but he was not going to show urgency.

"What's in the case?" The driver looked at Gil's bag. "They don't need hams in la Vella." That was the only town of any size in Andorra.

"Medical instruments." Gil didn't need to lie.

"All right, I'll take you for seventy-five pesetas. I'm Josep. You?"

"Romero, Doctor Guillermo Romero." He lifted himself to the seat, putting the valise on his lap, with his briefcase beside the driver. Then Gil undid the two belts holding the valise closed. When he opened it, a speculum reflected what little light there was. "So, not much value to anyone but a doctor, friend." Should he have said "comrade" instead of friend?

It was an old gravel road, running one lane west along the valley, but with no late-night traffic coming the other way to make the truck have to lay by. By midnight, Gil and the driver, Josep, had traded enough lies about themselves to become conspirators.

"Friend," Gil ventured, "if someone wanted to make it into France through Andorra, could he do it from Urgell?"

"La Seu is what they call it. But if you want to make it over the border, you are going the wrong way."

"What's wrong with Andorra?"

"The French border patrol at the Andorra frontier is tough. They know they can shake down every traveler for drink, smokes, scent. You want to go through Puigcerdá, not La Seu." It was a place Gil had never heard of. "Besides, it's half the distance." Josep brought the truck to a stop. "We just passed the turn for it."

"Can you take me there instead?" Gil was now making himself a hostage to Josep's trustworthiness.

"*Sí*. Same price though." He shifted into reverse and made a careful K-turn on the narrow road. As the truck started up, Josep went on, "Something else you probably don't know. Just across the border at Puigcerdá, there is a little part of Spain, really Cataluña, a sort of landlocked island, Spanish but surrounded by France. It's weird. The reason goes back to some treaty four hundred years ago." He stopped the narration to concentrate on the road, which had become more tortuous now that they were climbing due north directly into the Pyrenees, instead of skirting them to the west.

Gil was silent, hoping that Josep would tell him how to manage the border without his having to ask. *Stupid being reticent now*, he thought.

"This little piece of Spain is called Llivia. It's two kilometers from the border. Best thing about this border is that so many people go back and forth between Llivia and Girona on this side that all you need is an identity card and good Catalan. I've seen them take away people just for showing a passport when they try to cross. Your Catalan is good enough to fool the French. Show me your identity card. For an extra twenty-five pesetas, I'll be glad to drive you right to the border."

Gil pulled out the identity card from his coat pocket along with some Republican banknotes—he wouldn't need them anymore. The passport was in the briefcase, and the briefcase was locked. He said nothing.

At 1:00 a.m. Josep pulled the truck up to the border three hundred meters beyond the single street and stillness of Puigcerdá. The town behind them looked like it had slept soundly through the whole Spanish Civil War, every window dark.

The border gate barred the road, and Josep had to honk. After a minute or so, a dim light came on in the border hut. Then the door opened, and a man emerged, in a dirty undershirt, wearing the distinctive patent leather hat of the Guardia Civil—Franco's Guardia Civil, or maybe Stalin's. Josep must have felt Gil's shudder. "Not a *Guardia*. Just likes the hat, I think."

The man turned on an electric torch, shined it up to the cab, and put out his hand. Josep handed down the papers.

"What are you doing crossing at this hour?" He looked from the cards to their faces.

Gil could think of nothing to say and did not trust his imperfect Catalan. After a moment of silence, Josep volunteered.

"Doctor. Midwife sent for him. A patient delivering a baby with complications."

Coming around the truck, the border guard climbed the running board and looked at Gil, asking in Catalan, "What's in the case?"

Gil gave a one-word answer, "Look." He opened the case.

The guard shuddered slightly at the sight of the speculum. He jumped down. *"Pasad."* He raised the barrier and turned back to the hut.

Josep stopped at an intersection, leaned across Gil, and opened the door. "You are in France; in another minute you will be back in Spain." Gil held out his hand. Josep took it. *"Bon viatge."* Good travels. Two minutes later, Gil was still at the crossroads when Josep drove by in the other direction, going back to Spain. Each gave the Popular Front salute: a clenched fist, arm raised.

∽

A month later, in November 1938, Dr. Guillermo Romero was a gynecologist on the staff of the Municipal Hospital, Lvov, Poland.

It was remarkable how welcome Spanish doctors were in Poland. A medical man with Catalan certification had to be a good Catholic, unlike so many candidates for these positions.

CHAPTER FIVE

Rita, we must talk." Urs had just returned from the office. No doubt he had stopped at his mother's home again, she thought. Eager to deflect him from whatever subject his mother had put in his head, she turned toward the kitchen.

"Dinner is ready . . . It's *coq au vin*." It was a decidedly un-Polish way of cooking chicken, one that reminded Rita of other countries, other mores.

As they sat down, Urs cleared his throat. Rita could tell that he was not to be deflected. A set speech was coming. "In the two years since we married, we have made love approximately eighty-four times." He was going on, but all she could focus on was the fact that he'd been counting. "I know you have been worried about not becoming pregnant. I have not brought it up before because I thought the problem of our having no children might be mine." Evidently, for this automaton, sexual intercourse really was just for procreation. And suddenly the careful structure supporting Rita's equanimity collapsed beneath her. She could feel herself sucked down toward a question she could never answer: *Why have I done this? How could I have made this mistake? What was I thinking?*

The emptiness of things was overwhelming her, and it must have showed.

Urs made matters worse by mistaking the source of her anguish. He moved toward her and surrounded her with his long arms. She resisted his embrace. Without really noticing, he continued, "So, I read. I made a study." He spoke with clinical dispassion. "I have subjected my sperm to microscopic inspection in the clinic. They are sufficient in concentration per cubic centimeter and in motility."

Rita pushed free from Urs and stood. "So, the problem is with me?" She heard the inward command, *Get a grip on yourself!*

"I don't know. It could be a problem between us. But I want you to go to Lvov. I have consulted a physician there. No one here needs to know about our problem. Anyway, no one in a small town like this can help."

"Lvov?"

"Yes, there is a medical school, a large hospital, a women's clinic. After all, it's the third largest city in the country. No one will need to know anything but the doctor examining you. I knew him slightly in Krakow. Now he practices in Lvov. His name is Pankow. We have exchanged correspondence about the matter, and he wants to examine you himself."

Rita wanted to remonstrate. Urs had opened a correspondence with a stranger on the most intimate of marital relations. It hadn't occurred to him to secure his wife's permission first.

But then she thought, *Don't make an issue of this.* There hadn't been any issues between them, never any hard or harsh words, never any arguments, scenes, tears, or anger—in fact, no emotion whatever. Urs never seemed to have any, and Rita had by now taught herself not to. She had convinced herself that the lack of strong feeling was a sign of maturity. People driven by emotion, she had convinced herself, were less content than those whose lives were calculated. Now, recovering quickly from her momentary despair, forcing herself to think about matters this way, she tried to see Urs's point. Having married for comfort, she really had to earn it. Besides, she did want children—Urs's children, for that matter—both to fulfill the unspoken terms of the agreement and because he had many fine qualities. Yes, the course Urs had outlined was perfectly reasonable.

And then she thought, *At least I can get away from Karpatyn for a day. Spend a day in a bustling city, one much bigger than Krakow.* Calmly she asked, "When does he expect me?"

∾

A week and exactly one bout of marital intimacy later, Rita was in Lvov. It had been a one-and-a-half-hour train journey through the flat, steppe-like countryside of Southeastern Poland, bare since the harvest. Each village they passed looked like the last—slattern hovels of stuccoed timbers huddled around a Ukrainian Orthodox church. Hardly anyone alighted or descended at any of the half dozen stops between Karpatyn and Lvov. *And why should they?* Rita thought.

Lvov was a refreshing surprise. Why hadn't she come before? It was a metropolis. Electric streetcars slid noiselessly past the main station and ran down cobbled streets in three directions. Large black automobiles and still larger trucks moved quickly past the few farm carts. The buildings across the street from the station were four and five stories high, faced in dressed stone, with arched windows from which glowing lights shone into the gray midday. There was a café at the corner, crowded inside, but with a few tables still braving the chill. The street was alive with shoppers, a newspaper kiosk doing a lively business, even a chestnut roaster plying his trade at the curb. She looked wistfully at the café. No time for a coffee. Rita found a cab, an old but shiny Peugeot, and gave the driver Dr. Pankow's address.

Five minutes from the station, the taxi stopped before one of these formidable stone-clad buildings. Rita paid and stepped out. At the entry under an overhanging balcony, she sought the doctor's brass plate and entered. Beyond the lobby, white marble slab stairs wound around a wrought iron elevator cage, something she had not seen for almost two years. She waited till the cabin descended. It took her to the second floor, where she knocked at a frosted glass door. The physician himself could be heard to say, "Come in." He looked up at her from his desk, neither smiling nor frowning. "Pani Doctor Guildenstern?"

Rita was taken aback momentarily by a form of address reserved for her mother-in-law. "Yes, Doctor. How nice to meet you." It wasn't really nice. He was a formidable, stern-faced character, heavyset, with deep parenthetical wrinkles on either side of his mouth, eyes hidden beneath a heavy brow. Who did he look like? she pondered. Then she had it: Otto von Bismarck! To complete the image of unapproachability, Dr. Pankow was wearing a frock coat and wing collar. When had she last seen someone dressed this way? At an undertaker's?

With no ceremony, Dr. Pankow motioned to the cloth-covered folding screen at the side of the room and said, "Be so kind as to undress, and put on the gown you will find on the examining table."

She could hear water running as he washed his hands, and then Pankow came around the screen, now wearing a white coat and pulling on a pair of rubber gloves. As he examined her, he asked several obvious questions. "How regular are your periods? Are they painful? Irregular in their flow? Ever been pregnant and miscarried? Is intercourse painful?" She thought, *Why don't you ask any of the important questions? Why is your husband uninterested in sex? Why is he no good at it when it does occur to him? Why did you marry him in the first place?*

Dr. Pankow's examination seemed no different from others she had experienced, and she was beginning to wonder what special knowledge he might have. When he had finished, he put his instruments aside, pulled off the gloves, and said, "You may now dress, Pani Guildenstern."

A few moments later, they were again facing each other across the broad, heavy desk. "Well, everything seems in perfect order to me. But I want you to see a specialist."

Rita looked surprised. "I thought you were a specialist."

"My practice is limited to women. I want you to see someone who specializes in reproductive problems. I understand you have traveled some distance. I will call and try to get you an appointment today." He picked up a telephone on his desk and opened a notebook next to it. Meanwhile, Rita took a train schedule from her purse and began to see how late she could stay. By the time she had located a nine o'clock evening train, he was putting down the telephone. Pankow picked up a pen, dabbed it in an inkwell, and scratched out a few lines on a pad.

"Here is the address. It's the gynecology department of Central Hospital. A cab will get you there. Your appointment is at three o'clock." He pulled a pocket watch from his waistcoat, glanced at it, and went on, "May I suggest that you spend the intervening period at the George Hotel, an excellent tearoom? My wife enjoys it very much. Good day." He did not rise.

Rita took the address, her departure, and the advice. Outside she found the same old Peugeot taxi. Within three minutes she found herself at the George Hotel. She might have walked and saved a zloty. It was another four-story stone structure, with three ranks of balconies above the main entrance. Rita swept across the entry as though she really were Pani Doctor Guildenstern. The doorman bowed slightly and stood expectantly. "The tearoom, please," she said. Her eye followed his gesture beyond the arched stairway to double doors with triple brass bars across panes of frosted glass. As she arrived they were swung open by another liveried hand to reveal a scene of late Victorian probity. Elderly dowagers pouring tea for spindly spinster daughters, while fatter daughters-in-law polished off crustless watercress sandwiches. This was not a place Rita wanted to fit into, but it was too late to turn back.

She took a seat and looked around again. Here on display was the life she was now being relentlessly sucked into. Correct and censorious, these women were dressed in so many layers that motion was almost impossible. They were squinting at menus through lorgnettes and looking down on almost everything. If she were lucky and her husband took her to Lvov often enough, surely she would become accustomed to this room.

It took the better part of an hour to do justice to a pot of tea and a few buttered brioche. By then the thick damask of the tablecloths, the uncreasable starch of the napkins, the overbearing gleam of the silver metal tea service had begun to oppress her. She could not make herself remain at the George Hotel another minute, no matter how early she would be at the specialist's clinic.

∽

It was a ten-minute walk to the Central Hospital through what still seemed to Rita like a teeming metropolis. When she arrived without a wrong turn, there was still a half hour to spare. She found the main entrance and searched the directory for the obstetrics and gynecology department. Finding it on the first floor, she advanced to the sweeping double stairs. They were in the same proportion as those at the law faculty in Krakow. As she glided up them, she tried to recall the feeling of being a student again, instead of a matron.

Presenting herself at the reception desk, Rita began to address herself to a nurse obviously too preoccupied to look up at her. But when she explained that an appointment had been made for her that morning by Dr. Pankow, the nurse looked up with a start. "I have instructions to show you into the doctor's cabinet immediately." She rose and led the way down a wide hall. Its marble floor was flanked on one side by doors and on the other by tall windows, through which much of Lvov seemed slightly to shimmer in the aberrations of the wide panes of glass. The nurse stopped at a door, knocked, and without waiting entered, announcing as she did, "Pani Doctor Guildenstern."

A youngish man with a still slightly sunburned complexion, in a dark, well-cut suit with a velvet waistcoat, black mustache, and dark hair, stood to receive her. Rita could only gasp, but the nurse did not notice as she formally introduced him, "Dr. Romero. Dr. Guillermo Romero."

Rising, the doctor said rather too quickly, "Thank you, nurse; that will be all for the moment," and taking her by the elbow, hurried her out of the room. Then he turned and smiled.

"Guillermo Romero?" Before Rita could say another word, he put his forefinger to his closed lips and took her hand, leading her to a door that opened up to an examination room. Gil turned on the light, closed the door, and threw the bolt on the lock. He took both of her hands and looked intently in her eyes. She was reading the same look in his eyes, now gleaming as a tear welled up at each corner. Suddenly they were both weeping with delight. Gil leaned forward to kiss her, and Rita's mouth opened at the same time. It lasted fully a minute, after which Rita began to move Gil's fingers over the buttons and hooks that held her oppressive clothing to her body.

Skirt dropped, blouse opened. It was too much for both of them to wait till he had removed slip, camisole top, stockings, garter, underpants . . . She brought her hands to his fly and deftly undid every button as he loosened his belt. Leaning back on the examining table, Rita pulled down her underpants and drew up the slip for him. He took her—or more aptly, she thought later, she took him. Their mutual passion welled up too quickly to be paced or channeled. Almost before he had much penetration, climax overcame him, leaving her moist and unsatisfied.

"I'm sorry. It will be better the next time." Gil stepped back and began adjusting his clothes, while handing her a starched linen hospital towel.

She was still in a fever of excitement when the questions began intruding on the sensations. As she dressed, she could not decide which to ask first. How had this happened? What was Tadeusz doing here? How had he managed to get back to Poland? Why had he come back at all? Why was he masquerading as a Spaniard? Who was Guillermo Romero? Even before she could fully formulate the questions, the broad outline of some of the answers began to suggest themselves. But she wanted details.

"I really am Guillermo Romero now, Rita. That's what I am called; that's what my documents call me. That's how I think of myself." As he said it, he felt its truth. "In Spain I had to change everything. By the time I left, I was Guillermo Romero."

"But I still go to your mother's bookshop every week, and she tells me about Tadeusz in Spain. When the International Brigades were withdrawn, I hoped you'd come back . . . When I saw that picture in the magazine of the French gendarme leading those men across the sand in greatcoats carrying nothing but bedrolls, I looked in every face for you. Then your mother told me you were going to Mexico."

"I wrote to her, so she wouldn't worry. In Barcelona the return address was always '*poste restante.*' When the brigades were withdrawn, I had to think of something. I wrote her from Marseille that

I was going to Mexico, where I'd be safe. Lots of Republicans went there. Now I'm well settled here, but I haven't figured out what to tell her. Is she worried?"

"Not yet."

But Gil was already distracted from the problem his mother's anxiety might pose. "How long can you stay?"

"The last train back is at nine o'clock.

Gil looked at his watch and smiled. "Let's get some supper."

"Where?" Rita said with some anxiety.

"Nowhere public. I have a flat nearby. Meet me at the hospital entrance in five minutes."

∾

An hour later they were at last relaxed enough to begin really to exchange intimacies, recollections, and expectations. A few streets away from the hospital, Gil had taken Rita's arm, and she had willingly given it. There was no concierge to concern them as they passed through an arch into the courtyard of a large building. Within, patches of grass were still littered with the drying leaves of a large oak that dominated the courtyard. Gil pulled a latchkey from what looked like a military officer's belted trench coat and opened the door.

Inside, he reinserted the key and double locked it in a way that said, "We are now really alone." Rita was ready to fall into his arms again, but Gil was already moving to a small kitchen off the entry. She followed him to its open door.

"First, we eat, just a little." He reached into a small icebox, and she noticed that there was almost no water melted into the drip pan visible below it. It was almost as cold inside as out.

Still wearing his coat, Gil reached in, pulled out some eggs and butter and a bottle of white wine. He saw her shiver, so he put the food down. *A fire will be even more important*, he thought. Moving back through the hall into a sitting room, he bent at the small fireplace and lit a match.

She could hear the hiss of gas escaping just before the warm yellow light skipped its way along the twin pipes of the grate. Before he could rise from the fire, Rita began to take charge in the kitchen. She could feed them more quickly. It would leave them more time. While she prepared the eggs, Gil laid out two plates, filled two wineglasses, sliced two slabs from the loaf on top of the icebox, and put the butter dish between the plates that faced each other.

By the time they had finished their meal, the rooms had warmed. With some wine still in their glasses, Gil fished a packet of cigarettes from his jacket and offered Rita one. She thought for a moment and said, "Afterward." They both rose and went to the now warm sitting room, illuminated only by the fire in the grate.

They undressed themselves slowly, watching each other. Gil threw a goose-down quilt from the chesterfield to the rug, and they lay down on it before the grate. This time Gil was as patient as he had been the first time he made love to her the year before. *How many women had he slept with?* Rita wondered. The question was flooded away by the urgency he was able to call forth and then let diminish as he stroked her thighs. His mouth was at her nipples, just barely hurting them, but very surely readying her for him. Another random thought occurred to Rita: is this a doctor's clinical knowledge of a woman's body?

Meanwhile Gil was alternatively entering her, releasing himself ever so slightly, and then holding himself back, withdrawing to bring his mouth to the velvet tissue between her legs, and then moving up to kiss her mouth as he entered her again. When he finally began to thrust, Gil grabbed her right hand and moved it to her mons. She was well beyond any inhibition and did as he suggested, moving her fingers rapidly.

Afterward, as she recovered, she asked herself, now that it was over, whether she was ashamed, embarrassed, somehow repelled by the sheer carnality, the animality, and the dimensions of the pleasure attained. The answer was no, no, never. "I'll take that cigarette now."

They lay together, facing each other, heads supported by elbows, enjoying the aroma of Virginia tobacco for a long while. Each looked at the other, unaccountably and at the same time understandably, comfortable in their nudity. Then, stubbing out the cigarettes, they began to make love again.

It was dark when Rita noticed the large clock now audibly ticking on the mantelpiece. The light was too poor to see its hands. "What's the time?"

Gil looked to his wrist. He had left his watch on. "Eight fifteen."

"How far to the station?"

"It will be close." He rose.

They dressed quickly, walked out of the courtyard under the arch, and began looking and listening for a cab in the darkness. Silence. "Let's walk. We can just make it. We need to talk anyway." Gil led her at a rapid pace in the direction from which they had come. "Speaking as your gynecologist, I shall require weekly visits for treatment of your infertility problem."

Rita was not following. "What infertility problem?"

"You have none. And seeing you once a week is not enough. But I can't think of how I can get to see you here more often."

The train was pulling away. Rita leaned out of the compartment window.

Gil shouted, "I'll meet your train next Thursday morning."

Afterward, they would both be able to remember that date. It was March 16, 1939.

CHAPTER SIX

Two weeks later Urs began to wonder why he had received no bill from his Lvov colleague Dr. Pankow. He could well imagine Pankow forgoing a fee for the first visit. That was a common enough professional courtesy. But if Pankow thought he was expected to treat without charge a fellow physician's wife over the course of several appointments, he was very much mistaken. He decided to wait another week, and if no bill came, he would write to the good doctor, thanking him for his kindness, but gently chiding him for his misplaced generosity.

Certainly the treatments seemed to be doing Rita good. She would come back from Lvov with a good color. The first time she returned with stories overheard at the tearoom of the George Hotel. The second time she talked about the films that never made it to Karpatyn. She'd managed to bring back pastries. Even better were the back numbers of the medical journals she found for him at the hospital.

Only he would have to remember to write Dr. Pankow . . .

Late in the afternoon of the last Thursday in March, Gil broke out of a postcoital haze to ask, "Rita, what is going to become of us?"

"It's probably not up to us," she replied in an offhand way.

Gil lifted his head from her bare midriff and looked at her. "Who is it up to if not us?"

"Herr Hitler, I suspect." She frowned. "We'll be at war with him very soon."

"Poland at war with Germany?"

"Of course. We're his next target. Isn't it obvious?"

"No, no. You don't understand the international situation." Rita could tell a lecture was coming on. She sighed. Not noticing, Gil took a breath and began. "The Brits and the French have given the Polish government ironclad guarantees." He reached for her cigarette, drew on it, and handed it back. "We've got more important things to think about . . . us."

Rita was willing to argue. "I wish you were right. I wish we had the luxury to think about *us*. But I don't think we do. I think Stalin will give Hitler free rein in Europe. Then if Hitler loses his war against the Brits and French, Stalin fills the vacuum in Germany. If Hitler wins, then Stalin was not strong enough to beat him, anyway."

"Hitler and Stalin in bed together? That's the Trotskyite line, Rita? Where are you getting this from?"

"We'll find out soon enough if I am right. But just suppose I am, what will you do?"

"Fight for my country, I suppose."

"Your country, Guillermo Romero? Spain? It's already lost its war."

"Well, I'll fight for what's right."

"But what if right doesn't line up neatly with any of the sides you'll have to choose between? Fight for British plutocrats or the French bourgeoisie, or Stalin, who destroyed his own allies in Spain? Besides, for weeks now you've been telling me morality is just an imposition of forces of production, haven't you? How can you start talking about defending what's right?" By now she was slightly angry.

"Let me rephrase that . . . What I meant by right is nothing more than minimizing human suffering. If the Nazis win, the suffering will be immense. Look what is happening to the Jews in Germany. Surely we've got to resist adding so much human misery?"

Rita nodded. "Yes, but let's not fool ourselves into thinking there's some objective moral rightness that's making us act. We'll struggle against the forces—Hitler's, Stalin's, Franco's—that make millions of lives unbearable. We'll do it because our humanity, our emotions compel us to. Not out of some abstract notion of what's morally right." She looked at him without smiling.

Gil needed to break the spell. The day couldn't end like this. He rose from the bed and came back a few moments later with a box in the shape of a large cosmetic compact. "You asked what will become of us. Well, one thing I think we don't want to become, at least together, is parents. So, I got this for you." He handed her a diaphragm in its case.

Without opening the case, she knew what it was immediately. "I can't take this. If Urs found it at home, that would be the end."

"Would that be a catastrophe?" Before she could answer, Gil went on, "Don't worry. I will keep it here for you."

The letter came with the first delivery on a Thursday morning at the end of April, an hour after Rita had left for her treatment in Lvov.

April 28, 1939
Dr. Urs Guildenstern
14 Ulm Street

Karpatyn
Stanislava

Dear Colleague:
Thank you for your kind communication of 23 March. I have the honor to confirm that I did indeed decline to make any charge on account of an initial consultation with Pani Doctor Rita Guildenstern.
Had I entered into a course of treatment, I would have presented such a statement of account. However, after the initial consultation, I sent her on to my colleague, Dr. Guillermo Romero, a gynecological specialist at the women's lying-in section of the General Hospital.
I understand that Pani Doctor Guildenstern is now under his care. I trust he has been in contact regarding his statements for services.
I remain your obedient servant.

Dr. Stanislaw Pankow

Urs read the letter once, twice, a third time. What could it mean? He had certainly had no bill from this Dr. Romero. And Rita hadn't asked for money to pay for her appointments, at least three of them by now. She hadn't said a word about this new doctor, Romero. She had not even mentioned his name, leaving the distinct impression it was still Pankow treating her. Suddenly Urs felt himself becoming warm. He felt the perspiration beneath his shirt. Drops of sweat trickled down his arms toward the starched French cuffs. He removed his coat, unbuttoned the waistcoat, sat down behind his desk. Now he was perspiring uncontrollably. He loosened his tie, opened the collar. Then he detached it altogether from the shirt. Still the heat was rising everywhere in his body. It had happened once before, he recalled: that morning a year earlier he'd come home from an all-night call, early the morning after

Sommermann's visit, when he found the apartment door unlocked and Rita nude beneath the eiderdown.

The only way to get control of his body now was to go outside into the cold April air. He picked up his collar and tie and pulled his overcoat, hat, and scarf from the rack. Passing the mother and child in the waiting room, he said aloud, "Sorry. I have an emergency. Please come back tomorrow." Out the door, he was already a little cooler, dressing himself as he strode to the railway station.

The midday to Lvov was an especially slow one, stopping at every crossroad town to load the day's milk. There was only one passenger car, with open seating. Sitting there in full view of the other passengers, Dr. Guildenstern had to get control of himself. As he thought about matters, his suspicion about Rita did not recede. His rage alternated with despondency until both were displaced by shame.

At 3:00 p.m. he was standing before the reception at the women's clinic of the Central Hospital, presenting his card and asking for Dr. Romero.

"Sorry, sir. Thursdays he is not here. It's his day off. Doesn't see patients today. Would the doctor care to come back tomorrow?"

Suspicion strengthened, Urs replied, "No. It's a matter of professional urgency." The lie came easily. "Can you give me his home address?"

"Most irregular."

Urs proffered his card once more. "Nurse, I am a medical man. I do understand. I would not presume except for the urgency . . ." He was perspiring again. The nurse appeared to notice. She plucked up a pen, dipped it, and began to write in her careful hospital hand. She gave him the slip of paper. "It's in Ivana Honty Street, ground floor, between here and the station."

He looked at the slip, mumbled a "Thank you," and turned. As he walked down the broad corridor back to the staircase, it dawned on him that if his worst fears were true, he could not face them or the humiliation that would attend them. But the thought had no influence on his course out of the building, retracing his steps along Svobody Prospect. When he came to Ivana Honty Street, he turned right, and a few moments later found himself in front of the address he had been given. It was four o'clock on an overcast afternoon. But there were no lights shining from any of the windows overlooking the street, even as he walked round all four sides of the large building. Then he ventured through the arched entrance and inside found himself facing the vast oak tree in the middle of the courtyard. Only one set of windows was lit. Urs moved around the quad so that the oak shielded him from the mullioned windows glowing in the dusk. He found himself wishing that he smoked or had a flask to keep him warm and provide some Dutch courage. But liquor made him ill, and cigarettes just left him coughing.

All he could do was stand there hoping he was wrong. He fantasized this Dr. Romero opening the door, alone, and walking off to a restaurant. He tried to give the mental image detail . . . Urs would see the man lock his door, he would sigh in relief, hang back a minute, then head for the station, still mystified but relieved.

Next he tried out the worst turn of events: he saw himself hammering at the door, rushing in to find them both smiling, laughing even, naked, at ease and completely unashamed, merely amused by his outrage.

Then Urs began to sob. He tried to conjure up the innocent outcome again, the one that would do no worse than embarrass him. He couldn't do it. *Get a grip, man! Why are you crying anyway?* He could live without her if he had to. If she left him, Urs's life would be as it had been before they met—flat, but calm. He could deal with that. But that's not what his life would be like. Whatever he did, wherever he went, he would be trailed, or heralded, by whispers from women, mockery from men, titters from their children.

He couldn't bear that. He would feel their schadenfreude: "Poor Pani Doctor Guildenstern . . . his wife left him." The ridicule: "No surprise; I don't wonder." It would be as though he had been seen by the whole town urinating in public. He wouldn't be able to face his mother or his father. Sharing his embarrassment, they would have to walk the footpaths of town with their eyes cast onto the pavement. He thought back to Rita. He could live with her not loving him, never having loved him. He could deal with that private chagrin, that mortification. What he could not bear was the public ignominy. He might as well be dead. Now the sobs came in unremitting waves, one after the other.

Then he saw her, through the window, Rita stepping into a dress, and a man behind her, buttoning it up her back. The man came around from behind her toward the window. He knew that face. It took a moment. It was Tadeusz Sommermann.

Urs found himself staggering out of the courtyard. Through tears now coursing down his cheeks, he stepped out from under the arch and saw a cab. He stepped in and ordered, "Take me to the river."

"There is no river in Lvov, *Pan*. They covered it for a sewer when I was a boy." The cabbie laughed, but Urs had stopped listening.

"Is there a lake, a reservoir? Take me."

"Yes, *Pan*. Yanovs'kyi Stav. It's a big one, but it's thirty kilometers out of town, and the road is rather rough." The cabby hadn't noticed how distraught his passenger was.

"Take me there. Immediately." Urs leaned back on the seat and closed his eyes.

❧

At about five thirty, Gil and Rita returned from tea. They would still have time together before her nine o'clock train. Facing another week apart, they both knew that the languid afternoon had not sated them.

Waiting at the building's entry arch was a porter from the hospital Gil recognized. The man looked relieved when he saw Gil. Stepping toward him, the porter drew up to something like attention and said, "A message for you, Doctor, from the hospital. I am to wait in case there is an answer."

Gil took the envelope, opened it, read the note, and passed it to Rita.

Pan Dr. Romero,

The emergency department has admitted a physician. His name is Guildenstern. Your address was found among his effects. The police are here as it is a case of attempted self-murder. The orderly is instructed to await any message you wish to send.

It was signed by an emergency room physician Gil knew. Rita gasped. Gil turned to the porter. "Let's go." All three began to walk quickly to the hospital.

At the entry to the Urgent Care stood a man wearing the cap-and-badge livery of Lvov cabdrivers, along with a policeman and a young man in doctor's whites. Gil went directly to them. Rita followed. He addressed the doctor. "Geretski, what happened?"

"It's a doctor from out of town. Tried to drown himself. Lucky for him the cabbie here had the presence of mind to fish him out of the drink."

Gil and Rita turned toward the driver. Now they noticed his clothes were damp in spots and completely wet below the waist. Without prompting and with relish, the taxi driver repeated a narrative he had already given twice. "This guy asked to go all the way out to the reservoir at Yanovs'kyi Stav. Paid me off when we got there and told me he wouldn't need me to take him back. Well, it was getting dark, and there's never anyone there this time of year. I thought he was acting funny, so I drove away a few hundred meters, turned off my lights, and turned around. Then I just watched. The guy started walking along the shore picking up the largest stones he could find and put them in his pockets, overcoat, jacket, trousers, inside his waistcoat so they bulged. Didn't care if he was ripping the clothing either. Well, you don't have to be a doctor, pardon, to figure out what he was going to do. So I started the cab and drove back as close as I could. By the time I got to the shore, he was up to his neck."

"Thank you for saving my husband," Rita heard herself saying.

The policeman looked at her. "Does your husband know how to swim?"

Rita caught the tense of the verb. "He's all right?"

"He's out of danger now," said the physician.

"No, he can't swim, Officer." Turning back to the doctor, she asked, "Can I see him?"

"Follow me." The doctor turned, and Rita followed him.

"Officer." Gil cleared his throat. "I'll vouch for my colleague. No need to trouble yourself. Thank you." He tried to say it with authority.

It seemed to work. "Very well, sir. I suppose there's no need to take this further." The policeman clicked his heels, bent slightly at the waist, and left.

There was only the cabby left to deal with. "What did your passenger owe?"

"Well, he paid for the journey out. But there is the fare back."

"How much?" Gil found the money and added several zloty. "For your trouble and your wet clothes."

Darkness descended, and then the streetlight came on, a sphere of white surrounded by purple. Gil could see his breath as he stood beneath it, waiting, smoking.

Rita was in Urs's hospital room for over an hour. She emerged shriven. Seeing Gil, she walked over to him. "It's finished."

He had realized as much. Had she returned to him in only a few minutes, he would have known that they could remain together. The longer he waited, the vainer grew this hope. Well before the hour was past, he was beginning to prepare himself for the end of their idyll.

"I am going back to Karpatyn with him tomorrow morning," she said. She bit her lower lip to stop the tremble. Once in control again, she continued, "He's completely in command of himself. He said he would find a way to finish it . . . so coolly, no bravura . . ." Gil did not speak. Rita continued, "I couldn't live with that. I told him I'd go back with him."

"So, it's you or nothing for him? I can't think of Urs as driven by love."

"I'm afraid it's not love. It's shame. Mostly he talked about what people would say, what people would think. His parents, his patients, the whole town. When I said I'd go back with him, it was as though a coffin lid had been pried open. He started living again."

Now Gil knew what he was dealing with. His counterattack was ready. "So, he doesn't love you; it's *amour propre* that nearly killed him. Well, is that a reason for you to go back with him? Is it for his self-esteem that I . . . that we have to sacrifice our happiness? I can't say I care much for how a market-town doctor deals with his personal misfortune, even if I did grow up in the same market town. I don't live there anymore. You don't have to either." The words subsided. Gil waited a moment, gauging their effect on Rita. She was evidently not ready to reply. Perhaps it was moving her from her resolve.

Gil continued, "And what about you? What do you really owe him? Don't you have a right to a life? Why should he be able to trump your happiness just by threatening to throw himself into a reservoir? Rita, we need to break with this petit bourgeois morality."

Now Rita finally interrupted. The words came almost with contempt. "Stop lecturing. Listen to yourself. What you are saying is sheer hypocrisy, selfishness dressed up as moral philosophy." Before he could reply, she started again, now calm. "Remember what you said this morning? Doing right means nothing more than minimizing human misery. Well, that's what I am going to do."

"What about my suffering? What about yours? There are two of us. He is just one."

"You don't understand. I'm not adding up his misery on one side and our happiness on the other, and then seeing which way they balance out. That's no better than bourgeoisie morality."

"Then why are you going to do this to us?" Now there was resignation in Gil's voice. He took out a packet of cigarettes, slid it open, put two in his mouth, lit them both, and handed one to Rita. He wanted the aroma always to remind them of the afternoon they had just spent together.

Rita drew deeply, and the smoke emerged in streams from her nostrils. Gil was standing close enough to see the dust motes in the light of the streetlamp.

"I'm doing this to us because I can't do anything else. I won't dress it up as sacrifice, decency, obligation, doing what's right in anybody's book. I could live with the burden of his misery. But not his death. I'd be walking around the rest of my life trying to rid myself of the guilt. There is nothing I'd be able to enjoy . . ." She looked at him and reached for his lapel, smiling a little. "There's nothing I'd be able to take pleasure in with that thought forever oppressing me." She decided she had to make it concrete for Gil. "The image of Urs swinging somewhere from a noose, putting a gun barrel in his mouth, throwing himself in front of an express, taking an overdose of Seconal. I couldn't bear it. And that's flat." Her hand dropped from his coat.

The next morning Rita took Urs home. His clothes had been cleaned and pressed. He had a new collar and cuffs. His tie was straight and pinned with a pearl stick just above the waistcoat. No one would ever be the wiser. They rode the train talking inconsequentially, as if nothing had happened. Urs was calm; Rita was relieved. Really she was. At least she could live with herself.

Five months later, in the late summer of 1939, she realized she was finally pregnant. The child would arrive early in 1940. She was calm when she told him and watched him mentally count the month back to June and then smile. The child would be his.

PART II

DURING

CHAPTER SEVEN

It was a series of repeated blows to the head, so swift and so hard you couldn't recover before the next one. First the Molotov-Ribbentrop nonaggression pact. Soviet Communists making common cause with Nazis? Then, almost immediately, the Germans put an end to Poland. They did it so quickly the newsreels didn't have time to cover the campaign. Where, everyone wondered, were the French and the Brits? Two weeks later the Soviet Army moved into Poland from the east. The Germans even withdrew from parts they had already overrun, leaving almost half the country for the Russians.

Rita gave birth three months after Soviets marched in. They had decided to call the boy Stefan. She was unable to present her child to his maternal grandparents, however. There was now a border between them. It was the frontier between the western part of the Ukrainian SSR and German-occupied Poland. The mails remained efficient, however, and Rita was able to send pictures.

～

Leaving the hospital with a baby in her arms, Rita walked into an entirely new experience. Urs handed her a new identity card. She was no longer a Pole. She was a Ukrainian now, a Soviet citizen, the wife of the director of a government polyclinic, open to all. His privilege to practice medicine had turned into a right, no, a duty to socialism's future. The social order had been completely reversed. It was at least initially a rough meritocracy. The Russians demanded that things work. That took the ability to count, to read, to work a lathe or a telephone switchboard. If you could do those things, you were needed, and you were rewarded. The Soviet Union, she knew, was powerful but backward. Life would get harder, but not in every way worse, and in a few ways perhaps better.

Urs's unqualified enthusiasm for the new dispensation sometimes grated. Only once did they argue about it. "They want me to join the party." He said it proudly one day in February as he returned from the clinic.

"You aren't going to?" It came out as something between a question and a protest.

"Why not?" He drew himself up. "I'm director of a government facility. They won't really trust me unless I am in the party. As a party member, I can get what the clinic needs. I owe it to my patients."

"Urs. Think. Once you are in the party, you're subject to the whim of anyone above you. And you'll be their scapegoat whenever a conspiracy is needed to explain away failure."

"What do you mean?" The question was sincere. Could it be that Urs had not been reading newspapers or listening to the radio for the last five years? Of course, Rita suddenly realized, this wasn't hyperbole. Medicine had been the only thing that had absorbed him all that time.

"Do you remember the little terror of '37 and the great terror of '38? Do you know what I am talking about? Stalin's show trials in Moscow?"

"Those were Trotskyite wreckers and German agents."

"They were loyal old Bolsheviks. Urs, this is the government that sealed a pact with Hitler to divide and conquer. You can't get their blood on your hands." That was the end of the matter. Rita was relieved. There was one more reason Rita could give, though it would cause Urs pain—something she had learned only the day before.

⁓

Pushing her son in his pram a few streets beyond the market square, they had found themselves before what had been Jastrob's Bookshop. She had scrupulously avoided it since the day she and Urs had returned from Lvov sixteen months before. The urge to ask about Gil would have been too great. The temptation to tell them about Gil would have been overwhelming. She had no idea whether, living only one hundred kilometers away, their son had ever divulged his whereabouts. She missed browsing the shelves, changing a library book, scanning the glossy magazines, but she would not be tempted to visit. She told herself the baby gave her no time for reading anyway.

Now she was standing before the shop for the first time in almost a year. The sign above the door was gone, and the two front windows were both broken. The door hung askew, held by a single hinge. Peering inside she saw the shelves not just empty, but akimbo, and not a stick of furniture left unbroken. Then she heard something stir in the rear. Pushing the baby carriage down the side of the house, she saw an urchin breaking wood off what had been a coal shed behind the house. He stopped, expecting to be reproved by the posh lady with the pram. Rita remained silent, so he spoke. "Family's cold. Can't afford coal even when there is any."

Rita nodded as if to say, Go on. She looked at the back door of the house. "Where did they go? Do you know?"

"Week ago, some Russian police came. I was watching from my window that morning." His eyes indicated a small house just visible across the street. "Big black car, not Polish. Would've recognized the mark. Took them both away. Then they started in on the store. Burned the newspapers in the back. Hauled off all the books." He stopped, then remembered something. "My dad said they were . . ." He searched for the word and found it. "*Chekists*." Now Rita understood. The NKVD, the people's commissariat for internal affairs, the security police. Probably not smart even to hang around this place either, unless you were doing something innocent, like stealing firewood.

But she wasn't going to tell Urs anything that might remind him of Tadeusz Sommermann. Not even to warn him against joining the party.

∾

Things changed gradually. Polish staples disappeared. Soviet ones replaced them, cruder but cheaper. People learned the etiquette of queuing. The farmers' market persisted, and even Rita's mother-in-law surrendered her qualms about making use of it. Very soon Karpatyn was crowded with refugees from the Nazi occupation. Demand pushed up prices. The Polish zloty was for the moment still in use. It didn't matter to Rita. Urs was paid in rubles.

None of this was important to Rita. Only her child mattered. She had not expected to find herself besotted by a helpless, inarticulate infant whose needs and wants you had constantly to guess at. He was no worse and no better than other babies, but he was hers, and he was enough to set aside all her vexations, all her disappointments. Rita was almost shocked by how love for her child just crowded out everything else that had absorbed her thoughts, how it blotted out her regrets, even the end of her affair with Gil. All she ever wondered about the affair now was how to label it—a dalliance, a lapse, a brief, purely sensual adventure? Surely not the beginning of a real love, just something cut short by mature reflection, a cooler head, caution, loyalty, guilt . . .

∽

By a year Stefan was walking. A month later he began babbling distinct sounds, and his grandmother pointed out to Rita that he was talking. How stupid of her not to have noticed!

As he grew Stefan took after his father—dark curly hair, a widow's peak, a cleft in his chin, though not yet Urs's long, thin nose. Looking at Stefan, no one could doubt he was Urs's son. He was also quiet and serious like his father, given to long periods of sustained play. Urs began to wonder when he could teach the boy chess.

By June Stefan was a year and five months old. It was hardly possible any longer to keep him in his pram. Midmorning that Saturday, the 21st, Stefan was padding along between Rita and her mother-in-law on the bank of the Dniester River as they noticed a dozen or more twin-engine Soviet planes flying low toward the west. It was unusual to see military aviation moving toward German-occupied Poland. A half hour later as they came toward the *rynek*—the central square— they observed the head of the local NKVD and three subordinates get in a military staff car and drive off at speed.

At one o'clock Rita and Stefan were surprised to see Urs at the door. Normally he ate lunch at the polyclinic canteen. Besides,

Saturday afternoon was Urs's busiest day. Most people couldn't afford to miss work. Stefan had recognized the sound of his father's tread coming down the hallway to the apartment. "Pappy!" There was evident delight in his voice. Urs came directly into the kitchen. He looked at her. "You haven't heard?" She shook her head. "Turn on the radio."

"It will take a minute or more to warm up," Rita replied. "Tell me what's happened."

"Germans attacked, at four a.m., all along the border."

"How long will it take them to get here?" She resisted the urge to pick up her child.

"It's not the Poles they've picked on this time, or the French. The Red Army will stop them cold."

"With soldiers like the ones we've seen in Karpatyn?" Rita's tone was mocking. "The ones with felt wrapped around their feet instead of boots, scrounging garbage cans for food, while their officers get drunk on Polish vodka?" She caught her breath. "The army that has only one rifle between every two men?" He couldn't stop her. "The same ones who couldn't beat the Finns in '39?" Her voice was steely. "When will the Germans be here?"

Urs could only shrug.

Rita looked around, beginning to calculate what they should carry away with them. "Can we evacuate?"

"I'll try to find out." Urs rose. "I'll see what they know at the town administration." The next moment he was descending the stairs.

By now the radio was making static. Rita turned the tuning knob, sliding the indicator bar through the whole of the long wave band, then the shortwave. Nothing. Wrong time of day for broadcasts? More likely the stations in Lvov had already been abandoned.

She looked out the window. It was calm below. The few people along the street were going about their business. There was nothing to do but wait till Urs returned. Besides, why assume the worst? Her parents had been living under the Germans for almost two years now. They were suffering shortages and restrictions war always imposed on its losers. But no outright Nazi brutality had yet been visited on them. Indeed, they had hardly seen a German soldier in Gorlice, their village near the former Polish-German border. Perhaps what she had seen in the newsreels, what she had read in the Jewish press, perhaps even *Kristallnacht*, were exaggerations or aberrations. If not, well, most Jews had lived through them. Why should things be different here? There was no reason to panic. Saying so to herself did nothing to quell the emptiness in the pit of her stomach, the feeling of pressure on her temples, the disequilibrium when she rose and moved toward Stefan, still patiently mounting blocks on the floor across the room.

She had managed to get Stefan napping by the time Urs returned, now trudging slowly up the stairs to the landing, adrenaline evidently spent. He came into the kitchen and sat, heavily. Rita admonished him with a finger to her mouth and a nod to the nursery. Urs began in a whisper. "It's bedlam at the town hall. Only a little better at military district headquarters. But with the NKVD gone, people are ready enough to talk." He stopped and thought a moment about how to lay everything out. "Let's see, first, it looks like the heavier thrust is not coming this way. The local garrison was ordered north this afternoon. They'll be gone by tomorrow. Party officials have been told to make their way east. And all local officers have been militarized—police, fire brigade, anyone the army can use. That includes doctors, nurses, even orderlies, at the polyclinic."

"You?"

"I got the order this afternoon." He held up an onionskin flimsy. She grabbed it, unfolded it, and quickly read through the fuzzy typescript of a two-sentence carbon:

To Dr. Urs Guildenstern: You are ordered to report for military con-scription no later than seventy-two hours from receipt of this notice at the Karpatyn main railway station. Until your military activation, you will be held responsible for maintaining order at your facility and preserving its stocks for military use.

Below the scrawled carbon of an illegible signature were the words:

By order of the military district of the western Ukraine.

She looked up at him.

Reading her mind Urs replied, "Don't worry. I won't have to go. In this bedlam they can't enforce orders. They can't even be sure I ever got them. Let's wait a day."

Sunday morning it remained unclear whether Urs would have to obey the mobilization order. All that day they turned over the alternatives a hundred times, thinking through every possibility. By evening the chains of reasoning were ending up at the same conclu-sion every time they tried them out: he had to go. The conclusion was strengthened by each new scrap of information.

Rita was the first to voice the inevitable. "You must leave. You've got to obey that mobilization order. It may be your only chance. You can't stay in the clinic. Just like they did in the west, the first thing the Germans will do is shoot every doctor, lawyer, every edu-cated man they get hold of. Stefan and I will be in danger too." He didn't voice disagreement. She didn't say what she had been think-ing. It was cruel to admit, but with Urs gone, she would not have to manage someone too weak to even deal with a failed marriage. She and the child would be better off without him. They would fade into the town's population swelled by refugees.

Monday morning the clinic opened as usual. The staff was on hand and at work. All except the three Ukrainian porters. They were gone. So were the Ukrainian patients.

That afternoon Rita bartered some costume jewelry, a cameo, candlesticks, some lace, and an onyx box for a ten kilo bag of flour, three kilos of sugar, and tins of baking powder and soda, along with blocks of strong laundry soap. In the evening she helped Urs decide what to pack. As she did so, she monitored her feelings. Was this the right decision? Putting things out on the bed, choosing what he was to take and what not, only increased her resolve.

They woke on Tuesday, knowing without doubt that he would have to leave. It was all Urs could do to stifle the relief that welled up in his mind, a feeling he was utterly ashamed of, that he would admit to no one. Sometimes Rita read the shameful desire to get away on his face. And she was relieved. All she could think was that he would be just another burden to carry through a difficult occupation.

❧

Three days later there they were, at the eastbound platform of the Karpatyn railway station. In the bright glare of a morning sun, the quay was crowded. The men were all between the ages of thirty and fifty, a few in ill-fitting uniforms, the rest in coats and ties. Every lawyer, doctor, engineer, factory manager, accountant—every educated Jew and the few Poles that had remained in town—were on the eastbound platform. Most were surrounded by wives, mothers, sisters. But none of the women were traveling. There was only one valise among each party, and the women were there to bid farewell. Mostly they were putting up a brave front.

The military train had not yet arrived. It gave Rita and Urs a chance to cover the ground once again. They had lost count of the number of times they had turned the facts and theories inside out, examined them from every angle, weighing chances and probabilities, information and rumors, like every other family on the platform.

Urs went into the station and came back out on to the platform with a ticket in his hand. "There was another report this morning."

He didn't even need to explain. Stories had reached them almost from the first. The Wehrmacht had been ordered immediately to execute commissars, party members, and any representative of the Soviet state. Was the *Kommissarbefehl*—the directive to execute commissars—Russian counterpropaganda, circulated by the Soviets in order to stiffen their cadres? No, it was coming from the west— the wrong direction to be entirely without substance.

At first it had not worried them. "Thank God you kept me from joining the party," Urs had said. But now they were hearing something more. It wasn't just Germans checking for party cards in Lvov. The rumor was Ukrainians were eagerly identifying Soviet functionaries—party members or not—to the Germans.

Standing on the platform, Stefan holding her hand, Rita looked hard at Urs. He stared back unblinking, then asked, "You're sure?" She nodded. A sudden hoot in the distance, and everyone on the platform turned east, looking down the newly lain, wider, Russian-gauge track. Stefan clutched his mother's leg at the sound. A large steam engine pulled in, locking its eight massive wheels as it slid along the platform, small red flags flying from each side of the main pistons. Behind it were four second-class carriages and a dozen box-cars. The carriages carried consecutive numbers, and each boxcar also had a number chalked on its sides. Urs looked at his ticket, and his gloom lifted a little. He had been allocated carriage seating.

Once he had hefted his valise onto the shelf above the seats in his compartment, Urs pulled the wide window down and leaned out. Rita held Stefan up to him, but the child looked down to the gap between coach and platform and began to cry. She drew him back and leaned forward to hug Urs one last time. As she did so, he whispered. It was not the endearment she expected. "Behind the bedstead there's a loose baseboard. When no one is around, slide it up."

Now as the train began to glide out of the station, he had to shout to be heard. "Did you hear me? Do you understand?"

There was no point answering in the hiss of the released air brakes. She nodded, and suddenly he was another indistinct, flesh-colored oval leaning from the side of the train shrinking into the distance.

&

That night after putting Stefan to sleep, Rita took stock. She had a fair amount to sell: clothing (hers and Urs's), some jewelry, a fox collar, the dishes and silver, plus a second set, medical books in Polish, a radio and a German portable phonograph, the camera, a pair of binoculars Urs sometimes used for bird-watching, and a shelf of philosophy books no one would want. Then she remembered Urs's last words. She walked back to the bedroom, moved the bed, and slid out the board. Urs had proved himself not entirely a *Luftmensch*. Hidden behind the baseboard, in a doctor's clasped leather bag, there were two dozen morphine vials with a syringe, a sack of fifty Polish gold twenty-zloty pieces, and perhaps most fore-thoughtful, a small blue bottle marked in French *Poison, Cyanure de potassium*. How long ago had he bought that, and why?

CHAPTER EIGHT

Three days later Karpatyn was occupied, not by Germans in *feldgrau*, but by Hungarians in forest green. Everyone began to breathe a little. It was going to be another occupation—arbitrary, authoritarian, but not so different from the Soviets, or for that matter, the rigors of military rule many could still recall from the Great War. The only sign of German supervision was the requirement that Jews wear the yellow Star of David armband.

A month later the Hungarians were gone, on their way to the Russian Steppes, replaced by an SS Police detachment. Suddenly the world became an inferno. Even weeks after they arrived, Rita was still asking herself how long she would have to live with a constant knot of fear in her stomach. Once living with terror became everyday normality, some of the physical symptoms of fear lessened. The sudden cramps persisted, but Rita wasn't sweating through two or three blouses a day, each needing to be washed to eliminate the rancid, acrid odor of fear. The knot tightening in her gut always came with a question, one she couldn't really frame further than its first two words: Why this? Why now? Why us? Why me?

Sometimes she'd glance at the tomes of philosophy on the shelf in the living room. There were no answers to be found in any of them. Only Stefan was able to distract her, finding words, asking questions, growing more interesting every day, demanding her love, oblivious to everything pressing down on his mother.

∿

From the moment he arrived in Karpatyn that August 1941, *Obersturmführer* Peter Leideritz had a problem: sixty thousand Jews to deal with, and only a dozen SS/SD and Gestapo, along with eighteen or so Vienna policemen, to do the job. Even with the hundred Ukrainian auxiliaries he had been authorized immediately to recruit, the only way to do the job was terror. He didn't mind. It relieved the monotony. Leideritz was a policeman from Darmstadt who'd been smart enough to join the party when he came of age in '31. He'd been behind a desk since '38. The tight black officer's tunic was uncomfortable against his paunch, but he was glad to be back in the field. It wasn't the front, but it was important.

Leideritz managed to organize three good-sized mass killings by the end of 1941. It was heavy work and unpleasant after the first few moments. Russian machine pistols had been handed out to the Ukrainians. The clip held ten bullets, so reloading was not required after each shot. You couldn't stand too close: the front of your uniform, sometimes even your face, would be covered in human brain. Disgusting. One of the Vienna policeman had refused to participate in the *Aktionen.* The man had to be sent home on sick leave, and despite Leideritz's repeated requests, there was no replacement for him.

Later, when he attended Himmler's speech at Posen, Leideritz knew he had earned the accolade the *Reichsführer* bestowed: "Most of you here know what it means when one hundred corpses lie next to one another, when five hundred lie there or when one thousand are lined up. To have endured this and at the same time to have remained a decent person—with exceptions due to human weak-nesses—has made us tough. This is a page of glory never mentioned and never to be mentioned."

∽

Rita had thought out a daily scheme that would expose her and Stefan to the least risk. But it was still a matter of placing high-stakes bets at roulette. She would awaken the boy just at sunrise, and together they would take a walk while the police were still sleeping. Only in the early evening, when the goons had released men from the labor details, did she venture out again, leaving Stefan napping, hoping he would not waken. It was during those brief periods she made the rounds of the shops, whose provisions were daily diminishing. Rita didn't immediately fear running out of money or trade goods. The shops would probably run out before her reserves did.

What she really needed was someone to talk to, to share the days with, and even more, the long twilight evenings. That, she real-ized after a few weeks, was a problem she could solve. She had space. A lodger would give her company. Perhaps a refugee with a child for Stefan, even a bit of rent money.

Late one afternoon, two days after she placed a small card on the notice board outside the *Judenrat* office, she came back from the meager farmers' market to see a tall, very thin young man waiting at her doorstep. There was a large leather case at his side. He looked neat, even a little prosperous, less withered, less defeated than most of the men she had seen that day. His raven hair was pushed back from his forehead, above dark eyebrows that seemed to rise like two accent marks—grave and acute—above deep brown eyes. His ears stuck out, and his skin was dark, with visible pores. The face was dominated by a straight narrow nose that made a right angle with his long, thin lips. Handsome in the Jewish stereotype, she thought as she came up the steps to the street door.

"Excuse me," was all she said as she brushed past him and slid her key in the door. Before he could react, she was already putting the half-closed door between them. The stranger reacted to her evident anxiety, stepping back and raising his hands slightly as if to suggest he was weaponless. He smiled. "I came about a vacant room. Did you put the notice up?"

Shielding herself with the door, she nodded, frowning. "I don't think you'd be suitable. I am all alone with a small child. What would people think?" What Rita was really thinking was what would her mother-in-law say?

The handsome face frowned. "Here we are all living on borrowed time. You can't worry about what people will think." He looked at her again and peered behind her up to the landing, where Stefan stood looking down at them. The boy had heard his mother's voice and had come out of the apartment to the top of the stair. "Besides, I'm the best lodger you could possibly get."

Rita decided she was willing to listen. She opened the door wide, and they marched up the stairs, where the stranger put down his case and crouched to make Stefan's acquaintance. He was obviously trying to forge an alliance. Rita gathered Stefan up. "So, convince me you're the best lodger I could get."

"To begin, I have a steady job, with an ironclad work permit. If I take the room, you won't have to look for another lodger anytime soon. The district supply officer has given the SS/SD orders to lay off workers like me. So, the Ukrainians can't pick me up on their sweeps for forced labor. I'll pay rent in reichsmarks. In fact, it's the only way I can pay. But I can also use them to buy food for you and the child without risk."

"And all I have to do is rent you a room? What else do I need to do?" She didn't think she needed to insinuate further.

"Lady, you aren't my type." He frowned slightly. "But the Germans are quickly making Karpatyn a jungle. It won't just be Germans and their stooges you'll have to worry about. Very soon it's going to be Jews selling out Jews to survive. Me, I don't need anything you have except a room. And I am willing to pay." He smiled and reached out to tousle Stefan's head.

"It's the boy's room." She looked down at Stefan. "He will move into mine." She turned, and the man followed as she went through the sitting room and walked down the hall away from her bedroom to the nursery.

"I'll take it," he said, almost before he had looked around.

"But you haven't asked how much or seen the kitchen or worried about where I can get a bed and furniture that will fit. Why are you in such a hurry?" Rita turned and led him back to the living room.

"I can't stay where I was. I don't have time to look around much—"

Rita interrupted, glancing at the prosperous leather case. "I see that."

Ignoring the interruption, he went on, "—and I can't afford to spend a lot of time looking. By the way, how much?" Rita mentioned a figure. "I can afford that."

"Should I have asked for more? Mr. . . . . I think I should know your name if you are going to live here."

"Erich Klein, at your service." He plucked her hand and made to kiss it.

Rita pulled her hand back. "We had enough of that from the Hungarians."

So, she had a lodger, and someone besides an eighteen-month-old to talk to. From the first, she had to admit, she liked him. He was easy to look at, in an unusual way. More important, he was interesting, even deep, in some way Rita couldn't immediately identify. Confident, natural, composed, graceful in his movements, he knew instinctively how to share space. From the first, he took to Stefan. Erich Klein was going to be a pleasure to have around.

∾

Klein was the bookkeeper at the Terakowski garment factory. He'd been there for almost four years and, in fact, was its manager. The factory was on the west side of town. Before the war they had produced heavy woolen cloth for the British market. They were just starting to make greatcoats for the Wehrmacht. No one had bothered mentioning to the Germans that October was a little late to start producing garments for the Russian winter.

∾

Rita was avid for talk. The next evening when Erich came in from work, she invited him into the kitchen. She had only started putting kindling in the stove. It was still cold, and he kept his coat on. From it he pulled a long bottle that glowed yellow under the naked lightbulb. "It's an Alsatian. From Riquewihr."

"But how?"

"Spoils of war?" Erich shrugged and laughed as Rita uncorked it. She had not tasted anything so good since the Russian occupation had begun two years before. "What's for dinner?" he asked.

"Fried potatoes with the skin still on them. Get used to it. I hope it goes well with"—she sought the label—"a Pinot Gris."

Klein enjoyed her smile. "What did Stefan do today?" The boy was weaving his way between chair and table leg pulling a wooden train.

"He listened to several stories and had another reading lesson. He's too young, but there is not much else to do."

"Perhaps you will let me try to teach him some arithmetic."

"Double-entry bookkeeping?"

"Actually, I was thinking of tensor calculus." He said it under his breath.

"What's that?" she asked, but Klein ignored the question, straddled Stefan upon his foot, and began riding him back and forth. Stefan understood immediately that he was a horseman and began to whip his mount to move faster.

∾

Rita came back to the kitchen from putting Stefan to bed. There was still half a bottle of the wine, and neither wanted to leave it to the next night. There might not be one. "So," she began, "we've lived in the same town for four years and never met. How is that possible?"

"Different circles. Karpatyn is a big town," Erich said as he poured them both half a small tumbler. The lights were off, and the only illumination came from the glow of the open door of the wood-fired stove. Only the contours of their faces were visible in the dark. Both seemed to realize this would encourage conversation. "I'm from Warsaw. I came in '37 with a close friend, Sylvan Terakowski, the son of the owner of the textile *Fabrik*. Became the bookkeeper. Sylvan and his father were shipped off to Siberia by the Soviets when they nationalized the plant in '39." He paused. "How about you?"

Rita told him the broad outlines—her family, gymnasium with the Benedictine sisters, the law faculty in Krakow, Urs—but she was more interested in his history. "So, you qualified as an accountant in Warsaw?"

"No. I learned on the job here. In Warsaw I was a student. Mathematics." Erich sighed, then he said with great earnestness, "For a long time before the war, Warsaw was the world's center of mathematics."

"And you were there, in Warsaw? But you gave it up and came here. What happened?"

"Long story. I lost my faith."

"Lost your faith in God or mathematics? Is mathematics a religion? I don't understand."

"Something happened while I was doing my doctorate that destroyed all my confidence in math and made me into an atheist too."

"What was that?"

"It's technical."

Rita replied with a hint of annoyance. "Don't patronize me."

"Let's see, how to explain . . . I was in the middle of my studies when I found out that an Austrian—I guess he's German now—named Gödel had proved something terrible a few years earlier. It was 1931, I think. Shook mathematics so that it hasn't recovered. He showed that the only way a mathematical system could include all the truths about numbers was if it also contained a falsehood, too, a piece of plain idiocy, a contradiction, like 'two is an odd number' or 'three plus two equals forty-seven.' And the only way it could avoid such a falsehood was by deliberately being silent, incomplete about some mathematics we knew had to be true. When I found that out—that mathematics had to be either incomplete or contain a contradiction—I just couldn't go on; I had to give it up. I realized that math just turns out to be a game. It wasn't the only game, of course . . ." He stopped, momentarily taken by his simile. "That goes for arguments they teach about God's existence. Same logic, different game. So, now I am an atheist playing the accountancy game! Doesn't shock you, does it?"

"Being an accountant? No, I can deal with that." Rita smiled. "As for atheism, welcome to the club." By now the stove was cold.

CHAPTER NINE

Christmas came, with a falling off in the presence of the forces of order. Most of the SD—the *Sicherheitsdienst*—had gone back to Germany, and the plain policemen were home in Vienna for a well-earned rest. Even after New Year's, when the Germans returned and the Ukrainians had slept off their week of celebration, the streets remained relatively safe. Some began to suggest the worst was over. The Wehrmacht was at Moscow; the war would end by spring. Surely its excesses would give way to rationality. Perhaps the Hungarians would come back.

At six o'clock on a Monday morning late in January, Rita woke to the unmistakable sound of a German truck pulling up at the house. She was frozen in place by the sound, first of the front door being thrown open and then of jackboots on the stair. Her trance was broken by a rapping at the apartment door. It was one of those polite, prewar knocks, not the thud of someone who would break the door down if it were not opened immediately. Erich came to her bedroom door. "It's Germans. I'll get it."

She came out of the room carrying Stefan to see a military police sergeant and a single private carrying a rifle.

The *Feldwebel* spoke to Erich. "Dr. Urs Guildenstern. You must come with us. You have five minutes to pack a case for three days." He turned toward Rita. "You must pack him enough food for the journey."

"You've got the wrong man." Erich looked relieved.

"Four minutes to pack your bag." He pressed a button on his watch. "You're wasting time," the man barked. "We are requisitioning all doctors, dentists, engineers, and other skilled persons for priority war work."

Rita found her voice. "But he's not Dr. Guildenstern. He's my lodger. My husband was named Guildenstern, but he was killed by the Russians." Perhaps blaming it on the Soviet enemy might soften this *Feldwebel*. The sergeant looked at Stefan in her arms and back at Klein. Clearly no resemblance.

"*Leutnant,*" Erich promoted him. "Here is my *Ausweis*. My name is Klein. I am not a doctor. Here is my work permit. I am an essential worker at Terakowski *Fabrik*. There has evidently been a mistake." He handed the documents over.

The other man now cleared his voice, and the sergeant turned to look at him. "*Feldwebel?* Permission?"

"*Ja.*"

"The last man we put in the truck—the old man whose wife was making such a fuss, we had to put her down—he was a Dr. Guildenstern. Perhaps there is a mistake in the list, a duplication."

The sergeant took one more look at Erich's papers, dropped them on the table, and turned for the door.

They heard the lower door slam closed. Erich looked at Rita. "Was that your father-in-law?" She nodded.

Now in the eternal cold of deep winter, daylight was brief, but days passed more slowly. One painfully boring afternoon, seeking distraction for Stefan, Rita pulled the fattest of Urs's medical textbooks off the shelf. She sat Stefan on her lap and opened the book to its illustrations. There were pages and pages of glossy colored diagrams of organs, tissues, and vessels, and finally naked men and hairless women, the skin of their abdomens thrown open in flaps revealing the principal organs. Rita was put off. Stefan was fascinated.

So, for several days there was something to teach him, till at last, one evening when Erich came home, Stefan proudly identified every organ in the thorax. Erich laughed, looked at the suggestive anatomical diagrams on the succeeding pages, and smiled at Rita.

That night lying in her double bed, Rita was awoken by Stefan as he lashed out in a dream, from which, however, he did not awaken. She lay there awake, willing herself back to sleep, employing and discarding every device she had contrived over almost a year to find temporary oblivion. Stefan was warm next to her in the bed. Suddenly she knew why she couldn't sleep. She was thinking of Erich lying alone in the room three meters down the corridor. Despite the cold, she felt as warm to herself as the child next to her. And she began to feel wet, not with perspiration, but down below. *Think things through, Rita!* Too late to do that? Had she already decided? Finally, *Why not, Rita, if you can't think of a good reason not to?* Slipping out from the duvet, Rita rose, closed the door behind her with infinite care, and tiptoed out of the room.

She reached out to the knob on Erich's door. Unlocked and ajar. She felt the erotic surge well over her again.

He was on his back, hands behind his head. Was he lying there waiting for her? She approached. No, he was asleep. Rita drew the sheet and blanket and draped herself along the right side of his body, with her head on his chest. Then she reached back, pulling down his right arm so that it rested over her shoulder. Erich stirred, mumbled something. She whispered, "Sorry, I didn't understand." His voice came back "That's all right," and he turned over on his stomach facing away from her and began snoring lightly.

Rita was left with her cheek impaled on his shoulder blade. After a moment, she rose and tiptoed back to her bed.

The next morning there was no sign that he had been sentient during any part of the episode.

That evening Erich had taken Stefan into the bedroom to read a bedtime story. When Rita came in, the child was already asleep, and Erich was still reading.

"Stefan sleeps as soundly as you do," Rita said as they came into the sitting room.

She was hoping he would say, "How do you know?" Then she would tell him what had happened the night before.

He did not pick up on it. Instead, he said, "Do you believe in free will?"

"I don't have the energy for philosophy tonight, Erich." She had energy enough, but not for philosophy. "But the answer is no."

"Why not?"

"Helps me to sleep at night, knowing there is none."

"Why is that?" Erich persisted.

She didn't want to seem rude. "Without free will, none of those bastards is responsible for what they are doing. They are just sick, crazy, defective individuals we should pity. We have to protect ourselves from them. We can't help hating them, but it doesn't make any more sense than hating an avalanche." She believed it. But she couldn't feel it.

"But if the Nazis don't have free will, we don't either."

"That's right." Rita nodded.

"Rita, you have just made me feel much better about my whole life." Erich smiled mysteriously, rose, and headed toward his room.

I'm glad for you, she thought, *but I don't see why that makes life any easier.* This time she would not wait till he was asleep.

Ten minutes later, just as Erich blew out the candle by his bed, she slipped into his room, still carrying her lit candle. Its glow was reflected in the sheen of a black negligee she had bought for Gil and never worn for Urs. Standing before him, one strap fell from her shoulder. She smiled without adjusting it. He smiled too and made room on the narrow bed.

As she got in, she brought her shoulders forward to give him a view down the décolletage, moved her face over his, and opened her mouth, with a wet tongue ready to play against his. As their noses brushed, Erich turned his head away and gave a little laugh. "Rita, I'm sorry. You're not my type . . . I told you . . . that day when I first moved in. Maybe I was too subtle." He sat up in the bed and took a lone cigarette out of a shirt pocket on the chair next to him. "I was saving this. Let's share it." He lit up and passed the cigarette to her. Then he put an arm around her in a way she could only think of as brotherly. She inhaled, and he watched her nostrils flare around two shafts of smoke.

"I go with men." There, he said it. How would she react? Why hadn't she figured it out before? Perhaps she simply hadn't wanted to.

The words sank in. Rita was suddenly burning with embarrassment. How stupid! How idiotic! The hints and clues came back to her in a rush. The first morning his reassuring her she didn't need to worry, his urgent need to find new lodgings, coming to Karpatyn with a young man—a close friend, he had said.

She moved to sit up next to him and took another deep pull on the cigarette. She had not had one in months. She felt light-headed as she passed it back.

The gesture of sharing a smoke immediately relieved Erich. It was going to be all right. In the light of the candle, they watched the smoke curl up from the glowing end of the cigarette.

The intimacy, the darkness, the aroma of smoke, scent, and bodies emboldened Rita. "What do men do exactly?"

"Some of them do the same things men do with women." He was not going to be more explicit than that. "But I've never been able to. What I like is . . ." He didn't want to use the Polish. "Do you know the word *fellatio*?"

"Of course. Do you like to give it or get it?"

"Both . . . in equal measure."

After a moment Rita looked up, gauging his slightly sheepish smile, blew out the candle, and began moving down the bed beneath the coverlet.

CHAPTER TEN

Einsatzgruppen were not a solution. Too many Jews, not enough bullets. According to reports from Latvia, sometimes it took several days to dispose of twenty-five thousand people. Impact on morale was bad too, especially where shooting children was required. Leideritz had, in fact, lost two more subordinates who refused to carry out such orders. And there was always the chance, never so far encountered, of a thousand or so Jews overpowering a hundred men armed only with machine pistols. So, now a solution had been contrived, finally.

His Jews were to be herded into three ghettos, A, B, and C, a total of 520 houses. Each ghetto was to be repeatedly filled and liquidated. Disposal was to be at the extermination camp Belzec. The task of making Galicia *Judenrein*—clean of Jews—could be completed in a year or less if the facility at Belzec was properly run.

With a little warning, Erich had been able to think things out. In the days before the move, he chose a house at the edge of ghetto A, the largest of the three. The building was a two-story clapboard structure, with a front porch and a few steps. A short footpath from the rear door led to a privy. Immediately behind that, a boundary wall—really just a slatted fence—was being built to keep the vermin in.

As he led Rita and Stefan straight toward the house, she asked, "Why this one, Erich?"

"It's your lifeline. Biggest ghetto, longest fence, hardest to guard. With your house back up right to the wall, easy to trade across the fence."

He had been thinking ahead. They were only allowed to bring in what they could carry. For Stefan that meant a large stuffed dog. Only Rita knew it contained the morphine, the poison, and the gold coins Urs had left them. She knew Stefan would never lose hold of his stuffed bowwow, and guards would not search it on the way in.

When the three finally settled down in a room on the top floor at the back, overlooking the wall, they were surprised to find themselves alone. The house had been assigned twenty occupants, and they had the largest room on the upper level, with a small woodstove, to which five thin mattresses had been allocated. Erich headed back to Rita's apartment to carry in another bag of necessities. With a work permit, he could come and go with relative freedom before the curfew.

After Erich left an older man poked his head in, shrugged his shoulders, and took possession of a corner. His hair was white, short but still thick, brushed carelessly to the right. The matching white beard was not of the religious variety. Rows of wrinkles on his brow gave way to crow's feet that deepened so they almost hid his eyes when he smiled, as now he did. Once he had been heavy, and he still had the round cheeks of a well-fed Father Christmas.

He introduced himself, in a thick German accent. "Friedrich Kaltenbrunner. Excuse the poor Polish. I was raised in Germany, and only moved back to Poland in '38. Or rather was moved there . . ." He said this last more to himself than Rita.

"You're quite welcome." Rita smiled a little. "Still plenty of room. There are only three of us so far, if you count my child. Don't understand why we are so lucky."

"Don't you? That person you are with—no man wants to be in a room with him. He's a pederast. They are all saying so downstairs. Didn't you know?"

Rita said nothing, her welcome to the old man immediately wearing out.

Kaltenbrunner went on. "Doesn't bother me, though. I'm more broad-minded than the next man. Seen it all in Berlin anyway, before the Brownshirts cleaned up the place—not that there weren't a lot of queers in the SA anyway."

"If you are broad-minded, then be respectful of Herr Klein." She deliberately invoked the German. "He's my friend."

"Mine too," Stefan chimed in, unafraid to approach the old man.

"You are quite right, my dears. Besides, I'm too old to raise any interest in a young man. We'll be the best of friends! So will we." He looked down, reached out to Stefan's dog, and began moving it across the floor, making barking sounds. The boy was immediately won over.

Perhaps Kaltenbrunner would be all right. *It's not as if we have the luxury of choosing our bedfellows,* Rita thought.

"Stefan, stay in the room and play with your doggie." She looked up at Kaltenbrunner. "Can I leave him for a few minutes?" she asked. The old man smiled reassuringly and reached for the stuffed animal again. Instinctively she knew she could trust him. Were the eyes really the mirror of the soul? Of course not, but Kaltenbrunner's sought hers out and twinkled reassuringly. He was a schoolteacher, one with the best teachers' knack for putting pupils at their ease, and he was using it now on both of them.

Rita went down the stairs and into the street. It was not something she had done without great risk for a long time. It was silly, now imprisoned in a ghetto, but for a moment she felt free. A convict, liberated from solitary confinement, finally allowed to roam the prison yard with the other inmates. The feeling would soon wear off.

When Rita returned, the older man was unpacking his case. What was his name, she wondered. *I can't be so rude as to ask again* . . . Stefan came to the rescue. "Pan Kaltenbrunner says I can call him 'Freddy.'"

"That's not respectful, Stefan."

"We'll be living a little too close for the niceties, ma'am." Kaltenbrunner was taking two large books from the jumble of clothing in his case. Rita's jaw dropped perceptibly. Books! Did he think he was coming to the university? He put them at the head of his mattress. Noticing her widened eyes, he explained. "My pillows."

That evening they exchanged brief autobiographies. The older man's was wrapped in history. "I was born in Warsaw, but taken to Germany as a child, 1872." Erich and Rita started making the same calculation in their heads. *He's seventy*, they thought. "I was a student in Göttingen, and then a teacher in Stuttgart for thirty-three years—science—with time out for the Great War. I was in the west when we nearly captured Verdun." There was a twinge of patriotism in his voice, but the name Verdun meant little to his listeners.

"How did you manage to get out of Germany?" Rita asked.

"I was pushed. The Nazis were working to a deadline. Early in '38 the Polish government announced it wouldn't admit anyone from Germany without valid Polish passports after October that year. So the German government revoked residence for every Jew with Polish nationality, to force them out before the deadline. My Iron Cross second class didn't matter."

∽

Trade was the way of the world. Once an institution like the ghetto was established, a whole economy spontaneously arose to make it pay.

But first the *Judenrat* had to establish its police, the *Ordnungsdienst*—order service. This ghetto *Judenpolizei*—the *Jupo*—soon began to fulfill its function: ensuring the high prices of a thriving black market. Once ghetto rations were fixed at less than two hundred calories per person per day, service with the *Polizei* became a magnet. The opportunity to stand at the gates, charged to prevent smuggling, attracted men with ingenuity as well as a broad streak of sadism. Sharper than the German or Ukrainian guards just outside the gate, the Jewish police were not above finding the most intimate hiding places, stripping whatever food that workers had managed to get past the Germans.

A market in survival sprang up and flourished beneath, over, and through the ghetto walls. Gentile urchins could be called from the shadows beyond the wall simply by standing near it long enough to be noticed on the other side. They would scratch or rap on the wood to let you know they were there and ready to trade. Most anything was available for a price, if it was small enough to be tossed over or passed through, and if the price was right. Some of the Polish traders developed a reputation for honesty that earned them the ability to charge the highest prices. As long as there was the prospect of continued business, even the less well-established "firms" could be relied on.

Within a few weeks, a reliable postal service was established, though the rates to mail a letter were always transatlantic, and whatever came from elsewhere arrived postage due. It was through these mails that Rita learned of her parents' relative good fortune. Unlike

Karpatyn, their small town in the west of what had been Poland was now the Reich. The district was governed by a civilian *Gauleiter*, and none of the draconian measures of the *Generalgouvernement* had been imposed—no ghetto, no food restriction, nothing but the yellow star. Her parents were surviving, slowly trading away what they had.

Each morning the two men left for work—Erich to the factory and Kaltenbrunner to the school established by the *Judenrat*. Once they left, a morbid fascination would draw Rita to the windows. Day by day she watched the first month's triage eliminate the weakest—the ill, aged, and infirm—from the ghetto. Those who came without money or tradable goods immediately began to perish. From her window Rita could track the fate of a victim, from selling pencil stubs to begging, to listlessly sitting at the curb, finally to collapse, self-befoulment, and then death by a combination of starvation, the elements, typhus, and the implacable will to die.

The morning came that she could not bring herself to the window nor to venture outside. Her eye fell on the two volumes that really did serve Kaltenbrunner for a pillow. Reaching down, Rita broke the unspoken rule that no one's things were to be touched. She picked one up: Darwin, *The Descent of Man*, and then the other, Darwin, *On the Origin of Species*, both in German, well-read, annotated, dog-eared, both almost as old as Kaltenbrunner himself. She had heard of the more famous of these, and it held no interest. The other was unfamiliar to her. She slid her back down the wall, opened the volume, and read the subtitle, "Selection in relation to sex." She turned the page and began reading. The *Fraktur* print posed no problem, and the German was clear. All the rest of that morning she read, occasionally monitoring Stefan, who was content to play with wooden blocks and a few broken lead soldiers. She only needed to be sure he did not chew them.

As the afternoon ended, she realized that she had ignored Stefan, who had fallen asleep at his naptime, and she had neglected any preparation for the evening meal. Worst of all, she had violated the invisible barrier surrounding another's scant possessions. Carefully she put the book down, laid its more famous predecessor on top, and went about her business.

That evening, after a supper of gruel, Kaltenbrunner pulled Stefan into his lap. The boy was content to remain there with his stuffed dog. "So, how far did you get in *The Descent of Man,* my dear?"

Rita was mortified. "Freddy, I am so sorry . . ."

Kaltenbrunner waved her apology away. "I only know because you put them back in the wrong order. *On the Origin of Species* always goes on the bottom." Rita looked at him quizzically. Again he seemed to read her mind. "No, I'm not superstitious . . . that just brings bad luck." He smiled, and this time both Rita and Erich laughed out loud. Now Kaltenbrunner became serious. "*The Origin* on the bottom because it's the foundation. You have to read it first. Holds the explanation of the world, makes sense of everything, even the fate of the Jews."

"But you can't buy that stuff. Darwin is what the Nazis believe." There was heat in Erich's voice.

"Yes, and they also believe the earth is round. Does that make it false? Anyway, Nazis don't understand Darwin at all."

"You do?" Erich was still contemptuous.

"I've spent the last forty years on the subject, written a few books, corresponded with the leading evolutionists . . ." He paused to gauge the effect on Klein, who did not reply.

Here Rita intervened. "So, how does Darwin explain the world, never mind the fate of the Jews?"

Erich joined in. "Then you can get on to how the Germans get him wrong."

"That's easy . . . What Darwin discovered was the completely mindless, mechanical process that, repeated a million times, produced life, then human life, thought, language, everything people used to think needed a God to design and create. What looks like purpose, meaning, means and ends—it's all just blind variation and an environment passively filtering out the losers in the latest heat of a race that never ends."

It was now dark in the room. "We don't need another argument for atheism, Freddy. We have enough already. Just look around," Erich said.

"So, where did the Nazis get Darwin wrong?" Rita's question was earnest.

"They got almost everything Darwin taught wrong. To begin with, evolution has no room for higher purpose, still less, Nazism as fulfilling one. And there is no such thing as a master race. There are just temporary local winners and losers. The Third Reich is the transitory outcome of a vast process heading nowhere. Today's winners are sure to be tomorrow's losers when environments change. Think of the dinosaurs."

Rita's laugh was grim. "How many millions of years were dinosaurs around? Hitler's thousand-year Reich might as well be a million years as far as you and I are concerned. Anyway, how does your Darwin make sense of the fate of the Jew?"

Erich was silent. He knew that the Reich could not last more than a few years more, but why that was was too dangerous to reveal, even to his fellow inmates condemned to death.

Kaltenbrunner replied, "I'll tell you some night . . . when you're ready to listen."

The next morning Rita began reading *On the Origin of Species*. When she finished a week later, she turned back to the first page and started to read it again.

∾

A few minutes after ten o'clock on a gray morning a week later, Erich burst through the door. "Grab your coat; let's go." He swept Stefan off the floor too quickly for the boy to grab his stuffed dog. Erich's urgency brooked no hesitation. Rita pulled on her coat and followed him down the stairs. Erich turned at the bottom and made for the back door that led to the outhouse and the ghetto wall. Three boards were akimbo. Still carrying Stefan, he pushed Rita through them. Straightening the slats, he yanked Rita's yellow star armband off, took the arm, and began walking down the street directly away from the ghetto wall. At the end of the first block, he finally spoke. "We're just a nice Aryan family out for a stroll." Then she became aware of the noise rising from behind the receding wall.

Erich spoke under his breath. "Ghetto clearing *Aktion*. Just keep walking. You're not involved. You don't hear anything."

"What if we're caught out here without the armbands?"

"Stay inside today, and you're certain to be 'caught.' There is a double-reinforced German *Polizei* unit in there, along with the Ukrainians and the *Jupo* thugs, taking everyone without a work permit to . . . to wherever they have been taking them."

"Where are we going, then? We can't walk around outside all day."

"We're going to visit family friends, my dear." He patted her arm. Raising Stefan to ride on his shoulders, Erich led them through the town square, where a desultory farmers' market was in progress. Then they turned down the tramway toward the factory district.

The streets were deserted, sinister, bathed in gray halftones. Dazed, Rita asked, almost to herself, "Couldn't we just keep walking right out of town?"

Erich's reply brought her back. "To where would we just walk, without papers or money? We're a hundred fifty kilometers from the nearest city large enough to hide in, and even there we probably wouldn't last a week."

Twenty minutes later they walked past a large building with a peeling sign, *Terakowski Ready-to-Wear,* and came to a high wall with a gate. Turning in at the entrance, they saw a large villa. Rita felt the immediate relief of no longer being exposed on the street. They came up to the stairs to the entry. Erich dismounted Stefan from his shoulders and rang the bell.

An elderly woman invited them in. With some formality, Erich spoke. "Pani Terakowski, permit me to introduce Pani Doctor Guildenstern and"—here he turned to the boy—"Stefan." Turning to Rita he explained, "The Terakowskis own the factory. Pani Terakowski's daughter is in charge, now that her father is . . . gone."

"So pleased to meet you, my dear." The elderly woman led them to a sitting room. "May I offer you some tea?" Every seat seemed covered by antimacassars. The lady herself looked out of the last century: her posture was upright, gray hair swept to wide flat promontory above her forehead, held at the back by a pearl comb. Her black dress swished across the floor, lifting the fringe from the carpet as she moved across the room to a bellpull by the fireplace.

Rita found herself on another planet. "Very pleased to meet you. Yes, tea would be lovely." Lovely? Heavenly! Then she thought, *The ghetto is being brutalized, and I am sitting here preparing to balance a teacup on my lap?*

As she sat, Stefan came over to her and whispered.

"Excuse me," Rita said, embarrassed. "The child needs the toilet."

"How silly of me." Pani Terakowski put her at ease. "Yes, you both need to freshen up. It's just at the top of the stairs." Rita looked beyond the open double doors to the foyer. Up the stairs? She had nearly forgotten about indoor plumbing. By the time she returned, a servant girl was setting out the tea.

After a half hour of inconsequential conversation, a younger woman entered, brightened as she saw Erich, kissed him on both cheeks as though he were family, and introduced herself. "I'm Lydia. Excuse me, Erich, we need you on the shop floor." Evidently he was more than a bookkeeper. She turned to Rita. "Would you care to come too?" Rita caught the hint of something more than an invitation in her voice.

"Of course." She took Stefan by the hand and followed.

They went through the kitchen and out the back door to a cobblestoned alley separating the residence from a complex of storage sheds and factory buildings. Inside the largest of these buildings, a short flight of stairs led to an office with a large window overlooking the shop floor. Holding Stefan's hand Rita struggled to keep up with Lydia and Erich as they mounted the stair. There she turned to observe the factory floor itself through the window.

The workbenches were covered with field-gray German military coats, interspersed with sewing machines, large boxes of metal buttons, and bags from which cloth military insignia were spread out across the tables. The workers—men and women, some very young—were not at the benches. They were gathered in small groups, some sobbing, others rending their clothes. A dozen were shrieking as others sought to calm them. A few were at the doors of the building, physically being prevented from leaving by their coworkers.

Erich looked at Lydia, who began, "People have been coming in all morning, with more and more horrible stories."

"I see." He nodded, turned, and went down to the shop floor.

Looking down through the office windows, they could see him moving toward the other end of the building, where the largest group of workers was gathered. Rita could not hear what he was saying, but whatever it was, after a few minutes, his words seemed to be having an effect. Some went back to their workbenches; others began again to shift stock from place to place. A forlorn few remained where they had been.

Erich returned to the office.

"What did you tell them?" Rita asked.

"Most of them left kids in the ghetto this morning. I told them that we'd gotten word back, and the children had been hidden. Then I told them we had a quota to maintain, and lives depended on it." Erich sat down at a desk and pulled a ledger toward him. Then he dropped a piece of paper and three colored pencils to Stefan, who began entertaining himself on the floor. Lydia too busied herself with correspondence. Left alone, Rita walked down the steps and moved along the shop floor. She could see that at least some of what was being done did not require any skill and it would occupy her mind. She found a space at one of the workbenches and began sorting buttons.

CHAPTER ELEVEN

That night after curfew, they slipped back into the ghetto the way they had come. Upstairs in their room, they found Kaltenbrunner, trembling. They said nothing. Kaltenbrunner couldn't deal with the silence.

"You don't want to hear? Look out the window tomorrow morning. The bodies will still be there. They must have beaten a few thousand out of the ghetto by the afternoon. Anyone who didn't jump was shot, anyone who fell out of line was shot, anyone carrying anything was shot, until the *Feldwebel* told the goons to stop. Killing too many was going to prevent them from meeting their quota at the railroad sidings, he said."

"You heard this?"

"And saw it. Through a cellar window, where I was hiding, with about fifty children. It will be worse tomorrow or the next time when they realize they didn't get many of the kids."

"Tomorrow they are going to clear ghetto B," Erich observed quietly.

"How do you get this stuff?" Rita wasn't so much asking as expressing wonderment.

"Don't ask." He thought better of his answer. "Mainly through Lydia. There are always leaks."

❦

The Germans were as good as Erich's word. The next day they burned the smaller ghetto, along with all those still hiding in it, to the ground. It was the first time Rita experienced the smell, first of burning human hair, then flesh, and finally organs. The acrid smell gave way to a distinctive roasting odor, which turned treacle-sweet and then hung in the air like smolder-smoke. The only way to rid oneself of the smell was to sit in the outhouse. Even that did not work for more than a few minutes. Why did her child have to live through this?

The smoke cleared, but the smell never left her.

❦

That night Erich and Rita lay together, for warmth and humanity. Erich began to whisper. "They'll be back for the children soon." He fell silent, gathering his courage for a moment. Then he began again. "I think we can save Stefan." Rita didn't reply, so he outlined a plan. The last letter from Rita's parents in Gorlice reported the continuation of relatively good conditions there. Lydia could locate a Polish woman to bring Stefan to them. "He'll be safe, and then we can get you a work permit from the Terakowski works."

"No. I can't do it."

From the darkness they heard Kaltenbrunner, who had been listening. "You have to, Rita." He spoke between clenched teeth. "You must. Ever hear of the *Kindertransport*?" Silence from Rita. He continued, "In '39, everyone knew there would be war. The Brits organized ten thousand visas for German children. People took their kids to the *Bahnhöfen*—the railway stations—packed and labeled, certain to be safe and sound. At the last minute, dozens of mothers snatched their children from the train and ran home. Every one of those kids is dead today."

Rita was not going to argue. There would be no point to life without the child. Literally, nothing to organize her continued existence around. No reason to take another breath.

～

Rita thought the matter had dropped. In fact, she had become a creature to be manipulated by two men who knew better than a woman. There was little time to lose. Freddy began by finding her parents' address among her things. Within three days Lydia Terakowski had located someone—a Polish Home Army courier—who traveled between Galicia and the Tarnow region, where her parents lived. Then they sought the right time one evening to broach the matter with Rita.

Erich produced a Terakowski work permit with Rita's name on it.

"Rita, this will enable you to get out mornings and avoid the next ghetto clearance."

She looked at the form. "But what about Stefan? I can't take him to the factory."

Quietly, firmly, Freddy replied, "You must send him to your parents. It's his only chance to survive."

"I told you. I can't do that to my own child. I'd rather die."

Exasperation tinged Erich's voice now. "You'd rather both of you die than neither?" He could not control himself. "What kind of a mother are you?"

Freddy spoke. "People have to survive this war. You, your son, someone. Erich and I probably won't make it. Maybe you won't either. But you don't have the right to help them kill off more of us than they can. Someone's got to tell the world, to bear witness, to see that the guilty are punished."

Rita gathered her wits to reply. "Bear witness to their crimes before the bar of history?" She spat out her rejection. "That's not a reason to live. In a hundred years' time, Hitler will be remembered the way we think of Napoleon. In a thousand years, he'll be another Alexander the Great, saving civilization from the Bolshevik hordes the way Alexander saved Greece from the Persians!" She paused, troubled by the thought. "You're right; I don't have the right to help them kill. But my emotions are real, and they are screaming that I cannot send the boy away."

It was Kaltenbrunner who finally broke through. "Yes, your emotions are screaming at you. But your emotions have no foresight. They can't look ahead. They only look back to what enabled your ancestors to survive. If you allow them to overmaster you in the life-or-death choice you face, you'll regret it in a future that your emotions cannot see."

Rita was listening. But she was also doing something else. She was making herself give up Stefan. She was creating the emotion of loss, grief, horror, torture that she would experience when a German or a Ukrainian, or even a *Jupo,* tore Stefan from her and did something so despicable to his body she could not bring words to it, even as the images moved across her thoughts. She was inwardly watching a man push Stefan's body off his bayonet with a jackboot and then clean the gore from his shoe, drawing the heel across a curbstone as if befouled by a dog. She made herself watch invisibly while Stefan danced, begging for a crust, in a group of children. In her imagination they were picked off one by one, so many clay targets moving across a carnival shooting game. Finally she pictured Stefan in a soldier's grasp, held tight by his arm until the soldier opened his grip, letting the small body fly into the brick wall. The emotion she produced flooded away the pain she felt at the thought of sending him away.

"Very well."

Erich began quietly. "We don't have much time. Tomorrow they'll sweep through ghetto C. Then early next week, it will be our turn again." She nodded. "You must have him ready to leave tomorrow afternoon. Lydia's contact might be ready to go that soon."

∾

In fact, it was late in the afternoon two days afterward that Erich slipped back into the ghetto through the fence and led Rita, holding Stefan close, out into the street on the other side of the wall. The contact Lydia had found was a very tall, straight-backed woman, in a long coat and cloche hat with a Robin Hood feather, and a face half covered by a net veil—rather chic. The veil's fine black tracery of lines and nodes ended just above her mouth, which had a slight but pronounced tilt to the right. Was it a stroke, or more likely a birth injury, the last mark of a difficult forceps delivery? The doctor's wife in Rita wondered. Then, as she passed Stefan to the woman's arms, she noticed the finely manicured varnish of the nails on her fingers. The woman put Stefan gently on the pavement. Rita proffered a small bag, but the woman refused it. "We two cannot look like we are going away for any length of time."

"I see. You have done this before?" The woman nodded. Rita looked at her closely, trying to memorize the face. She needed to know this person. The veil made it hard. "Can you tell me your name?"

"I am sorry. I can't risk it. I am Home Army." It was the indigenous Polish resistance. "Mainly I am a courier. There is a unit in Nowy Sacz. They'll get the boy to his grandparents in Gorlice.

I have learned the address by heart." She looked down the alley both ways. She pulled a small piece of hard candy from her pocket. "Here, Stefan, now kiss Mommy, and we'll go for a walk."

Erich was standing aside, feeling that he should do something. "Rita," he whispered, "what about his stuffed dog? At least he can take that."

She shook her head. "I have to keep something of him." She waited till Stefan turned the corner before beginning to sob.

～

The next morning was a Saturday. For Rita, now living on time paid for by forced labor, it was a workday. Up in the dark, she followed Erich out the ghetto gate, showing her pass with studied boredom, keeping a few paces behind, expressing no wonder at the open streets beyond the gate. Despite the gloom and the cold, the walk to the Terakowski works felt almost like freedom.

After a very hot, thin tea and a piece of rye-and-sawdust bread with more margarine than she had seen in a month, Rita was assigned to buttonhole making. This was a process done by hand that required good eyes and consistent stitching, but had little risk of ruining a greatcoat. She sat at the bench working steadily all day and the next, willing herself not to go up to the office each time she saw Lydia come in. Since there was nothing she could do anymore for her child, knowing his fate wouldn't make a difference. Besides, not knowing, she could enjoy imagining Stefan in his grandmother's lap, cosseted and fed, clean and warm.

By Tuesday Rita had played this trick on herself so often it was no longer distracting her. She was at work on the buttons of a *feldgrau* greatcoat when Erich came over and sat down. "We just heard. The woman, the courier, was taken by the Gestapo." She gasped. He put a powerful hand around her wrist and forced her to respond to the pain before she could cry out. "They don't know when or where exactly. She was carrying Home Army documents. They don't have any idea whether she had already delivered Stefan safely or not."

❦

Two weeks later came a letter from Rita's father. It was his last. Conditions had changed in the regions absorbed into Germany proper. The old Gauleiter had been removed, and the new one had begun ruthlessly to impose the new order on their town. Remaining Jews had been told to pack bags for a journey to the east and report the next morning. Rita's father knew they were to be sent for extermination. She read the letter three times. There was nothing in it about Stefan.

❦

All three were sitting on the floor, each slouched against a different wall, staring at the candle in a lantern equidistant among them in the middle of the room. Like a family no longer on speaking terms, the silence among them was ominous.

Erich's voice cut into it. "Freddy, something you said a few weeks ago, it keeps coming back to me. Something I don't understand at all."

Kaltenbrunner replied listlessly. "What's that?"

"Well, you said Darwin explains everything, including the fate of the Jews. There's nothing about Jews, Germans, or even human history in his books, is there?"

Rita looked up. She recalled the question lingering with her after the others had fallen asleep. "Yes, tell us, Freddy. Tell us how your Professor Darwin predicted that the Germans would exterminate the Jews."

"Quite the contrary. They won't exterminate the Jews. And the Germans will lose eventually."

"Eventually, when we are all dead?" Eric's tone was quiet but fierce.

"Not all of us, Erich. They will kill off a lot of us. But not all of us."

Rita broke in. "Why are you so optimistic?"

"Look, Rita, think of Nazism as a disease carried by a bacillus, one that is highly contagious and invades brains by playing on people's hatred, fears, greed. For years it barely subsisted without spreading. Then the environment changed—the Depression—and it began to breed and spread."

"Hasn't infected us, but it will kill us," Erich interjected.

"Maybe . . . probably. Under the right conditions, Nazism spreads from brain to brain. Like any parasite, it kills its carriers, so it has to spread faster to survive. Think of all those Nazis dying on the Eastern Front."

Rita interrupted. "Why be confident the disease will be wiped out, instead of wiping everyone else out?"

They couldn't see Kaltenbrunner's smile at the question he expected. "Like any disease, Nazism breeds resistance. Think about the bubonic plague in the fourteenth century. The plague killed off thirty percent of the whole population of Europe. But it created a new environment for itself, one that selected for anything that could defeat the plague. It left an entire generation resistant to it. We've never had another Black Death. The Nazis will do the same thing."

Rita was persistent. "And why shouldn't the Germans kill all of us off long before Nazism is burned out or burns itself out?"

Kaltenbrunner was silent for a moment. Then he began, "I don't know the answer to that question. No one does. Darwin realized there is no way to predict when or where or even what variation will blindly emerge and begin to exploit its environment. Only that there will always be one. Somewhere, sometime, somehow, perhaps even already, some variation has emerged—some response, triggered by the new environment Nazism has created for itself, that will destroy it."

Erich had been listening, thinking, *Freddy, you are right, and your reason isn't too far off the mark. If only you knew.* There was something that was already working to destroy Nazism. And Erich was sworn to secrecy about it. Would it make any difference for them? He couldn't see how.

CHAPTER TWELVE

A fter April orders came down to suspend the ghetto-clearing *Aktionen*. Leideritz wondered what the problem was. Perhaps other larger ghettos—Lvov, Lublin—had priority. Never mind, typhus and starvation were doing some of his work for him. It was only important to prevent infection from spreading beyond the ghetto. That would require really severe discipline. He had already had to threaten more than one unshaven *Polizei* with the Eastern Front for slovenliness.

Passage through the ghetto gates was a twice-daily challenge to appear completely inconspicuous. Never be first. Never come late. Carry nothing. No bright colors, no tatters, and above all, no eye contact with anyone, inmate or *Polizei*. At least once Rita thought she'd copped it.

Coming in late, as the curfew siren began to blare, she was jostled in the crowd and brushed a German sleeve.

"*Entschuldigung, Mein Herr,*" she said, as sincerely and obsequiously as she could contrive.

Perhaps it was the faultless German, but the words jolted the *Gefreiter,* bored by the passing tide of flotsam. He grabbed her coat and pushed her to the ground. "Too close, Jew-sow." Rita watched him reach for the lanyard on his belt to guide his hand toward the sidearm, heard the snap of the metal holster clasp and the slight squeak of stiff, polished leather. The sequence seemed to proceed in exquisite slow motion. She tried to make eye contact. Impossible! His face was shaded by the high-peaked cap and its black brim. Now the blue metal pistol barrel came into view. She could even smell it—Cosmoline? Gun oil? Cartridge powder?

A *Leutnant* came out of the guard shack. The corporal straightened up. "As you were, *Gefreiter.* Can't waste bullets anymore, especially on workers." The officer walked away, and the soldier merely kicked Rita in the thigh. She rose and walked away as though nothing had happened. Nothing had, she decided.

❧

The Terakowski textile factory was a vast conspiracy. Most employees had contrived to add a relative or two to the work rolls. Now there were several hundred in the buildings every day being fed, kept warm, and out of harm's way. Each piece of clothing produced went through exhaustive, obsessive examination for defects, and almost everything needed restitching somewhere. The work was spread out over the available hands.

❧

A few days after Rita began stitching buttonholes, she noticed the young woman, a girl actually. She couldn't help noticing. Small, dark, her hair in a pageboy that seemed always to look as though it had been newly washed and cut by a French coiffeur—how did she do it without shampoo or even hot water? Dark eyebrows, and the worry lines between them, above a prominent nose gave her a serious look Germans would have called Jewish. But it was the eyes Rita couldn't stop making contact with. Small irises in whites so large there was no trouble at any distance telling that the girl was glancing in her direction.

On the third morning, looking up from her steaming mug of tea, Rita just openly smiled at her. By that afternoon the girl was at the bench behind Rita's work space, perched on a high backless stool, a belted gabardine coat before her, with a small book half hidden by the folds of the coat. Without dropping a stitch, Rita asked, "What could you be reading?"

"*Lord Tadeusz.*" Her whisper carried. It was the great classic of nineteenth-century Polish literature, suppressed by the Russians and the Austrians, celebrated by the newly independent Poland, compulsory in all the schools.

Rita smiled slightly. "We all grew up on it, didn't we?"

"Funny. I hated it in school. It was the set text in three different classes in the gymnasium I was sent to." She paused. "My name is Daniella, after my grandfather. But they call me Dani. I know yours . . . Rita. You're a friend of Erich's, right?"

Rita nodded. "Why are you reading it again if you hated it?"

"They made us read it. That's why I hated it."

"So, now you love it?" Rita reflected for a moment. "All I can think about it now is how it seduced us into Polish patriotism." She looked down at her needlework. "Look where that got us. Patriotism is for Germans! Not for Poles, certainly not for us."

Dani would not be bullied. "Still, it's beautiful."

Rita had to show that she was no philistine. She put down her needle and thimble, closed her eyes for a moment, and began to quote a line of the poem,

O mother Poland, in your fresh grave
We lack the strength your doomed life to praise.

She looked up at the girl. "And our doomed lives? Shall we spend them praising Poland?"

"It's beautiful." Dani would not be gainsaid.

"Yes, the poem is very beautiful, but that's all it is. Think about the words, glorifying a country that has forsaken you entirely. Let the Germans take Poland—to devil with it . . ."

"Stop." Dani said it so loud the workers at the benches around them lurched in their direction, ready to break up a catfight. But Dani was hugging Rita and whispering to her, so only she could hear. "It's beautiful, and that's all it has to be." She released Rita, and taking up her work, she began to recite from memory.

At first Rita was not listening. She was still in the fierce grip of Dani's embrace well after the girl had released her. Why? It wasn't just the human contact. It was a frisson she couldn't classify, one she had never experienced. Finally the feeling subsided. Rita began listening to the poetry. When Dani finally finished, Rita asked, "Why do you need the book? You know it by heart."

"I don't know the whole poem yet. I am trying to memorize it."

"All of it? How's that possible? It's four hundred pages."

"It rhymes. That's how. The *Odyssey* and the *Iliad* were sung from memory long before they were written down. When I know the whole thing, no one will be able to take it from me. I'll be able to escape from all this whenever I want." She passed her hand before her face dismissively. Then Dani cut a thread with her teeth and finally put down the piece she was working on.

❧

Within a few days, Rita and Dani were inseparable at their workbench. Rita would listen to long passages from *Lord Tadeusz*, sometimes closing her eyes, calmed by the rhythm of the girl's distant voice. Some days there was silence, as Dani's lips would move silently, repeating over and over passages she had not yet learned, the book held open by cloth on her workbench. Rita would not distract her. From time to time, in the evenings they would walk back to the ghetto together. Those times there was no opportunity for talk. Dani would use the twenty minutes or so to test her day's memorizing. One night Rita realized that the only thing she had to look forward to was the completion of the task Dani had set herself.

As they separated inside the gate, often they would smile, reach out, and brush hands. But Rita never asked her where she lived or where she had come from, whom she was with, or even what she prized besides the epic poem. Rita didn't want to know any of this. It could only burst the spell they shared. And Dani was equally incurious.

She knows Erich. Perhaps he can tell me about her, Rita thought more than once. But she never remembered to ask him.

∽

Five months later, toward the middle of September, as they moved through the passageway between the main factory buildings and the street, Erich passed Rita muttering, "Walk with me." She caught up to him. From prudence alone they rarely moved together between work and the ghetto. Now Erich spoke. "There is going to be a general registration. Lydia has asked me to prepare a real list of essential workers, two hundred at most out of the 650 we're now protecting."

"When does it need to be finished?"

"I told her I can't do it. I won't make up a list of people to be killed, some immediately and others later."

"You can't be sure that's what will happen. Besides, you'd just be doing what you're told to do."

"Listen to what you are saying . . . Everyone knows what's going up the rail line to Belzec. No one is going east for resettlement. I'd be writing out death warrants."

"So, you are going to let Lydia or one of her foremen do it? Just to keep your hands clean?"

"Rita, have you never simply refused to do something just because you couldn't bring yourself to do it?"

Once, Rita thought, and then she said it under her breath.

$\sim$

Approaching their ramshackle house, Erich and Rita both saw the body on the pavement near their door. Nothing unusual in that. They did not even quicken their pace until both realized the body had tracked blood down the pavement and that it was still writhing. But nothing really reached their emotions until they saw it was Kaltenbrunner.

They carried him inside and moved him up the stairs. Laid him down carefully on his pallet. Rita bent over his face as Erich began to examine him.

Kaltenbrunner was whispering. "They raided the orphanage today . . . We had five minutes' notice, and I was trying to hide a few of the youngest. But they had dogs . . . It was no use . . . They took them all. Then they started in on the teachers."

Erich finished his examination. "He managed to crawl back here with a compound fracture of his femur . . . Don't look." He stopped her as she began to move a hand down to his leg. "He's lost a lot of blood, and I think he has internal injuries, maybe a ruptured spleen, from where the bruises are. He certainly has a concussion." Erich looked down at Rita's left hand. It had been cradling Freddy's head and was dripping red. Without thinking she wiped it on her skirt.

Erich said, "I doubt he'll last the night. Let's try to make him comfortable."

"Shouldn't we send for the medical emergency team?"

"There are hardly any of them left. Besides, the only thing that Freddy needs they don't have—morphine."

Rita rose, walked over to her mattress, and pulled Stefan's stuffed dog from beneath the bedclothes. She pulled at a seam. Out tumbled two small sacks. She picked up one and brought it over. "Morphine."

Erich emptied the sack, looked the contents over, and took one vial of morphine and the syringe, putting the rest back in the sack. Then he pulled his belt off and handed it to Rita. "Pull up his sleeve and tighten the belt around his arm above the elbow." She followed orders as he drew 50 ccs into the syringe. She watched a vein rise in Kaltenbrunner's arm. Erich inserted the needle and pulled enough blood into the syringe to begin to redden the liquid. Then Rita fainted. A moment later she had come to, ashamed of her weakness.

"It's very common to faint at the sight of the injection and the blood. Happens to most people. Happened to me the first time I had a Wassermann test." Her look showed she knew nothing about venereal diseases, and Erich was not going to enlighten her. "Usually the doc or the nurse tells you to look away." Erich looked down at Kaltenbrunner. "He'll be comfortable now for a while. If he's still alive in a few hours, we'll give him some more."

Erich now looked at the two sacks. "Where did you get this stuff?" He hefted the sack of morphine vials and then the coins.

"My husband left them for me when he joined the Red Army."

"But this is your lifeline out of here, Rita." Erich was almost ebullient.

"The money?"

"No. A bag of gold coins like that—just a magnet for blood-suckers. But with morphine . . . you can get people to do things without ever coming back at you."

"Spell it out, please."

"With a few vials of this stuff, Lydia can probably get every stamp on a Polish *Ausweis* you'll ever need. And anyone who takes morphine in exchange is not going to sell you to the Gestapo. They would go down with you." He stopped for a moment, then he became peremptory. "Tomorrow morning, don't go to work. Take a decent dress to the ghetto photographer and get some pictures made. Don't bother telling him you need passport pictures. That's the only kind they can make anymore. You don't wear the dress; you put it on when you get there. And you don't tell him what the pictures are for."

"Are there any other mistakes I might make?" She smiled but without energy.

"Sorry." Erich began again. "We've got to do this in the next three days."

Rita looked at him. "Why?"

"That's why they want the worker lists. That's why they closed down the orphanage and took the kids. The *Aktionen* are starting again." Erich pocketed three of the vials, thought for a moment and added a fourth. He handed her back the remaining half dozen, unscrewed the needle, and separated the plunger from the syringe.

"What about you?" she asked. It had struck her that Erich was talking only about her. "If it's just a couple of vials we need, there's enough for you."

"I have other plans. Besides, for a man, even real papers wouldn't be enough to hide behind."

It did not take much more to keep Freddy comfortable before he died. By the time Erich had finished off the second vial of morphine, Rita was no longer fainting at the sight of an injection.

Still, she found herself unable to sleep. It wasn't the dead body lying between them. She'd been close to enough of them. It was the third little sack inside Stefan's stuffed dog that was keeping her up, the one containing a small blue bottle marked *Cyanure de potassium*. Suddenly it was clear to Rita. This was the best way out. Stefan was gone. One way or another, Erich, Dani, everyone who meant anything to her would soon be dead. Even if she somehow escaped, she didn't want to survive without them. She could not live in a world created by Nazis with daily reminders. There simply was no reason to continue.

"Erich," she whispered, "are you awake?"

"Yes," came the voice from the other side of Kaltenbrunner's body.

"Don't put me on your list. Don't bother getting me the documents. I'm not going to get those pictures. I want out now. I don't want to wait longer."

"I told you I'm not going to make a list. But you are going to survive."

"I've got another way out, and I am going to take it."

"Something else hidden in that stuffed animal, Rita?" She was silent. *How could he know?* "Well, Rita, it would be a mistake." She made no reply. "The Germans are going to lose the war. And you have a good chance of surviving . . . maybe even of finding Stefan."

Now she responded in a sarcastic undertone, "Don't ply me with more of Freddy's theory. I'm sure he was right, but meanwhile the Reich could still last for a thousand years." She shook her head once, sharply. "No. Leave me to it, Erich."

Erich had crept around the body separating them and was now a few inches from Rita's upturned face.

"No, Rita. The Germans will lose. It's a matter of a few years—two or three, no more. And you will be alive to see it. I know something. But if I tell you, it could put Germany's defeat at risk."

"Well, then, keep it to yourself." Her reply was indifferent.

"Listen, Rita. And then try to forget . . . End of September '39, the Polish government came through Karpatyn—the commander in chief in his shiny boots, the prime minister, everyone—on the way to Romania. Well, one of the war ministry staff looked me up. We'd been close in Warsaw at the math faculty. He was carrying a typewriter case handcuffed to his wrist." He stopped for a moment, and Rita realized what Erich meant when he had said he and his visitor had been close. Then Erich began again. "And he told me why. The general staff had brought the case to the math faculty with a 'typewriter' inside it, in 1938. Only it wasn't a typewriter; it was a German code machine. Some of the research students had been put to the task of figuring out how the machine worked and to crack the code. Well, they did it. They broke the code. We started to read German signals. Too late to help against their blitzkrieg in Poland, but with the ability to read the most secret German radio messages, the Allies can't lose. Once they are fully mobilized, they have the key to winning the war. And you'll be alive when they do."

Rita was skeptical. "But if they have the code, why has the German army cut through Russia like a scythe? What use has the code been to the Soviets?"

"The Reds don't have it. The general staff wasn't going to tell them when the Russians were Hitler's allies in '39. The secret is with the Brits, and they don't trust Stalin any more than the Polish government did." Rita nodded. "So, Rita, stay alive! Do anything to still be there at the end. Because it's coming, and coming sooner than anyone realizes . . ."

"But if what you say is true, it would be crazy for me to know. The first time a policeman starts checking my documents, I could give it all away. It's a story you've invented to save me, maybe to make up for my losing Stefan. You wouldn't risk the whole outcome of the war—that would be madness . . . even if I believed you for a moment."

"Believe me, Rita. What I have said is true. As to whether it's crazy to tell you, well, there's a line about that in your favorite philosopher, Hume."

She looked back at him with a wan smile. Reaching up through the darkness for Erich's face, Rita whispered the words as if they were an endearment. "'Tis not contrary to reason to prefer the destruction of the whole world to the scratching of my finger."

CHAPTER THIRTEEN

As eight o'clock approached on the morning of reregistration, about two thousand people were standing before a line of trestle tables set up in front of the *Judenrat* offices. To some it seemed farcical that both the Jews and the Germans were trying to look their best for one another. Germans in full uniform, belted and helmeted, with well-oiled weapons, clicking their heels in the direction of *Untersturmführer* Leideritz. Before the tables were faces washed and even rouged with children's crayons, lips red with the remains of lipstick, hair bobbed and ribboned, suits, and dresses hanging from skeletal frames among the women, some wearing cloche hats. Among the men, most wore work clothes, stout and clean as could be contrived. There were few aged to be found in the entire crowd, but many of the women were sheltering children under their arms, all admonished to appear well, stand straight, and look old enough at least to fetch and carry.

Untersturmführer Leideritz cleared his throat and began. "First registration, lumber mill workers." A large man in a check shirt came forward with a list. But Leideritz dismissed him with a wave of the hand. "Lumber workers forward!" he shouted. Forty men came forward and counted themselves out as Leideritz looked each one up and down. "Good. To the left." The throng visibly relaxed. "Next, brick factory." Here several hundred stepped toward the tables as the rest of the crowd fell back. Among them were women and children. Leideritz took a flimsy from the table and waved it at no one in particular. "This list has four hundred names on it. Preposterous!" He stood, riding crop beating at his boots, in an unconscious parody of himself. "Women and all children below fourteen, get back." Aided by officious *Jupos*, the Ukrainians filtered through the group, pushing men to the front and women to the rear, along with their children, a few of whom were pushed or tried to move right with the men.

"Line up," a *Feldwebel* shouted at the men. The file was led to Leideritz's place at the table. As each man gave his name to the clerk, the riding crop would flick out, right or left. When he was finished, seventy-five of the younger men stood at the left, and about the same number of the older, smaller, more emaciated stood at the right. They were moved off, along with the women and children. A new selection began.

The process took most of the day. At lunchtime everyone was ordered to remain in place, guarded by the vigilant *Juden Polizei* while Germans and Ukrainians were sent off to their canteen. Attempts to move across the line of demarcation were dealt with by truncheon blows from the *Jupos*.

Satisfied with their midday meal, the clerks returned to their typewriters. By three thirty Jews had been standing, crouching, or sitting in the open square for seven and a half hours. When it finally came the turn of Terakowski Ready-to-Wear Fabrik, Leideritz had grown tired of shouting and had passed the giving of orders on to his adjutant. He had not, however, passed on the task of selection. Once the textile factories' turns came, it was both men and women to be selected. The clerks' fingers flew as the riding crop indicated his choices. Leideritz prided himself that it took a practiced eye to sort workers with skills that were not obvious. But it was clear to those lining up before him that one's chances were just a matter of good looks among women and physical size among the men. Rita passed quickly to the left and watched with morbid interest to see who among her coworkers would also be deemed adequate cutters or seamstresses. She was watching mostly for Dani and found herself relax slightly when Dani was sent to the left, though she watched two people who must have been the girl's mother and father—a large workingman by his appearance—ordered to the right. She had never even heard of them from Dani.

Now Erich stepped forward. A noncommissioned officer leaned over to the *Untersturmführer* and said something. Meanwhile Erich glared, making eye contact with Leideritz in a way calculated to enrage. The *Untersturmführer* responded to the provocation. He looked back at the sergeant and shook his head. The riding crop pointed right. Erich nodded, and Rita could see him looking satisfied as he moved to the now swollen group composed of women, children, the lame, and the old.

It was well after dark before they finished. A long day's work for even the most ardent policeman.

All those who had been sent to the left were ordered to move out of the ghetto gates. Sentries lined their route, and short work was made of the few who sought to evade the orders. The line of demarcation was wide and well guarded enough to prevent any final exchange between the elect and the damned. On both sides there were only mute exchanges and lingering stares. It was already too dark to make faces out beyond a meter. The line of march took them through the town square to the railway marshaling yard beyond the station, where cattle cars and grain wagons awaited them.

Rita stood in the gloom. She had kept her eye on Erich's silhouette for hours. Emotions of loss and fear welled up in her. She had not felt them when Urs left, nor for her in-laws when the news of their fate had come. It was different from what she felt when she sent Stefan away or what she felt when learned of her parents' fate. Rita was feeling the loss of someone she loved in the romantic way, the carnal way, the way one feels, she knew, when one loses a life partner. Suddenly she recognized that Erich had banished the persistent fear she had lived with before he had moved in. Now it was back, to knot up her stomach, make her perspire that rancid sweat she could smell, in spite of the cold.

Finally she saw him stand up with the others, stretch almost nonchalantly, and move out toward the cattle cars. As he passed her, Rita saw a grin on his face, almost sheepish, conspiratorial. *Somehow*, she thought, *Erich must know what he's doing.*

❧

The next morning in clean work clothes, Rita presented herself at the ghetto barrier, where she turned in her old work permit, had her name found on a list, and received a new one. Unlike the last, this one had an expiration date three months hence.

Toward the end of the afternoon, Lydia sent an office boy down to the shop floor. As he passed Rita, he nodded toward the office. "She wants you up there."

Rita finished her buttonhole, rose, and moved along the floor to the foot of the office steps. Lydia came out of the office, down the stairs, and led her into a storage shed. "Listen carefully. I will have a set of identity papers for you tomorrow. If there is anything you want to take with you, pack a case. Take it to the back wall behind your place tonight at ten thirty. Someone will take it from you. You cannot carry a case out of the ghetto. You can't carry one from here to the train station. You'd be picked up before you got there. But you have to have one when you get there. Someone will get it to the station left-luggage before tomorrow night. I'll get you the claim check. Any questions?" Rita shook her head. "For God's sake don't do anything stupid in the next twenty-four hours." Lydia walked out of the shed, leaving Rita alone.

What to pack? She had almost nothing. Well, then, some under-clothes and something to sleep in, a toothbrush that had not seen paste or powder in six months, a scarf that might once have been brightly colored silk, and the dress in which she'd had her picture taken. There were only a few other things she would not part with: the contents of the stuffed dog and Freddy's two fat volumes in German. For a second time, she ripped the stitches out of the toy, pulled out its contents, and mindlessly sewed it up again, while she thought about what to do with the two small sacks. She sewed the six morphine bot-tles, spaced evenly, around the hem of her coat, dropped the syringe's metal plunger and needle among a nest of sewing needles in her kit, and put the glass tubes in a now-empty jewelry case. Would she ever own any jewelry again? She felt her earlobes. The piercing had healed over. Oh well. Then she sewed the gold coins into the hem of the dress she would wear. Rita harbored no illusions about these hiding places. They wouldn't survive scrutiny. Then she finished packing, snapped the clasps on the valise, and belted it. Creeping down the stairs in the dark, she went out the back and sat in the outhouse until her watch read ten thirty. How had she managed to keep this watch? Then she remembered: she had been about to trade it for food when she began working and eating at the factory.

The transfer was wordless. All she saw was a man's hand reach for the bag through a slat in the fence she had shifted. Then she heard a match lighting a cigarette and footfalls moving away. Oh, for a smoke.

⁓

Morning came. No Erich; no one in the room at all. The gauntlet at the gate. Far fewer passing through than before. So few that each pass could be checked and each worker eyed by the German sentry. No *Jupo Ordnungsdienst* strutting in their shadows. The slog through the streets, looking up and down at normal people coming and going. Will I ever be a free person, one of them again? No. Then she realized, *I'll be one of them tomorrow. Keep your head down, no eye contact with anyone.*

Another worker at the *Fabrik* caught up with her. "Why did they send Erich down yesterday?" She shrugged. He made the obvious observations: "Perfectly fit. Probably top of the list. I don't understand it." Again Rita made no answer. He walked on past her.

The day crept along with glacial slowness. Rita surreptitiously watched both the main doors and Lydia's office-loft all day. There was no sign of anything out of the ordinary. At least one German came through the main gate, pushed his way onto the loading dock, and simply took a Wehrmacht greatcoat from a consignment. With soldiers being earmarked for Eastern Front duty every day, this was not unusual. The coat had to be replaced, and they took the one Rita was finishing. At quitting time, six forty-five, Rita made herself the last to leave. As she turned out of the building to the main gate, a hand reached out and pulled her back in, meanwhile shutting the door. It was Lydia, who now led her out a side door and across the path to the house where Stefan and she had been entertained to tea three months before. Nothing was said till they were inside.

"Here." Lydia handed her a Polish government identity card, complete with the passport photo Rita had given Erich a week before, neatly over-marked by the edge of a government rubber stamp. The second item was a birth certificate, and the third was a paper written in Ukrainian Cyrillic. Finally, there was a receipt from the railway left-luggage depot.

"We'll need to put two fingerprints on the identity card." She took Rita's right hand and moved it over an inkpad on her desk, then deftly pressed two fingers on the space in the inkpad. "Wash your hands well. You can't afford to smudge these documents. And it's a giveaway if your fingers are inspected tonight." She pointed to a small washbasin on a sideboard.

As Rita dried her hands, Lydia continued, "The Cyrillic document is your baptismal certificate. You are now Margarita Trushenko, Ukrainian Catholic with a *Volks-Deutsche* mother. That should help a little. Here is a catechism pamphlet from the local church. Memorize it." Lydia handed her a little booklet. Rita put it in her coat pocket. "Most important, memorize every detail on the identity card—your birthday, your parents' names, where you were born, where and when they were born. Everything, Rita. You're Margarita Trushenko now. That fourth piece of paper is the receipt for your bag at the left-luggage. Pick it up at the station. Here is a ticket to Lemberg, *Panna—Miss* Trushenko—one hundred zloty and some reichsmarks."

Rita looked confused. She repeated, "Lemberg?"

"The Germans have changed Lvov's name." Lydia now rose from the desk and said, "Margarita"—Rita's new name—"come into the kitchen and have a little supper. Your train doesn't leave till nine o'clock." Rita smiled at Lydia's effort to instill the new identity. "Any questions?"

"Yes. Why are you doing this? Do you know anything about Erich?"

Lydia began warming a saucepan. "You know Erich was a dear friend of my brother's." There was no innuendo in her voice. "So he was close to my family for many years. He asked me to help get you these papers, and I couldn't refuse him."

Rita interrupted. "Why did he do that for me? Why did he let himself be sent to . . ." She was unable to finish her sentence or even her thought.

"Well, he loved you . . . like a sister, he told me. And he felt that the fate of your child was his doing, his responsibility, because he pushed you so hard to give Stefan up."

"But he was right to force me to do it. And besides, we can't be sure Stefan isn't still alive somewhere." It was the first time she had given voice to the thought.

Lydia was surprised. "But the courier was taken by the Gestapo."

"I had a letter from my father, written weeks after she was supposed to have delivered Stefan. It was a farewell letter smuggled out on the transit to Belzec." She reflected for a moment. "There was no mention of Stefan in it at all. Not a word. Surely my father would have said something if he were with them."

"So, a reason to hope. As to why Erich didn't try to save himself—he is trying. But in a different way. Erich was sure that the rest of the ghetto would be cleared in the next few weeks. The extermination camp at Belzec is up and running at full capacity. This part of the *Generalgouvernement* has to be *Judenrein* by the end of '42. He knew he didn't have a chance with German papers, his looks . . . well, you know." She was reticent about the obvious. "So, he spent the last few days making a strong bolt-cutter he could hide on his body. His idea was to cut his way through the barbed wire on the feeder hatch of the cattle car or break the hasp on a wagon door, jump, and take as many others with him as he could. Then make for the Pripet Marshes on the old Soviet border and join the partisans."

She set out a dish before Rita, and put another one on a tray. "Now, if there are no more questions, I am going to take some soup to my mother. Have some supper; study your new identity. You know where the station is. Let yourself out the front door and turn off the light. Godspeed . . . Margarita." With a kiss that surprised Rita, she was moving up the stairs.

The German soldier checking documents at the platform barrier actually said *Danke* when she handed him the *Ausweis*, and again *Danke* after she had opened her case for inspection. *If you knew the truth, you'd sooner shoot me down than be* korrekt, she thought. There was a vacuum of fear sucking at her intestines, giving her the sort of cramps she had lived with through the first weeks of the occupation. It was starting again—the dread, the feeling someone was playing Russian roulette with your life. She knew it would be constant again for days or weeks. She decided to sit as near to the soldier on the quay as possible. A soldier offered protection. Rita—or rather Margarita Trushenko, *Volks-Deutsche*—needed it, waiting for the Lemberg train in a vast and empty train station at night. She took out her catechism booklet and tried to study it. Perhaps memories of gymnasium and the Dominican sisters would distract her from the raging angst.

At 20:48 the express came in—from Lemberg, Warsaw, Dresden, Berlin—full of officers and men on their way to join the Wehrmacht divisions in the Donbas, still cutting through whole Soviet army groups. Fixed on her catechism, Rita did not notice the two Germans in civilian dress descending from the first-class carriage.

The German sentry did. He came to completely respectful attention as he examined their papers: one was an *Oberst*—a captain. The other was Friedrich von Richter, major general, *SS-RSHA*—Reich Security Main Headquarters—evidently traveling out of uniform. Of course, neither the sentry nor anyone else in Karpatyn that night could know that Richter wasn't SS at all, but *Abwehr*, military intelligence and an officer in the first section, responsible for code security.

"Herr *Generalmajor*," said the sentry, "there is no car awaiting you here."

"We were not expected. Get on the telephone to Leideritz. Tell him to send a car immediately." Evidently Leideritz wasn't expecting to see him, but Richter was expecting to see Leideritz. That was clear to the sentry at the station.

❧

Twenty-five minutes later, Peter Leideritz was standing to attention in first-class uniform as Richter and his adjutant strode into his building and led the way to his office. *How*, wondered Leideritz, *does this officer know where my office is? He's never been here before.*

Richter sat down, at Leideritz's desk, no less. His adjutant stood behind. He did not invite Leideritz to sit. "We are looking for someone, a Jew in your jurisdiction. Name of Klein, Erich Klein."

"May I ask why, *Generalmajor*?"

"Of course not." Richter glared. "Just tell me where he is. In the ghetto, on a work detail, where?"

Leideritz turned and called out to the clerks, who had all by this time assembled in the outer office. "Schmitz, bring the registers of workers with authorizations." He held out his hand. It was only a matter of seconds before they were delivered. He began to work through the list, glad to see it had already been alphabetized.

"Joachim, Junkers, Kalfuss . . . Klepfiz . . ." He looked again. "Sorry, *Generalmajor*, no Klein."

Richter glared for a moment, then was all business again. "Account for him if he is not here. Where is he? Did you let him escape?"

Turning again to the outer office, Leideritz shouted, "Schmitz, list of Jews transported to Belzec." The list was in his hands only a moment after he had demanded it. It was a massive sheaf of onionskin sheets, organized by dates. Leideritz began from the most recent transport, the one from which he knew there had been escapes. Running his finger down the list, he breathed a sigh of relief. "Yes, here it is. He was sent to Belzec four days ago. Probably already dead." Could this SS major general discover the truth— that he might have been among those who escaped from one of the cattle wagons? Not unless he cross-checked lists at Belzec. Leideritz would have to hope that there was no need or time for such formalities before marching Jews to the gas chambers.

Richter broke through his calculations. "Close the door. Sit down, *Untersturmführer*."

Leideritz did so, visibly relieved.

"So, let me tell you why this is important. We are pursuing an intelligence matter and need to be certain that this Klein did not have classified information." *How much more to say*, Richter considered— *that he was a mathematician before the war in Warsaw? No, too close to cryptography. Don't make him that important.* Richter continued, "He may have seen scientific papers about industrial processes that are now secret." It seemed enough to satisfy this Leideritz. It wouldn't do to make someone else more curious than necessary.

"Well, he's dead now. Case closed, *jawohl?*"

"Not quite." Richter cleared his throat. "Even if he's dead, we'll need to know about people he might have communicated with, lived with, worked with, who are still alive."

Another chance for Leideritz to show his efficiency and initiative. He rose, opened the door, and for the fourth time shouted, "Schmitz, Jewish quarter housing assignments and work assignments, *sofort*—immediately."

Within a few minutes, smiling broadly, Leideritz had what the *Generalmajor* wanted. "So . . . Erich Klein, work assignment, Terakowski Textile Fabrik, residence assignment . . . ghetto A, housed with Kaltenbrunner, deceased; Stefan Guildenstern, infant, missing, presumed deceased; Rita Guildenstern, nee Feuerstahl." He switched back to the work lists. "She works at Terakowski Fabrik. So, *Generalmajor*, only one person to track down."

"Bring her in, immediately."

Leideritz clicked his heels. *"Zu Befehl, Generalmajor."*

∾

The next morning *Generalmajor* Friedrich von Richter left for *Abwehr* headquarters in Berlin. He didn't have this Rita Guildenstern woman to interrogate. But he had enough information to worry about her, and more than enough, he thought, to find her. It was just a matter of sending out a description to every police station in the country. Something would turn up.

PART III

MEANWHILE

CHAPTER FOURTEEN

It had been a hard war for Gil, six months of discomfort and even some danger. But now, in the spring of 1942, with any luck, it was over.

The worst moment had been a dive-bomber attack on the rail line somewhere near Uman during the thousand-kilometer retreat to Dnepropetrovsk. He'd been in the Red Army less than a month, assigned at Lvov to a mobile field hospital. At first he stumbled from one duty to another, with no real supervision, amid the chaos of a withdrawal in which the order of the day seemed to be *sauve qui peut*—every man for himself. Somehow the field hospital had been assigned to the headquarters of the 15th Rifle Corps of the Fifth Army. That got it a locomotive and six passenger cars, which were immediately painted—top and sides—with large red crosses. The train had been ordered east from Kiev a few days before the whole southern group of armies, 650,000 men, had been surrounded.

As it stood in a marshaling yard waiting to water and recoal, air-raid warning sirens began to shriek. Then Gil heard a throbbing, increasingly loud whine. Looking out the large window of his carriage, he could see the gull wings of a Junkers 87 *Stuka*. A bomb was just beginning slowly to move from between its talon-like undercarriage. Freed from the weight, the plane lurched back upward and out of the window frame. He knew little of military aviation, but the *Stuka* was a type he recognized from newspaper photos in Spain. The German Condor Legion had flown them for Franco. The shriek, the anger of flames spitting from its radiators, the menace in its very shape, a predatory mechanical bird of prey, had made it an icon on both sides of the Civil War. But he had managed to avoid seeing one on the wing before now.

Gil rushed down the corridor, jumped off the carriage onto the gravel roadbed, and scurried under the train's wheels for protection. From beneath the carriage, he saw an orderly ten meters away raise his head out of a slit trench, urgently imploring Gil to crawl over and slide in, along with the others from the train. Frozen in the sudden silence, Gil could not move. Instead he stood, waiting for the next group of four *Stukas* to go into their dive. When the second set of dive-bombers had finished, Gil was temporarily deaf and trembling uncontrollably, but otherwise unhurt.

The last carriage of the train had been derailed by the closest of the blasts. Fortunately, it could be abandoned, since the commander of the field hospital was not responsible for rolling stock. Soldiers and officers stood around as the trainmen decoupled the damaged car. Another medical corps officer came up beside Gil. "Well, Captain Romero, rather brave of you to stay with the train." He was shouting over temporary deafness. "Seen it all before, I suppose . . . in Spain?"

"What do you mean?" he shouted.

"They say you were with the Republicans in the Civil War. The orderlies thought you were a damn fool staying with the train when everyone knew it was the target. But the chief said you knew what you were doing. Those dive-bombers frighten, but he figured you knew they aren't very accurate."

Gil would pocket the compliment, but inwardly he was mortified at his own stupidity. Inexperience could masquerade as bravura
once too often. He had to find a way out of the field hospital service, well away from the front.

⅋

After five months of retreat, the unit had detrained east of Voronezh,
setting up an evacuation hospital. Till that point they had been
moving back too fast ever to see any real casualties, except for a
brief period after they passed through Dnepropetrovsk. One night
Gil had duty with triaged patients for whom nothing further, and
in many cases nothing at all, could be done. It was said that in the
Wehrmacht, frontline medical orderlies and even evacuation medical staff carried small caliber pistols to put such cases out of their
misery. It seemed to Gil to be a good idea.

The dying man beside him was still in the remnants of a uniform, with the red tabs of an NKVD captain. So, here was a political commissar, a surprise to Gil since they were rarely to be found
in harm's way. This one had the stomach viscera of someone who
had taken enough shrapnel to destroy a company. He was coming
out of a morphine-induced sleep, and Gil began to wonder if there
was any more available. Catching sight of his white coat, the captain
asked, "Am I going to die, comrade?"

"Of course not." It was Gil's automatic answer. The dying man
beckoned him close and, with a powerful grasp Gil had no reason
to expect, took him by the throat. "That's a lie." Gil could taste the
spittle, he was so close to the man's face.

"All right, yes, you are going to die, and probably tonight." This
man deserved complete candor for the distress he had just caused
Gil. "I was about to give you enough morphine to see you through
to the end."

"First, you have to listen. I can't die without telling someone. There is something I did; it was wrong. Something we did, the NKVD. It's changed everything for me. I have to tell someone."

Gil shook his head. He had no need to learn NKVD secrets. "Whatever you did was for the Soviet state, for Comrade Stalin. Rest quiet now."

The captain closed his eyes. "I've been in the security organs since '37, when we were beating confessions out of the old Bolsheviks—harmless . . . old comrades. It was for the good of the party, yes? We had to send a signal to the wreckers even if it meant liquidating some innocent true believers." This was just what Gil didn't want to know. But at least the man was whispering, and there was no one else on the ward that night to overhear. The wounded man stopped momentarily, and Gil breathed a sigh of relief. But then he continued. "Even when Stalin made the pact, we believed he was playing for time, that we weren't ready."

Here Gil was finally able to agree. "Yes, that's right, Comrade Stalin understood everything."

"So, why did he kill thousands of Polish officers who could have helped us fight the Fascists once we were ready?" Gil wanted to stop up his ears, but now he was hypnotized by the dying man's words. What was he talking about? "Once Stalin got his hands on Poland, we were ordered to take them out of the POW camps and shoot them, one after the other. Was this Comrade Stalin's way of preparing for war with Germany? To kill men whose only crime was to have fought against the Germans? No. He wasn't getting ready for war against Hitler. He was going to join Hitler's war, and the enemy of his friend was his enemy too. Our country is in the hands of one of Hitler's pawns . . . who only fights him now because his loyalty was betrayed."

Gil almost reached up to cover the commissar's mouth before he realized they were the only ones still awake or even alive in the ward. *No one can talk like this, not even a dying man,* he thought. As for those Polish officers? If there had been any, it was hard for Gil to work up much sympathy for them. They were probably catechizing Catholics, foppish second sons of landed families, happy to compete in dressage and attend embassy parties, indifferent to the sufferings of workers and especially minorities in their new Polish state. These dead officers were probably men with nothing much against their German fellow officers, combined with three hundred years of hating Russians and Jews. Surely Stalin knew what he was doing when he liquidated this potential internal threat. This, at any rate, was what Gil was going to convince himself of now that he had learned what he didn't want to know.

Of course, the NKVD captain could have been making everything up. Perhaps it was even a test. Might it be that if he didn't report these remarks, he'd be in trouble himself? Would they maim someone like that just to set me up? No, that was too paranoid even in a nation where paranoia was the key to survival.

The NKVD officer began again. "We just followed Koba." This was Stalin's pet name. "I betrayed the revolution. I became an unworthy person." He lay back and smiled. "Now I've confessed." After a pause, he smiled again. "I am a Soviet person again." The dying captain fell asleep, exhausted by his exertion, and the morphine wasn't needed. He was dead before Gil's shift ended the next morning.

When his replacement arrived, Gil asked, "Comrade captain, do you believe deathbed confessions are to be trusted?"

The answer came back, "Yes, when they come from enemies of the state." Like every sensible person, his colleague was ever on his guard.

Don't make waves. Don't get noticed, not in Stalin's Russia. Gil was familiar with the maxim. But there was nothing for it. After the withdrawal from Dnepropetrovsk, Gil knew he had to act before the steady stream of wounded turned into a flood. He had to find a way out before the front caught up with him again. There was really only one chance.

Putting on a clean uniform, he made himself look as military as he could. The tunic fit nicely. Good-quality cloth, fully lined. There was smart beading down the trousers, the leather officer's belt ready to carry a sidearm. As a medical officer, of course, Gil didn't carry one. But there were officer's tabs and epaulets. Hair cut short, but still the thin mustache. He'd put on a little weight, but his color was good. All that time in the outdoors during the retreat, no doubt. He enjoyed catching glimpses of himself in uniform. He would regret giving it up. But it wasn't worth his life.

Steeling himself, he went to the colonel's tent and asked to speak to him. He was shown in directly.

"Yes, Romero?" Colonel Volodin, commander of the evacuation hospital, was not a physician, nor was Leutnant Colonel Briansk, the party commissar who stood behind the seated colonel.

"Sir, as you will recall, I came to Poland from Spain before the war. The Soviet government has concluded an agreement with the Polish government in exile to allow former Polish residents here in the Soviet Union to join a Polish Army now forming on Soviet territory."

"Yes. I am familiar with all this."

"Sir, I request permission to be detached from this unit so that I can join these new forces."

"You want to join Anders's ex-POWs out east in Orenburg? That's central Asia, man—there's nothing there." Apparently Volodin knew more about the matter than Gil did. He even seemed to know who was in charge of this fledgling army of Poles. "You'd be joining an army with no weapons, that probably won't even get fed. The whole thing is just another stupid waste of manpower. I need you here, anyway." He was about to conclude "Permission denied" when Briansk, the commissar, audibly cleared his throat. Gil tried not to notice its decided effect on Colonel Volodin, who turned. "Leutnant Colonel, what do you think about this request?"

"The first secretary, comrade Stalin, made this undertaking to the Poles, sir. He even had their general, Anders, taken from the Lubyanka to command it. Were Romero to file a grievance, he would have some grounds."

Gil laughed inwardly. No one filed grievances in the Red Army. But his face remained immobile. Was this grievance talk coded language?

"Very well." Volodin turned to Gil. "Report back for your orders tomorrow morning."

࿎

He was packed at 6:00 a.m. the next morning and still waiting at the adjutant's tent at eleven o'clock when his orders were finally cut.

Detached from this command. Major Romero will present himself at Polish Military headquarters, Moscow, for reassignment.

And now he had been promoted to major. Perhaps Volodin didn't want Gil to remember what the colonel had said—"another stupid waste of manpower"—just before the commissar had mentioned the Lubyanka prison.

࿎

A major didn't have to ride "hard class" to Moscow, though it did involve three changes. There was no rush. His orders were undated, and so long as he wore the uniform, he could eat at officers' messes along the rail route, stay warm in officers' waiting rooms, and even get a *musjik* to carry his bag along the platforms from one train to another.

Taking maximum advantage of his situation required some thought and some information too. Arriving in Moscow on November 24, Major Romero showed his orders at Paveletsky Terminal, received a billeting order, and checked his bag. He would explore Moscow on foot long enough to stretch his legs. Turning to look at the station's vast structure as he left the building, Gil caught a glimpse of old Europe in its Baron Haussmann-like proportions, its rounded black mansard roof, and its entry arches, three levels high. The reminder of the D'Orsay Station beside the Seine in Paris made him feel worldly for the first time since he had left Barcelona.

Late November 1941 was hardly the moment for sightseeing. The Germans were rapidly approaching, and much of Moscow's industrial capacity had already moved east. Romero didn't know it, but *babushkas*, grandmothers in head-scarves, were digging tank traps in the western suburbs. There were suggestions that the Politburo was clearing out. These rumors Gil would not believe when he heard them a few days later. But there seemed to be an absence of NKVD in the railway station, traffic was thin on the streets in front of the terminal, and none of it seemed to be heading in the direction the street signs marked toward Red Square.

But people were moving, walking rapidly through the station and out of it. Moscow was the largest city he had been in since he left Barcelona. He was thrilled at the anonymity it afforded him. A snow squall began as he turned right out of the lofty station onto a double-laned boulevard, still lit by high streetlamps against the winter gloom. Gil began looking for a café or bar, someplace where he could have a drink and perhaps begin to figure out the lay of this new land. The almost complete absence of shops, stores, and businesses immediately struck him. How did a city of millions function without them? It couldn't. So, where were they hidden?

He found himself walking across the Moscow River, or at least a canalized section of it. The snow squall had stopped, and the heat of the traffic made the pavement glisten. Here he saw men and women striding purposefully in both directions over the bridge—some carrying briefcases, others sheaves of documents, still others empty-handed—each, including the women, striding manfully, apparently on a war-urgent mission. None appeared to need the watchful eye of a security service to make them do their utmost. This was something entirely new in his short experience of Soviet life. Never in the vast tail of logistics that stretched endlessly away from the front lines had anyone ever worked hard when no authority was around. Until this very morning in Moscow, he had no idea how Russia could win the war. Now he was reassessing his pessimism. Suddenly he wanted to be part of something larger than himself.

The next morning Gil found himself the only person seated in a waiting room inside one of those vast courtyard blocks only a few streets from his billet and the station. The room was warm with men coming and going, and it was awash in Polish. Some of the men entering and leaving were dressed in Polish uniforms badly the worse for wear, others in the enlisted men's garb of the Soviet army, and a few seemed to be dressed in cleaned-up prisoners' coveralls. All were thin, some scrawny, but they carried themselves with an unreasonable élan.

A door opened, and someone shouted in Polish, "Major Doctor Romero." Gil rose and took four steps into a smaller room with a desk, behind which sat an officer in one of the weather-beaten Polish uniforms, one of those absurd four-pointed cavalry officer's caps from before the war hanging on a coatrack behind him. *Probably a prop*, Gil thought. The officer took Gil's heavy woolen greatcoat, hefted it, and smiled, putting it on the coatrack. "Handy in this weather. Wish I had one of those, major." Gil suppressed the urge to try barter. "I'm Colonel Radetksy." He offered his hand, then looked at Gil's papers spread out before him on the desk: Soviet identity, military orders, Polish residency papers, statements from the hospital director in Lvov, medical certificates from Marseille and Barcelona. "So, you want to join the Polish Eastern Army." He looked at the papers again. "You're not a Pole."

"Is that a problem?" It was one Gil could solve by opening up a seam in his medical case and pulling out his real papers—Tadeusz Sommermann, Polish citizen.

"Not really. You're not Russian, so you're covered by the Sikorski-Mayski Agreement. But all that did was make anyone who became a Soviet subject when they invaded along with the Germans in '39 a Polish subject again as of July '41. You're free to join the army General Anders is organizing or not. If you don't, you can take your chances in Russia as a civilian."

The option surprised Gil. "I see. What happens if I join up?"

"You go east to Totskoye in Orenburg and wait. Maybe you get to fight with the Russians against the Germans; maybe you sit out the war. Maybe Stalin changes his mind and re-Sovietizes us. Maybe he sends us back to the POW camps. That's where most of us came from. Maybe we fight our way out of the country. The Czech Legion did it in 1920—twenty thousand men, all the way from the Eastern Front across to Vladivostok." Gil knew of this feat of arms. He had met a few of its veterans in Spain, still seeking adventure in late middle age. It didn't interest him except as a footnote to history.

Radetsky read Gil's silence correctly. "It's not for you, is it, our little Polish army? Frankly, we want willing volunteers, Poles who are ardent for the nation. We've already lost a fair number of recruits, men who took one look at Totskoye and decided it wasn't for them. General Anders has issued orders that they are not to be stopped. It's not a cause for the national minorities." This, Gil understood, was code for Jews. "Poland was never really for the minorities. And you are really a minority—a Spaniard in Poland!"

"I think you understand, Colonel Radetsky. What do you suggest?"

"Well, I'll give you enlistment papers. They should be enough to get you out of the Soviet medical corps. Then come back and we'll cancel them. You'll have papers that should keep you out of trouble as a civilian, to the extent that's possible in this country."

"How can I thank you?"

Radetsky merely shook his head while taking Gil's extended hand to shake. However, the answer to his question immediately suggested itself to Gil.

A week later a package arrived at the Polish Eastern Army headquarters. It was labeled *Attention: Colonel Radetsky.* When he opened it, he was surprised and pleased to find a best-quality military greatcoat, shorn of all its Soviet military insignia.

❧

By the time the battle of Moscow was over, Guillermo Romero was hard at work at Maternity Hospital Number 6, Moscow's oldest and best lying-in clinic.

With the German offensive roaring into the suburbs, Gil reckoned he could be choosy. Fainthearted physicians had suddenly found pressing business to the east, leaving vacancies urgently to be filled. Childbirth did not take a holiday either for Christmas or the Wehrmacht's timetable. Thus he reasoned, and found his way to City Maternity Hospital Number 6, on Miusskaya Street. It was still called the Apricot by porters and orderlies, after a local chocolate factory, an unpatriotic name that was still undetected by the state security organs. The building took up the better part of a city block, three stories high, a turret on each corner connected by bays of nine windows, and surrounded by mature trees, leafless now in winter. When the spring came, a lovely garden would bloom within the building's quadrangle.

Finding an apartment on Miusskaya Ploshchad overlooking the broad square behind the hospital was not difficult for Gil either. Lots of important bureaucrats "called away" beyond the Urals to the east were eager to have the concierge sublet their flats.

He had been right to think that Moscow would be held. Gil prided himself on his powers to predict these matters on which life, and comfort, for that matter, depended. By the time the house staff returned after the battle of Stalingrad a year later, he had made himself indispensable. Gil would ride the war out here very nicely, thank you.

CHAPTER FIFTEEN

Finishing his examination, Dr. Romero snapped off his rubber gloves. "You may dress now, Comrade Madame Malov. Then please come in and sit down." Gil turned and moved back to his consulting room.

After several months supervising midwives on the delivery floors, Gil had found his métier in the gynecology department, just as he had in Lvov. It was a combination of his skills, his way with female staff—a willingness to listen—and his manner. The romance of his name and his exotic history did not hurt either. But mostly, he thought, his advantage was that he liked women, including the young woman now seated before him. She was only a few years out of the Komsomol, her red skirt over a white blouse practically an homage to her time in the league of young party members.

"Can you tell me when your last menstrual period was, comrade?"

"I have missed two cycles, Comrade Doctor." Most women in Moscow could recall such matters exactly. Hunting for sanitary products had been a monthly task even before the war. Now it was a mission, and women noticed when a month had gone by without having to find some.

"My congratulations. You are pregnant."

Comrade Madame Malov choked slightly. "That's what I feared."

"Feared?" Gil had seen enough patients not to be surprised.

"It's not convenient, Comrade Doctor. It's worse. It will devastate my husband, ruin my marriage, harm a friend for life . . . What can I do, Doctor?"

They both knew perfectly well what she was really saying. Only a few years before, it would not have been an issue. For a long time after 1917, abortion was a matter of women's reproductive rights. Contraception was widely available, and the double standard was condemned as a vestige of bourgeois morality. But as the five-year plans took hold, sexual freedom began to seem too revolutionary, almost Trotskyite. Then in 1935 the Supreme Soviet had passed strict prohibitions, largely, it was said, to accelerate population growth.

"I can't help you, comrade. We both know the relevant laws."

"Doctor, listen. My husband has been out of Moscow for eight months, first in the Far East and now at the Leningrad front. He is almost forty, much older than I am, professional military, and very senior, a division commander. I made a mistake with a young friend from the party. If I have the child, everything will be ruined. My husband's subordinates will find out and laugh at him, his superiors will condemn him, my friend will be ruined in the party, and my husband will repudiate the child. Please, you must help me." It didn't seem to be working. The doctor was not even looking at her anymore. Instead, he was writing something out on a pad.

She decided to change her approach. Breathlessly she said, "Doctor, I'd be very grateful," . . . and she began to unbutton the white blouse beneath its flag-red scarf.

"Stop that at once, young lady. I have just conducted an examination of your uterus. Do you think I also need to conduct one of your breasts?"

Now she was in tears, beating her chest and beginning to moan so loud Gil expected a nurse to barge in.

"Quiet down. My dear, I am going to help you. I don't know why. Call it an act of patriotism."

"Thank you, Doctor. Thank you. I will find the money to pay you."

"No money, please."

She misunderstood his demurrer. "Well, then, *valuta . . .*"

Did she have access to gold in coins, in foreign currency? This was a worse crime in the Soviet Union than abortion. How deep was he sinking into danger, helping young Comrade Madame Malov?

"No. I don't want anything. I am going to help you, and you are going to give me only gratitude in return, do you understand?" One never knew when gratitude would be useful, especially if you were keeping the secret of a party member married to a division commander. Influence, access, protection were more valuable than gold. He handed her the piece of paper on which he had been writing. It was his home address and a date a week hence.

It would take a week to organize matters. Things were in such short supply Gil could only take small quantities of what was required—a bit of ether, gauze, and some disinfectant. He had the speculum and curettes he needed in his personal medical kit bag at home. There was a sturdy dining table under a bright light in the apartment that would enable him to conduct the procedure. He had done a simple D and C many times before, in Barcelona and Lvov, to deal with a variety of women's complaints, and, discreetly, abortions.

Madame Malov—he couldn't think of her as comrade, though it was the only acceptable style of address—knocked on his door at the stroke of 8:00 a.m. on a Sunday morning. Gil opened the door. "I assume that you have nothing planned the rest of the day. I am going to insist on your remaining long enough to be sure there are absolutely no complications."

When he was finished twenty minutes later, he helped his wobbly patient into his bedroom and supported her as she lay down on a towel spread across the bed. "Please don't move around. Take a nap." He closed the shade on the window against the gray sky and tiptoed out.

In the late afternoon, Gil was just turning on the lamps against the impending gloom when Madame Malov appeared at the bedroom door.

"How do you feel?"

"Well, thank you, Doctor. You have never called me by my name. Do you know it?"

"Yes, it's on your record. Irena Yaraslova."

"Please call me that. No more Comrade Madame Malov."

"Very well, Irena." He did not add the patronymic. He never did. Not doing so was part of his Spanish persona. "Now, you may go. Bathe when you wish, but no intercourse for a week."

"Not for a year."

"As your gynecologist, I cannot advise such abstinence. But I can provide you with something that will prevent a recurrence of your problem. Come to my office next week."

"Without fail," she said, pulling on her winter coat. But Gil was not listening. Writing the note to himself to secure a diaphragm, there came a stab—Rita's face, that last afternoon in Lvov, as he handed her the diaphragm. Rita. Rita. Rita. A score of images all expressed themselves in that one word sounding silently across his mind. What had become of her?

Gil knew enough about what had happened in Karpatyn after the Russians came. He understood the fate of his parents. The letters, addressed *poste restante* to Marseille and forwarded to Lvov, had stopped early in 1940. When he saw what became of the bookshops and their owners in Lvov, it became obvious what had happened in Karpatyn. He knew he was not going to do himself any good by making inquiries. But Rita? Where was she? Alive, dead, escaped . . . He decided to think about something else. Comrade Madame Malov's breasts, for example.

∼

Daily life in Moscow was difficult, but never boring, even exciting for a time. Once the immediate German threat had receded, people began again to feel they had a future to look forward to. Later they became more guarded, reticent, suspicious, much more careful about their opinions. But in the first flush of realizing they would not be defeated after all, Muscovites felt almost free. War news was grim, especially that spring of '42 when Germans began their second full-scale offensive across the entire Eastern Front. But the catastrophes of the first summer—635,000 encircled at Bryansk, 650,000 surrendered at Kiev, 300,000 at Bialystok—were not being repeated. With the English bombers holding down a million Wehrmacht soldiers on antiaircraft duty and the Americans finally in the war, expressions of confidence in the outcome were no longer made just to keep security organs off one's neck. There was enough straight reporting in the newspapers so that people knew what was really going on. Boredom was not possible.

Even after people and supplies came back to Moscow, there was little to choose from in the shops when it came to food, cigarettes, or liquor. Gil finally began to recognize the retail stores—rare, small, and bare, hidden in corners, beneath railway underpasses, on sleepy backstreets, their shelves a disorderly array of the few goods on offer. Most people survived on what they were fed at work and what they could bring home from canteens for their families. No one left for the day without carrying a "just in case" shopping bag. Almost everything that was worth eating, wearing, buying, or smoking could, of course, be secured under the table, "*nalyevo*"— on the left—for a price beyond the reach of most people.

But money couldn't secure nearly as much as did a strategic location in the intersecting webs of party, military, and government. That was just where Gil found himself now. His maternity hospital was in the center of the old city, known since before the revolution for the excellence of its care. Its semiofficial, accepted name was the Krupskaya, after Lenin's estimable widow (still alive and hard at work building socialism). It turned out to be a node in all three of these networks of special treatment. When the Krupskaya lacked for anything, you could be sure the commodity was really in short supply. And when it came to the wives of the vanguard of the proletariat, their newborn infants, and those who cared for them, creature comforts could always be found somehow. So, most days Gil ate well in the canteen, wore a freshly starched white coat, remained warm in his consulting rooms, read his newspapers on wood spools each morning in the doctors' lounge, had real coffee with his colleagues, served in prerevolutionary china, and could tipple from a sideboard of Georgian brandies and liquors—gifts from grateful husbands.

In spite of the privations and shortages, he would later look back on wartime in Moscow as the best years of his life. He knew he was part of something important and good—like being with the Spanish Republicans, but this time winning. Now when he heard the words of the International again—now in Russian, not Catalan—again he found himself wanting to sing along. He did sing along!

༄

Gil was bringing examination records up-to-date one morning when his phone rang. "Ministry of Foreign Affairs for you, Comrade Doctor." Before he could clear his throat, a strident voice was speaking all too rapidly and loudly down the line from . . . from where? Probably the Kremlin. "Third secretary Dalglashin here, Doctor Romero. I need to see you urgently at the ministry. Can you come now?" Gil looked his diary, but before he could respond, the voice went on, evidently speaking to someone else. "I see, I see." Then, evidently, to Gil again: "Not now after all, comrade. This evening? I will send a car for you at the hospital. Shall we say 21:00? Good-bye."

Gil had not said a word, not one word. How could this man—what was his name, Dalglashin?—even been sure he had the right party?

Could he find out who this person was? There was certainly no directory he could consult, and inquiries might be treated as suspicious. What had he done, anyway, to attract the attention of the foreign ministry? Surely the Spanish NKVD's search for Tadeusz Sommermann in 1938 could not be a concern to the Soviet foreign ministry in 1942.

Normally Gil would be finished by six or six thirty each evening, but that night he found enough work to keep him busy after the entire daytime staff had left. Minutes before nine o'clock, he went to the cloakroom for his coat, fur-lined hat, and gloves, and was standing at the main entrance when a large black ZIS-101 came to a gradual stop at the curb. A uniformed chauffeur got out. Opening the back door, he said, "Dr. Romero?" Gil saw that there was no one else in the car—a good sign. He nodded to the driver and entered.

Through the checkpoints at the Kremlin wall, up to a large squat building, then a series of identity checks. Romero was a name on a list they had. "Go right ahead; you are expected." Up a carpeted staircase, Gil followed the driver. Then along a marble-floored hallway that magnified the sound of the driver's metal toe-tips as they struck the floor. No one was to be seen in the hallway. Finally the man stopped before a double door, a pair of doors that must have been two meters high, that opened up to an anteroom, guarded by no one. He led Gil through still another polished wooden door, at which he stopped, knocked once, nodded to the office's sole occupant, waited till Gil had entered, and quietly left, closing the door behind him.

The room's occupant was a very tall man with a long horse face, dark hair parted in the middle but combed back away from a wrinkled forehead. The eyes were so deep-set Gil could not tell their color. Two deep parentheses bracketed his mouth, and his cheeks showed the stubble of someone whose beard grew fast. He wore a double-breasted gray suit too fine to be made anywhere in Moscow, and he was smoking Gitanes—Gil had never forgotten the aroma. "Sit down, Comrade Dr. Romero. Cigarette?" He offered the packet, and Gil took one. The man handed him a heavy desk lighter.

Gil must have looked as alarmed as he felt. "Please, no cause for disquiet, Doctor. You are in no difficulties. I am Comrade Dalglashin, Vladimir Dimitriov Dalglashin, third secretary of the ministry, responsible for . . ." He stopped. "Well, that's not important. I have asked you here on a personal matter. Your name was given to me by my daughter, Slava. She is a close friend of Irena Yaraslova Malov." Gil was so visibly relieved that a broad smile Dalglashin could not understand broke out across his face. "Irena Yaraslova has told Slava of . . . a service you performed for her and of the complete discretion with which you were able to accomplish it."

Gil decided this was a good time to break in. "And your daughter has mentioned it to you, as she finds herself in the same predicament." He said it as matter-of-factly as possible. Then he changed tone. "I regret that Irena Yaraslova broke confidence with me. I helped her because I believed pregnancy would disrupt her role as an example to others of the New Soviet Woman. I violated Soviet law in order to protect the morale of a husband at the front. I refused to take any payment. And for this Irena Yaraslova betrayed me." Gil enjoyed the sound of indignation in his voice.

"Calm yourself, Doctor. She has not betrayed you. No one has found out beyond my daughter and me. No one will. But if you allow me, I will explain the circumstances, and perhaps you will see your way to helping another worthy young person who has made a misstep."

Gil didn't need to listen. But he waited the anxious father out before agreeing to his proposal.

❧

Young people's bodies are resilient. They endure procedures older people cannot tolerate well. They come through them quickly, with no long-lasting consequences. Not one of the women that Gil was able to help over the next three years perforated; not one ever became infertile, or at least they all continued to have normal cycles. On two occasions he had to intervene again. He also tried to solve their problems more permanently. Alas, his access to a supply of diaphragms was limited. He couldn't get his hands on more than a half dozen at a time. By the battle of Kursk in August 1943, they had altogether disappeared.

A few of Gil's patients were young women private soldiers, taken by officers as campaign wives and dismissed when they became pregnant. Others were middle-aged Bolshevik matrons, raised on the early Soviet acceptance of free love and still militantly committed to it. One was a nurse at the maternity hospital, who would later show her gratitude more than once during quiet nights on the lying-in wards.

Gil had spent years among the bohemians on the Left Bank in Paris. Now he saw the same willingness in young people to take risks, incur dubious reputations, to experience everything in life at least once, and generally to throw caution to the winds of war. He was certain it was the same everywhere. He disapproved of it nowhere.

∾

Once they began parading German POWs through Red Square in the fall of '44, Gil felt he had to make some changes. Moscow might not remain cordial once the war was over. Prudence demanded something fungible he could carry with him if needed. So he began to accept the payments offered.

Gil was an excellent gynecologist, and he was remarkably discreet. His clientele was invariably so well connected, he concluded there was no significant risk of apprehension. Finally, he was circumspect about how late in a pregnancy he would intervene. Accepting payment did not appreciably reduce his business, but it introduced him to the circulation and variety of gold coins in the Soviet Union. After twenty-five years of Communism, Russia was still awash in Nicholas II twenty-ruble pieces, Louis Napoleon twenty-franc pieces, and twenty-dollar US gold coins, now as illegal in the United States as they were in the Union of Soviet Socialist Republics. Within a few months, Gil had several of each of these. As the hoard grew, the danger did as well. Just being apprehended with such coins was a death-sentence offense. Where to hide them?

Finally he decided: in the hospital library, behind the twelve copies of *History of the Communist Party of the Soviet Union (Bolsheviks): Short Course* written by the Commission of the Central Committee of the Communist Party of the Soviet Union (Bolsheviks). This work was rumored to have been authored by the first secretary, Comrade Stalin himself. There was no such thing as having too many copies in a scientific library.

Well before Gil had begun to charge for doing his patriotic duty, his freely offered help had opened many doors, including at least one door he didn't want to walk through at all.

CHAPTER SIXTEEN

Comrade Dalglashin of the foreign ministry had a wayward daughter. He also had a wife with complaints more frequent in older women. The daughter's reports of Gil's bedside manner came to her mother. Soon the entire family—father, daughter, and wife—had made his acquaintance. Once Gil had made Madame Dalglashin more comfortable, with attendant benefits for Comrade Dalglashin, it was inevitable that he would be taken up by their circle of friends and acquaintances. Besides an agreeable manner, an exotic name, and international experience, Dr. Romero played chess, something Dalglashin valued. He was also a deft hand at contract bridge, a game Madame Dalglashin had learned in a Western posting and that they did not wish to share with Dalglashin's fellow party members.

A few invitations to make up a fourth, sometimes along with Madame Dalglashin's younger sister, began to give Gil an insight into the *Nomenclatura* that governed the Soviet Union. Dalglashin's apartment was not much different from upper middle-class life Gil had glimpsed in Paris and Barcelona: large rooms, warm and subdued, with heavy curtains to ensure privacy; carpeting a little too deep to be very old, under dark furniture on which rested more than one bright brass converted samovar lamp. There were family portraits in silver frames littering the top of a baby grand piano and landscape paintings that might have been by Corot, lit from above by gallery lights, labeled discreetly at the bottom of the frame. A set of decanters on the sideboard revealed a taste that had moved beyond vodka to French liquors and American cocktails.

After two rubbers of bridge one evening, Madame Dalglashin excused herself for the evening and retired, followed out of the room by her sister. Dalglashin looked at his watch. It was just before 10:00 p.m. "On call, Doctor?" Gil shook his head. "Well, it's too early to call it an evening. Come with me. I'll introduce you to my favorite watering hole in Moscow."

It was the last of the summer in Moscow and a pleasant walk from Dalglashin's apartment through the quiet streets. "We're going to the Metropole Hotel. Best bar in Moscow."

∽

The Metropole turned out to be Moscow's idea of a large Art Deco building, suffering, like most prerevolutionary buildings, from recent remodeling. It stood next to the river and only a few minutes from Red Square, which glowed behind the hotel.

The door was opened smartly by a doorman in a livery that made him look every inch the White Russian Cossack. "Good evening, comrade minister." Holding the door, he bent ever so slightly at the waist. Gil anticipated a heel click, but it was not forthcoming.

Across the lobby the entry to the bar was visible. The space itself was not large. The counter was contained within an alcove held up at its corners with four marble columns. Beyond it the room was furnished in a parody of a London club. Wing chairs with leather backs held down by a tracery of brass tacks, each chair fitted with its own side table, on which a small lamp glowed. A radio was playing

the only song that seemed safely Soviet and yet sufficiently romantic, *"Katyusha."* There were a few thin and leggy younger women in
the bar, but it was populated mainly by men in dark suits speaking
quietly to one another.

As Dalglashin and Gil entered, a man rose from one of the
wingback chairs, spread his arms wide, and smiled broadly, beam-
ing Mediterranean warmth. Dimples on his large cheeks gave the
man a disarming air of innocence. His dark hair and tanned skin
made him look like the star of some Hollywood cowboy film. His
suit was ill-fitting, but he rose from the deep chair like a very strong,
very fit man.

"There you are, comrade. I had almost despaired of your coming tonight." So, this was not a chance visit to the Metropole, nor
were the introductions about to be made entirely casual.

"Enrique, here is the young countryman of yours I told you
about. Comrade Doctor Guillermo Romero, permit me to introduce Comrade General Enrique Lister." The buckling of Gil's legs
must have been evident, for Dalglashin put a firm hand under his
elbow. Then Lister took his hand in a steel-clad grip.

"Que bo coneixer-te." It was Catalan, and Gil could see he was
expected to reply in the same language.

"General Lister, *tinc l'honor de conèixer-la.*" He really was honored to meet the most successful and charismatic military figure on
the Republican side of the Spanish Civil War. The name was as well
known to him as any he had learned in Spain; neither the prime
ministers—Negrin and Largo Caballero, not even La Passionara,
the communist woman orator Dolores Ibarurri herself—none had
not outshone the fame of Enrique Lister.

Lister indicated chairs on either side of his, and all three sat
down. Switching to Russian for the benefit of Dalglashin, Lister
asked what they were drinking. Dalglashin said "Georgian Brandy,"
and Gil nodded agreement.

"I am so glad at last to meet a fellow countryman, and a patriot too, Dr. Romero. Your reputation as a physician precedes you. But I know nothing of your experiences in our homeland. In that regard, perhaps, you have the advantage of me."

Gil replied with as much Iberian courtesy as he could muster. "My knowledge of your exploits in the war is unavoidably considerable. No one in Barcelona could have been ignorant of your victories at Madrid and your valor at Brunete, Belchite, and Teruel. In Cataluna the 11th division's sacrifices on the Ebro were honored every day until the end." Gil hoped the recitation would stand him in good stead.

Lister nodded. "Not everyone in Barcelona was so happy with my war. When they sent me to Aragon to break up the anarchists and put an end to the POUM, the bleeding hearts bled, and the Trotskyites screamed for my blood."

Gil had no trouble remembering how he had almost been caught up in this purge when the NKVD started looking for Tadeusz Sommermann. But this was not the occasion to show any recollection of the matter. "I was a doctor in the maternity unit of the Hospital del Mar and didn't have time for politics then."

"Do you now, Doctor?" Dalglashin's question might have been menacing. Gil couldn't tell.

"Impossible. I hardly have time to breathe at Maternity Number 6."

Lister was happy to change the subject. "*Joven*, how did you manage to get out?" No one had called Gil *joven* for a long time, and Lister couldn't be many years his senior. Was he using it as a term of endearment? Gil hoped so.

"I left with the sixty thousand or so who ended up at Gers." This was the largest of the camps set up for refugees by the French Popular Front government. It had been chaotic but humane in its way, quickly built in the rolling fields near a country town in the

foothills of the Pyrenees. With the connivance of complaisant gen-
darmes, escape from Gers was not difficult for those who spoke
French and had a place to go. Gil had met several of its escapees. If
he had actually been at Gers, there might not have been a record,
and he would not have had to stay long even if he had registered. It
was a safer lie than the truth. After all, he had fled from the prospect
of a roundup in which Lister had played a leading part.

"Ah, yes. Gers." Lister turned to Dalglashin. "What does the
ministry know about affairs in Spain these days, comrade? Now the
bloodbath has ended, does Franco still have a grip on things?"

"The Americans are keeping him out of the war by feeding the
entire country."

"Out of the war? There is an entire Spanish Division—the
Blue—fighting against us on the Leningrad front. Ferocious too!"
There was a little pride in Lister's voice.

Dalglashin clarified. "I meant that Roosevelt is keeping Spain
out of the war against the Americans and the Brits. Franco could
take Gibraltar tomorrow with a couple of *Guardia Civil*." He
paused and then continued in an effort to find common ground
with Lister. "What we also hear is that Franco is allowing some of
the Republican prisoners out, if they are low rank and if they have
some Fascist family to vouch for them. Some Republicans have even
joined this Blue division in Russia to prove their loyalty or to get
family out of the prisons."

Lister snorted. "He must have shot fifty thousand when he
finally got control. I am surprised there was anyone left to send to
prison." Then he brightened. "Any chance the western allies will
topple him?"

"None, so long as he stays out of their war. Remember, it's only
a few years since Churchill was praising Franco and attacking the
Republic."

"Things can change, yes? After all, it was only two years ago that Stalin was supporting Hitler."

Dalglashin quickly but furtively looked in each direction. This was an obvious truth, but dangerous to assert or even allow to pass unchallenged. He spoke a little louder than was necessary. "Enrique, you are being wicked now. We all know Comrade Stalin was playing for time. We were not ready in '39."

"And you were ready in '41?" Lister was completely unabashed.

Dalglashin ostentatiously looked at his wristwatch and rose. "Enrique, I must go. Comrade Molotov has called a staff meeting for eight a.m. Can't keep the Minister of Foreign Affairs waiting." Gil took his cue from Dalglashin and stood as well. Lister remained seated, smiling affably, making no effort to delay the third secretary of Molotov's ministry. But he reached out and clapped a hand on Gil's wrist. It was the same powerful hand Gil had experienced when they had shaken hands. "*Joven*, Comrade Molotov doesn't need you tomorrow morning. Stay." There was that warm smile again, but the grip was exigent.

Gil returned to his seat and waved to Dalglashin, who was already turning to leave. "I'll find my own way home. Best to your family."

Lister began speaking Catalan. "Well, all that candid talk got rid of our friend quickly enough, *joven*." So, it was intentional.

Gil replied in Catalan. "Yes. But aren't you a bit frightened to talk like this?"

Now Lister began speaking in a much quieter tone, but still in Catalan. "To tell the truth, I am scared to death." Gil remained silent. "I don't see how I am going to survive in the USSR. You know the history?" He didn't stop for an answer. "Well, maybe not. *Pravda* isn't going to announce it, but Stalin has gotten rid of almost every important foreign communist who has come to Russia since his pact with Hitler. The rumor is he is going to shut down the Comintern and dispose of everyone."

Gil repeated the word, to indicate his ignorance. "Comintern?"

"Com . . . intern . . . the Communist International. You really are nonpolitical if you don't know what that is. It's the organization of all the real communist parties around the world. If you are not Comintern, you're a Trotskyite. Mark my words, by next year, even if you are Comintern, you'll turn out to be a Trotskyite. It's a mania with them, or at least an excuse for Stalin to dispose of anyone he wants to. And what he wants least are loudmouthed foreigners with their own ideas and any experience of what it's like outside the USSR. He doesn't like educated people or Jews much either, but I don't make that list."

"But why?" *Always best to play the ingenue*, thought Gil.

"But why?" Lister mocked him. Then he whispered, "*Joven*, if you had been awake for the last fifteen years, you would know that's the way Stalin has stayed in power: being a paranoid megalomaniac. If you kill off everyone who might be a threat, there's a good chance that you've killed off some real threats among them."

Gil would have no part of this blasphemy. "Comrade General, I won't listen to this."

"*Joven*, call me Enrique. I'm not telling you anything new. You were in Spain. You know as much as I do about the famine in the Ukraine, the show trials . . ."

How can I stop him telling me this? "Famine? The Kulaks were hoarding."

Lister's laugh was derisive. "And I suppose you think Kirov was killed by a petty thief?" Gil remembered the assassination of the most popular of the Soviet Union's political leaders in the early '30s. The murder was investigated by Stalin personally. But Lister was continuing. "The only thing they managed to keep quiet was the way they killed off Marshal Tukhachevsky and the rest of the Red Army general staff in '37." Now there was venom in Lister's tone.

"What?" Gil could barely absorb the information. It was truly explosive. He had known nothing about the trial of the leadership of the armed forces. Was this why Stalin signed the nonaggression pact with Hitler—because he had killed off most of the officers needed to staff his army?

"Have you forgotten, or did you never hear this. The trials weren't secret. In 1937 Hitler was still the enemy. Stalin purged forty thousand officers from the army and had about seven thousand shot for being German spies—spies since the First World War, in some cases."

"Why?"

"No reason. Stalin's whim . . . paranoid fear of being overthrown, jealousy of trained military officers. No one knows. But everyone is frightened. It could start all over again, in the politburo, the party. I think it's already started in the Comintern. The foreign party heads in Moscow are falling over themselves to show their loyalty and save their skins."

"So, what are you going to do?"

"What are we going to do, *joven*?" Lister patted Gil's hand. "Yes, *we*. I am sure you are going to help me."

"Yes?" Gil was trying not to decline immediately. He didn't even want to ask what Lister had in mind. Inviting Lister to go on was all he could think of.

"Romero, your Catalan is wonderful for a Galicianer. Better than mine."

"I'm not from Galicia."

"Not the one in Spain, *joven*. I am from that Galicia. You are from the one much closer, the Austro-Hungarian Galicia. You're probably a Pole, and you certainly never saw the inside of Gers."

"I beg your pardon?"

"Beg as you wish, Dr. Romero." He gave the name a mock dignity. "But you really can't fool me. To begin with, I have the ear of a native speaker, even if I don't have the tongue of one. You're no Catalan. And I have the list the Spanish party composed of everyone who went through Gers. You are not on it. I've checked."

There was no point in denials, though Gil was not going to help Lister learn the full provenance of his identity. With a sigh he asked, "So, what are we going to do?"

"We are going to build me a little protection, in case the first secretary of the Spanish party, Diaz, or that witch Ibárruri, decides to sell me to the NKVD."

"La Pasionaria?" It was the only way Gil had ever thought of Dolores Ibárruri. The name was synonymous with *"¡No pasarán!"*— They shall not pass! "What could she possibly have against you?"

"You are not listening. She and I, we both want to survive in Stalin's scorpion cage. So we both have to be ready to sting each other. I'd sell her out with as little qualm as she'd hand me over, if that's what it takes so I can continue to fight for Spain."

"But what could she do to hurt you?"

"She may have trumped-up party documents that implicate me with the ICL."

This was a set of initials that Gil wished he had never heard. But he had, from Lena in Paris that summer of 1936. The International Communist League. "General, no one could accuse you of supporting Trotsky. You led the Republican divisions against the POUM yourself in 1937."

"It won't matter. I'll only be accused of killing them to cover my tracks. It's the twisted logic of the NKVD." Gil nodded regretful agreement. "That's where you come in, *joven*. I've got some dirty linen too. And you are going to store it for me." Suddenly there was a sinking feeling in the pit of Gil's stomach. Lister was going to make him part of history whether he liked it or not—a dangerous part. Gil shook his head. Lister mistook it for disbelief. He nodded. "Yes, sister Ibárruri was playing footsie with the anarchists, the left deviationists, even the socialists. She was doing it even before Stalin and the Comintern called for the Popular Front. So, *we* can fight fire with fire." An index finger poked painfully in Gil's chest as Lister emphasized the *we*.

"My friend, over the next few weeks and months, I am going to get you the original Spanish Communist Party archive, with security reports going back to the early '20s. You are going to hide them somewhere very clever, somewhere no one will think to look. You are not going to tell anyone, including me, where you will hide them. All you will do is send a letter to someone in Alma Ata, in Siberia, an envelope with nothing in it, but with the location where you hide the material as the return address. That is all, *joven*. If I don't know where you have hidden it, I can't betray that location to the NKVD or anyone else."

Gil couldn't help admiring this man, but he was not going to take risks for him. This was worse, much worse than the knowledge he had been burdened with by the dying NKVD captain's confession. "But I can betray it," he told him, "and I will spill everything if they torture me."

"Relax, *joven*. With luck the security organs will never know of your existence. With a little less luck, you will be back in Poland or wherever you come from by the time they do find out about you. And with the most luck of all, none of these unpleasant truths about *La Pasionaria* Ibárruri will need to be revealed. Let's just say this is the price you pay for being allowed to continue to masquerade as a Catalan hero of the Spanish Civil War. If you refuse, the least we will do is make you look like a real spy."

᷎

Gil began trying to think out the problem even as he walked through the lobby of the Metropole Hotel that night. Turn the material over to the security organs immediately? Impossible. He'd be swept up for a Polish spy as soon as they had his identity, and dead even before they discovered his Paris connections. Do as Lister demanded—hide the documents away? That would be a death sentence too if Lister ever had to use the material.

How could he extricate himself? He couldn't entirely. But he could make the whole thing look like a cock-up. That might help him wriggle off the hook.

The packages started coming in October 1942, about one a month, wrapped in brown paper, tied up with string, marked "Medical Journals." With the first one came an address in Alma Ata to which he was to send a card with the hiding place in the return address. That evening Gil remained late at his desk, updating his patient records. Then he climbed three flights to the medical records department, a vast open space surrounded by filing cabinets with patient records going back to prerevolutionary times. Walking around the room, he made a mental note of the file cabinets containing records more than thirty years old. They were the next batch to be burned at the end of the year, numbers 43 to 63. He then went to the typing desk, removed an envelope with the hospital's return address, and put it in the typewriter. Above the words "Records Department, Maternity Hospital No. 6," he wrote "files numbers 43–63," typed the Alma Ata address, smudged any fingerprints he might leave on the envelope, and left it in the "out" tray. If anyone ever looked for them, they would learn the files had been burned as 30-year-old medical records.

Then Gil took the unopened package of "Medical Journals" home. When he arrived he opened the coal grate, stoked up the fire, unwrapped the package, and carefully consigned each page to the flames, trying as hard as possible not to read any of it.

~

The Comintern was indeed terminated in June the next year, just as Lister foretold. One evening during a bridge game at the home of Dalglashin, the third secretary of the foreign ministry even mentioned the matter. Had Gil been ordered to elicit something indiscreet by his Spanish friend? *Was the room wired for sound?* Suddenly Gil lost all track of the cards that had been played.

"Comintern dissolved?" Gil tried to sound indifferent.

"Yes, Comrade Stalin's way of assuring the western allies that their local communist parties will be loyal to their own countries, not to Moscow. If he means it, I don't know what all those foreign party secretaries here in the Soviet Union will do to survive." Gil made no comment.

He went home that night consumed with fear. What if someone now came for the records?

A year later the packages ceased coming. When Enrique Lister began to appear on the cover of patriotic magazines in the uniform of a Red Army general, Gil was able to breathe easy again.

CHAPTER SEVENTEEN

The war's most pressing problem for Gil turned out to be less world historical and more cosmically coincidental than infighting among Spanish communists.

One morning in late 1943, a new patient file came to Gil's desk for a young Muscovite housewife named Karla Guildenstern. Quickly he ran his fingers down the patient's details until he came to husband: Urs Guildenstern. Place of birth: Karpatyn, Western Ukraine. Occupation: Physician, Red Army, on active service, evacuation hospital, Leningrad front. Of course he'd get priority for his wife at the best hospital he could get. That meant the Krupskya.

Gil had to think. Could he risk seeing this woman? Her husband was a doctor. She was sure to discuss the examination with him. He would ask what her doctor's name was. He would remember the history, the shame. Even if he didn't, a pregnancy, if that's what she had come for, would eventually lead to a meeting with Urs at his wife's bedside.

Then what would Urs do? Ignore it, pretend nothing had ever happened, turn his back, ignore the pain Gil's affair with Rita had caused? Or would Urs make a scene? Still worse, would he unmask Gil Romero as Tadeusz Sommermann?

Now different questions washed these out of his consciousness: If Guildenstern had remarried, then what about Rita? Did she get out? Had they divorced? Was Rita alive or dead? Did Urs know? Did he know anything about her fate? The only way to answer these questions was to do the thing he could not, at all costs, do: reveal himself to Urs Guildenstern.

Gil's decision was quickly made. He picked up the telephone and called the waiting room nurse. "I am feeling ill. I must go home. Please shift all my intake for the rest of the day to Dr. Ivanoff." He took off his white coat, slipped out his door, and was walking away from the building within a few moments.

A few days later, Gil called for the file on Guildenstern, Karla, Mrs. She was indeed pregnant, due May 15, 1944. If she was going to deliver in his hospital, in the Krupskya of all places, the likelihood of meeting Urs would be close to a certainty. Gil had six months to deal with this problem.

∽

By the end of 1943, people in Moscow could already see the end of the war, though it was still years away. At Stalingrad the previous winter, the Germans lost 600,000 men and their commanding officer, von Paulus. Hitler had made him field marshal when already surrounded, knowing that no German field marshal had ever before surrendered himself. Von Paulus turned out to be the first.

As the war receded from Moscow, its café society was still willing to risk some visibility. And it had taken up exotic and interesting people such as Dr. Guillermo Romero. Gil and Lister made it a point of never finding themselves in the same bar, party, or reception after the night they had met. But for many in Moscow, the Spanish Civil War was a fragrant memory, a badge of honor unsullied by tactical compromise with Nazis. These people were eager to have a Catalan for a guest, even if he made no claim to membership in the International Brigades.

Standing alone one night, with champagne cocktail in one hand and an American Lucky Strike cigarette in the other, Gil was surveying the guests at the party, especially the women. He had just been assailed by the scent of Arpège cutting through the tobacco smoke. It brought Paris back with a stab of longing. Suddenly he wondered, *Could Lena possibly be somewhere in this crowd?* His reverie was interrupted by a tall man smoking a pipe, who walked up to him making such strong eye contact Gil was momentarily afraid he was about to be arrested. The man's graying hair was parted nowhere at all, and some of it hung lank over his brow. His clothing was rumpled, high quality, and professorial. When he proffered his hand, it was ink-stained. Drink in his left hand, Gil had to put his cigarette in his mouth to shake the hand. The stranger gave his name, but Gil did not quite hear it in the noise around them. "Sorry," Gil said, "I thought you said 'Ehrenburg,' a writer I used to read in Paris."

"That's what I said, Ilya Ehrenburg."

Despite himself, Gil's eyes opened wider. He did not even realize he was repeating the name out loud. "Ilya Ehrenburg?" He closed his mouth, thinking, *Next I'm going to be introduced to Charlie Chaplin!* Gil had indeed first read Ehrenburg's journalism, stories, and novels in Paris. In the romantic imagination of the left, he was second only to Hemingway as the iconic foreign correspondent in Spain. Unlike Hemingway, Ehrenburg had made his way to the front and remained there long enough to become something of a hero among the Spanish.

Gil put down his drink and grabbed Ehrenburg's forearm as if to see whether he was an apparition. "*Con mucho gusto!* I am Guillermo Romero."

Ehrenberg smiled warmly and replied in Spanish, "We had better speak Russian. You never can tell who may want to listen." He changed to Russian. "They tell me you are from Barcelona and you were a Republican stalwart."

"I did not fight, alas. I was a doctor there, as I am here, in a maternity hospital. I was in the western Ukraine and joined the Red Army medical service when the Germans attacked. Technically I am a Pole, so I was demobilized when the Anders army formed."

"Did you see much fighting before you left the service, Romero?"

"It was a six-month-long retreat, but we started getting some business when the army took its stand at Dnepropetrovsk." The unwelcome recollection of the NKVD captain's deathbed confession came back to him.

"Tell me, Doctor, does the Hippocratic oath require you to treat Wehrmacht wounded or Waffen-SS soldiers?"

"I am afraid it does."

"Even though the Wehrmacht's medical service doesn't treat Soviet soldiers." There was a question in the statement.

"The Hippocratic oath has never given much pause to German military medicine, comrade. Their medical orderlies carry sidearms to put their own soldiers out of the misery their fatal wounds cause." Gil offered this bit of intelligence even though it had come to him as rumor.

"I'm afraid I side with them in this matter. We need to kill them all," Ehrenburg admitted.

"I know. I have read that article you wrote in *Pravda.* 'Kill.' Wasn't that the title?"

"Do you disapprove?"

"We can't kill them all, and they aren't all Nazis. Think of the Germans in the Thälmann Battalion in Spain. There must have been a difference between them and Nazis. Besides, articles like the one you wrote will make it hard to get any of them to surrender." Here he was, a nobody, criticizing Russia's preeminent wartime correspondent, one of his own few genuine heroes. But Gil needed to make a mark on Ehrenburg. This was someone Gil wanted to remember him.

Ehrenburg threw up his hands in mock surrender.

Gil said, "Enough politics."

Ehrenburg replied, in Spanish, "Not enough, but not here."

"Back to the Hippocratic oath then? How do we reconcile it with Marxism-Leninism? This is a question I have been struggling with since I was a student in France."

"What is the problem? It's just a relic of the outworn bourgeois class structure that gave it birth," Ehrenburg replied.

"That won't do, comrade. The Hippocratic oath was propounded two thousand years before the advent of bourgeois capitalism."

"I suppose you are right."

Gil didn't notice the concession. "Besides, suppose we write off the Hippocratic oath as a bit of middle-class morality, frothy superstructure, a device to control the proletariat in the interests of the capitalist classes. Why can't the same analysis apply to our own socialist morality? What reason is there to extol the higher morality of 'From each according to his ability, to each according to his need'? Isn't that just more superstructure, the product of a new socialist substructure?" Ehrenberg was not interrupting, so Gil just went on to the end of his little lecture. "There's really no basis for morality at all." If Lena were not in the room, Gil thought, her ghost was certainly haunting it.

"I see." Ehrenburg seemed impressed. "Lenin once quoted Proudhon's line, that property is theft. He went on to say, 'Yes, but theft is theft too.' I think there is a moral in what you have just said for Lenin's observation." He smiled. "But I can't think of what it is at the moment." Gil laughed. Then Ehrenburg said, "Let's meet again. Do you play chess?" Gil nodded vigorously. "Which is your hospital? I'll track you down there sometime."

"Maternity Number 6."

"Aha, the hospital of the *Nomenclatura*. Very good."

❦

All that winter and spring, Ehrenburg would call and arrange to meet Gil at some chess club or other. They'd play three games, smoking and nursing small tumblers of vodka, usually drawing one game and splitting the others. Then they would go for long walks. Both understood that real conversations had to be reserved for the walks. It always remained a mystery to Gil why a world-renowned journalist would seek him out almost as a confessor, he who was uniquely unsuited to the role!

It was also suspicious to Gil that Ehrenberg never mentioned Enrique Lister, though they must have known each other well in Spain. Like Lister, Ehrenburg was wholly committed to Soviet power and the ideal of communism, but torn by the horrors of Stalin's rule. Ehrenburg never hinted at any knowledge of Gil's real origins. His Spanish ear was not good enough to detect Gil's nonnative pronunciation, and he had no Catalan. It was entirely possible that between Lister and Ehrenburg, their mutual acquaintance with a Catalan gynecologist might never come up. More improbable things had happened, such as Guildenstern's new wife ending up in Romero's waiting room.

Ehrenburg had been in Paris in the teens, '20s, and '30s, long before Gil arrived. He told endless stories about Diego Rivera, Modigliani, Picasso, André Gide, his marriages and love affairs, his novels, screenplays, and even a movie or two he had made. He would recount the times he had been in favor and out of favor, arrested by the Cheka, predecessor to the NKVD, deported by the French, censored when his reporting on Nazi Germany ran afoul of the Molotov-Ribbentrop pact. Ehrenburg's eyes glistened as he described the fall of Paris to the Germans. "I was the only foreign correspondent there besides the German ones." It was an experience made possible by that very treaty that joined Nazi Germany and Soviet Russia as allies, since few other non-German reporters could remain there. He talked about his friendship with the Spanish anarchist leader Durrutti and about the POUM, for whom he had a warm spot of which surely Lister could not have approved. Together they remembered sultry nights on the Ramblas—the Flamenco bars, the dives. Once when they were both drunk, each promised the other they would walk together down to the waterfront at Barceloneta once more.

❦

Mainly Ehrenburg gave Gil war news he couldn't print in *Red Star*, the Army newspaper he wrote for. It was read by more than two and a half million Soviet soldiers. Ironically, the first time Ehrenburg came for him at the hospital, it was Gil who put the great reporter straight.

Ehrenburg had won all three games, and they were leaving the chess club. When they got to the open street, he began to speak. "You heard the latest German propaganda? The Germans say they have found twelve thousand bodies buried near Smolensk. 'Doctor' Goebbels is trying to get the world to think the Russians shot twelve thousand Polish officers in '40." Ehrenberg was mocking. "And the lengths they've gone to dress the whole thing up—dragging in forensic detectives from the occupied countries, foreign POWs, as if these people have any choice but to sing Goebbels's tune. And the Poles in London believe the Germans! Outrageous!"

"Ilya, what if it were true? Would it make any difference?"

"What are you saying? How could it be true? It's Nazi propaganda."

"Listen, Ilya. When I was still in the army in late '41, I treated a dying NKVD captain." Gil tried to repeat what the man had said to him before he died. "This was two years ago, Ilya. Long before Goebbels could have gotten hold of those bodies." Why was he telling Ehrenberg this? Why was he even remembering it himself, putting himself and Ehrenburg at risk? Because he admired this man so much. Because for a moment, he wanted to tell dangerous truths, to rise to the nobility he saw in his friend. "Does it really make any difference?"

"It makes a difference. It adds to the burden we have to carry inside. It's another lie we have to bury for the good of the cause." Tears were running down Ehrenburg's cheeks. "No, it only makes a difference where it counts, in one's conscience."

The words left Gil unmoved. He carried no burden. Gil consoled himself with a thought: *I suppose the reason I am no artist is that I lack his emotions.*

∽

"We are winning, but the costs, Gil!" Ehrenburg mused one afternoon as they walked through early spring slush.

"What do you mean, such costs? War always costs!"

"For everything that has gone well, the Soviet people have been made to pay a much higher price by the madness, the stupidity, the suspicions of Stalin. To begin with, any fool knew the war was coming months before the Germans attacked. Stalin was warned by Churchill, by the Americans, by his best agents in Japan. He did nothing—worse than nothing. He ordered the Red Army to stand down along the borders: 'No provocations,' he demanded. So we lost a million and a half men in the first six weeks of the war, just because he had wanted so much to suck up to Hitler."

"How do you know this?"

"Zukov told me." Ehrenburg named the most successful of Stalin's marshals. "Came back from the Manchurian border and saved Stalin's neck. Anyway, Zukov thinks he's mad."

"Do you really think Stalin's mad? You know him, Ilya."

"I know Stalin is not fit to lead a country at war. And it is only his bodyguards that have kept him in power. For a month after the German attack, he cowered in his dacha, depressed, drinking, sleeping all day, unable to stir himself. Finally the politburo came to arrest him. Everyone knew his crimes. Instead, when they got there, they were disarmed by Stalin's guards. Then, in his fury at his own friends, Stalin finally bestirred himself. And to do what? To order futile counterattacks that lost us another 750,000 men. A reserve lieutenant could have organized the defense of the motherland better."

෴

When they met a few weeks later, Gil was ebullient. "You have read the news? Stupid of me! You must have written it." Ehrenburg waited. "The new Stalingrad, the encirclement on the Dnieper. A hundred thousand Germans?"

"Yes. But self-congratulations are not in order, Gil."

"As usual, you must know more."

"More than I want to know. It's always that way. It was half the number we announced. And we lost more men than the Germans in that victory—twice as many—and five times the number of tanks."

"Why?"

"Many reasons. Because the army throws men away instead of using weapons. Gil, do you know what trampers are, or blocking formations?"

"No, never heard of them."

"Blocking formations are machine gun units deployed behind our lines, with orders to shoot down our own solders retreating . . . not just the occasional deserter, but whole units. Why are whole units withdrawing, fleeing against orders? Are they cowards? Fascists? No. It's because they are senselessly ordered to charge into German fortified positions. When the war began, they were being ordered to advance without weapons! Think of it, Gil! Even after the victories of 1943, the army still needs blocking formations!"

"And trampers . . . what are they?"

"Punishment battalions, filled with prisoners, deserters—people whose willingness to fight is suspect. Or zeks from the gulag, and worst of all, our own soldiers—prisoners of war we've managed to liberate. They're used as human minesweepers. You fill them with vodka and march them in straight lines into a minefield. Whoever walks to the other side has found the way through for the rest of the army. Does the general staff order this because they lack mine detectors? Do they do this because they are sadists, or because they are ordered to do it?" Gil had no response to all this. "It's hard to cheer victories when you know what they cost."

❦

In 1944 March passed into April, making the problem of Karla Guildenstern more pressing. Every few weeks he had called for her chart among many others and seen that her pregnancy was proceeding normally. Worse luck, the final lifting of the German siege of Leningrad meant her husband would almost certainly be able to come to Moscow for her lying-in. As a physician Urs would be accorded all the courtesies of a colleague, including the doctors' common room, the cafeteria. He'd be introduced all around. There would be no way to avoid him. What to do?

By May Day the matter was urgent. The next morning, the medical staff was called to a meeting by the hospital director.

"Gentlemen and ladies," he began (there were several women among them), "I have been ordered to seek volunteers for a"—he was searching for the right word—"an unpleasant . . . uh, a difficult mission. It will require the volunteer's absence for two weeks to a month and will begin in a week's time. I am not allowed to say more than this: medical officers are required to accompany a large forced deportation to the east. It's a nationality that has given aid and comfort to the Fascists during their occupation. Conditions will be very severe for these people, and no picnic for those who are required to carry out the deportation. Party members are expected to volunteer. Others are invited to do so."

He paused, considered, and went on, "Do not volunteer if you are uncomfortable with the concept of collective responsibility or the guilt of a people as a whole."

Everyone listening realized that the director was himself taking a risk making this observation in the presence of several physicians who, as party members, would be obliged to report his remarks. Gil's admiration for the director's bravery was immediately followed by the realization that volunteering could get him out of the hospital and out of Moscow for just the period Karla Guildenstern would be in the hospital.

"If you wish to volunteer for this assignment, see the hospital party secretary. Meanwhile, this matter is confidential, and no one is to discuss it. That is all, colleagues."

∾

So Guillermo Romero spent sixteen days on a train that started with 2,498 Crimean Tartars, a few old men, but mainly women and children. They were to be moved from their homes on the Crimean peninsula five thousand kilometers to Samarkand in trackless Central Asia. When it was over, he reflected that no matter how hard it had been for him, at least he had the food and the warmth of an NKVD guard car. The poor Tartars had been given thirty minutes' warning to leave their homes and then were marched to the railway line, where they were crammed into cattle cars and moved without letup for two weeks through the barren landscape of war-ravaged Ukraine and the empty desert of Kazakhstan, only to be left to shift for themselves in the steppelands north of Samarkand.

Gil had been briefed about their crime before the deportation began. They, or at least too many of them, had welcomed the Germans as liberators. Worse, they were guilty of sending large numbers of their menfolk to the Wehrmacht, where they fought ferociously against the Red Army, even after the Crimea had been retaken from the Germans. And this after twenty years of Soviet enlightenment, electrification, schooling, the mechanization of their agriculture. Twenty years after scientific socialism had freed them from the feudal yoke of their religion. All this, and they were still disloyal to the state.

He did his best for these Tartars, delivering three pregnancies, one of which survived, treating the wounds of adolescent boys brazen enough to taunt the guards, even treating several shot while trying to escape. There was nothing he could do for the elderly, dying of exposure and hunger. Gil was able to enforce hygiene firmly enough that he did not have to deal with typhoid, though there was nothing he could do about the dysentery. At the end he estimated that three hundred of his train had died along the way. The chief medical officer of the deportation congratulated him; some trains had lost half their consignment. There were hard figures on how many people had been forcibly relocated, about 200,000. But there had been orders not to keep track of fatalities.

When the exercise was over, almost forty thousand NKVD security personnel were to be moved back to the Ukraine. On the return journey from Kiev, Gil found himself in a compartment of physicians who had participated in the deportation. For three days the train rattled north to Moscow. The whole compartment argued about the morality of what they had done. Gil had no interest in the debate.

PART IV

ENDURING

CHAPTER EIGHTEEN

Margarita Trushenko, *Volks-Deutsch*, was standing on the platform as the 21:00 Warsaw express glided to a halt at Karpatyn station.

She knew herself as Rita Feuerstahl, not even Rita Guildenstern—she had never been able to call herself that. She never would again.

So Rita Feuerstahl was standing there on this night in late October 1942, trying as hard as she could to change her identity into Margarita Trushenko. She began by concentrating on the catechism she had once known by heart, back in the gymnasium of the Dominican sisters. Inevitably, her mind began wandering.

I'm not the same person who learned these sentences by rote the first time fifteen years ago. Ten years from now, everyone I know will have been thinking of me as Margarita Trushenko for so long and so completely that I really will be her.

An initially imperceptible hum now gave way to an increasing roar as the passenger train rumbled in from the east. Once the engine, bearing two swastikas, had passed, the line of carriages slowed until the entire train precisely bracketed the platform.

As each coach glided by, Rita could make out the effaced Polish national railway markings underneath the Reich Bahn insignia on the doors, until finally one stopped and swung open before her.

Lifting her case into the rack above her head, she felt its uneven weighting as the two heavy volumes within shifted from one side to the other. She knew why she had taken them. It wasn't to remember Freddy. She needed them. The books had become a center of gravity, and not just in the valise she had raised up to the luggage shelf above her seat. They had become her center of gravity. It was ironic that in the ghetto, where what she had really needed were food and shelter, she had found exactly what she'd always been looking for: the real why of things she'd been searching for as long as she could remember. Reading them over and over, those two books had slaked a thirst that had been with her since the Dominican sisters' gymnasium.

She settled herself in a seat. In a few minutes, the blackness of the darkened town and then the night turned the window beside her into a mirror. She couldn't see through the reflection of her face, and so she began to stare at it, trying to make it the face of Margarita Trushenko. Changing her identity shouldn't be so hard. Starting now, everyone around her would help, assuming she lived long enough for them to do so. *Myself, me, my identity. Just a useful illusion, like much else foisted on us by natural selection. What quick work Darwin makes of the philosophers' great puzzles.*

The train was rattling through a countryside that in daylight would have reminded her of journeys to Lvov three years before, which would have made her remember the slightly nervous anticipation, the rush of pleasure at seeing him—was it Gil or Tadeusz?—on the platform in Lvov, the pure sensation of sexual release, the intimacy of a shared meal, the chagrin of returning home that last time with Urs. As it was, she remembered none of this. She was already a different person from that Rita.

Noiselessly the conductor came up behind her and cleared his throat to alert her to his presence. Not noticing how his German uniform had frightened Rita, he doffed his cap and asked for her ticket, in German, which he duly punched and walked on.

$$\backsim$$

At ten thirty Margarita Trushenko alighted from her train and walked up the long quay beneath the glass and wrought iron roof of the Lemberg *Hauptbahnhof.* That's what the signs said everywhere—not Lvov, Lemberg. There was not a Polish sign to be seen. She was greeted by *Fraktur*—gothic printing everywhere. Directions to the *Befehlshaber*—military headquarters; *Wartehallen*—waiting rooms; the *Gepäckaufbewahrung*—the left-luggage.

Rita decided to head for the *Gepäckaufbewahrung.* Surely the rules in force in Karpatyn were to be followed here. Wandering around in the night on the street with a suitcase was an invitation to police inquiries. She walked directly to the open bay and passed her bag across. In return for a few groschen, she was handed a small claim check. As she turned around, a rather nice young man in an overcoat with a turned-up collar came up to her, took off his hat, and hugged her. He was clean-shaven, shorter than Rita, with curly brown hair.

"Darling." It was a voice too loud for her ears only. "I'm so glad to see you." Then, in a whisper, his mouth at her ear, "Your name, dear, quickly."

"Margarita," she whispered back, her cheek still brushing his ear.

Again, just a little too loud: "Margarita. Thank goodness you're back." He took her arm and walked her out of the station and into the square beyond. He paused to light a cigarette and offered her one. "Take it, even if you don't smoke. It helps." They stopped, and Rita looked back at the glass ceiling of the entry hall, barely illuminated against the black sky, then turned to the brighter arch of the station entrance. It had not changed in four years. Everything else had.

"I do smoke. Thanks," she said, exhaling. "What does smoking help? Who are you; what is this all about?"

The young man smiled. "My dear, smoking helps because nice women don't smoke in the street, especially nice Jewish girls. Back there were about a half-dozen SS and Gestapo, ready to pick you up and send you straight to Lemberg ghetto—or would have sent you there, if there still was one. Didn't you see them closing in on you?" He nodded back to the station. "I saved your pretty little neck in there." They walked along, and he continued, "Coming in alone from the east on a late train is a giveaway around here."

"I have nothing to hide from the police," Rita insisted.

"Of course not. That's why you gave a complete stranger such a warm hug and your first name. Any little Jewess would have shrieked for protection against this masher, yes?"

"Really! Take me back," Rita huffed. "I insist." But when he stopped, shrugged, and began to turn, she resisted. He had called her bluff. As they resumed walking away from the station, she asked his name.

"Jerszy Sawicki, at your service, ma'am."

"And why are you risking your neck for me?"

"Patriotism, my dear, pure patriotism."

"Where are we going, then?"

"A hotel not far from the station. We'll be there shortly."

A few moments later, they were at the Hotel Nowozytny, a run-down nineteenth-century tenement grayed by fifty years of coal dust, with a single door and two windows facing the dark narrow street of similar buildings. A man in shirtsleeves and a leather vest was sitting on a milk can leaning back against the outside wall. He rose as they approached and entered the hotel ahead of them.

The door opened to a small lobby with a narrow counter in front of a row of pigeonholes with keys in them. There was a steep staircase going up, and beneath it a back door, *probably*, thought Rita, *for an outhouse*, which had ceased to be used only long after the hotel had been built.

The leather-vested man who'd entered before them was the clerk. He took a toothpick—or was it a matchstick—out of his mouth and spoke. "Jerszy, bringing me another guest?" He looked at Rita. "Staying with me, or your own room?"

"How much is a single?"

"Two marks. Identity card, please. It will be returned in the morning." She laid it down with a thump, along with a reichsmark note. The man copied her details into a thin, worn, stained ledger, handed her a key, and walked back outside into the night air, muttering, "First floor, number 2, best room in the house."

Jerszy took his own key off the row, number 5, and they moved up the stairs.

Rita reached the first door and began fumbling with the heavy skeleton key. Jerszy offered to help, but she refused. When it was finally opened on the third try, he tried to invite himself in. Rita blocked him. "It's been a long day. I am tired. Perhaps tomorrow." She tried to smile as she firmly closed the door.

The narrow room had a bare overhead bulb, a single bed with the springs showing beneath the mattress, a rickety cupboard, a window that looked down on the street above the hotel entrance, and a door behind which stood a sink. A showerhead dropped from the ceiling, with a drain in the middle of the floor. There was no toilet in the room.

❧

The next morning Rita was up at dawn. She dressed quietly, put on her coat with its cargo of coins and morphine sewn into the hem, and made her way down the stairs. The same clerk was on duty, but snoring, with his head on the counter. There was no point in taking her key with her. She had left nothing in the room. She placed her key into its pigeonhole and slipped out the door.

Now, where to go? *Be careful, Margarita!* She knew exactly one person in Lvov, or rather Lemberg: Dr. Stanislaw Pankow, the physician Urs had sent her to and who, in turn, had referred her to Gil. Now, where was his office? She began by retracing her steps to the station. From there, one turn and then another led her back to Pankow's medical cabinet. When she arrived at seven thirty, it was far too early for a doctor's practice to be open. The safest thing seemed to enter the building and wait on the staircase landing above his office.

As she sat on the wrought iron stair tread, the chill rose from it through her body. Repeatedly she stood to shake it off.

Promptly at nine o'clock, she heard Pankow arrive, unlock his door, and switch on his light against the winter's morning gloom. Rita came down the stairs, remembering that for this meeting she had to chance being Rita Guildenstern again, and knocked on his door.

"Come." The command was peremptory. He wasn't expecting a patient. Pankow looked up from his desk. He did not place her. "Do you have an appointment, *Panna* . . . or is it *Pani?*"

"Dr. Pankow." She paused. "I was a patient of yours briefly, four years ago. Rita Guildenstern."

Pankow thought for a minute, and then his face grew red. He put his pen down, straightened in his chair, raised both of his hands to his waistcoat, and began smoothing it down, obviously disconcerted. "Yes, I remember." His face had turned to a glare. "How dare you come here? Your conduct was a scandal in the local profession. It was intolerable. Please, go immediately." By the time he finished, however, his dudgeon had been replaced by anxiety. It was as though she were contagious.

Rita's sense of danger made it impossible to feel any chagrin. "Please, Doctor, I am alone in this city and know no one. I don't know where to turn. Can you help me? I don't need money or a false identity. I only need somewhere to stay, at least for a few days."

"I am unable to provide you with any assistance whatsoever." There was anger in the tone, incongruous with the fear in his eyes. "It would endanger my practice, my patients, and my family." *Not to mention yourself,* she thought. "Please leave immediately." He rose and gestured toward the door with a finality that brooked no further importuning.

Rita had a hand on the doorknob when Pankow said, "Stop a moment. I cannot think why I do this, but your paramour visited me in July 1941. He was about to decamp with the Reds, as one might expect of a Spanish communist." Pankow stood, went over to a cabinet, opened it, and handed her a small package. "He asked me to get this to you. Now I have. Take it. Go!" He walked to the door and gestured her out. Rita could hear him lock it behind her.

Returning to the hotel seemed the only immediate option. They still had her *Ausweis.* When she arrived Jerszy was in the narrow entrance, passing the time with a new clerk, whose look added no new charm to the hotel. "Your identity card, miss." The clerk handed it back with a palpably suggestive look.

"Where have you been, Rita?" Jerszy was relieved to see her. He looked at the small package she carried. "What's in the box?"

"I went out for breakfast." Why had he called her Rita? Had she been betrayed already, or slipped and given the wrong name?

"Shall we go up to your room, Rita?" He said it again. How did he know?

"Yes, let's. But my name is Margarita."

"I know, but it's a mouthful. So I shortened it," he explained as they mounted the stair.

She opened the door, and they entered. With the door closed, Jerszy moved toward her. "I enjoyed that hug last night at the station. Can we try it again?"

"Maybe when you come back from the station with my case." Rita fished the claim check from her coat pocket.

Jerszy brightened. "Good idea, kid. Don't move a muscle. I'll be right back." He left the room, and she could hear him bouncing down the stairs. She went to the window. Looking down, she could see he had stopped to talk with the clerk, now lounging on the other side of the narrow street. Quietly she opened the window and listened.

Jerszy was answering a question. "I was going to have some fun before I pass her along. But maybe there is something in her bag worth taking first." He held up the claim check. "Back in a jiffy. Did you have to give back her papers?"

"I thought she was a call girl, not some pigeon you'd brought in."

Rita didn't like the image, but it gave her an idea. She closed the window and went to her coat. Removing one vial of morphine, she took it to the washroom. Then she remembered the package Pankow had given her. She picked it up from the bed and unwrapped it. There was no note, no label, only the diaphragm in its powder-blue case that Gil had tried to give her that last afternoon they were together.

A knock at her door. She opened it. Jerszy stood before her, slightly breathless, holding her case. Foot barring the door, she held her hand out for the case. He handed it over. Rita said, "Go take a shower, Jerszy, then come back."

While he was gone, she inspected the case. It had been opened by a penknife at every seam. Jerszy evidently had some experience at this sort of search and was no doubt still carrying the knife, if not a second, more dangerous one.

In the jewelry case, Rita found the syringe parts, and in a small sewing kit, the needle, apparently undetected by Jerszy. She put them together and placed them with one vial of morphine in the bathroom medicine cabinet. Then she took off all her clothes, putting back on only her slip.

When Jerszy knocked again, she let him in. With no preamble whatever, he approached her and placed his mouth over hers. To his surprise she was responsive. Maybe she wasn't a prim Jewess after all, he thought. Yid or not, she was a modern girl. Good. Holding her with one arm, he moved the strap of her slip off her shoulder to uncover a breast, which he began inexpertly first to squeeze, then to kiss.

Despite herself Rita was becoming aroused. She could feel his erection, and it was having an effect on her—nipples hardened, her body now disregarding the cold of the unheated room. It had been two years since she had last had intercourse, and four since she had been satisfied by it. When Jerszy began to undress, she said, "I've got a diaphragm I'd like to use." She reached for the case.

Ah, so she really was a modern girl, Jerszy thought. "Very well." He released her, and Rita went to the washroom. A few minutes later, she was back, holding the syringe and vial of morphine.

"Jerszy." Her voice was throaty and moist. "Have you ever made love with a little extra stimulation? Opium, heroin, morphine?"

He had not. Was he going to let this little tramp teach him new tricks?

She opened her hand to reveal the vial and the syringe. "It's beyond your wildest experiences, Jerszy. You must try it with me."

The temptation was strong, but he was still cautious.

"Let's do it." She smiled.

He nodded. "You first."

She nodded. "Give me your belt." Jerszy sat down on the bed and pulled the belt from the loops of his trousers and handed it to Rita. She pulled it tight around her forearm, remembering the procedure she had learned the night she helped ease Kaltenbrunner's death. She looked at Jerszy, willing him to follow her every action, willing him to respond to blood's bloom in the syringe as she had. If he did not, she was in trouble.

Filling the syringe with a massive dose of morphine, she found a vein in her arm, pierced the skin, and pulled the syringe back. Blood filled the cylinder, confirming contact with a vein, and there it was—the sight of it drawn into the syringe toppled Jerszy off the bed. In the ten seconds before he recovered enough awareness to realize what had happened to him, Rita had quickly withdrawn the syringe and expressed the blood, leaving the original dose for him. "Never mind, Jerszy, it happens to everyone the first time they see blood come up in a syringe. Give me your arm. I need to do this to you quickly, before the effect takes hold of me." A moment's bleary hesitation, then he rolled up his sleeve and laid his arm on her lap. Rita belted his upper arm and found a vein. This time Jerszy closed his eyes. Within fifteen seconds Jerszy had slumped unconscious to the floor. A dose this large was surely enough to put him out for a day, if not kill him outright.

Rita disassembled the syringe, dressed, and packed her case. Then she pushed Jerszy over, went through his wallet, and took his money—375 reichsmarks, some zloty. She burned his identity card. How much trouble would he have explaining how he had lost it? Then she found his latchkey.

Carrying her case she mounted the stair and stole into his room. As she searched through his meager possessions, she thought, *They've turned this nice Jewish girl into a thief.* If that's what it took to survive, Rita was going to be a good one. She found the knife he had used, a hip flask that might be sterling, a few silk ties and a wool scarf that might fetch a mark or two from a used clothes dealer—if there were any left in Poland—and a tin of tooth powder, a luxury she had not seen for two years. There was almost a carton of cigarettes, Polish but smokable, and a pair of fine leather gloves, men's, but small. These she assembled on his bed and packed into her case. By now it was midmorning, and she could hear the charwoman trudging up to the top floor, there to begin cleaning vacant rooms. She put a do-not-disturb sign on Jerszy's room door handle and her own.

A glance over the window ledge showed the day clerk sitting in front of the building, just where the night clerk had met Jerszy and her the night before. Rita put on her coat, picked up her case, quietly walked down the stairs, and made her way out the back door. She came out of the alley between the hotel and the next building with her back to the clerk, who was chatting with someone and too busy to notice her departure. Ten minutes' walk, and she was back at the station queuing for a railway ticket to Warsaw.

CHAPTER NINETEEN

How not to make the same mistakes in Warsaw? That was Rita's problem now, or would be if she reached Warsaw. But reaching Warsaw was beginning to look increasingly unlikely even as the train moved tentatively out of the Lemberg station.

Why, Rita asked herself, *in this almost empty railway car, is a large man in a trench coat coming toward me, smiling more and more broadly as he approaches? Why, given all the empty seats in the carriage, has he decided to sit down on this bench right next to me? I might as well have let Jerszy turn me in.*

The large man had gray hair cut short in a fashion that suggested the military. He took his raincoat off to reveal an ill-cut suit and a loud tie on a badly ironed shirt, with one collar bent across the lapel of his jacket. Without formality or introduction, he opened the conversation. "I am Milkolaj Bilek, Metropolitan Police, Lvov, uh, sorry, Lemberg. Hard to remember when you have called it Lvov for fifty-three years." He didn't let Rita get a word in. "So, you met our friend Jerszy, and now you want to get out of town fast. Don't blame you. Not a very nice customer." Rita would have been unable to break into the flow of his words even if she had any idea what to say. "I wonder how you managed to extract yourself.

Must be a resourceful girl. You couldn't have done it with money. Money is the one thing that will make our Jerszy and his 'friends' stick like leeches." Here at last he stopped, ready to listen to a comment on all this.

All Rita could manage was a hesitant, "I don't understand," as she fished her identity card and other documents out of her handbag.

He studied them in a cursory way. "Yes, yes. Very nice. I hope they work for you. But in Warsaw you'll need a *Kennkarte* if you are going to get past the Blue Police."

Kennkarte was something Rita knew: an identity card issued by the Reich to every German and to Aryan-enough Poles in what was left of Poland. Blue Police, however, was something she didn't understand.

"I don't understand, Pan Bilek. Are you going to arrest me?" Rita's fear was quickly being supplanted by perplexity. "What is the Blue Police, please?"

"Arrest you? Have you broken any Polish law? Don't answer . . . Arrest you for being Jewish?" He smiled. "Not against Polish law last time I checked. Of course you aren't Jewish, are you? Says so right there." He indicated the paper he had returned to Rita, still lodged in her hand. "Ukrainian Catholic, and letter-perfect with your prayers too, I'll warrant. But I think you need a little history lesson and a tourist guide. Blue Police, that's the street police created by the Germans, but mainly composed of former Polish police. Not all professionals, and more than its share of anti-Semites and pro-Nazis. You are lucky it was regular police, or what's left of us, who found you. I'm Home Army."

"Home Army?" Rita interrupted. She knew well enough. She had sent Stefan off with a Home Army courier. But she thought it better to sound naïve.

"Maybe that's really an innocent question. I'm going to risk a lot telling you. Home Army is the main resistance movement in

Poland. There are a few others—fascist, socialist, communist—but we are the ones with links to the government in exile in London, and we have the most men, weapons, and the best organization. The Home Army has even worked its way into the Blue Police." He chuckled. "Anyway, I was keeping an eye on Jerszy and his friends. That's how I spotted you in the station last night, greeting him so warmly. I figured you for a working girl." Rita tried to look as though she didn't understand the term. "Prostitute," Bilek explained, indulging her. "That's why I was surprised to see you get on a train out of Lemberg so quickly."

"Well, I am not a prostitute." She tried to be matter-of-fact about it. If she did look like one, so much the better perhaps. "But Jerszy was going to turn me over to the Germans."

"No, he wasn't, or at least probably not right away. First he was going to force himself on you, and then he was going to sell you to the gang of *szmalcowniks*—blackmailers, extortionists, toughs who keep him as their pet Jew."

"Pet Jew?"

"Sure. It takes one Jew to sniff out another one. Jerszy is a Jewish hood who has been getting into trouble with the Lv' . . . eh, Lemberg police since he was a kid. Now he's valuable to the underworld of extortionists in town, the ones who live off of all the Jews in hiding. They don't turn one into the Gestapo till they have sucked him dry. The bounty for Jews is pitiful—fifty zloty. Compared to what you can get from most Jews still living on the outside, that's nothing. So, Jerszy was going to milk you for some and then turn you over to the gang for the rest. Maybe they'd get more from your family or friends too. Then when you were picked clean—only then, mind you—they were going to sell you to the Germans."

Now Rita was seriously confused. "Why are Jews preying on Jews? And if Jerszy is Jewish, why is he moving around freely in Lemberg?"

"I can't answer the first question. But as to the second, most Polish people are not going to turn in Jews to the Germans. We hate Germans as much as we hate Russians. Of course, there are the crazy anti-Semites. The Germans have found most of those and put them to work. But most places they are outnumbered maybe twenty to one by the decent Poles who are not willing to help Germans at all. Polish people are not going to take sides in this war the Nazis have going against Jews. In fact, most people will turn their backs on someone's being Jewish, never report them, maybe even help them a little, if there is no risk. Police are the same. If some *Untergruppenführer* puts a gun to my head, I'll give him a Jew to save my neck, but I am not going to help those bastards. So, Jerszy goes free. As for his gang, well, they're connected to some people in the Blue Police, so there is not much I can do about them unless they do something serious. Shakedowns like yours are not serious. In fact, there are plenty of Blue Police on the take too. It's survival."

Rita took it all in. She sighed and decided that there was nothing for it but to come clean. Perhaps there might be something to gain. "Look, Pan Bilek, I have been living for the last year in the ghetto of Karpatyn. I am completely lost. I don't understand what is going on. I don't think I am going to survive a minute in the *Generalgouvernement*. Can you help me?"

"OK. Some rules. First, never, ever tell anyone what you just told me. Second, don't carry large quantities of money. You are likely to get hauled into alleys all the time in Warsaw. If you have enough money, an extortionist will take it, and keep taking it till it's gone, then sell you off to the Germans for the head money. You're better off with no money and a solid *Kennkarte* than being a Yid millionaire in Warsaw. Third, don't hang around with other Jews. A girl like you can blend into the Polish scene completely. Don't try to help another Jew. They'll be spotted and drag you down with them."

Bilek paused for a minute, then apparently felt he had to explain things a little more deeply. "There are a million people in Warsaw. You can trust 950,000 of them. But 50,000 extortionists is more than the Germans need. Besides, there's little work, less food, almost no coal. It's not surprising that extortion has become a regular business, with its own rules. Learn them."

He became practical again. "When you get to Warsaw, find a room with an anti-Semite, someone with a reputation for hating Jews." Bilek took out a business card. On the back he scribbled an address. Then he carefully put a small blue dot under the letter 'l' in his last name. "I am going to get out at Zhovkva and go back to town. Take this card to the address on the back. Show it to the lady. She is Home Army, and she will help you, at least temporarily. Get off at Warsaw East Station, in Praga, on this side of the Vistula." This was the river that divided Warsaw, as it did Krakow and all of Poland. "Turn left out of the station, turn left at the first street, walk four blocks back down next to the tracks, and you will be there. Please, my dear, look like you know where you are going. If someone approaches you—anyone, man, woman, child—swallow this card, or it will go hard with you . . . and me." He got up and was out of the railway car before she could say another word.

❧

Warsaw on a winter evening. Steam spreading from the brakes on the carriage wheels, merging with condensation from the breath of travelers as they hurried down the quays. Only the station *Kommandantur*—the Wehrmacht office—was lit up against the gloom.

Rita needed to melt into this flood of travelers. She needed to do as they all did—no hesitation, no searching around, no inquiring looks. She walked past a man in uniform—surely this was the Blue

Police, from the color of the tunic—scrutinizing a shabbily dressed passenger's papers, his ticket, his face. Move past, not too fast, not too slow. Out of the station, turn left, left again, Topazowa Road, four streets down, parallel to the tracks. Rita tried hard to look like a Warsaw girl eager to get home after an eleven-hour rail journey. Like any street facing the noisy, grimy tracks of a city railway terminal, it was a line of narrow tenements, with few lights, some small bars and cafés, and hardly a person on the streets. At number 46 she rang the bell marked only "4th floor." There was no buzzing her in. Instead, she heard the clop clop clop of wooden shoes making their way down the stairs. When the door was opened, a hand reached out. Rita put Bilek's card in it.

The door swung wide. "Come in, please." It was a tall woman with brown bangs, in her late thirties, thin, and rather studious-looking, wearing a white blouse over a navy blue skirt, and a heavy woolen cardigan sweater that looked as though it had been made for a man. After a more careful examination in the light of the room, the woman smiled, handed back the card, and offered her hand. "I am Krystyna. You are . . . ?"

"Margarita, Margarita Trush—"

"Let's stick with Christian names. It's safer. Come up. Let me take your case. It's a long way to the fourth floor." When they arrived Krystyna carried her bag into the flat, its windows overlooking an air shaft formed by contiguous buildings, covered by a black sky. She turned to Rita. "A cup of tea, Margarita? Then I think you'll want to go to bed."

"I am full of questions, but I suppose they can wait."

In the morning Rita slept in. In fact, she was still asleep at noon, when Krystyna slipped in and woke her. "I must go out for several hours. Please stay here. Make yourself at home. You will find some bread and margarine in the kitchen. You can also make some more tea." She paused. "Can I call you Rita? Margarita is such work." A ghost of a smile, then she was off.

So, Jerszy wasn't the only one to shorten her new name back to her old one. Perhaps it was safe to continue to think of herself as Rita.

Rita spent a while wandering around the apartment. There was nothing much to see. This was a Home Army safe house, and it wouldn't have an identity that could give someone away. She took a tepid bath and made herself a bit of a meal. Then she curled up with one of her Darwins. The volumes were an endless fascination and a persistent source of insights.

Krystyna came back at nightfall, with a string bag filled with several root vegetables no one would have found appetizing before the war. Rita sat at the kitchen table as Krystyna steamed the vegetables and fried some potatoes in lard.

"How much can I ask you about the Home Army?"

"Well, I can tell you everything the Nazis already know. Sabotage, intelligence, protecting Allied soldiers, coordination with the other resistance groups, even the communists once Germany attacked the Russians, some of the Jewish underground too. But I don't know much. Mainly I am a courier around Warsaw, and I never read what they give me."

Rita's interest quickened. "Do you know other Home Army couriers? Ones that operate outside of Warsaw, in the east, maybe?"

"We aren't even allowed to know what each other looks like, let alone names. When couriers pass on messages or documents, we try to do it without making eye contact or looking anyone in the face. So, no, I don't know anyone. And I don't want to. All I need to know are passwords and dead drops." Rita looked blank. "Places where I can leave or pick up a message without meeting the other person delivering it or picking it up. Listen, we have more urgent matters to discuss."

"Yes."

"You can't stay here more than a few days. It's not safe for me. You have a Polish identity card, yes? And a baptismal certificate?" Rita nodded. "Good. You must go to the *Generalgouvernement* bureau across the river to get a German *Kennkarte*. With your looks it should not be difficult. You tell them you are a refugee from the east. Complain about the Russians. They like that. If you can get a card, you can look for work, you can rent a room, and fade into the population. Find a room by looking through the newspaper classifieds. Better on this side than across the Vistula. This is a workers' area, and they are used to transients and newcomers." Rita nodded. She could do that.

"You speak Polish like a Pole. That's critical. Any German?"

"Yes."

"Don't use it around Poles. Some will hate you; others will decide you are educated and shake you down as a Jewess. The Germans don't know that's a tip-off with Poles."

Rita took the opportunity of a pause in her instructions. "Krystyna, I have to ask, have you ever heard of Home Army couriers saving Jewish children or taking them to safety, hiding them—anything like that?"

"I haven't done anything like that. But I know it's been done. There is a liaison from Home Army to a Jewish organization, the *Zegota*, that mainly channels money to Jews hiding here in Warsaw and around the country. They may do something like that to save children too. Why do you ask?"

Rita now sighed. She'd have to tell Krystyna if she was going to learn anything. "Maybe the *Zegota* could help. I have a child. He was with me in the Karpatyn ghetto till last spring. I gave him to a Home Army courier to bring to my parents, who seemed to be doing all right in the west. But they were taken in an *Aktion*, maybe before my child arrived. The courier was caught by the Gestapo before I could find out what happened to my son."

"I see."

"Is there any way I can find out what happened to him?"

"No chance the Home Army will help you. Just for starters, we have our own share of anti-Semites, and even the ones who aren't won't sacrifice security to help look for lost children. Look, there is still an orphanage in the Warsaw ghetto. If your son never got to his grandparents, perhaps he was taken there."

"What do you mean, still an orphanage?"

"Well, there was another one, famous really, but it was shut down a year ago, and all the kids deported to the east. But there is another one there now, I hear."

"How could I get to it?"

"Are you mad? You're free; you might even survive. You want to go into the ghetto?"

"It's my child, Krystyna."

"Going into the ghetto is a one-way trip—except for the criminals, the Jewish mafia, the gangs that operate on both sides of the wall."

"There are Jewish gangs in Warsaw?" Rita realized she shouldn't have been surprised about this after her experience with Jerszy.

"There have been several, one pretty much emerging every time another one was eliminated by the Germans. First, when the occupation began, there was Group 13, named after their main office, 13 Leszno Street. These thugs might just as well have been Nazis, a branch of the Gestapo. They took on the *Judenrat*'s own police for a while. Then they switched to smuggling, and extorting, under the cover of a medical service. But they were liquidated. Other groups filled the vacuum. The Germans are too busy with the Russians to really keep a lid on things. The Blue Police are corrupt; there are still enough Jews in the city to blackmail, extort, sell protection to—why shouldn't some of these parasites be Jews? It's groups like them that make it difficult for the Home Army to know who it is dealing with in the ghetto. There are even rumors of a new gang called Zagiew, actually fighting for the Germans against the Jewish resistance in the ghetto. It beggars the imagination. Anyway, if there still are Jewish gangs operating on both sides, they are not advertising it the way they used to."

"I see."

Krystyna was not going to say more. "Look, Rita, like I said, tomorrow, out you go. Find a place, get a *Kennkarte*, disappear."

"Krystyna, I think I have something the Home Army can use. But I need some help."

They were sitting at the breakfast table. Krystyna's agitation was evident. So was Rita's, for that matter.

With a look of annoyance, Krystyna responded, "Yes, what?" She might as well have said, "Yes, what *now*? Jews, never grateful, always wanting more. Why did I ever get involved with you . . . ?" *Well*, Rita thought, *can you blame her, either for her response or for her anxiety about the risks she is running? No. So, be patient.* Rita stood and went over to her coat, brought it back to the kitchen table, and began to rip the seams out of the bottom. Out onto the table came the remaining dozen vials. She laid them across the table and then went into her garret, coming back with the three parts of the syringe. "Morphine."

Krystyna visibly relaxed. "Something we can always use."

"It's a gift to the Home Army."

"And in return?" Krystyna was back to business.

Rita tore more of the seam out and began fishing out gold zloty coin after gold coin, until eighteen of the twenty coins were on the table. She left two still hidden in the seam. "I can't go anywhere in Warsaw with a hoard like this, can I?"

"No. It would be stripped from you piece by piece or all at once. Just having it on you is enough to prove you are a Jew in most people's eyes."

"Yes. I've been told I am safer with nothing of value on me. I'd give these coins to the Home Army too, but I think I am going to need them. So, I need someone to keep them for me."

"Well, it won't be me. I told you when you arrived, you can't stay here. You can't come back here, ever. You have to forget all about this place and me. Besides, what are you going to need all that money for? You'll get a *Kennkarte,* no problem. And then you'll be safe."

Rita drew a breath. "I have to get into the ghetto. I have to find the orphanage. I have to look for my child." Krystyna was shaking her head. "I have to. It will take money. I need someone to keep it."

Krystyna was still shaking her head, and now closing her lips into a tight grimace.

"Look, you told me yourself, yesterday, there are ways . . . what did you call them, dead drops? You can hold my money and pass it to me without anyone knowing, without any risk to you. You can even keep what I don't end up needing."

Krystyna was weakening, Rita could see. After a moment's thought, Krystyna said, "All right, I am going to get zloty for this from the Home Army. They need hard currency and will give you a fair exchange." She stopped. "There is a café down the street. It's called *Le Chemiot*, French for trainman. You passed it coming here. I stop there in the early evening for a glass of wine—terrible stuff, but I do it every day at 18:30. If you need money, go in, have a beer or something, ersatz coffee, whatever. Hang your coat on the coatrack at the back, always inside out. That way I'll know which is yours. When I come in, do nothing. When you leave, there will be money in your coat.

"I don't know why I am doing this. It's dangerous for you, for me, for the resistance." Rita knew why. Like most humans, Krystyna would respond to human emotions with kindness, especially if there were something to gain. "Now, here's a key. Out you go. You know where to go and what to do. When you come back for your things, I won't be here. So put the key on the top of the doorframe when you leave. You are tall enough to reach it."

An hour later, Rita was across the Vistula, in Three Crosses Square, central Warsaw, queuing at the *Generalgouvernement* Internal Passport Office, documents in her hand. After thirty minutes or so, she found herself in front of the bars of a window grill, confronted by the pinched, birdlike face of a man addressing her in German-accented Polish. "Tak—yes . . . ?"

Wordlessly Rita handed across her Polish identity, her birth certificate, her baptism certificate, and the completed application form, along with the required photo, taken that morning at a little studio in Praga. The little man put a series of ticks against various items on his checklist, looked up, and addressed her in Polish: "Come back in a week." Rita was ready for this. She began in her rehearsed German, "But, *Mein Herr Inspektor*, can't it be today? I cannot go around Warsaw without papers, and I am applying for a job today, with the *Generalgouvernement*." Then, with all the stealth she could muster, she slipped one of the reichsmarks banknotes Julia had given her that last night in Karpatyn across the counter. At the going rate of exchange for zloty, it was at least a week's salary for the poor bureaucrat. At the same time and in the most pliant tones she could muster, she pleaded, "*Bitte, Mein Herr*, could you not do it for a good *Volks-Deutsche*?" She put her finger on her mother's names in the baptismal certificate.

He grumbled. "Always the same. Special treatment." Then more quietly, "Come back before we close at five thirty." Then he looked up. In a voice louder than he seemed capable of, he called, "Next."

❦

On to the labor exchange, though how she was to negotiate this office without papers was beyond her. The office was in the next building, a holdover from the prewar Polish government office. Rita studied the listing of positions available in a glass case on the wall. She found one that might be promising—shopgirl in a department store—and moved to a bench. Again, another form to fill out on her lap, this time demanding work experience. Her only relevant experience was having been a customer in such a store. But that wouldn't work here, so she mentioned positions at a few shops in Lemberg. Would they check?

"So, you are interested in the salesgirl position at Jablkowski Brothers? Not too many girls want to work there."

"Why not?"

"It's the neighborhood. Close to the ghetto. Lots of identity checks." She looked straight at Rita, as if to say, "Jewish? Don't take this job."

"No problem. Please give me the address."

"Very well. Report there on Thursday at eight thirty. Take your documents." That gave her a day to find lodgings.

It seemed safe to ask the one obvious question a stranger might ask. "Exactly where is the Jewish quarter?" This was the ghetto's official name. "With my luck, I'd end up on top of it."

"It surrounds Mirowski Square, a few blocks north of the Jablkowski Brothers Department Store on Bracka Street. It's easier to avoid now. Much smaller than it was." Rita did not have to ask why.

It was almost noon when she came out of the labor exchange, too late to begin looking for a room. Everything decent advertised in the newspaper would already be taken. Besides, walking the pavement without a document in her purse would be madness. There was nothing for it but to find a hotel for the night and convince them she could show papers by the evening.

Rita joined what passed for noontime bustle. At the first intersection, she surveyed the streets in four directions. Three-story stucco buildings, all attached, all painted creamy pastel colors, mainly ochre, and visibly deteriorating after three years of occupation. Not many cars, and those bearing marks of German requisition. A few horse-drawn carriages. One felt sorry for the horses and their drivers, in that order. Both looked as though they knew their lives would end before the war did.

There, down the street, halfway back to the Internal Passport Office, stood a decrepit-looking building with a small sign she could just make out: a German name, Hotel Handel—the Hotel Commerce. She began walking toward it. From the moment she crossed the street away from the labor exchange, she felt a presence behind her. As Rita passed a narrow gap between two buildings, she was pulled back into it. She turned around to see two young men— boys actually, both smaller than she was—one brandishing a broken penknife blade. The slightly larger one began, "*Tak, suka Yid.* [So, Jew bitch.] One hundred zloty, and you can go."

Rita looked at them, two urchins, probably starving in the streets, but prepared to threaten a woman for a zloty or two. The knife was real enough. But if she was going to survive in Warsaw, she had to be able to deal with this. In her loudest German, she began to shriek, "*Hilfe!* German lady being attacked by Polak street thugs. Someone, anyone, help a German woman undefended." Then in Polish, "Do you hear? I am a German woman, and you will be in for it if they catch you . . ." Back to German: "*Hilfe! Hilfe!*" The boys looked at one another twice and began to scamper down the alley.

～

The clerk at the Hotel Handel was a wizened spinster, or at any rate, wore no wedding ring. "Yes, we have a room. No luggage? Well, payment in advance, fifteen zloty. No visitors, no Jews; you have to register with the police by tomorrow. Your papers." She held out her hand.

Rita gestured with her head. "They're just being issued, at the office up the street. I'll bring them by at six o'clock. I'll get my luggage from the station and come back when the papers are ready."

The woman shrugged. "If there is one thing the *Szkops* can do right, it's issue papers on time." It was the first time Rita had heard the word in Warsaw. "*Szkops*" was an abusive Polish term for Germans. This woman evidently had no more love for them than for Jews.

By six o'clock Rita had papers, good anywhere in the Reich until 1948, bearing her photo, endorsed by an eagle gripping a swastika, and registering her in Warsaw. After slapping them on the hotel counter, Rita boarded a streetcar and traveled back across the Vistula to Praga, thinking hard about where she was going to hide the last two gold coins in Krystyna's apartment. They would be her reserve, and she had a good idea that she would need them.

As Krystyna had promised, no one was in the flat. Rita packed her few things quickly. Then she began to seek a hiding place for the two gold coins. *Somewhere dark where it would be hard to shine an electric torch*, she thought. In the kitchen she dropped down to her knees in front of the large enamel iron sink. It stood beneath a window overlooking the air shaft. Reaching the back of the sink, she pushed her hand up until she could feel the gap between it and the wall it was bolted to. She wrapped each coin in enough cloth that it could be pushed into the space and remain there. Then she stood at the sink, pushing and pulling at its frame to try to dislodge the coins. She could not move it. Satisfied that the coins were held fast, she closed her case and left the apartment, placing the key high enough on the doorframe to be invisible to anyone who was not looking for it. "Thanks, Krystyna," she whispered.

CHAPTER TWENTY

Rita lay there in the dark on the narrow, creaking bed, trying to warm the damp sheets and shape the lumpy pillow, unable to cover both shoulders and her feet with the thin, short blanket. The hotel's small but annoying blue neon sign was flashing through the translucent blinds every seven and a half heartbeats.

Sleep was not coming. Her thoughts kept returning to what she had learned in only a few days since escaping the ghetto. As if Nazis weren't enough. There were Blue Police, the Home Army, a sea of factions, and add to the mix Jewish thugs preying on Jews, Jewish gangs trying to control the ghetto. Was there no end to the spawning of new predators?

The question started out in her mind as purely rhetorical. But then it turned into something Freddy had said about the Black Death. Don't think about people as the agents who perpetrate the horrors. Think about us as a fertile environment, a niche that diseases invade, occupy, change. We are the prey, the hosts, the victims that the virus or bacillus, the parasite carrying the disease, feeds on. The infection of Nazism had created breeding grounds that selected for other, different parasites, even infecting Jews and spreading a new parasite among them that made their hosts scavenge on the Germans' prey.

Then she thought, *Rita, your mind is a breeding ground too. What parasitical idea in your head is surviving by making you survive?*

The next morning Rita set out from the hotel to find a room as close to Marszakowska Street as she could get. This street ran from Mirowski Place, where the two parts of the original ghetto had been connected by a wooden trestle pedestrian bridge over the tram tracks, down to Aleje Jerozolimskie, a block from the department store on Baska Street. She didn't think it would be hard to find a room along Jerozolimskie Street. By now the ghetto was much smaller than it had been at its origin in 1940. So many had been deported to extermination that the Germans had closed the little ghetto that had been connected to the larger one by the pedestrian bridge. Still, Poles probably didn't want to live near even an empty ghetto, and Jews in hiding certainly didn't. It would surely be the part of the city where the Germans checked for papers more than anywhere else. Yet the newspapers had no adverts for rooms in the district. And as she walked the street up from the store and back down from the German ghetto administration office, there didn't seem to be many "for let" signs in the windows. She rang every door with a sign. But evidently something about her was putting off the owners. More than one lady with rooms to rent didn't like a brand-new *Kennkarte*, and a few others accused her to her face of being a Jew on the run. Others would not rent to a single woman: "Who knows what line of work you are really in, dear?" By late in the afternoon, Rita had given up hope and resigned herself to another night at the Hotel Handel, with no chance to look the next day. She had to report for work on Thursday.

She was practically back to Baska Street, where the department store sat. The lady at the last door she tried was at least genuinely regretful with her—"No, nothing." As Rita turned to descend the stair, she called out, "Wait. A friend told me today that she had lost her lodger. Perhaps you can take the place. Let me give you the address." She wrote out Widok 44. It was a street Rita already knew from wandering through the district. She thanked the lady and turned to leave. As she left, the woman said, "She'll like you. The last tenant was a man, a Jew she had a lot of trouble getting rid of. Finally she just had to call the police."

At Widok 44 Mrs. Kaminski was suspicious, especially since Rita could not remember the name of the lady around the corner who had given her the address. "Sorry, I don't have any room."

"But your friend, *Panna*—Mrs. . . . Anyway, she said you just lost your lodger . . ." No response. "She said you had to get rid of him. He was a Yid." How could she break through? "But as you see, I am not a Jewess. I am Aryan, *Volks-Deutsche*. Please, I am new to Warsaw and have no place to stay." Finally, "I'll pay in advance! Please."

The door opened slightly, and now Mrs. Kaminski was reconsidering. "No visitors, no Jews, no noise, do not ask to use the kitchen. Bath only twice a week. Lights off at 10:00 p.m. Twenty zloty a week. Police registration slip . . . I have to have it tomorrow."

"Yes, yes, agreed. Thank you." Rita pushed the money into her hand and practically barged through the door. "May I see the room?"

"I suppose so, as you have forced me into renting it to you." Mrs. Kaminski did not even smile at her own unintended joke.

The room wasn't much better than what Krystyna had provided in Praga. Still, it was where she needed to be if she was ever to find her way into the ghetto and back out again, with her son if she could find him.

∽

Jablkowski Brothers Department Store was still an imposing building, one that must have been a splendid emporium in prewar Warsaw. Now it was living on its past and on what its buyers could scrounge in the wake of German requisitions throughout Europe.

Without even bothering to examine her perfectly valid papers, the floorwalker engaged Rita instantly and led her to the stationery and school supplies. All she had needed was her German and an obsequious air about her. She was handed a brown smock with the lettering "Stationery" embroidered over the heart and sent to the fountain pen desk to learn her duties. The stock was displayed under glass in a long counter, across from the revolving door at the store's main entrance. To the left were perfumes and cosmetics, stocked with whatever the French had left to export after the German occupation troops had taken their fill. To the right were hats and gloves, scarves and baggage. In each department there were one or two salesladies—in many cases, just girls. All seemed to Rita to be watching her, sizing her up, guessing at her secrets, as she was led across the floor to her station.

The floorwalker was dressed in a cutaway, with a waxed mustache and hair parted in the middle, reminding Rita of a character out of a Charlie Chaplin movie. She almost wanted to stay the night, put on roller skates, and dance them across the wide space between pens and the revolving entrance doors. He led her to her station, more concerned with making an impression on customers, especially German ones. This floorwalker, she could tell, would rarely notice what was really going on among his charges.

Shortages had reduced trade in the store's main line of business, textiles and clothes. Rita knew why this was so from the inside, so to speak. Almost all of Poland's textile production was now fashioned into uniforms by slave labor exclusively for the Wehrmacht. But some luxury goods, especially ones from Germany, such as fine fountain pens, were still coming into Warsaw. They were going out again, back to Germany, because here they could be bought for zloty at the exchange rate that made a German corporal better off than a Warsaw lawyer.

The main thing the floorwalker was not noticing was that his staff seemed to be composed of two sorts of people: rabidly anti-Semitic clerks and Jews on false or no identities. This fact about the employees became clear to Rita when she entered the canteen for lunch that first day on the job.

She was motioned over to a table by her counter mate, a young woman named Lotte. Once seated, Rita was invited to participate in a round-robin of abuse and vituperation directed at the Jews of Warsaw, Poland, and Europe. It wasn't what she was expecting.

One of the few older women employees began. "You just started, right, sister? You should have been here when this place was a Jew-business. Owned by Jews, catering to the Yid trade. Never gave a Christian even a chance to rise above floorwalker. Fired people for the littlest offense—taking home a trinket no one would have missed, cutting out of work early on saints' day. What did it matter when they were so rich?"

Here Lotte observed, "Every Jew I've ever seen is a millionaire. The *szmalcowniks* shake down the same people week after week. The Yids never run dry, and these pests just live off the proceeds, never doing a stitch of honest work and making a lot more out of it than a poor honest shopgirl. I feel like turning some of their targets in myself just to get back at those scroungers."

A girl from cosmetics wondered aloud, "The Jews were rich, so why were they all soft on the communists and socialists? When the Jablkowskis owned the store, the unions had the run of the place. They made Catholics pay union dues even when the Cardinal Archbishop told us not to have anything to do with the Reds."

Before she could stop herself, Rita asked a question. "Did the nonunion workers get pay raises when the union people got them?"

Lotte was perceptive enough to catch the drift of a subversive question. "Of course. That was only fair. If the Jews had openly favored their union pets that way, we would have gone on strike. What's your point? Jew lover? Socialist, Red?"

Rita would have to be careful around this one. She beat a retreat. "No, just curious. I am sure things are much better now that the Jews are gone. I worked for Jews in a shop in Lvov, before the Russians came. Then I had to work for the Soviets."

"Poor girl. You'll have to tell us about it." The older woman rose, and they all went back to work.

~

The next day just before lunch, Rita saw a large and obviously German car pull up in front of the revolving door at the main entrance across from her fountain pen display. Three men entered, in full-length leather, each a different stereotype of the Gestapo officer. The floorwalker approached, bowed, and *Heil Hitler*-ed. They clicked heels, snapped a slight bow from the waist, turned, and began walking right toward Rita. They reached her display, wheeled left in unison, and came to a halt on either side of the perfume counter across from her. Behind it stood a young woman. She was petite, dark, with large eyes and a clear complexion that went well with her department store smock. Once the three men had deployed themselves at the counter, she slowly unbuttoned her smock, picked up her purse, and came out from behind the counter. Refusing to say anything at all to anyone, she took up a position among them, and all four walked out. The calmness in her movement, the look of acceptance in her eyes, the furrow lifting from her brow, all sent an unambiguous message: "I am glad to stop hiding, living every waking moment in apprehension, wondering when I will be taken. It's over, and I can surrender at last."

Who did she remind Rita of? Who did she look like? It came to Rita with a stab that made the girl's fate suddenly completely personal to Rita: the girl had the coloring, the carriage, even the calm of that girl at the Terakowski factory, back in Karpatyn, the one who was memorizing *Lord Tadeusz* . . . Yes, Dani.

For a long moment after the Gestapo and the girl had gone, there was a silence. Everyone seemed to be holding their breaths, afraid to show a reaction, wondering if the little drama was really over. Some appeared to be silently saying Hail Marys; others looked about as if they could detect who had betrayed her. Then the buzz broke out across the floor. Meanwhile, the floorwalker fluttered about in his cutaway shushing the salesgirls and reassuring the tut-tutting clutch of dowagers among the clientele.

A few moments later, Rita was polishing fingerprints off the glass top of the counter when Lotte slid over, leaned forward, and spoke under her breath. "I knew she was a Jewess, first moment I saw her. Just a little too refined, manners too nice." Rita nodded. "Then, she ate too much at the canteen for her size. It was probably her only meal every day. A giveaway when you've been watching them for as long as I have."

"Shove off, sister," Rita said, taking her cue. "If I don't clean this counter, the Goddamn floorwalker will have me by the short hairs." Was this crude enough? Or was Lotte's ear going to catch out her irony again?

Perhaps. Lotte went on, "Half the girls in this shop must be Jewish. Maybe you are too."

In a voice loud enough for one or two customers to hear, Rita blurted, "Jesus Maria!" She glared at Lotte. "Go on like that, and I'll think *you're* one! Want to see my baptismal certificate?" She reached for her purse under the counter. "Where's yours?"

"Calm down, sister, calm down." Lotte was still whispering. "You know, I saw her last weekend, that girl they just took. She was out with a Wehrmacht noncom, a sergeant, I think. Probably wouldn't come across when he wanted it, so he turned her in."

Now it was Rita's turn to be upset. "Do you think a German soldier would turn in a girl just for protecting her virtue?"

"Sure. Why not, if he knew she was a Yid?"

"Lotte, I'm from the east; I haven't been in the big city long. Explain some things to me. Why would a German soldier have anything to do with a Jew-sow? Why would a girl tell a German soldier if she was Jewish?"

"Jewesses sleep around. They all do. So, they're the only girls a soldier can get. As for the soldiers, not all of them are Nazis, and even the ones who are, well, there are limits to their loyalty to the party, right? Girl's willing to sleep with a German, she's probably Jewish. Girl refuses, well, then let her prove she isn't. Simple."

"I see. Thanks."

CHAPTER TWENTY-ONE

Mrs. Kaminski was pleased with her lodger. Never brought anyone home, never asked to use the kitchen, quiet and neat, out
every evening doing something in town presumably. But no
trouble. Eventually she warmed to Rita. Finally one evening, she
broke her own rule and invited Rita into the kitchen for tea, offering to let her cook. She had been relieved to learn that her tenant
took meals at the department store canteen and didn't need to cook.
Still, a young lady could always learn something from her elders,
and both of them were alone in this world apparently.

Mrs. Kaminski's husband had been killed by the Reds during
the Polish-Russian war in 1920. She had been alone, renting rooms
ever since. She would be glad of some company, especially on long
winter days. Sunday mornings she invited Rita to accompany her
to Mass, and Rita was glad to go. When Mrs. Kaminski first offered
to teach her how to cook, Rita politely declined. The smells from
her kitchen eventually broke down Rita's resistance. Somehow Mrs.
Kaminski could turn a little flour, lard, and some water into a pas-
try dough. Then by stretching and pulling, throwing on a few raisins, wrinkled old apples no one could want, and the walnuts that
were one commodity still unrationed, plus a little precious sugar

and some cinnamon, she could roll the whole thing into a strudel any Gaulieter would be pleased to serve. Watching her once or twice, Rita begged the chance to try her hand. It was a way to make Sundays after church go by.

The only problem about Mrs. Kaminski's place was that it was a little too far from the ghetto. Every night Rita had to go some distance to court disaster. After work ended at six o'clock, she took to walking up Marszakowska Street toward the ghetto, doing what she could to attract the attention of the extortionists. All too often it was only a German soldier whose interest she piqued. Apparently she needed to look more furtive, less Aryan. How, short of putting a yellow star on her arm?

She was desperate to be victimized by the shakedown artists, to attract the attention of those she should have feared most. Every night she forced herself to do it. A few zloty in her purse, her documentation at the ready, even a copy of the German Warsaw newspaper in her coat pocket to add to her false identity. But then, how to put on the face of a Jew on the run? It shouldn't be so hard. That was just who she was. After a time she realized that sauntering, strolling, making a display of herself was part of the problem. No one took her for a fugitive. She was just another tramp on the streets. She couldn't have looked more like one if she had been standing under a streetlamp smoking a cigarette, adjusting a garter.

As she walked along, Rita would repeatedly see people plucked into side streets, being shaken down. But never her. Twice in the first few weeks she was in Warsaw, she saw Gestapo convoys, a truck and one or two cars, pull up before a row of flats. A half dozen very large Waffen-SS, led by an officer in the precise-fitting black, rushed a door and broke it down. In moments men pointing their automatic weapons were herding trembling children, mothers clutching infants to their breasts, gaunt, broken men out into the street. They made pathetic attempts to climb up the back of the truck, falling away from lack of strength and inability to reach the handles or the tailgate chains or even just the floors of the open-gated truck beds. The rain of rifle butts and pistol barrel blows failed to contribute in the least to their success, only increasing their frantic clawing. Finally the soldiers simply had to lift and hurtle each of them into the back, where hands eventually reached out to break a fall or catch a child.

Rita knew she had to watch the bystanders and learn how a Pole—or better yet, a *Volks-Deutsche*—reacted to such a scene. Some stared, openmouthed; others smiled, a few even jeered, most slunk away. This last Rita could do with no trouble.

What she needed to find was a Jewish thug, someone like Jerszy in Lemberg. But when she finally began to be noticed, all she seemed to attract were Polish *szmalcowniks*. These she faced down when she could. "Leave me alone. I am *Volks-Deutsche,* and you will get into a lot of hot water trying to drag me in to the Gestapo." She would burst into a flood of German, loud enough to be heard by any passing Blue Police or German soldier. That was usually enough. She knew enough to identify a Jewish extortionist—the accented Polish, Yiddish intonation or expression. The few times she was in doubt, dragged into an alley, held at knifepoint, threatened with immediate harm, she would surrender the money in her purse and condemn the thief as a common criminal. But she would listen carefully for their Polish. Was it native? Was it colloquial? Was it fluent?

Christmas passed into the new year. *Happy 1943* said the somewhat forlorn sign over the inside of the revolving doors at Jablkowski Brothers Department Store. There was a very small bonus in the paycheck and a desultory attempt at a Christmas party. Surely if anything was going to give away the identity of the Jews working in the store, it would have been the way they celebrated, or rather didn't. But the Poles at the parties were evidently some combination of too drunk or too nice or too indifferent to notice.

∞

Rita kept moving closer and closer to the ghetto in her nightly peregrinations. Sometimes she was stopped by sentries for papers. More often she was cautioned that the area was dangerous. The Blue Police were *korrekt*. "Desperate Jews, criminals, even partisans— best steer clear, *Panna*," or just as often, "*Fräulein*."

But it all seemed very quiet. After her experience of the Karpatyn ghetto and its repeated *Aktionen*, she couldn't understand why the Warsaw ghetto was being left alone. A few men coming and going from the ghetto, showing their papers at the gates, but no German entering at all. Were they just starving the ghetto? They evidently weren't liquidating it anymore. Was food getting in somehow? If so, perhaps she could find a way in with it.

Rita's weekly wage was not enough to meet her needs, pay her rent, contribute to Mrs. Kaminski's kitchen, and pay off the urchins and impoverished extortionists—more like beggars—that she was attracting. So, early one February evening after work, she dropped in on the Chemiot café in Praga precisely at six thirty. Krystyna was alone at one end of the *Zinc*—it really was a bar counter from Paris, shiny, smooth silver metal. Rita came in, hung up her coat with the lining out, and sat down at a table. Seeing her, Krystyna went to the back of the bar, evidently heading for the toilet.

A few moments later, nursing a beer, Rita found herself making eye contact with a Wehrmacht soldier. It was brief, but not brief enough. Encouraged, he was coming to her table. What to do? She couldn't leave. Smile, you're a *Volks-Deutsche Mädchen*. Give some small comfort to a German boy far from home. She smiled, pushed open a chair, and moved her beer to make room for him.

"Good evening, *Fräulein*. Can you spare a few moments of your company to a soldier on his way to the Eastern Front?" His German was singsong—was it Swabian?

"With pleasure, though I have a train to catch myself." Her German was as casual as she could make it. "How did you know I was German?"

"Looks, I guess. But I was just hoping. I have no Polish to use on the girls here."

Small talk, then, Rita thought. "Can you tell me where you are going? No, don't answer that." She smiled. "Military secrets. Not even a German girl can be trusted. Tell me instead what you have been doing. A furlough at home from your unit?"

"Afraid not. Worst assignment you can get short of the Eastern Front, and now I am getting that one." He paused. "My unit was doing guard duty at the Jewish quarter." He used the official designation.

"Why so bad?" Rita tried not to appear particularly interested.

"The place . . . disgusting. You can't stand being near it. Decaying corpses on the streets, desperate people. The way they smell, the walking dead. Worst of all, the starving children. No matter how important it is to rid the world of those people, it's hard, really unpleasant work. Even the party members sometimes ask themselves, is this suffering really necessary? Can't we put them out of their misery any faster? Well, the thing is, we were putting an end to their suffering, clearing large numbers of Jews out, sending them . . . away." He would not say what he really meant, and Rita couldn't afford to finish his thought aloud. He took a sip of his beer. She emulated. Then he began again. "But the whole operation stopped a week ago."

Dare she ask? Will he go on? The wait was an agony of several seconds. He looked around, hunched over a little more, almost as though guarding his beer, and began to speak under his breath. "They are fighting back. Somehow they've got guns, a few of them, anyway. Maybe from the Polish resistance, maybe on the black market. Last week they started shooting during a roundup. When our unit disarmed them and took them out, they broke up a transport, outside the ghetto. Jews running for cover everywhere. Hundreds of them, loose. There weren't enough guards to round them up. It all got back to the ghetto, of course."

His urgency allowed her to ask, "What happened then?"

"Four days of street battles with terrorists inside. We took a lot of hostages. But it didn't stop them. The *Oberkommando* thinks the Jews are preparing a bigger armed revolt or some sort of surprise for us."

"What will your commanders do?" she asked, though what she wanted to ask was when this would happen.

"I don't know. For the moment they have stopped the deportation from the ghetto. At some point they'll have to go in with force. But not my problem now." He stopped. "I'm going east. They're combing the units to send out replacements. Slightest infraction, and you're gone."

"I'm so sorry." Should a *Volks-Deutsche* commiserate, Rita wondered?

Staring into his beer glass, the soldier went on unbidden. "I cut a little corner, and now it's my death certificate."

"Don't tell me if it will get you in trouble."

"Can't get any worse than the Eastern Front. I was a code clerk, perfectly safe in headquarters company. Anyway, there were so many messages to send. But they made us change the code settings on the machines every day. That was too much trouble."

Rita stopped him. "You mustn't tell me any more, soldier." All the while she was thinking, *Could Erich have been right about their code? Is this why the Americans and Brits are winning in Africa? Is this why the Royal Navy is sinking more U-boats every week?*

He wouldn't stop muttering. "Code's unbreakable anyway. So, once in a while, we didn't bother to change the settings. Somebody noticed higher up, and now I'm for Army Group Center on the Volga." He lifted his glass and spat out a bitter, "Prost."

Rita followed his gesture with her own toast. They finished their beers together.

By this time Krystyna was back at her place at the bar. Rita had never even noticed her putting anything in the coat she had hung up. It would be a perfect dead-drop exchange. She rose and grasped the soldier's hand firmly. "I wish you the best of luck."

He replied, "*Heil Hitler*," with no enthusiasm whatever.

The reply formed in her mouth almost without thought. "*Heil Hitler.*" She turned and left.

∽

Now Rita had a deadline if the ghetto was finally to be cleared. It was urgent she find the right extortionist. She had to let it be known in the right places there was someone looking for a way to get inside before it was too late.

She began taking longer and longer walks, later and later at night. No longer just walking, either. Rather, she tried walking fast enough to attract attention, brushing past people, making them wonder where she was going in such a hurry—even better, she thought, what she was hurrying away from. It worked. Soon enough she had been stopped and shaken down by the same few extortionists several times. Finally she gathered her nerve and began to ask, "Do you know any Jew in this business?" "Why?" was the only reply. Her answer was, "Don't ask. But if you can bring me one, I'll make it worth your while." She couldn't chance missing a contact. She had to give her address. It was the worst thing she could do, but now she was as desperate as any Jew in hiding. Unlike them, she needed to be found.

One morning in the middle of February, Mrs. Kaminski came to her room as Rita was dressing. The knock was peremptory. Then, before she could answer, the older woman was in her room. "I told you no visitors, and especially no Jews! I am sorry, but you will have to leave."

"Jews? What are you talking about, Mrs. K.?" Rita's emotions were mixed, fraught and excited.

"One of those street-corner shakedown artists brought a Jew to the door last night, looking for you. I told him to go away. He left this note for you. It has your name on it. I told you, no Jews." She handed over the note. "Be out of here tomorrow."

"I can't possibly find another place that quickly, Mrs. K. Give me another day."

"Very well, Wednesday." She shut the door with finality.

Rita read the note.

I'll be under the ghetto bridge on Mirowski at 14:30 two days from now. Be there. Bring one hundred zloty, or it's the Gestapo for you.

Was it the right contact? Was it a trap? Would she have enough to make these people do what she needed? She went to work behind the pen counter in a fever. Before lunch she went to the women's room several times and finally asked the floorwalker to excuse her for the day. "Cramps." Squeamish, he wanted to hear no more. Yes, she could go for the day.

She got off the streetcar a hundred feet from the ghetto bridge. She made a point of arriving by streetcar so that there would be no doubt she had a right to pass freely, to use the very services Jews were strictly forbidden. Her contact must have noticed. He was there with the kid she'd dealt with two days before. They stirred from the shadows of the footbridge and came forward. Before they could say anything, Rita held out a twenty zloty note to the boy who had made the contact for her. "Here. Now beat it. I don't want to see you again."

When he had gone, the haggard wraith stepped forward. "Hand it over, lady." His accent was reassuringly uneducated, Yiddish, and hungry.

She pulled him into an alley, *a new experience for him*, she thought to herself. "Here's the hundred. There is another hundred zloty for you if you can get me someone who used to work for Group 13, or someone with contacts in the *Jupo*, someone who can get me in and get me out of the ghetto. Understand? When you find him, don't come to my address. I'm not living there anymore. You'll find me walking Marszakowska Street from here to Aleje Jerozolimskie between 19:00 and 22:00 the next three nights. Any tricks, no hundred zloty."

The next night after work, Rita went back to the Chemiot. Entering, she could see Krystyna propping up the bar as usual. She left as soon as she noticed Rita, who had ordered a glass of tea. She gulped it down, and went straight to Krystyna's building, pushed enough buttons to get someone to buzz her through the front door, and mounted the stairs to the fourth floor. A few minutes later, Krystyna appeared. She was red in the face from fury or exertion or both. "I thought it would be you. What are you doing? I told you never—"

"I know. This is the last time you will ever see me. I left two gold coins hidden in your apartment. I need them now."

"I know. I found them. You Yids can't be trusted, even by people who risk their lives to help you. Eighteen gold coins just seemed like an odd number to carry around. I figured there were at least two more, and it didn't take me long to find them after you left. You don't deserve them, Jew cow."

Rita crumpled into tears. Krystyna had a right to be furious. Her trust had been betrayed. But Rita had to do these things. "I need the rest of my money now, and those two coins . . . it's the only way I'll ever get a chance to see if my son is alive."

"Wait here." In a moment she was back. "Here." She handed Rita the two coins. "The Home Army's not going to be your safe deposit box anymore. We're keeping the rest of it. Consider it carrying charges. Now get out." She slammed her door.

❧

That night Rita walked the kilometer or so between the ghetto and the department store several times, this time looking unconcerned and exuding unapproachability. Not even a prostitute would have lingered so brazenly at each intersection. But no encounter. It was after eleven o'clock when she returned to 44 Widok Street. There was a note pinned to her door: *Out. Tomorrow, or I confiscate your belongings and turn you in.* She packed that night.

In the morning she left with her case. When she presented herself at the Hotel Handel, the clerk remembered her. "Yes, I'm back in town for a week or so. I know the drill. I'll register with the police tomorrow." She asked for a room with a sink, as close to the shower and toilet in the hall as possible, and went up to it directly.

Another day behind the fountain pen counter with Lotte droning on about the rationing, her family, encounters with men, offering her offensive opinions. It seemed endless. But at 19:00 Rita was out again walking Marszakowska Street.

About 21:00 her nameless Jewish contact finally whistled her into an alley and then on to a backstreet. From there he walked her north toward the ghetto, wordlessly. At Plac Bankowy they climbed through the boarded-up entrance of a gutted building and groped their way in the dark down into its basement. When they arrived someone in front of them struck a match, lit a cigarette, and offered Rita one. She took it. When her eyes adjusted to the light of the match, she saw a middle-aged man, face weathered but not broken. There were several lines of wrinkles at his neck, rising behind his mouth and across the sides of his face, climbing into his brow line. His hair was thin as far as she could make it out. His lips were large, as was his nose, which had also obviously been broken. But his eyes showed life and defiance. He was dressed in what looked like rags, but he didn't look hungry.

"Well, you've found the person you're looking for. Don't imagine I'm alone, even in this hole in the ground. What do you want?"

"I need to get into the ghetto."

"So, go in the front door. It's open." It was his way of telling her to stop wasting time and get on with it.

"My child might be in the ghetto. I have to find out. I want someone who can take me in and get me out, with my child if I find him in the orphanage or what's left of it. Can you do it?"

"Maybe. How much is it worth to you?"

She opened her palm to reveal one gold coin.

"Not enough, and why shouldn't I just take it from you now and turn you over to my friends in the Gestapo?"

"Because there are several more just like it, and you would miss out if you did either of those things."

He didn't ask how many. He was obviously going to get every one she had, no matter how many there were. "I may just be able to help you. When do you want to go?"

"Now. We both know there isn't much time before the ghetto blows up."

CHAPTER TWENTY-TWO

Now? You want to go right now?" he repeated. "Not dressed like that. Those clothes would be ripped off your back. Not even a brute like me could protect you. And then there are people in there who would kill you just for looking healthy and Aryan." He thought for a moment. "Maybe we can do something about your clothes. Follow me. Watch your head." They moved down deeper toward a tunnel just large enough for her guide to move through, stooped over.

As they walked Rita broke the silence. "What is your name?"

"No names. I don't want yours either. We don't need them, and we won't have any in the pits they'll bury us in." Rita suppressed the question that immediately arose: so, why do anything for a few gold coins?

They were evidently in a tunnel, a long one, moving downhill as it went along toward what Rita thought must be the west, the direction of the ghetto. After a hundred meters, the tunnel began to rise. It ended in a room, where two men sat on the floor, evidently guards. They nodded at Rita's guide, but said nothing. Her guide looked around. "Any rags we can fit her up with?" Lethargically one of the two rose and picked over some torn garments, handing up a torn skirt and a threadbare coat. Her nameless host passed them to Rita. "Change into these." She hesitated. "No time for modesty, lady. They may look, but they won't touch." He turned to his henchmen. "Don't harm the golden goose, boys." There was nothing for it but to remove her coat and dress and put on the rags. The only thing she took from her coat was the envelope containing her documents.

"So, I am going to take you to what's left of the *Judenrat* office. If there is anybody there, we'll have a way of getting them to check records or getting to the kids still in the ghetto." Rita nodded, and he led her out of the tunnel and up into the first circle of hell.

She was grateful for the darkness cloaking the misery around her. But the darkness could not veil the smell. It was not the smell of burning flesh still reeking in her mind's nostrils six months after the Karpatyn ghetto fires. It was more familiar in some respects, but overpoweringly rank. It was the smell of excrement, of befoulment, of dysentery and vomitus, irregularly punctuated by the smell of putrid meat or some organic substance—human bodies?—gone very bad. The odors were coming at her in waves that effectively prevented her nose from accommodating itself so that the smell's offensiveness might dissipate into the background. Rita began to feel herself involuntarily swallowing, and then starting to vomit. Her nameless guide handed her a rag that had been dipped in gasoline. "Here, cover your nose with this." A smell she normally found repugnant rescued her, and she was able to continue.

In the darkness, several times she tripped over bodies, mostly dead, but some responded with a slight moan. And once she inadvertently stepped on flesh that gave way and spread a slime over her shoe top, seeping in around her ankles. Better not to think of what was making her foot slap in her shoe with each step she took.

In the darkness too, it seemed to her, there lurked shadows that retreated as her guide went past, not prepared to confront him or anyone he was guiding. But Rita instinctively closed up the space between the two of them.

After a ten-minute walk, they found themselves in an open square. On one side of it, Rita could make out a gallows. It was twice or three times as long as the one she had known in the Karpatyn ghetto, and there were still bodies hanging from it. She could tell even in the dark: the heads akimbo, outlining ovals slightly darker than the night sky behind them, waists narrowed by the ropes securing their hands. She looked down—involuntarily, she realized—seeking and finding the marks of excrement that the executed always lose. She forced herself to look up and away from it.

Suddenly it dawned on her. She had not seen a single other person actually moving through the ghetto streets. Pulling away the gasoline rag for a moment, Rita shouted ahead to her nameless guide, "Where is everybody? Is the ghetto empty? We haven't passed anyone."

He stopped for a moment. "This ghetto used to hold 350,000 or 400,000. Now there are only about 50,000 left. Overcrowding is no longer a problem. Anyway, all the able-bodied are underground, literally, building bunkers and hiding in them. They know the Germans are coming." She thought, *"They," not "we"? Where does he think he's going?* "There is nothing much to do out in the open at night, except get knifed by people like me." There was a mordant laugh. He turned to continue. "We're nearly there."

The *Judenrat* headquarters was a two-story building, with a raised triangular crown. It must have been a school or a government building before the war. It too seemed deserted. They entered and began moving down a corridor. Her guide obviously knew exactly where he was going. *Here at last, sleeping on the floors, were people, living people*, Rita thought with a little relief. Picking their way through the sleeping bodies, occasionally they woke one by the noise or their footsteps, but invariably the body simply turned over and went back to sleep. Finally they found themselves before a closed door. Rita's guide pushed it open, struck a match, and extracted a short candle end from somewhere inside his coat. Seeing a body in the corner of the room, he went over and shook it awake. "Are you in records? We need some information."

The man stirred. The guide grabbed him by the lapel, yanked him to his feet, and kept a grip on his neck in a way that made it clear the man had no choice but to respond. He turned to Rita. "Ask him what you want."

"Are there records for children brought here from outside—orphaned children or children sent here from other ghettos?"

She could only make out bleary eyes in the candlelight, but the voice answered, "There had to be, for the rations. But since last fall, they have been hopelessly incomplete." He turned, put his hand out for the candle, and began looking at ledger books. "Arrivals are listed by date. Do you have a date the child arrived?"

"April last year. Stefan Guildenstern. He would have been two and a half. " Then she added, to no one in particular, "He was already speaking—Polish. He knew his name."

The clerk moved the candle across a shelf, with his finger on the bindings. "It's gone."

"What do you mean, it's gone?" Rita demanded. "What's gone?"

"The ledger for that month."

Rita was firm. "Look further. It's probably just out of order."

"Lady, if April '42 were here, it would be on this shelf." He scanned back and forth. "I'm sorry, but people have been coming and going in this room for months. Taking ledgers and bringing them back, cutting out pages to use for handbills, documents, anything. Half the volumes are gone." He stopped. "Besides, if you're looking for a kid, go to the orphanage. There is hardly anyone left, but if he got here, maybe someone will remember him."

The guide tightened his grip. "Where?"

"You're hurting me. It's not far. It's opposite Gesiowka Prison on Smocza. You know where that is?" The grip was relaxed.

"All right; let's go." He didn't bother looking toward Rita but simply barged out the door, sending bodies in the corridor sliding away. Not bothering to go back to the main entrance, he blew out the candle and made his way to a side door.

Outside the stench regaled Rita again, and she reached back into the tatters of her garment for the gasoline rag. Here some street lighting from beyond the ghetto gave more illumination than Rita wanted. She could see the shreds of broken life before her in every way: no doors, no window glass, shattered sticks of furniture, upholstery stuffing, an icebox, plumbing, mountains of trash, detritus of every kind, the carcass of a horse, stripped of flesh and rotting. And everywhere bodies she could now not avoid seeing in the eerie light: flies buzzing on open wounds and ghostly white maggots crowding the eye sockets of the dead, decaying at the curbsides. Here and there, as in Karpatyn, a dead child at its mother's side or cradled in a dead lap created by the *rigor mortis* of legs straightening while the corpse remained upright at the curbstone. As they walked she thought she saw curtains move ever so slightly. They were being watched . . . by whom? The already dead, those too weak to bestir themselves? Or was it the few predators left—like her guide—watching, stalking?

Now she was frightened. This was not a fool's errand. It was a suicidal mistake. Rita was beginning to tremble and sweat uncontrollably in the cold air, no longer moved by pity or sorrow, human sympathy or care. Suddenly she couldn't breathe. She was drowning, being smothered, paralyzed in a nightmare that was swallowing her up. She reached out to her nameless guide, still striding along. "I can't go on. Take me back."

He was gruff. "Nearly there. Get a grip."

She felt a sharp slap and regained some semblance of control over herself.

An eternity later the man stopped in front of one of the derelict tenements. "Here you are. Go ahead in. Be careful. If there are any children left in there, they have been untended for long enough to have gone feral." Rita was struck by the word. Where had this man picked up a word like that? Then it struck her. He had been moving in and outside of a region of feral animals for months, years. Surely the word was one he had heard often. He handed her the candle and struck a match.

Carefully she pushed open a door that hung by a single hinge and looked within. The first thing she saw was a half dozen, then a score or more forearms rising to foreheads, protecting eyes from the brightness of the candle. Then she saw the children, ranging from toddlers to ten-year-olds, some so closely intertwined on the ground that they must have been older and younger siblings. All in tatters, blue with cold, filthy in every way. Once adjusted to the light, those with any strength surged forward, hands outstretched, some piteous, some threatening, all ravenous, all emaciated. The only children who did not move were already dead, bloated by malnutrition beyond the ability to stir themselves, or too young to recognize the disturbance as a potential source of food. Staring at them, nothing to offer, Rita suddenly could not even remember why she had come, what she wanted.

The man broke her hysterical trance. "Well, do you see him? What's his name?"

"Stefan," she whispered. Then she shouted it, "Stefan? Stefan Guildenstern. It's your mother."

A dozen of the older boys, even a few girls old enough to understand, rose weakly, began to wave an arm so thin any cloth remaining on it fell away. "It's me . . . I'm here, please."

Rita ignored them. Instead, she brought the candle down to the toddlers, moving quickly from face to face, rushing through her search, more eager to get it over with than to find her child. She came to the last child. Then she forced herself to search again, pushing aside the arms and the bodies of children old enough to seek a savior, too old to be her child. Finally she addressed a girl who seemed the oldest. "How long have you been here?" The girl did not respond. Rita passed a hand across her blank stare. Her eyelids did not close. She was close enough to smell death on the child's breath that matched the pallor of her skin.

Standing up, she said in a voice that reached across the space, "Anyone know a boy named Stefan?" Rita recognized the pointlessness of her question even as it left her mouth. She was now feeling foolish, cruel, fearful, and grief-stricken all at once, trembling with cold and sweating at the same time. Children began to surround her, almost threatening in their numbers, if not their strength. A strong hand reached in and pulled her back, then guided her out into the street, now almost backlit by lights behind the ghetto walls. "I've got to get you back out of here before daybreak if I am going to get me any more of those gold coins of yours." The guide led the way out of the building and into the street.

Two steps away from the building, Rita turned back unnoticed and slipped into the doorway again. When she came out ten seconds later, her guide was turning around looking for her. "What happened to you?" he whispered as she reached him.

"I got dizzy," she replied. "I lost you for a moment."

"Can't afford to lose you now." He grabbed her wrist and began pulling her along. They wound their way through a maze of alleys and open streets, each as much a grim witness to the ghetto charnel as the rest. The journey seemed to Rita an endless torture. The gasoline smell of the rag had long weakened to ineffectiveness, and she was retching up acid with every breath as they finally found their way to the place where they had begun. Her nameless guide pushed her head down as they entered the basement, meanwhile deftly reaching into the coat she wore to remove the envelope of documents she had carried into the ghetto.

"Give me that," she hissed, and began to scratch at him. He had no trouble warding her blows off with one hand as he held the envelope aloft. She stopped, exhausted. "It's just my papers. The gold coins aren't there. Would I be foolish enough to carry them with me?"

He opened the envelope and satisfied himself. "Well, where are they? We're not going to let you go without the rest of the payment."

"Just get me back to where I left my clothes." She retched out the words. He turned back, not relinquishing her envelope.

A few minutes later, they were at the tunnel opening. Holding her firmly, the man reached down to the ground, picking up her dress and coat. Carefully the hand began to feel through the garments, feeling for coins. "No payoff, no papers."

"The second coin is back there in the building where the children were. On the lintel of the door. Just go back and reach up for it. I went back and put it there when I told you I got dizzy." His smile was slightly rueful. "For the next one, and the ones after that, you'll have to give me my papers and let me go. I know you'll have me followed. So, you'll know where I live. Send someone you trust up to my room when you think it's safe enough, and the rest will be there."

With a look of admiration, he handed over the papers. "Jewess or not, you're a clever one. But you're right. You won't go far unless you come across with the rest. And if the second coin is not where you say, you'll be in the hands of the Gestapo by suppertime." He let go of her wrist, handed her the documents, and went quickly out back into the ghetto. Rita dressed and crept back out into the Warsaw streets.

She could feel herself being followed before she could see who it was. Perhaps the street urchin following her had been told to make it obvious. She made no attempt to lose him. By now it was dawn, and they were alone on Marszakowska Street. She let the boy follow her all the way to Aleje Jerozolimskie, walking in the direction of her hotel. In the distance she could see the first tram of the day coming up behind her. It was three stops away, full of early morning riders headed to work. She gauged her pace so that she arrived at a stop just before the tram pulled away, jumped on, and paid her fare. The boy was left on the other side of the street, grimacing. Rita could only hope that he was not prepared to attract attention by running and that he might even be a Jew, forbidden on the trams under any circumstances.

It was going to be too easy, she thought, outwitting these *szmalcowniks*. But what if she had found her child? This plan would never have worked. Did she really think she would find him? Did she even want to do so? Was the entire horror something that she had to subject herself to, knowing that she wouldn't find him—or, finding him, would have condemned herself to death along with him? Did she need to know what she had learned about the Warsaw ghetto? Did it do anything more than add to her own personal hell in the Karpatyn ghetto? These were questions without answers, questions one was driven to ask oneself. Fatuous questions. She had to convince herself they were as pointless as they were answerless. Alas, willing them away just didn't work. But now her tram approached Warsaw Main Railway Station.

Rita walked off the tram and into the station. Surreptitiously she looked around for Gestapo, though she felt confident enough to pass their scrutiny. She was more anxious about the extortionists preying on the foot traffic coming into the station. Perhaps entering without a valise, a grip, or a bag of any kind, she might not attract their attention.

But there, leaning against the railing of the ticket barrier, was one of the two men from the darkened ghetto tunnel. Back there, even in the dim light of the entry to the ghetto, he must have gotten a good look at her as she changed into the rags. Despite the dimness of the candlelight back there, she had no trouble identifying him now. In a moment it also became clear to Rita that he had recognized her. Would he approach? Would he simply make it impossible for her to get away? He pushed himself away from the ticket barrier and began moving in her direction.

Rita reached into her coat pocket to pull out her left-luggage receipt. All her clever planning—finding a way to save her Darwins, getting her few other things from the room without checking out, finding a cheap case at the station the day before, packing it and checking it—all would be for naught. As she pulled the claim check out of her coat pocket, another bit of paper came out with it. She looked at it. *Milkolaj Bilek, Detective Inspector, Metropolitan Police, Lemberg,* with a small blue dot under 'l' in the word "Bilek." She looked up and then around the vast space of the station. There, between her and the left-luggage, stood a uniformed Blue Police constable.

"Officer, can you help me? A policeman in Lemberg gave me his card. He told me to show it to any Blue Policeman if I ever needed help."

The man looked at her, then at the card, and handed it back. "Be off with you, woman. I am not here to help damsels in distress."

"Please, sir." Rita proffered it again. "Might you not look at it a little more closely?" Her finger pointed to the ink dot under the name.

Grudgingly he looked a second time. Then knowing eyes sought hers. "May I be of some assistance, Miss?"

Rita felt she would have disrobed for him then and there, she was so grateful. But all she did was give him the winningest smile she could contrive. "I have a bag at the left-luggage. Then I need to get a ticket to Krakow and make my way through the barrier. My papers are all in order." She looked directly at him, as if to say, *There is no risk in all this for you.* "Then I think I will be fine."

"I'll be pleased to accompany you." He smiled conspiratorially and clicked his heels. Rita put her arm through his.

❧

It didn't take more than two days for Lotte to realize Rita was not coming back to work at Jablkowski Brothers. No one could afford to miss a second day and expect to keep her job at the department store. At the same time, it came to her that she could profit nicely from this unannounced resignation. Just before opening, she pocketed four of the nicest fountain pens from under the glass and immediately approached the floorwalker with her suspicion that Rita had quit and taken property with her. What is more, she suggested, Rita might have been a Jewess. "She was talking like a communist only a few days ago at lunch, sir."

"Thank you, Lotte. I will file a report and take the matter up with the *Kripo.*" That was the criminal detective police. And he would. Pilferage was the most serious offense in the floorwalker's catalog of crimes. He went to his office and picked up the telephone. Now, what was her name . . . Trushenko, Rita Trushenko.

CHAPTER TWENTY-THREE

Karpatyn to Lvov/Lemberg, Lemberg to Warsaw, now Warsaw to Krakow. The rattling, rocking, lurching train moved south and west toward a city she thought she knew and understood. When was Rita's luck going to run out? How long could she continue to play roulette with her life and not lose? The thought held Rita briefly until fatigue overwhelmed her and she fell into a sound sleep.

She was awoken twice, once by the conductor seeking her ticket and then later by a Gestapo *Shutzpolizei*, demanding to see her *Kennkarte*. He handed it back and reminded her that its Warsaw registration would need to be amended to Krakow if she intended to remain there.

Now she was awake and traveling through familiar scenery: the bleak winter landscape of small-hold farms hedged around by broken stone fences and brushwork hedges that would become impenetrable even to sight in the summer. The fields were dotted with boulders unmoved over centuries, surrounded by derelict stubble. No farmer and team of horses were to be seen in any of the fields, nor even cows lolling around sloughs. Smoke curled out of stone and timbered farmsteads. Were the lives within so different from what they had been five or ten years ago?

The train slowed along a curve. Through the window for a moment, Rita could see the engine banking slightly, and then in the crescent of the curve a cemetery. Was that a gravedigger? No, a watchman, a farmer, approaching a tall woman holding aloft a white cloth against the strong wind, at her feet a brace of hunting dogs digging at something. It was as though someone were staging the scene from *Lord Tadeusz* that Dani had been learning that first morning Rita spoke to her in the Terakowski works. How did the verse go?

> *Their dogs dug in the ground,*
> *And howled furiously, as though the scent*
> *Of death their frantic tunneling unearthed*
> *For war or starvation these things portend.*
> *The forest watchman was not the first*
> *To have seen, wandering through cemeteries,*
> *The Maid of Pestilence, tall as the trees,*
> *Waving a bloody kerchief in the breeze.*

And then the rhythm of the words gave way to an echo of the frisson Rita had felt when Dani had held her in what now seemed a world away—that afternoon months ago in the ghetto factory.

The man and woman in the cemetery were the only humans in the winter landscape of stolid farmhouses, from each of which rose two or more steady columns of smoke. *These Polish peasants were at least sometimes warm through a long winter*, she thought. Even their animals were out of the elements. Not her. Rita felt she had been continually cold as far back as the Soviet invasion of Poland, certainly since the German attack in the east. In fact, she realized the only time in her whole life she'd been warm in the winter were those months after she had arrived in Karpatyn. Being cold was just the normal order of things, to which now could be added being hungry. Nothing but a perpetual cold was really to be expected in this world.

There had to be some point to her being cold, being hungry, being alone. There had to be some meaning to it. Judgment, punishment, test, trial, strengthening—something that made sense out of it. Some scheme into which what was happening could all be fit—Rita, Urs, Tadeusz, Stefan, Erich, Freddy . . . A story from which she might at least learn something about herself and her life. At the end of it, when the war was over, if she survived, there would be a plot with a natural beginning, a long, painful, tension-filled middle, villains and heroes, and a satisfying end, or at least one that brought the story to a close—her survival. When it was all over, the story would stitch together everything that had happened—her perpetual discomfort and danger—even if it didn't make sense of the horrors visited on the millions somehow suffering through the demented melodrama that would end with her survival. Yes, there would be a story at the end, if she did survive—a plot with dangers and escapes, in which her actions and everyone else's would make sense. But would it explain how and why she survived?

No, Rita knew well enough. The real explanation would be just blind chance! The odds were in her favor, slightly, but enough to make her survival unmysterious. The meaning of it all would just be dumb luck. The explanation would not be satisfying. It would merely be true. She wouldn't delude herself.

The fact was, most people were not prepared to take the trouble involved in turning her in. There just weren't enough real Nazis, virulent real anti-Semites, crazed Polish nationalists, prepared to take pains to rid the environment of their racial, cultural, or class enemies. Most people were no worse than indifferent to other people's fate. The Mrs. Kaminskis of the world would rather just walk on by than act on their prejudices, especially when dealing with individuals they knew, especially when the Jew they had to turn in was a familiar face. To do that required an incentive, some gain, and little risk.

But what about the compliant Blue Police constable at the ticket barrier in the Warsaw station? Wasn't that a miracle, the hand of God, like winning a thirty-six-to-one bet at the roulette table? Think, Rita. What was the chance that that cop was Home Army just like Bilek in Lemberg? Forty percent? Fifty percent? Higher? What was the chance that, even if he had not been Home Army three months before, he was now? The Germans had lost the battle of Stalingrad two weeks before. Maybe the smart money in Poland was turning against them?

Throw in her Aryan looks, her twin plaits of blonde hair, her faultless Polish, her excellent German, her *Kennkarte* and baptismal certificate. The odds were stacked in her favor. Rita's chances were improving every day.

It's just that the stakes are so high, Rita told herself, *and my estimates of the chances likely so inaccurate. It's easy to think survival is a fluke, a miracle, and then try to make sense of it all.* As though the obvious explanation for all the bullets she had dodged was God's will, or divine providence, or that somehow she was meant to survive.

Thinking things through the right way would make her more cautious. That was good. It freed her from taking some misplaced credit for surviving. It might even relieve her of a weighty burden of feeling guilty about surviving. But, Rita asked herself, was she an unfeeling monster for thinking this way? Were cold, calculating probabilities depriving her of her humanity, anesthetizing her grief over her losses—of parents, in-laws, even Urs, probably Tadeusz, certainly Stefan? She could still cry, couldn't she? She was still moved by the hollow in her life created by the loss of her son. She could still hope against all evidence and reason that he lived. She could risk coming right up to the edge of the cliff, even climbing down into the abyss beyond it, on the chance she might find him. Surely for all the rationality she forced on herself, she was still completely human.

Why was she alive? Intelligence, foresight, the right decisions? How foolish to think that. Better to ask why thought always seeks stories, meaning. Why do we endlessly try to make sense of things? Why are we never satisfied with the right answer—dumb luck? Why do we always crave a motive? And why did rail journeys always provoke interior monologues of philosophy?

Krakow is a city I know, she tried to reassure herself. She would not have to wander around pretending to be going somewhere. Still, there would have been many changes since she left in the spring of 1936. To begin with, Krakow was probably *Judenrein*. Of the sixty thousand or so Jews who had lived there before the war, ghettoization and *Aktionen* surely had left at most a remnant, one too small to muster any possibility of resistance, as in Warsaw. Would the town be honeycombed with Jews in hiding? What of the university? Would there still be anyone at all who might recognize her? No. It had been too long since she had been a student, there was such a turnover every year, even the number of women in the faculty of law was great enough for her to have been relatively anonymous. And of course, no names were ever taken in the vast lecture theaters or examination halls. The ghost of Rita Feuerstahl wouldn't haunt Margarita Trushenko.

Everyone knew that Krakow had become the capital of the German administration of Poland, the headquarters of the *Generalgouvernement*, installed in the Wawel Castle, beside the cathedral just off the town square. Would the Germanization of the city make it harder to survive on false identity, or easier? She'd find out soon enough.

Off the railway coach, up the platform to the station building, through the ticket barrier, past the identity check, leave your bag at the left-luggage, buy a newspaper, and find a room. Clockwork. There it was, the absurdly vast space made by the plaza before the equally out-of-scale three-story nineteenth-century railway station, still frowning under its overhanging balustrade, still the ochre color of an Italian palazzo. Just as she had left it . . . except for all the *Fraktur* signage.

The main square, where Rita had lurked that night Urs had first dined with her, was lousy with Germans. Officers carrying leather briefcases under their arms would stop one another, come to attention, raise an arm instead of saluting. They would make a display of snapping their cases open, exchanging onionskin flimsies for countersignatures. Noncoms bearing stripes and service ribbons from the Eastern Front would pose before the cathedral or the castle for each other's 35 mm Leicas and Retinas. Older men in gray flannels and dark ties scurried from one side of the square to the other, usually carrying files and stacks of paper tied neatly into bundles. The scene was correct, normal, civilized—a continent away from the mayhem these men were imposing on a region that stretched from Riga on the Baltic to Athens.

Rita moved through the square quickly and found that her old habits were leading her directly to the Jagiellonia and the lecture halls of the faculty of law. Out past the western side of the square, in a few minutes she found herself in an almost deadly calm among the streets where before the war young people had thronged. Cafés were crowded, pushcarts sold street fare, student life spilled out from shops in fierce competition with one another. Now, nothing.

An eerie quiet, punctuated by an occasional pedestrian's footstep audible in the silence.

The newsagent's shop was still there on the corner, where students had purchased their pen points, ink, and notepaper. But it was doing no business at all when Rita stepped in. Opening the newspaper to the rooms-to-let pages, Rita began hunting for locations past the university. She had seen the signs in German pointing to the Jewish Quarter in the other direction, across the river, in the crowded tenements where she and so many students had lived before the war. *Let's stay as far away from there as we can*, she told herself.

With no students in residence, rooms in Krakow were a buyer's market. Rita visited a half dozen. Some she ruled out because she did not fancy their officious landladies, setting out the rules even before showing the rooms: no cooking, no gentlemen callers, above all, no Jews. This last seemed in a few cases to be a ritual pronouncement, made to establish the *bona fides* of the house. But twice it was elaborated upon. In one case, the lady of the house lamented that she had been blamed by the Gestapo for harboring the vermin. "How was I to know? They were very quiet, neat, paid in advance." She answered her own question. "I should have caught on when they paid so promptly and never fell into arrears." In the other case, the landlady related her experience with prewar students: "Socialists, communists, political meetings, parties till all hours, posters on the wall. Rich Jews, no loyalty to the government, the church, anything." Some rooms were dusty from lack of occupants.

Rita could afford to choose. After examining six, she went back to the third one, closest to the law faculty, on Wenecja Street, mainly because she had hit it off with the landlady. The middle-aged woman had asked few questions, but had volunteered that she missed the bustle of students coming and going, the enthusiasm of young people, their romances, and even the noise of their arguments.

"You're back," Mrs. Wilkova greeted her on the second visit.

"Yes. I'll take the room if it's still available, please."

"No one has come since your visit an hour ago, dear. No one is likely to, unless they open the university again, and there's not much chance of that."

Rita didn't want to make the university a topic of conversation. She was just a girl from the east, who had lost her family in the Russian occupation and escaped to the west. For the German authorities, there was the additional claim that she was a *Volks-Deutsche Mädchen*, but that was not going to make a difference among Poles. "Mrs. Wilkova, can you tell me where the labor exchange is?"

"In the main square, just next to the *Blue Polizei* Bureau. You won't fail to register, will you, dear?"

She felt like replying *Sofort* and clicking her heels. But instead she merely nodded. "I'll do it on my way back to the station for my things." The landlady handed her a latchkey.

Rita's path led her back past the Fac'. Suddenly she found herself before the building where she had first met Urs in the winter of '35. Looking both ways down the street, she could see no one at all. Just the gaunt plane trees and the lines of weeds growing between the once carefully maintained paving stones. Even the café where she and Urs had first become acquainted now appeared derelict. She mounted the three steps anyway and opened the oversize door. It crashed with a loud report behind her. This was followed by a light going on behind a frosted glass door under the great marble staircase. Out came an elderly little man, with a growth of stubble, a mop of white hair, and a familiar look about him. Yes, the same old man she had seen as a student. He had been a bit of an eccentric and a vocal patriot, rather a pet of the Green Ribbon nationalist bullies, cheering on their harassment of Jewish students. Would he still share their enthusiasm after three years of Nazi occupation?

She approached. "I used to be a student here. Where is everyone?"

"Well, *Pani*." He stroked the white stubble and thought. "The Germans closed the faculty in early 1940. Took the professors all away, don't you know?" It seemed obvious from his tone the little man had not understood why. "Almost none of them ever came back . . . Germans even took their families." He pulled a dirty kerchief from his overalls. "The cardinal archbishop got one or two back. They say the rest were shot. I saw them one day, the two who came back, but they looked too old to lecture. Besides, what good would two lecturers do? There were no students anymore."

Rita found herself feeling sorry for the old anti-Semite. Could he be part of the Home Army? She wanted to ask, but feared doing so. "Why are you still here, *Pan*? What is the building used for?"

"I still get a pay packet every week, so I come. Even without heat it's a little warmer than home, and there is an electric light. Besides, the Germans have used the lecture hall once or twice. I even saw the head of them all, *Gauleiter* Frank, come in for a speech to a lot of men in black. It was all German, so I didn't understand . . ."

Tentatively she probed, "Ever see any Poles here now—former students, people from the university?"

"No one. You're the first person to come in for a long time . . . except for the Germans, that is. You said you were here before the war, *Pani* . . . " He looked at her, unsuccessfully trying to place her. Rita said nothing. "Well, it's cold in this hallway . . ." He turned and without a parting word returned to his cubby beneath the stairs, closed the door, and turned off the light.

∾

The clerk at the *Blue Polizei* registry office made a careful study of Rita's documents. He was evidently acquainted with the forger's art and disinclined to laxity so close to the German headquarters. "Very well," he said, more to himself than her, added to a register her name and details, along with her local address, and countersigned the second of the four places available on her *Kennkarte*. Without even looking twice, he handed back her documents.

A few moments later, she was staring at the vacancies in the labor exchange's wall postings. Rita saw that several of them required German, had slightly higher salaries, and expressed a racial requirement: "*Volks-Deutsche* applicants only." These she took note of, submitted her name, and waited her turn along the benches. There were few other applicants that morning. Why? Did the unemployed know something she didn't?

When her name was called out for the second time, "Trushenko," she started. For a moment she had forgotten her alias. Not a mistake to make. She rose and went to the desk.

"*Tak*—well," said the woman, looking at her form. She switched to German. "You want this job as a *Hausdame*—a housekeeper? It's for the Fiscal Accounting Service, Reich Tax Inspectorate. Qualifications?"

"I worked in a hospital and a hotel," Rita lied in fluent German.

"Can you cook for Germans? They don't eat pig's knuckles, flaki, or kasha."

"I can make an excellent strudel." *Thank God for Mrs. Kaminski*, she thought.

"Starching and ironing? How many shirts an hour?"

Rita had never lifted an iron over a man's shirt. She had no idea. "Fifteen."

"No! Really? I'll hire you myself!" Evidently this was too high a number. She appeared to treat Rita's answer as pardonable exaggeration: "Very well." She handed across an address. "They will expect you tomorrow morning. It's a trial." The woman stared at her, altogether too knowingly.

That evening she asked Pani Wilkova, as casually as she could, how many shirts a good laundress might starch and iron in an hour.

"If she is fast, perhaps six."

CHAPTER TWENTY-FOUR

The Reich Tax Inspectorate was two streets north of the main square, on Świętego Jana, St. John's Street, in a newer two-story block opposite a chapel. She mounted the stairs from the street entrance to the first floor and knocked. The door was opened by a small man, peering at her over rimless reading glasses. Wisps of gray hair were combed over his pate from left to right. The skin on his face showed no exposure to the sun, but it displayed at least two shaving nicks. Four straight wrinkle lines ran across his forehead, and he lacked any sign of a chin. The gray eyes were matched by an open gray waistcoat.

His shirt cuffs were covered by ink guards. He had evidently just risen from his work at a set of account books. Looking up at Rita, his first words were in German. "At last you are here, *Fräulein.*"

"They told me to report this morning, *Mein Herr.* Am I late?" Rita looked at her watch. Spot on 9:00 a.m.

Impressed with her German and her punctuality, he replied, "No, no, my dear young lady. It's only that I have been in urgent need since we lost the last housekeeper. My name is Herr Lempke, and you are . . . ?"

"Fräulein Trushenko." She proffered her placement notice from the labor exchange and her papers. Rita decided not to ask why he had lost the previous housekeeper.

He pushed the papers aside. "It's quite all right. How soon can you begin?" Behind him a door was open to a kitchen in disorder.

"Immediately, sir."

"Very well. Please begin in there. We will discuss the details of your work when I can spare a moment this afternoon." He walked off down a corridor with at least six doors opening onto it. At its end, Rita could see a large office, and there another woman, a secretary, laboring over a very large typewriter with an extra long platen, evidently for the many columns an accounting ledger required.

Off the entry where they had been standing was a large dining room, with furniture even heavier, darker, and much larger than her own dimly remembered dining room in Karpatyn.

Rita took off her coat, enjoying the warmth rising from radiators beneath each window, and attacked the dishes in the sink. When she finished she surveyed the kitchen more closely. It was well stocked, and there was ample clean linen in the pantry. She had found herself transported back into a world she thought no longer existed.

At noon Herr Lempke entered the now orderly kitchen with a sigh of relief. He motioned Rita to a chair, sat down himself, and laid out what was expected of her. His manner was tentative, if not diffident. It was almost as if in describing the job, he feared scaring Rita off.

Her duties would include keeping house and cleaning the offices, as well as cooking and laundry for the staff. There were usually two or three tax inspectors from the Reich visiting at any one time. Lempke was the senior resident, though he returned to his family in Germany from time to time. His wife remained in Mannheim with their six children. There would be an allowance to do marketing and as many zloty as she needed to provide for Herr Lempke and his associates. They would bring certain things in short supply from Germany—wines, liquors, other delicacies. There were two rooms off the kitchen for servants. She could choose either of the two rooms, and she was to have a salary of three hundred zloty a month, or the equivalent in reichsmarks, along with two afternoons off a week—Wednesday and Sunday. Was all this acceptable to Fräulein . . . uh . . .

Rita supplied the name again, "Trushenko . . . and yes, it is perfectly acceptable." She had never expected to be satisfied with domestic bliss. But here it was, hers for the keeping, and she was going to hang on to it for dear life.

"Herr Lempke, I have a room in town. May I keep it, or must I reside here?"

"Well, Fräulein Trushenko, you sleep where you please so long as you are here before breakfast each morning." In the end she would move in—food and warmth made up for lack of privacy—but for a few weeks, she kept the room at Pani Wilkova and stayed there from time to time. This would prove to be another piece of blind luck.

"Dinner for three tonight, seven o'clock." He rose and was about to leave the room.

"Including your secretary?" Rita looked over his shoulder down the hall.

"Fräulein Halle? No. She does not board."

෨

Were the farmers' markets still in the same places they had been before the war? Was there anything much still for sale after four winters of German occupation? Were the stalls still open this time of day? What could she find in the larder? The first meal had to be beyond complaint if she were to keep this job. Best to begin with some advice from her landlady. So, after taking stock of a canned ham, a bushel of potatoes, and some shriveled onions in the pantry, Rita marched back past the law faculty to Wenecja Street.

"The farmers' market is still there, on Biskupia, and the Germans haven't stolen everything." Was this a political remark? Rita explained her new position and her intention to keep her room.

∽

The amount of food Rita was able to assemble that night would have fed a large family in the ghetto for three weeks. With dried apples, raisins, and nuts from the market, the amount of butter she found in the cold larder was enough for a strudel far richer than anything Mrs. Kaminski could have made. When the three German bureaucrats pushed their chairs back from dinner that evening and asked her to join them at the table, she knew that the job was well and truly hers.

"So, Fräulein Trushenko, where did you learn to cook so well?" Lempke proffered a cigarette. Rita decided to decline. She could not afford the mark of sophistication or comfort when consorting with the haute bourgeoisie.

"My father ran a hotel in the east, and my mother learned to cook from her German grandmother, who bequeathed her a cookbook of Silesian dishes. She taught me." Rita decided not to amplify. One of these three men could be from Silesia for all she knew.

"And your parents?"

"Taken to Siberia by the Russians, sir. They were considered capitalists. I never heard from them again. My mother was weak. I don't think she could have lived long."

"The strudel is Viennese, my dear. Where did you learn to make it so well?"

"Years of practice, sir."

⁓

That evening after clearing up, she found some stationery and an envelope, sat down at the kitchen table, and began a letter:

Dear Lydia,
You will see by the envelope that I am now an employee of the German Reich Tax Inspectorate.

Suddenly it occurred to her that even letters from Reich offices were likely to be censored, especially when sent east. She decided that this letter would have to be much more circumspect than she had planned. She began again.

I am well treated and grateful that we Volks-Deutsche *are so warmly welcomed in the Reich. After an interesting trip from Lvov and a few weeks in Warsaw, I am now settled in Krakow. I am writing to ask whether you have heard anything from cousin Erich since he left to join the forces fighting in the East. I would be glad to learn how he is doing and where I can send him some socks and other warm clothes that I am knitting for our brave soldiers.*
You may write to me at the address at the top of this letter.
Best wishes,
Margarita Trushenko

Reading the letter over once more, she crossed out "Lvov" and wrote "Lemberg," sealed it, found a stamp in one of the offices bearing Hitler's profile in Prussian blue, and placed it in the outbox. It would be carried to the post office with the rest of the mail in the morning by the secretary, Fräulein Halle.

No reply ever came back. But she was to receive far more by way of reply than any news about Erich she had hoped for.

∾

The next morning Rita made a point of inviting Fräulein Halle into the kitchen for a cup of ersatz. No one was drinking real coffee anymore in Poland. The woman was German, grateful for the company, and garrulous, at least about their employer. Taller than Rita, willowy but not undernourished, she had the stereotypical features of an Aryan woman—cheekbones so high they would not have looked out of place on the Mongolian steppe, but deep blue eyes and the inevitable blonde hair, permed into the Babelsberg version of a Hollywood hairdo. She wore no ornaments and an unladylike pair of trousers, along with a white blouse.

Rita broke the silence first. "What's Herr Lempke really like?"

"He's a bureaucrat. Just another *MussNazi*."

"How do you know?" Rita was relieved, but wanted reassurance he wasn't a true believer.

"They hardly ever '*Heil Hitler*' in here. I've even overheard them joke about the uneducated, greedy, slovenly *Gauleiters* who have come through Krakow. And now they are all scared. They think there is no way that the Germans can hang on to what they have taken in Russia. They tell themselves the only thing to do is to divide the Allies from the Russians, play for a truce in the west, and hold on to the Ukraine, like they did for a couple of years after the Great War."

"But if they talked like that, they'd be shot!" Rita was pleased but surprised. They sounded more pessimistic about Germany's war than she was!

"That's why you may not hear them say anything like that. But among themselves, well . . ."

"And you? *MussNazi*?"

"No. I'm a Berliner. We never had time for that crowd in Berlin. Just a German girl who wandered into the wrong office in the civil service. Pay is good here; the RAF and the US Eighth Air Force don't bother us this far east. Lempke is harmless. So I'll stay for a while."

"Here, have the last piece of strudel." Rita smiled, feeling confident she had finally found an ally, perhaps even a friend.

❧

Two weeks and things had settled into a routine that was allowing Rita to sleep nights, gain a little weight, listen to radio concerts from Berlin, and chat with Pani Wilkova a few evenings a week. She was reluctant to move her two vast Darwin tomes to Świętego Jana Street. They weren't subversive, just seriously incongruous with her cover. What would the daughter of an innkeeper from the eastern marches of Poland be doing with Darwin on her hands? So, she kept them in the case under the bed in the room she continued to rent. She had read them so many times, by now they had mainly sentimental value. She almost laughed out loud as the words flitted across her consciousness.

One morning in Rita's third week at the Tax Inspectorate, returning from the farmers' market, she found herself looking up the stairs from the street entrance into a dark face under a kerchief. The woman came down to the vestibule. Her clothes were dirty and torn, and her smell was rank. With the sun behind the open door shining on her, it began to dawn on Rita—first the realization that this was someone from Karpatyn, then from the Terakowski textile factory, and finally she knew. It was Dani, the girl whom Rita had listened to for months, reciting the Polish epic *Lord Tadeusz*. It was Dani, threadbare, with a haunted look in her eye, thinner even than when Rita last saw her, leaving the factory for the ghetto the day Rita had escaped. Then Rita remembered the electric warmth the brief moment her body had touched Dani's the first day she had found her reading at the workbench.

Though Dani had detected recognition in Rita's face, she still said nothing. She remained silent so long Rita began to fear that she had become a mute. Had her tongue been ripped from her mouth? Had she lost her hearing to a blow on the head?

Mute or not, there was no time to exchange a word. Rita began to mount the stairs, pulling Dani along. "Follow me and be quick." She led her into the foyer, through the dining room, and into one of the unoccupied maids' rooms. "Stay here. Not a sound. I will come back with some food as soon as I can. I need to start their midday meal." Rita pointed down the hall. Closing the door firmly behind her, she tried to regain control of herself.

Going about her duties, Rita began to think through how to deal with Dani's arrival. It had destroyed an equilibrium that Rita had carefully constructed. It had put her back in a danger she had managed to escape. The worst thing for Rita was to be associated with someone who looked Jewish, lacked papers, had no means of support, and might for all she knew produce Yiddish when she tried to speak German. And yet all these problems were defeated by the fact that it was Dani. It wasn't just that suddenly Rita had someone to talk to, to share her experience with, someone who needed her help. It was Dani who had turned up, Dani whom Rita had not even realized she missed, Dani whose poetry had eased her misery on the shop floor in Karpatyn.

An hour later Rita came into the small room with a cup of sweet tea, some toast, and a bit of strawberry preserves. Dani was fast asleep and was awoken only reluctantly. But there might not be another chance to talk for several hours.

"It's you, it's you! You of all people!" She repeated the words as she woke the sleeping Dani with a hug—and was rewarded by a smile. These were not the words Rita had intended. What she had intended to say was more on the order of, *What the devil are you doing here? Why are you putting me at risk? Who told you to seek me out?* But all these questions her instinct for survival drove her to raise were beaten down by the overwhelming emotion of gladness. "Quickly, tell me how you found me, how you got here, what happened in Karpatyn?"

Dani sat up. "So . . . you got out in late October. The week after, they started the final clearance of the ghettos." For a moment Rita thought Dani would break down, but she gathered her forces. "Once they had found as many of the old, the sick, the children as they could and herded them onto the cattle cars, they burned the second ghetto. That left only the large one for the few hundred workers that had been granted the new work permits." She stopped for a minute, gathering her thoughts, organizing her narrative. Then she continued.

At the end of that week, Karpatyn was finally to be made completely *Judenrein*. The last workers were to be stopped at the ghetto gates and redirected for transportation to Belzec. The morning before, she had overheard two *Jupos* behind a latrine share the rumor from the Viennese *Schutzpolizei*. That evening, when everyone left the Terakowski Works, Dani hung back and hid herself on a pallet in the rafters, among the bats and sparrows that nested there when the lights were turned on. The next day vindicated the two *Jupos'* source: no one came to work; the factory floor was still. Dani remained in the rafters as long as she could. Then she climbed down and, scampering to the outhouse, found everything deserted—the factory yard, the loading dock, the machine shop. No workers at all, not even the few Poles. She decided there was nothing to do but try to hide in the factory at least till it reopened. Then she'd leave with the first shift of new workers.

Over the next few days, moving cautiously between the workbenches, through the canteen, among the storage sheds, even up to the office, Dani managed to uncover a few well-hidden crusts of bread, a dried salami end. Not enough to curb the pangs of hunger but enough to keep her alive. After five endless days, there was not another scrap to be found, and Dani was bloated from the tap water she was drinking to fill her stomach.

That fifth morning she watched from the rafters as the owner, Lydia Terakowski, led a man around the shop floor, pointing out the sewing machines, the cutting tables and the pressing irons, the conveyer belts on tracks above the tables, and the rest of the equipment. Dani would learn that Lydia could tell that things were slightly wrong, that they were not as they had been left—cabinets were open, drawers were unclasped, doors were ajar. She betrayed none of this to the man, with whom she spoke in German.

When the man was gone, she returned. "Who is that? Who is hiding here? Come out. You won't be harmed or sent away." Dani climbed down from the rafters in the roof and stood before her. "How long have you been here?" Lydia did not look friendly.

"Since the last day. How long has it been? I have lost track," Dani admitted.

"Five days. Come with me." Lydia led her across the yard and through the gate down to the house. Once in the kitchen, she put together some food and sat waiting as Dani wolfed it down. "Look, the last ghetto has been razed. There are no more Jews in Karpatyn, unless like you they have managed to hide. You have to get out." Then, more to herself than to Dani, Lydia said, "But you're a dead giveaway."

"Why is the factory closed?" Dani asked.

"Without the ghetto manpower, it can't operate. Now a German has come in and is forcing me to sell the works. The offer is outrageous. You'd think this was a Jewish business they were stealing." Lydia stopped, realizing she'd been too candid. Before the war in Germany, the standard rate for a Jewish concern was one-fifth its market value, with the sale financed by an interest-free loan from the owner. This deal was going to be just as bad.

Lydia was now alone in the house. Her mother had gone back to Warsaw for the winter. Her only concern in hiding Dani was the irregular visits of German officers passing through, making courtesy calls before politely stealing greatcoats. The prospective buyer, representing one of the large textile mills in the Ruhr, came only by appointment. So Lydia was able to shelter Dani through December and into the winter.

The one thing Lydia could no longer do was provide papers. The local priest had ceased to be cooperative, hinting at pressure from the bishop. Forgers had left the area. Business dried up once the ghetto had been liquidated. Inquiries would almost certainly bring the Gestapo down on her head.

By late January the sale, such as it was, had been closed, and a date set for the removal of the factory to Germany. Railcars would be brought up the Terakowski siding and everything put aboard by a Wehrmacht engineering detachment conveniently lent for the occasion by the local *Befehlshaber*.

Then Lydia received the letter from the Reich Tax Inspectorate, Krakow. She actually found herself shaking as she opened it. Would she be audited by Nazis as well as stripped of her factory? From the relief of reading Rita's letter, she felt a plan emerge. Once the machinery had been placed on the freight cars, Dani could hide among the large crates. When the train slowed at Lemberg, with any luck she could sneak off. In a bigger city, she might have a chance. There was, however, neither time nor money to acquire any papers for her. All Lydia was able to give her was Rita's address in Krakow.

On an afternoon four days later, a little better fed and cleaned up as much as Lydia could manage, Dani jumped off the freight car as it slowed to enter the Lemberg marshaling yards behind the main railway station. She managed to wend her way through strings of boxcars and passenger carriages until she found herself at last walking down a road next to the tracks. Soon enough the road became a city street. It was there her luck ran out. Or so she thought. As she walked along, a Blue Policeman caught up with her. He grasped her shoulder and turned her around. "Papers."

She looked blankly, then said, "None. I'm a farm girl from a small village. We never had any papers. I didn't know I needed them."

"Sorry, sister. You're about as Jewish-looking a girl as I have ever seen. Come with me." Despite Dani's protestations, he led her off toward the town center. Dani tried everything, including some Hail Marys and as much of the catechism as she could remember. Then she began cursing him in a Polish that only a policeman could ever have heard from a woman. Nothing worked, and despite herself, Dani was reduced to sniveling. After a ten-minute walk, the policeman and Dani found themselves at a street corner waiting for a slow cart and horse to pass. The Blue Policeman looked behind him into a café, turned back to Dani, and said, "Wait here. I am going in for a beer."

What to do? Escape? Remain? Follow him in and demand a drink? What would an ignorant farm girl do? Obvious: remain rooted to the spot she had been left at. Dani did so. An endless quarter of an hour later, the policeman came out. "Still here? Well, then you can go, my dear. No little Jewess would be foolish enough or stupid enough to wait." He looked at a pocket watch. "Besides, I'm not on duty anymore." He sauntered off.

Just then another man came out of the café. "Come along, my dear; perhaps I can help you." He took Dani to the same police station the Blue Policeman had been heading for, sat her down at a desk, and asked her name. He mulled it over. "Danielle Cohen. That will never do." He put a piece of paper in the typewriter before him. "It won't be much help, but it may make a difference in a pinch somewhere." He thought for a minute. "Let's see. You're not Cohen anymore. Do you like Nowiki?" Dani nodded. He pulled the paper from the typewriter and signed it. Then he took her to the station and bought her a ticket for Krakow.

"And here I am."

"Can I see the letter you got in Lvov?"

"I have it here." She reached down the front of her dress and pulled it out, unfolding it carefully.

Metropolitan Police
Central Office
Lemberg

This is to confirm that Danielle Nowiki came before me and filled out a report testifying to the theft of her documents. Replacement will be difficult as Stanislava Records office has been destroyed by fire.

Signed
Milkolaj Bilek
Inspector, Blue Polizei

There was a small blue dot under the 'l' in *Bilek*.

CHAPTER TWENTY-FIVE

So, Dani Cohen was now Dani Nowiki. It was one more thing to remember. That afternoon Rita spirited her out of the Inspectorate Office and into her rented room with Pani Wilkova. But after a week, the landlady was not happy. Dani had not registered with the police, and she looked suspiciously Jewish even to Mrs. Wilkova's unpracticed eye. Each day for a week, she drew a line in the sand, and each evening she relented for one more night. Something had to be done.

"Herr Lempke, there is so much work. So many people are coming through from Germany. I fear I am having difficulty keeping up with both the housekeeping and cleaning the offices. Might I be permitted to have a local woman come in daily and help?"

"Capital idea, Fräulein Trushenko." Lempke called the secretary out of the office. "Halle, ring up the labor exchange. Post a job for an undermaid, Polish. We don't need to pay for a German speaker. Fräulein Trushenko can deal with her."

"Very good."

That morning Rita came back from the farmers' market. Poking her head into the office, she said to Halle, "I think I found a girl for us at the market. A bit coarse, but experienced, healthy, honest-looking. Would save us the trouble of going through the labor office. I told her to come at teatime."

Halle agreed. "I'll check with Herr Lempke." A few minutes later, she came back into the kitchen. "Very well."

There were three German tax inspectors at tea that afternoon— all middle-aged, highly respectable, and very correct—when the doorbell rang. Rita answered it and came back into the dining room trailing a woman who looked like a cross between a country girl and a woman of the streets. Her appearance and demeanor were scrutinized by those present. Anyone with a bit of Polish would have detected the heavy, even exaggerated, working-class accent.

That the woman was uneducated was clear even to non-Polish listeners. Though she was modestly dressed, this young woman also managed to convey an air of dishabille.

One of the guests wondered aloud what her previous experience might have been. The other pronounced her too slovenly for the situation. Herr Lempke was not so put off. "Can she work?"

Duly translated, they awaited her reply. After a few phrases from the woman of what sounded rather like invective, Rita said, "She says, excuse me, *Hell yes. She's been doing it all her life.*"

"Looks a thief to me, as well as a bit louche," observed one of the other two.

Halle now intervened, and Rita could have kissed her for it. "Fräulein Trushenko can watch her carefully. Let's give her a week. If she doesn't work out, we'll go to the labor exchange."

This proposal overlapped with a statement from the Polish woman, which Rita translated. "She says she has to know right away. She has something else lined up, and it won't wait." Dani went on, and Rita caught up. "She says she's worked in lots of fancy places before, including for Catholic priests, even for Jews. Does windows, parquets, and ironing." This was a slightly sore point with Lempke, as his shirts were not being laundered and pressed to the standard he was accustomed to.

"Very well; take her on trial, Fräulein Trushenko. You may dismiss her without recourse if she doesn't work out. And tell her, this is a highly respectable house. See that she understands what that means."

Rita turned to Dani. In plainest Polish she said, "There are to be no male visitors whatsoever, understood?"

Dani nodded.

They had not even asked her name.

〜

There was a deep stillness in the suite of offices. The tax inspectors had all retired immediately after dinner, and Fräulein Halle had left as well. Rita sat down in the kitchen at her household accounts, deciding what she needed to market for in the coming days.

After dutifully cleaning Dani retired to the tiny maid's room. The room's small window overlooked a patch of grass between the building and another one. This building across the courtyard was entirely unlit against the night and obviously more offices of the *Generalgouvernement*. Next to the door, against the wall, there was a narrow bed, covered in a terrycloth spread that had lost all its color and acquired a layer of pilling. Beyond it a small side table supported a dispirited little lamp—transparent glass around a dimly glowing filament visible through a cracked parchment shade. This was the only light in the room. The walls were light blue but stained around the radiator below the window. Still, there was a radiator. And at the moment, it was making the small room pleasantly warm, a luxury only Germans could hope to experience in Poland. The wall opposite the bed was taken up with a raw wooden cupboard and a cold-water sink.

It took Dani literally a moment to unpack the meager belongings she had acquired during the week she had remained in Rita's rented room. Responding to the room's warmth, she took off the smock she had been wearing, unbuttoned her dress, hung them both up, and began contemplating the sink. Instead, wearing only her slip, she slid down onto the bed, leaning against the wall, lighting one of the German cigarettes she had swiped from a silver box in the dining room.

Dani looked up to see Rita now leaning on the doorjamb, a bottle of Moselle open in one hand, two small glasses in the other. "When was the last time you had a glass of wine?"

"In a previous life sometime in the last century." Dani watched Rita drop onto the bed. As she too leaned against the wall, her added weight made the bed slip away from the wall. They found themselves both draped over its side, laughing, heads close together.

Rita took a long breath and put a hand on Dani's forearm. "I should have been worried about the risks of hiding you. But I couldn't care less about the risk." She stopped. The words were not coming out right. "Let's have some of this stuff." She poured the amber-colored wine into the short tumblers, and they both drank them off to the bottom. Rita immediately refilled the glasses, somehow eager to substitute drinking for talk. She drank half the second glass and stood. Walking over to the window, Rita attempted to open it. It was painted shut, and she noticed the pull ropes on either side had been severed. There was no point trying to open it. "It's so warm in here."

"Well, take off your smock."

Rita did so, and then her dress, hanging it carefully on a hook she noticed behind the door, which she then closed. As she stood in her slip, her form silhouetted by the dim lamplight behind her,

Dani looked up at her appreciatively. "The female form is so much more interesting than the male."

"Interesting?" Rita remained standing, but took up the theme. "I'd always rather look at a woman, wouldn't you?"

Dani nodded as she patted the bed. "You'll still look good sitting down next to me." Rita complied, this time holding some of her weight off the wall. It was a posture difficult to maintain. Soon she found herself first leaning on Dani's shoulder and then resting her head in Dani's lap. Sipping the wine, Dani stroked Rita's hair. Then she began pulling hairpins out so that the plaits fell away from her head. Once the pins were all piled next to Dani at the end of the bed, she dropped them on the floor. Now her hand moved down across Rita's face and neck, finally resting on her chest. Dani's forefinger and thumb discovered the nipple of Rita's breast under the thin covering of the viscose slip. Unconsciously she began toying with it.

Rita's first reaction was a stiffening of her spine as her body readied to repel this delicate assault. But instead, she fell back and began to enjoy it. After a moment she reached her left hand up and pulled the slip's shoulder strap down her arm. The signal was unambiguous, and Dani reached her hand beneath the material onto the naked breast and the now erect nipple. When Rita could no longer bear to remain still, she rose slightly and pulled Dani's face to hers, her tongue searching for Dani's tongue. She had never done this with a woman. Yet she felt driven to it.

After a few minutes of this, Dani pulled away. "Now what do we do?"

Rita rose from the bed, pulling Dani up with her, thinking all the while about her night with Erich a year before. "I'll show you." She pushed the straps of Dani's slip off her shoulders, letting it fall. Then very slowly she began tracing narrowing spirals over Dani's chest until they culminated at her nipples. Dani was now weaving slightly back and forth in a rhythm that matched the motions of Rita's fingers. Rita pushed her back so that Dani was leaning against the cupboard. Bending her knees, with two hands Rita rolled away Dani's loose-fitting underpants, opening her legs, and began to stoke the insides of her thighs. Suddenly Rita was rhythmically squeezing the top of Dani's labia together by the forefingers of each hand. Then a finger moved down, and from Dani came a shudder of desire. Rita pulled back, promising herself she would be as slow as Erich had been. But Dani was exigent. Soon her hands were pressing Rita's head firmly against her mons, her body demanding almost to be bitten until she was overcome by the spasms of an orgasm.

Rita decided that for a first experience, this would be enough. Mutual pleasure could await another night.

Once Dani had fallen into a deep sleep, Rita crept off to the other maid's room. The next morning a reticence reigned between them as they went about their duties.

∽

Later that morning an air-raid warden came up the stairs to the office. "*Fräulein*, are you in charge here?" Rita nodded. "Well, there has been a complaint. Light at a back window last night, violation of blackout. Someone noticed and filed a complaint. See to it." He raised his right hand. "*Heil Hitler.*" Rita replied as required, and he was gone.

What else had they seen last night? Had they broken a law? Might they be sent to a concentration camp, forced to wear the pink triangles? Surely a Peeping Tom would not have reported them. Rita said nothing, but added blackout curtain material to her shopping list.

That afternoon she came back with a valise and announced, "I've moved out of Mrs. Wilkova's room. I'll be here from now on." Dani smiled, and nothing more was said.

❧

Dani dared not go out much. A few forays to shops close by, some walks to the main square at night. Never alone, always with Rita. Just hanging laundry out to dry or beating the dust from a carpet in the back of the building seemed a risk. One morning as she hummed away, hanging sheets, a voice came down from the opposite side in Polish. "Quiet out there. No yodeling. This isn't a Yid shtetl." Was the complaint voicing a suspicion?

Asking Lempke to help Dani get papers was too much of a risk. He might have been a *MussNazi*, but he was still a Nazi. And for all anyone knew, Dani was supposed to be just someone off the streets, someone who could find her way back on them without anyone in the house being concerned. More than once Halle or Lempke found themselves trying to send Dani far afield on errands that Rita simply had to countermand. "She has work to do. I will go," she would insist. Both Rita and Dani knew that besides the risk Dani ran as a Jew, without solid German papers she might be swept up at any time in the daily roundup for forced labor workers at German projects in the city, or even sent off to more distant locations.

Krakow was a wholly different city for Rita than it was for Dani. Her *Kennkarte*, her German, her job, her connections provided the best of covers. She could safely go anywhere. But as in Warsaw, it soon began to be apparent to her that many of the *Echt-Deutsche*—real Germans—she met every day were Jews hiding in plain sight, invisible to Germans because Germany had been *Judenrein* for so long that Poland's educated, affluent, urban Jews were hard for them to tell apart from its Poles. These were the ones who had survived almost four years of the relatively coarse filtering sieve, culling Jews from the Krakow environment. These people went about their Aryan business day by day, probably suspecting one another, but never willing to put their hypotheses to the test. Jew would meet suspected Jew. Both would greet one another, "*Heil Hitler*," giving nothing away.

Did it make Rita safer, knowing that none of these people were going to expose her? Or should she have felt less safe, knowing there were so many Jews around her that a day's sweep by a zealous Gestapo officer would easily fill a boxcar?

The bureaucracy had established special German shops where good food, especially food not available to Poles, was sold. Going to and fro among these shops, moving through the government blocks, daily passing the same officers and bureaucrats, Rita became a familiar figure in the city center, just as others became recognizable to her. Sometimes she could almost forget her fugitive state, even occasionally experience the feeling of freedom and lightness she had felt as a student, now almost seven years before.

Krakow had been spared by the Germans' campaign in '39. It was too distant from Britain and too unimportant for Allied strategic bombing. And it had been cosseted by the Reich under the pretense that for centuries it had been an island of German culture in a sea of Polish backwardness: an Aryan outpost on the Slavic marches of the Reich. But the atmosphere in the restaurants and cafés—of which there were still many—and in the offices began to acquire a certain edginess as winter gave way to spring 1943. The defeat at Stalingrad, culminating in a field marshal's surrender of 600,000 troops, could be hidden here even less than in Germany itself. The quiet voice of doubt whispered that Germany could not win a two-front war, now in its fourth season, especially on the night the surrender on the Volga was announced by the *Grossdeutscher Rundfunk*.

It was followed by a long period of funereal music. If only Rita and Dani had been able to listen alone that night!

∽

One evening in early March, Rita found herself in a *Kino*, a cinema for Germans. She watched with a mixture of revulsion and fascination the speech of "Dr." Goebbels in Berlin *Sportpalast*, ringing changes of irony, hauteur, sermon, and most of all bombast, as the demagogue openly admitted the threat from the east. A podium had been raised high enough so that the little man with the clubfoot towered above a fanatical host of uniformed Nazis, nurses, soldiers, militants of the party, and upper civil servants. Behind him was a great banner, "*Totaler Krieg, Kürzester Krieg*"—"Total War, Shortest War." But the banner was belied by the speech. The rhetoric wasn't a call to full mobilization. It was a warning. Goebbels was telling Germany that it could lose, in words for all to understand.

Rita had heard the speech two weeks before as the entire Tax Inspectorate office had gathered before the radio. But now, on the screen, the effect, the message, the signal that Germany could lose the war was more powerful, and in the darkness of the *Kino*, Rita could smile and laugh silently as well. In the *Sportpalast* the audience rose and fell back to their seats as one, *heiled* their *Führer*, and responded to the exhortations of his minister of propaganda. But, Rita recalled, around their radio the week before, there had been no such enthusiasm from the *MussNazis*.

She left after the newsreel, a bit of a spring in her step. That night, behind a well-made blackout curtain, the two women lay side by side, sharing a cigarette before snapping off the table lamp. The bed was narrow, but it was reassuring when one woke in the night to feel the other close by.

"I saw Goebbels's *Sportpalast* speech in a newsreel tonight. They know they are going to lose the war." Erich had to have been right—Africa, now Sicily, the surrender of Italy. The "strategic withdrawals," "shortening the front," the admission of defeats—all were coming too regularly. She had wondered whether to tell her lover.

"I suppose they will lose." There was the sound of indifference in Dani's voice.

"Don't you care?"

Dani sat up. "So, they lose. What will they take down with them? What have they already destroyed? What about my family, my life, my humanity? I'll never get any of it back. I'll go to the grave with this experience emptying the meaning out of everything I'll ever do." Rita had no reply. "Even if they lose the war, why did it ever happen, what kind of a God would allow it, what kind of sense can anyone make of it? You and I, we've seen human bestiality so far beyond what we could have imagined, it's hard to go on living. When it's over, it will still have happened. I don't think I can live with that . . . can you? Most of the time, I really just want to die."

This was not the moment for atheism, for determinism, for explanations. Rita could only hold on to her lover, her friend, her companion, and suppress her own answers to these questions, ones that carried her through the same events and through the same emotional response to them. She could not help thinking that for all the weight of Dani's lamentations, tomorrow Dani would awake and move through her day, stifling the occasional pang. She would find little things to take pleasure in. She would make plans that would lead to small satisfactions in days; she would, in fact, continue to live, despite the future her thoughts, emotions, and memories combined to condemn her to.

Dani began again. "If I survive, I'll torture myself with the question, why me? By what right do I survive? Where's the value in that, compared to a million other people? If they lose this war, I still won't have any answer to this question."

Rita let her friend sob herself to sleep. The question, she knew, no longer troubled her.

CHAPTER TWENTY-SIX

April 20, 1943, was a Tuesday. As on any other day, like clockwork, at 16:00, Herr Lempke, Fräulein Halle, and a visiting inspector rose from their ledgers and typewriter and came into the dining room for tea. Dani and Rita had it ready when they arrived, along with a few small sandwiches, biscuits, and the Polish poppy-seed cake German visitors were especially fond of. The swinging door to the kitchen had been propped open so that Rita could come and go easily carrying the tea things. As she pulled the cozy off the teapot, the front door opened, and another of the Germans entered and sat down.

"Interesting news from Warsaw," the new man said. "That SS-*Oberführer* with the double-barreled name, von Sammern-Frankenegg . . . he's been fired."

"Really. Never heard of such a thing. Law unto themselves, those *Oberführers* are. Who ranks high enough to dismiss him? What's he done, anyway?"

"Himmler. Too soft on Jews, apparently. Turns out there's some kind of revolt in the Warsaw ghetto. They got hold of pistols and rifles, even a couple of machine guns. Anyway, he couldn't put it down. Berlin was furious. Polish flags and terrorist banners flying, even visible outside the walls. Dozens of Wehrmacht killed."

Rita said nothing. She stood still, hoping they would not notice her listening to every word. Dani had quietly come as close to the dining room as she could. Both listened for more. Rita put the news together with what she had heard in Warsaw and what she had seen in the ghetto. It sent a shiver through her.

But the matter was not sufficiently distracting to tax inspectors, and they moved on to a subject of more immediate concern, the correct rate of depreciation for Polish rolling stock taken into Reichsbahn capital accounts.

There was nothing to do but wait until late enough to risk listening to the BBC news broadcast in Polish at midnight. The radio stood on the sideboard. It was a rather large prewar model, more powerful than the *Volksempfänger*—people's broadcaster—in most German homes and offices. It came with a sticker warning users not to tune to foreign stations under a *Führerbefehl*—an edict directly from Hitler. Punishment was severe.

A few minutes before midnight, Dani flicked the on/off button but left it at zero volume. Three vacuum tubes, unshielded by a back cover, began to shine a reflected orange glow on the wall of the darkened room behind the set. There was nothing they could do about this, even though it would make what they were doing evident as far away as the corridor's end, down to the last office in the suite. It would take at least three minutes for the set fully to warm up and begin receiving. As the two women waited in the gloom, anticipation made them fidget. Then, turning the volume up only enough to be able to tune in a station, Dani began to slide the tuning knob away from the *Grossdeutscher Rundfunk* toward where they knew the BBC wavelength was. Finding it, she stopped and raised the volume slightly. There was the BBC, giving a full report of war news from around the world: "Mopping-up operations by victorious Allied Forces in Tunis. Further western movement of Soviet forces against German Army Group South. Heavy nighttime and daylight bombing of German industrial centers, Bolivia enters war against Axis . . . " Nothing, not a word about Warsaw. Rita tuned back to the *Grossdeutscher Rundfunk,* turned the radio off, and they retreated to their room.

"I have to know." Dani's voice cut through the night.

"It's too dangerous. Maybe we'll hear something tomorrow."

∽

"How can we contact the Home Army?" Dani wondered. "They might know something." They were standing at the kitchen sink the next morning after breakfast.

"Dani, the Home Army has very little interest in what happens in the ghetto. There are people in the Home Army who think Jews are as alien to Poland as Germans or Russians. If they are doing anything for the ghetto, it won't be much. And the chances someone here would know anything are nil." Rita was trying to convince herself as well as Dani. "Besides, Krakow is the worst place in Poland to look for the Home Army."

"I'm going out," Dani announced. "I'll find a bar with *Polizei* or Waffen-SS soldiers and listen for news. I can't stand this."

"*Verrückt.*" Rita used the German word—crazy. "Are you completely mad? You want to throw away your life, probably mine too, on the chance you might find out what is happening hundreds of kilometers from here, something that you can't do anything about anyway?"

Dani looked at her lover with something akin to hatred. She hissed, "Better than sitting here wiping the Germans' asses and licking crumbs from their table, trying your best to be an Aryan

Mädchen." Dani rushed at her, her nails digging into Rita's arms. Fending her off, Rita gasped. Surely the words could be heard all the way down the hall. A door opened. There was Fräulein Halle, the secretary, marching down the hall.

"Lempke sent me out to find out what this disturbance was about . . ." She looked at both women, still struggling. "What's going on? I thought you two were lovers."

Equally startled by this observation, both women turned and gaped at her. Under her breath, Halle spoke. "I wasn't born yesterday, girls." Then she smiled to reassure them. "I told you I was from Berlin. These things are familiar to us." She followed the two women's eyes as they looked back toward the offices. "They don't have the slightest idea. Those little gray men in there are devoted to double-entry bookkeeping. They don't even realize you're Jews."

From down the hall came the call, "Halle, let's finish that letter."

"*Jawohl.*" She said it out loud. As she turned to go back, she said quietly, "We'll discuss this at a more opportune moment."

⌒

Halle's head leaned through the kitchen door. "So, what was that fuss about this morning?" It was 6:00 p.m., and the office was closing.

"We're desperate to know what's going on in Warsaw," Rita said. "The Jewish quarter, what's left of it is resisting."

Rita was going to go on when Halle interrupted. "Jews fighting back? Not before time too!"

"Anyway, we can't find out anything. Not even on the BBC." She was giving more away with each interchange. "Dani was threatening to leave the house to look for information. I tried to stop her. We argued."

Halle looked at Dani with a mixture of admiration and incredulity. "It matters that much to you? Can't think why. Much too late for them. Nothing you can do to help, even if it's true."

"What do you mean, 'if it's true'? You heard the talk at teatime yesterday."

"Look, if neither of you do anything foolish, I'll pass by the office of the *Befehlshaber* on some pretext and scan the teletypes from Wehrmacht headquarters or the SS/Gestapo offices. At least that source will be reliable."

Dani was grateful. "Would you?"

Rita was anxious. "Won't it put you at risk?"

"Actually, the staff in the Krakow military *Kommandantur*—military headquarters—are more frightened of people from the Reich Tax Inspectorate than they are of the Gestapo. They won't bother me."

෴

The next evening Halle came back after dinner and sat down in the kitchen. Until that moment they hadn't even known her Christian name. "I'm Magda. Magda Halle, sounds like Matta Hari, the spy from the Great War." Everyone on both sides knew that name.

Between Nazis and Berliners, they learned from Magda Halle, there was no love lost. She came from a family split between allegiance to Rosa Luxemburg, the communist revolutionary, and Friedrich Ebert, the social democratic founder of the postwar Weimar Republic. This spanned across enough of the left to make for at least a decade of bitter acrimony in Halle's family. For ten years between the end of the Great War and the arrival of the Depression, the arguments were ceaseless. But the Depression sealed the family's united front against the Nazis. Too young at first to avoid the *Bund Deutscher Mädel*, Magda Halle was fully inoculated against the regime by the experience. Instead, she had gravitated to what was left of Berlin's Weimar culture. She had modeled for Yva, the famous Berlin fashion photographer, and even had a fling with Yva's protégé and apprentice, a young man named Helmut, who was constantly importuning her to take her clothes off. A stint at secretarial college had led her into the civil service and eventually to Krakow. Rita and Dani learned all this the evening Magda Halle came back from the Krakow *Kommandantur*.

"Nothing yet on the teletype from Warsaw Wehrmacht headquarters, but I think I'll be able to get some reliable news from the SS."

The two women sighed.

"How ever did you know we were Jewish?" Rita asked.

Before Magda could answer, Dani interrupted. "How did you know about . . . us?"

"It wasn't hard, the way you two swish by each other and find occasions to touch. As for your being Jewish—Dani, you look like the description of Rebecca the Jewess in the English novel we had to read in school . . ." She searched her memory. "*Ivanhoe*, by Walter Scott. And you, Rita, you speak Polish like a Pole and German like a German, and there are two volumes of Darwin on your shelves. You can't just be a Ukrainian Catholic girl who grew up in her father's inn on the Russian border. In fact, when I noticed those books, I thought you might be a Nazi. It's only Nazis I have ever heard going on about Darwin—you know, survival of the fittest, hygienic breeding, evolution of the master race, the *Ubermensch*."

Rita was defensive—and it had not even registered on her that Magda had been snooping through her things. "The Nazi version of Darwin is all rubbish, just what you would expect from uneducated street thugs who picked up their wisdom from *Mein Kampf*."

"Their version of Darwin sounded pretty convincing when I was a schoolgirl."

"In fact, the reason I carry those books around is because they're the only things that ever made sense of the horrors of Nazism."

Magda looked at her quizzically. "How's that?"

"Go ahead, Rita, explain it," Dani challenged. "I don't get it. Neither will Magda."

"There is only one thing to get, Magda, or maybe two. Evolution is inevitable. But the process isn't going from lower to higher. It's just going from different to different—today's fittest are likely to be tomorrow's unfit. It's environments that decide fitness, and environments change. Maybe too slow for us to notice. But the reptiles—the dinosaur—used to dominate, and now the mammals are on top. Why? Change. Maybe in the climate, weather, a new disease the dinosaurs couldn't handle. A million years from now, the reptiles might be on top again, or it'll be the cockroaches. Think of the master race as dinosaurs—or better, cockroaches."

"So, evolution isn't always progress?"

"Just ask the dinosaurs." Rita smiled.

Dani was not satisfied. "Then why did evolution produce us, higher beings, humans with language, culture, religion, meaning?"

"Doesn't seem so hard to explain." Rita waited a moment, then went on. "Humans are a pretty puny bunch—just hairless apes, after all. No big teeth, not very strong, can't fly. We don't even run very fast. Not much to make us the 'higher' beings. Once we left the jungle, we had to start struggling to survive against mastodons, lions, hyenas, wolves. The only trick that would work was ganging up to protect ourselves from them. Without that we would have become extinct. So, there must have been very strong selection for anything—especially gestures, grunts, signs—that made it possible for people to gang up, to cooperate. That's how language, and culture, emerged by natural selection."

"And everything else about humans comes from that, does it?" Dani sounded unimpressed.

"Is there a better story? One that involves God—Adam and Eve, maybe?" Rita challenged. There was no immediate reply, so Rita went on, "My story certainly explains religion, tribalism. In fact, it explains Nazism."

"How's that?" Magda asked.

"The ideas that make cooperation in your tribe possible are just like any other parasite, only they invade the brain instead of the liver, say. The brain parasites survive and spread because of what they do to and for their hosts—us. So ideas that make us band together, especially against strangers, are going to be encouraged by the same forces of evolution that made it possible for us to kill off the woolly mammoth, right?" The others nodded, Dani grudgingly. "Give natural selection a couple of hundred thousand years. It's sure to find ways to make you hate strangers who might be threats to survival. Better safe than sorry. Hate all strangers. The best way of making you hate strangers who just might hurt you is the way religion does it. It even gets you to give up your life for some greater cause—protecting your tribe from the strangers."

Magda was thinking. "Back to the rats and cockroaches for a minute. If humankind were ever to kill itself off and the rats or the cockroaches end up the dominant species on the planet, Darwin tells us that won't be any reason to think rats or roaches are the best, just the ones who happen to be able to survive on the detritus we end up leaving behind. Right?"

"Exactly." Rita was pleased. Magda had understood. "Nazis, Aryans, the master race, whatever they call themselves, are people infected by the temporarily dominant brain parasite. If they win, if their ideas end up making civilization, culture, or even humanity extinct, all it will show is that being savage sadists is a way of life suited to our time, but not all time."

Rita paused, but they seemed still to be following, so she took up the thread. "That brings up the Nazis' second huge misunderstanding of Herr Darwin. He never thought that there was anything morally good or right or best about surviving, or even becoming the dominant species in an environment. There is nothing in Darwin that says might makes right. Nothing! So the two things the Nazis think they take from Darwin aren't there at all. No master race, no progress, just change. No glorification of violence or overlordship as morally right."

"Go on; tell her the rest." Dani turned from Rita to Magda. "She thinks that Darwin showed there's no right or wrong, no meaning, no purpose to anything." Dani smiled as if revealing a bit of scandalous gossip.

Rita took the challenge. "You see, Magda, Darwin showed that purpose in nature is an illusion. Whatever looks planned and organized to attain some end is just the result of blind variation that gets filtered by a passive environment—whether in nature or culture." Here she looked at Dani. "Denying it is turning your back on science. Meaning, purpose, that's just wishful thinking. Something we can't afford. We can't waste time wondering what this war means in human history. Human history doesn't mean anything. The war is just a catastrophe no different from a new ice age, only happening much faster, more like the Black Death."

Dani finally remembered the news Magda had come with. "So, the Jews fighting in the ghetto against the SS are engaged in a struggle for survival that means nothing?"

Rita had to answer the question. "I am afraid so. When you add up all the human actions that make up history, who wins and who loses doesn't reveal meanings. The path is just blind variation, Darwin's process of selection operating on history." She stopped for a moment. "What is the cosmic meaning of the fact that Jews are finally fighting the Wehrmacht in Warsaw? There is none. Can we stop ourselves searching for it? No." The other two were silent.

As she carried the last dishes back into the kitchen, Rita wondered what ideas were parasitizing her own brain. Which ones were selected because they caused her to act in ways that just happened to preserve them, even to spread them?

For the next three weeks, every other day or so, Magda would stop at the kitchen and summarize the teletype's report. The news about the uprising in the Warsaw ghetto was never good, often painful, and finally tragic. The only benefit that emerged from these three weeks was the bond it forged with Magda Halle, and later, a decent set of documents for Dani.

Magda brought the last report to them on May 17. "It's over. The Wehrmacht's been using flamethrowers for several days, setting fire to everything. The Germans estimate the number of people killed by the fires was about six thousand. Another seven thousand killed, either fighting or by collateral damage. And now they've taken the last fifty thousand out." Rita thought back to her night in the ghetto. Could there still have been that many people in it?

Dani asked, "German casualties?"

"Officially, sixteen dead, eighty-five wounded. But in a month of fighting . . . well, that's probably a lie."

"And we sat here, in cozy Krakow, doing nothing." Dani began to weep. The other women did nothing to stop her.

A week later Magda brought in a Leica 35 mm and took a picture of Dani. "We can't have Rita doing all the marketing and running all the errands. So, I am getting you a *Kennkarte*. Got five hundred zloty you can spare?"

"*Gewiss!*"—German for "Sure!"—"Nothing else to spend my pay on cooped up in here," Dani replied, smiling gratefully. When she came back into the kitchen with it, Magda was already gone. Rita had been quicker to find the money.

A week later Dani had papers. "They are real . . . or as real as the *Generalgouvernement* can make them!" Magda grinned. "But you'll have to go to the *Polizei* to register for Krakow. It's just down in the main square. Do it early in the morning before the real Nazis have slept off their boozing."

PART V

ENDING

CHAPTER TWENTY-SEVEN

Almost a year later, Rita left for Germany. By the spring of 1944, the *MussNazis* in the office knew not just that the war was going to be lost, but that the defeat was going to come not on Russian soil, but probably in Poland, and perhaps even in Germany itself.

In late March the *Grossdeutscher Rundfunk* announced a tactical withdrawal west of Lemberg. That meant the occupation of Karpatyn by Soviet forces. There was nothing to cheer Rita or Dani in the news. For them Karpatyn had simply become a location on the map, nothing more. But Lempke and the other accountants in the Tax Inspectorate were continually aware that the Eastern Front was washing back toward them. A tide that had gone out with a rush was returning inexorably toward the sand castles they'd built along the Vistula River. Each of the officers was making longer and longer visits back to Germany, taking larger and larger bags with them as they left, returning with smaller and smaller valises.

One morning in April, Lempke called Rita into his office, a very unusual step. Magda was at her desk in a corner, typing columns of numbers. She did not even look up.

"Fräulein Trushenko"—he was still calling her that after fourteen months living under the same roof—"soon I return to the Reich.

I propose to send you to my family in Heidelberg." He looked up, smiling at his generosity. Rita did not know how to react. Her face remained immobile. "Don't you understand? A chance to get away from the war, to live in Germany, perhaps permanently if you measure up." She nodded. It was enough assent for Lempke. "We have a large house. Six children. My wife cannot cope with it all. You will be housekeeper. I will secure travel papers, some ration coupons, and rail tickets. You may leave"—he looked at the calendar on his desk—"next Thursday."

All she could say was, "Thank you very much." All she could think was, *My God, leave Dani?*

∾

"Well, you don't have to go," Magda was musing. "You could just melt into the Polish population, go back to Warsaw or somewhere else. But you won't be able to stay here. He'll dismiss you in a minute if you decline the post."

Dani was nodding her head. "A *Volks-Deutsche* would never turn down an offer like that. You'd raise suspicion immediately. You don't have a choice. You have to go."

Why was Dani taking this line? Surely they meant too much to each other. The thought of losing the only person still alive that Rita loved made her feel that she was drowning. She found herself gulping for breath. Meanwhile, that very person sat beside her coolly calculating what Rita had to do, apparently without a thought to how it would tear them apart. Was this a signal? Was the comfort she had given Dani wearing off? Certainly Rita craved Dani as much as ever. Might her lover have even begun to think of what they had found in each other as wrong, unnatural, repugnant? No. That couldn't be. She reached out for the reassurance of Dani's hand, and it came to her grasp willingly.

But Dani was going on, piling up reasons Rita didn't want to hear. "You're much safer in Germany. When the Russians come, people with *Volks-Deutsche Kennkarten* are not going to be safe. Working for the Germans, you're really going to be in danger." Rita was going to interrupt, but Dani preempted her. "Sure, sure, it's crazy, but just try convincing a commissar standing between you and a dozen soldiers. He won't have time to check your true identity with whoever got you your forged papers."

"They aren't forged."

"All the worse."

"But what about you, Dani?" Rita was succumbing to her logic now.

"That's another thing. If you go to Germany, maybe you can find a place for me. That's the only way we'll both have a chance."

$$\sim$$

It was only later that the penny dropped.

Magda and Rita were sharing a cigarette in the kitchen. "You looked so bowled over this morning," Magda said, "when Dani told you to go."

"Yes. I can't understand why she's so eager to get rid of me. I see the logic, but there was an urgency, a hardness that I hadn't seen in Dani before."

The smoke came blue from Magda's nostrils as she breathed out. "You really don't see, do you?"

"What?"

"She needs you to go." Rita stared at her. "Until you leave, she can't do what she has to do. That's why she's forcing you."

"What are you saying?"

"She can't leave you. But she needs to do something in this war . . . I'm not sure what. Maybe join the Home Army. Whatever it is, she can't do it till you are gone. In Germany you'll be safe, and you won't be able to stop her. That's why she wants you to go."

"And how do you know all this? Did she tell you?"

"Not in as many words. It's a guess, but I think a good one. You've seen how restless she's been, how terribly bitter, since the ghetto uprising in Warsaw last year. She takes risks in the street. I've seen it. Tearing down proclamations, pulling faces at Germans. She asked me too many questions about where the *Kennkarte* I got for her came from. Last week she brought home a Home Army leaflet she found in the street. Imagine if Lempke had seen it!"

"Anything else?" Rita was becoming convinced.

"One more thing. Really scary." Magda put out her cigarette. "Something putting both of you at risk, and maybe me. She goes to confession too often for a Jewish girl."

"You think she is becoming a believing Catholic?"

"No. I think she is asking priests how to make contact with the Home Army. If she asks the wrong one, all three of us could become passengers on a freight train." Magda left the kitchen.

∾

Lempke handed Rita her tickets and travel permits on a Monday morning and left Krakow on the sleeper to Berlin that evening. She was to leave for Heidelberg the following Thursday morning, third-class coach through Dresden to Berlin, and Berlin through Leipzig to Heidelberg.

As she put the Darwin volumes in her case—the same case she had arrived with over a year before—Rita could see how little she had accumulated in twelve months. Now, with the few bits of clothing and personal effects folded away, the room looked unoccupied, forlorn. Dani had kept her distance all afternoon and into the evening. Rita looked around the room for what she might have forgotten. A quiet knock on the door. Dani came in. Her eyes were red, but she was not crying. Rita closed the case and took it off the bed. They settled at each end of the small bed, like two schoolgirls, knees forward, legs bent, easily within reach of each other. Nothing was said. Instead, as slowly as they could, they let their two bodies share the bittersweet farewell—brief touches, distracting caresses, then fingers of one hand searching deep while the other played across a breast. A long while later, their bodies found themselves lying on their side, heads resting on each other's thigh, succumbing to *la petite mort* over and over. *Why can't the real death come now?* Rita thought. She'd welcome it. When they had their fill, they slept, too exhausted for words.

Both women woke with a start very early in the bright morning. By mutual but unspoken agreement, they made love one last time. It would be the last thing each remembered. After, Rita rose. Dani remained in the narrow bed, most of her body emerging from its covers, letting the perspiration cool from her chest and thighs. Rita watched Dani's nude body as she slowly dressed, a kind of seduction in reverse.

❧

The train, mainly full of lightly wounded troops and a few officers on leave, crossed into Germany just after noon. The smell in the compartment was a mixture of disinfectant, wet wool, and strong tobacco. Helmets on the baggage racks clicked against one another and sometimes slid along the shelf from one side of the compartment to the other as the train negotiated a curve in the track. Rifles had to be moved as legs stretched and crossed, sometimes in a single orchestrated movement. There were no *"Heil Hitlers"* as men moved in and out. Even the sole officer in the compartment was not demanding salutes, but buried himself in a small volume of dense *Fraktur* print. Goethe? Schiller?

Rita was the only civilian in her compartment, and she had not been called upon to show her papers once she left Krakow. Instead, heels clicked as she handed over her ticket and travel permit. The soldiers were overly solicitous—"By your leave" and "Please excuse," "Mind if I smoke" and "Will you have one too?" They were hardened by the front, but young enough to still be softened again in the company of a woman. Rita was unable to summon up any hatred for them, taken one at a time. A private with a bandaged right hand needed her to fish out a cigarette and light it. With another soldier, she exchanged seats so he wouldn't have to clamber over her on his crutches. A third told her more than she needed to know about how he would spend his leave in Lubeck.

Mainly Rita studied the contrast in landscape as the train moved farther and farther toward Dresden. Germany was different from Poland. The farm fields were larger here and planted with grain, not potatoes. The herds and flocks seemed bigger too. *Ironically*, she thought, *in Germany there was more* lebensraum—*living space—what the Germans made the war to acquire.* As she left Poland, small statues in the fields honoring the Madonna disappeared. Woodlots became more common. She had half expected tractors and mechanical reapers, signs of German efficiency, but the farms were no differently equipped here. Still, towns came thicker and faster, buildings stuccoed white with distinctively narrower Protestant church steeples instead of the rounded, crenellated turrets favored by Polish church and nobility. In every town the train raced through, there were shops facing the station, and automobiles.

Dresden materialized outside her window as the tracks and sidings began to multiply and spread away from her vantage point on the slowing train. Rich, clean, bustling, untouched by war, the classic buildings marred only by the long red banners with the swastika shouting its domination from between Ionic columns. The train slowed smoothly and almost glided into the terminal. Alas, she thought, no time to explore. Rita had to find the express to Berlin. Leipzig was much closer to Dresden, but a *Volks-Deutsche Mädchen* didn't qualify for the direct connection. She would have to journey through the capital on a third-class ticket.

$\sim$

Berlin was in the early twilight of an April evening. The conductor was coming through the carriage, opening compartment doors. "Berlin, Anhalter Bahnhof." But Rita could see no mainline station, only rubble on each side of the tracery of tracks surrounding the one she was coming in on. Arriving from the south, she had already seen enough bomb damage to make her wonder why Dresden had been spared, but she wasn't expecting the Reich's largest train station to be in ruins. The train had stopped just beyond a narrow canal in the middle of the marshaling yard. There was no quay or even a platform beside the carriages, just a yawning drop to the gravel roadbed. A young man in the *feldgrau* of the Wehrmacht helped her down.

"*Danke.*" Rita looked up at him. "Please. Is this Berlin main station?"

"I'm afraid so. It's as close as we will get to it by train this evening. The station was knocked out pretty much completely last winter. Please, let me show you the way." He grabbed Rita's case from her before she could muster serious resistance, and together they clambered along, next to the now empty carriages, in line with the rest of the passengers. "Between them the RAF and the American Eighth Air Force have pretty much closed the station, along with a lot of other things in Berlin."

"But I just passed through Dresden. And it's untouched."

"I guess that's because most people in Berlin aren't Nazis and most people in Dresden are." He smiled conspiratorially. Rita was taken with his bravura.

"Are you a Berliner? I need some information."

"Yes, ma'am."

"I have to get to the station for trains to Frankfurt and the west. It's the Zoo Station, yes? Can you tell me how to get there?"

"I'm going in that direction. I shall be glad to take you along as far as I go."

Ten minutes later they were passing along the crumpled iron-work of the Anhalter Bahnhof's glass roof. Then they turned toward Potsdamer Platz. As she read the sign directing them, Rita began preparing herself for what was supposed to be the busiest intersection in Europe.

The tumbledown relics, the bombed buildings, the fire damage, and the flotsam along every street leading away from the station was worse than anything Rita had seen in Warsaw. The desolation around her was hard to reconcile with the almost Prussian blue of the still bright sky above. It was as though she were walking through a black, white, and gray photograph displayed under a full color sky. Would Potsdamer Platz be different?

As they reached it, the young man spoke as though reading her mind. "You should have seen it before the war, or even when we were still winning." Again this irreverence. The cheeky young soldier was courting a lethal charge of defeatism. Was he soliciting an indiscretion from her? She promised herself she wasn't going to indulge him. "That domed building used to have every kind of restaurant in it. Down there"—he pointed to an open rectangular square of broken facades and collapsed buildings—"was the biggest department store in Berlin. Wertheim's—a Jewish business. They tried to hang on to it by putting it in the owner's wife's name. Didn't work." Rita wasn't much interested in history. What struck her was that amid the ruins, there were cafés full of people, drinking, smoking, talking, actually having a good time, something she had not seen since perhaps the summer of 1939. Somehow Berliners were refusing to take reality seriously.

"Are they drinking real coffee?" She didn't even realize she had voiced the question aloud.

"Not a chance. But we remember what it used to taste like, and that's sometimes enough!"

They were beginning to march up the main street leading away from Potsdamer Platz toward the Brandenburg Gate, Berlin's magnet even for nontourists. Halfway there her escort pulled her away, up a side street leading to grass and trees. "You don't want to go that way, Miss. It's Göring-Strasse. Used to be Ebertstrasse, after the social democratic president. Now it leads right to the Reich's chancellery, Hitler's headquarters. Too many soldiers."

"What's the problem? You're a soldier, no?" She was breaking her promise to herself. Perhaps she could smoke him out a little more without taking any risks.

"I'm Wehrmacht Medical Service, a conscript soldier. I don't carry anything more deadly than a mercy-killing pistol. Up there, those guys are Waffen-SS. You don't even want to get close. Besides, the park is much prettier." He looked toward the green.

Soon they were walking along a wide, finely graveled path through generous rhododendron bushes beneath large trees beginning to come into leaf, filtering the still visible but sinking sun. After a few moments, they found themselves walking along a vast avenue cutting through the greenery. At one end Rita could identify the Brandenburg Gate, and at the other, the Victory Column of the Franco-Prussian war. She knew them as the iconic picture postcard images of her childhood, the way children in Western Europe knew the Eiffel Tower and the Arc de Triomphe. They were symbols of

Berlin and Germany, the great cultural engine of change bringing Eastern Europe into the new century. She was glad her first views of Berlin were these and not the *Reich Chancellery*, surrounded by goose-stepping robots in black.

The soldier noticed her turn her head from east to west and back again along the avenue. "Those buildings are—"

"I know." She smiled, appreciating his proprietary feeling about Berlin. "We knew all about them in Poland. I didn't realize you could see one from the other."

"You couldn't, until the *Führer* moved the whole Victory Column into the park a few years ago." They were silent for a moment. Then the soldier began to point out ground-clearing projects. "We think the city government is going to allow citizens to set up vegetable garden allotments in the park. They are beginning to worry about food. Nothing is coming in from the Ukraine anymore. There have always been garden allotments in Berlin, but not here in the Tiergarten. Mainly people grew flowers in them anyway. Now it's going to be potatoes. Last summer thousands of people slept in the Tiergarten every night during the RAF bomber offensive." He led her away from the wide boulevard and back into the paths sheltered by lateral tree branches and hidden by banks of foliage. It was easy to forget where you were or even when. A velvet silence descended, and neither wanted to break it.

Ten minutes later, however, the young soldier began to frown as they approached a massive concrete turret emerging from out of the ground like a black ogre, looming over the large trees that surrounded it. Rita had never seen something so formidable, immovable, impenetrable, lowering, threatening. It seemed the nightmarish keep of malevolence itself.

"That's where I work. It's the Tiergarten Flaktower. There's a military hospital on the third floor. The top has the antiaircraft guns. The bottom is an air-raid shelter."

"It's the ugliest building I have ever seen. Please take me away from it."

"Sorry, I can't take you away. It's where I'm going. My post. But if you continue straight ahead, you'll come to the canal that runs through the park. Turn right. When you come to the second bridge, cross it, go past the café in the park, and you will come out at the train station you want, Zoo Station."

She felt safe with this soldier of the Reich. "But can't you take me the rest of the way?"

He looked up at the tower, back at Rita, and shook his head, turned, and began walking toward it.

CHAPTER TWENTY-EIGHT

It was dark, but there was still a spring mildness in the air when Rita arrived at the Zoo Station. Entering, she went to the waiting hall and sought the train indicator board. There were no trains for Leipzig on the board at all. She looked around for an inquiry desk and saw none. There was only the ticket windows, with a long queue stretched away from them. Finally she saw a cleaner, pushing a broom against the tide of dust, newsprint, food wrappings, and discarded tickets. "Excuse me. Is this the right station for Leipzig?"

He continued to sweep, but said distinctively enough for her to hear, "Yes, but you won't get a train tonight. Bombing on the line south. They've stopped everything going that way for the night at least." He moved on past her.

Could it be right? She needed a more reliable source. Rita stepped over to the queue and attached herself to its end. In front of her were a mother with two children, one coughing and wheezing. With them was another, older woman.

In fifteen minutes the queue had made no appreciable progress. But the proximity of the women had made their faces, their postures, even their smells, familiar enough to break through the anonymity. It was no surprise to Rita when the older woman asked, "Where are you off to, dear?"

"Leipzig. But there are no trains there tonight." She looked toward the departure board above the steps up to the quays.

Overhearing, the woman with the two children intervened. "Hilde, remember, just when we got here, they announced no service to Leipzig till morning. There is an air raid on the line at Bruck."

"Yes, that's right."

Rita decided to be friendly. "Where are you going, ma'am?"

"Magdeburg," was the answer, but it came amid the blast of loud sirens echoing painfully throughout the building.

"What's that noise?" Rita could not suppress the question or the sound of fear in her voice.

"Air raid, dear. Come along, children . . . " Everyone in the station was surging out. Rita followed the two women and their children. Without thinking, she took the hand of the elder boy, who looked up at her for reassurance. The crowd was flowing out of the station and moving down a broad street, but Rita's group was not moving fast enough. Even before they arrived at the U-Bahn station on Kurfürstendamm, the older woman was saying, "We'll never make it."

She was right. Breathlessly they reached the stairway down only to be confronted by a thick metal barrier (and a sign that announced, "No Jews"). "Nothing for it but the park," said the younger woman, and all five turned back, hurriedly retracing their steps back past the railway station, under the elevated tracks, and into the park. Well before they reached its entry, the boy was coughing uncontrollably. Rita swept him up and carried him along while the child regained his breath. As they reached the park, she set him down. The boy smiled up at her.

They were not the only ones seeking the sanctuary of the park. By the time they arrived at the entrance, many others—families, couples, single men and women—were streaming in, some carrying cushions, even bedding. Rita was still holding the young boy's hand as they reached the café by the canal, now closed, and seated themselves at one of the outdoor tables.

The mother had taken note of Rita's care for her child. She smiled. "Thank you for helping. Maybe he likes you. Not many adults he holds hands with. My name is Flora." She took the child to her lap.

"Rita." She offered her hand to each.

The older woman settled herself and turned to Rita. "Ingrid is my name. Not from Berlin, are you?" Before Rita could reply, she said, "Never been in an air raid before. That's how I knew."

Rita looked up at the bright lines of white sent up by the searchlights, moving like pencils across the black sky. Then she heard the distant thud of what must have been either bombs or antiaircraft artillery. "No . . . I mean, yes. This is my first time in a raid."

"Wish it were my first time," said the younger woman.

Looking at the boy on Flora's lap, Rita asked, "What's his name?" When she misheard "Stefan," she gasped slightly and repeated it to herself.

"No. It's 'Sylvan.'" His mother went on, "He's four—big for his age."

The child began to cough again. "Do you have any more of that cough syrup you got from Dr. Cohen last year?" Ingrid asked Flora.

"I went round last month, but they told me he'd been deported. Gave me a good talking to about letting a Jew doctor treat an Aryan child."

"Right they were too," scolded Ingrid.

"Jew or no Jew, he was the only doctor in the neighborhood who treated you like a human being. Sometimes you have to make exceptions."

They turned back to Rita. "Where are you from, dear?" Ingrid asked.

"Poland, the part Stalin took in '39." Rita pulled out a packet of cigarettes, offering them to her two new friends.

Flora, the younger one, pulled a face. "The *Führer* hates tobacco."

It was a clue Rita missed as she lit her own. Had she picked it up, she certainly would not have gone on as she now did. "Back at the underground . . . the sign on the shelter, 'No Jews.' Are there still Jews in Berlin?"

Both women replied at once. "Yes, thousands." "Of course. They're everywhere."

"Probably out in this air raid looting my flat right now!" Flora observed.

"It's all Goebbels's fault, running things in Berlin. The government is far too lenient with them. Thousands of *Mischlinge*—half-breeds—hundreds of full-blooded Yids married to German women, committing race crimes every time they go to bed at night . . . and there's nothing can be done about them!"

Rita was surprised. "Why not?"

Ingrid answered, "It's the law, the silly stupid law. All those by-the-book civil servants, you'd think they were Jews the way they enforce the Nuremberg laws. If someone is less than three-fourths Jew or was married to an Aryan before '35, you can't touch 'em."

"She knows the law." Flora indicated her older friend. "Knows the status of every Yid in our district. If it weren't for those untouchable Yids, she'd be in a decent flat by now."

"Been waiting ten years, I have," Ingrid agreed. "I'll die before they kick one out and give me the place. I ask you, how long does someone have to be a Nazi to get what you deserve?"

"You got that nice fox collar from *Winterhilfe*. Wasn't that enough?"

"What's a used fox collar? You got a nice flat easy enough. Once those *Ostjuden* across the hall from you went for resettlement, you were allowed to move in right away."

"That was five years ago."

"Well, they're getting softer on Jews all the time." The old woman looked toward Rita. "You're not from here, so you wouldn't know. Last winter they tried to round up those Berlin Jews married to German women. The wives protested on the street for a week. Instead of shooting them, they released their husbands! Unbelievable."

"Spineless, these wishy-washy national socialists Goebbels lets run the *Schutzpolizei*. It's as bad as the way they caved in to bleeding hearts before the war."

"What do you mean?" Rita couldn't help wanting to hear more.

"They were making a real start on eliminating the social parasites, those who eat but don't contribute—the dumb, the mental defectives, mongoloids, and genetic defectives. But the pastors got wind of it and whipped up churchgoers to protest. We wouldn't be scrounging for ration coupons to buy meat, butter, and eggs now if the Race Purity Office had been allowed to do its job."

"What can you expect from that little man?" Now they were obsessing together and ignoring Rita. "He has already got the *schnorrers* extorting honest people for the *Winterhilfe* collections." Rita couldn't suppress a laugh at the Yiddish word. Not noticing, Flora continued, "Did you get the new contributor's button last week? If you're not wearing one, they'll make you pay double this week." The older woman nodded.

Rita wondered, *Could one freely abuse Goebbels for his disability? Did they really think he was soft on Jews?* This was a slice of public opinion she had been missing. And *schnorrer*—beggar. They had no trouble helping themselves to Yiddish either. She never should have gotten them on to this line of conversation, but now it had transfixed her, listening to these two women. She was about to make a serious blunder. "Flora, Ingrid, I don't understand. Twice you mentioned resettling Jews to the east. Your child's doctor, Cohen, and the people who were in your flat, right, Ingrid?"

"Yes. All the non-German Jews and the German-full Jews have been resettled. All the Jews in the former Poland have been moved to the east."

"Well, the east, that's where I come from. And I have never seen any Jews resettled there."

"Probably farther east than where you come from, *liebes Kind*." Ingrid's "dear child" was slightly ominous.

But Rita was beyond any self-restraint. "Maybe. But in the part of Poland I came from, the Waffen-SS and the Wehrmacht just took thousands of Jews out of the towns, shot them, and buried them in shallow graves."

Both women turned to her, aghast. "What are you saying? That is the vilest libel on the German Wehrmacht and the security services I have ever heard." Ingrid was spitting the words out.

Now Flora joined. "You sit here protected from the Mongol hordes the Bolsheviks have unleashed against German womanhood, uttering slanders against our soldiers."

They were now both shrieking. The men and women at tables nearby turned their heads and began to listen. "*Polizei! Polizei!*" Both women were standing, shouting freely. Flora gathered her children to her for their protection, and Ingrid was rising either to strike or take hold of Rita. Ingrid's surprisingly strong arm was suddenly clamped on Rita's forearm.

Suddenly everything was drowned out by the roar of four Merlin aeroengines throbbing under the wing of an Avro Lancaster flying much too low. Whether it was disabled and about to crash or off course and on damaged instruments, no one could tell. Whatever, it was more than enough of a distraction for Rita to pull free, grab her case, and begin running out of the park, into the danger of bombs now audibly and visibly falling on the Ku'damm. "Thank you," Rita said aloud under the drone of the engines in one of the few English phrases she knew. *Better,* she thought, *to chance her life to the RAF's carpet bombing than to have to explain herself to Goebbels's Jew-loving* Polizei.

Rita reached the park exit at the station still running. Instead of going down toward the U-Bahn air-raid shelter, she decided to follow the elevated tracks of the aboveground S-Bahn as it curved south and west away from the station. The closer to a military target, like railway tracks, the safer she would be from the *Polizei.* After ten minutes of sprints broken by the need to catch her breath and the pain of a stitch in her side, she found herself in a square, trees splintered and cut down, surrounded by a number of buildings already derelict from previous bombings. There was an entrance to the S-Bahn at the end of the square, and a light still shone on the station name, Savignyplatz. The name rang a bell for Rita. Then she recalled the Berlin address Magda Halle had given her back in Krakow. She reached into her purse and pulled out the piece of paper: *Directions: S-Bahn to Savignyplatz, two blocks west to Schlüterstrasse, 21,* Halle's family's home in the Charlottenburg district. Bombs were still falling, but the sounds were definitely moving away. Rita turned toward what she reckoned had to be west.

A few minutes later, she found herself before 21 Schlüterstrasse, or what was left of it. The building number was still clearly visible on the lintel of the burned-out entryway. It had been a substantial art nouveau structure in pastel peach. Now all that remained was blackened peach stucco topped with broken white windowsills. Above the second-story walls, black sky was visible through broken rafters and timbered beams. Derelict parquet flooring cascaded in a frozen stream down toward the ground floor. Through the main entry, Rita could see a staircase going up to nothing at all. Behind it was the charred rear of the building, where a courtyard and a large burned-out tree were visible in the street lighting that cast the facade's shadow back to the next street's bombed-out structures. If Magda had any family left, they were not to be found hereabouts.

There was nothing to do but to continue to put distance between herself and the women in the Tiergarten. Fifteen minutes' farther down the street brought Rita to still another small park, in the middle of which hundreds of people were sitting out the air raid, evidently excluded by lateness or other disability from the Fehrbelliner U-Bahn station at the foot of the park. Rita laid out her coat, setting her head on the case, and was quickly asleep.

∾

Even before the all clear had sounded, Flora was urging Ingrid and the children back to the station. She was aflame to report this woman, who had defamed the Wehrmacht and was probably a Jew or a spy or at any rate a disloyal person.

There was a lone *Orpo—Ordnungspolizei*—pacing the station waiting room. Not much need for order police to regiment the bombed-out Berliners sleeping on the benches and the floor.

"*Herr Polizei,*" Flora called across the waiting room, wakening several of those who could do no more than doze. The *Orpo* turned and brought a finger to his lips, "Shhh . . .," then closed the distance between him and the women.

With a subdued click of his heels, he whispered, "*Gnädige Frau?*" making his salutation a question.

Flora began, "I have to report a crime, and the criminal may still be about . . ." She looked across the waiting room, searching the benches and alcoves for Rita.

"What is it, ma'am? Theft, assault?"

"No. Slander against the Wehrmacht."

Suddenly the Orpo realized what he was dealing with. If he didn't make a show of taking this matter seriously, he would shortly be the subject of another complaint to be taken seriously. He withdrew a small notebook, poised a short pencil above it, looked up at Flora, and said, "Details, please."

Both volunteered, "Her name was Rita." Flora continued, "That's what she said, anyway. Didn't give a surname. From the east, Poland probably."

The *Orpo* was taking it down carefully. "Description?"

Flora and Ingrid had her to a tee. One corroborated the other's report of Rita's outrageous statement. Well, he would file it with the *SS-Kripo* and make a carbon for the *RHSA*—the Reich main security headquarters here in Berlin. But he wasn't going to turn over the station looking for someone who was probably already gone.

Rita was back at Zoo Station the next morning. Before joining the queue for a new ticket to Leipzig, she scanned the waiting room. She didn't want to meet Flora and Ingrid again, so before seeking her train to Leipzig, she searched the departure board for their train to Magdeburg. This time she made no friends, or even eye contact, on the line. After an hour of waiting, she had new tickets, this time with no changes all the way to Heidelberg. There was a train to catch immediately. Owing to cancellations it was full, and until Leipzig she had to sit on her case in a corridor, along with many others. Finally, seated at a window, looking back in the direction from which the train had come, she watched the agricultural landscape pass by, hoping ghoulishly to feast an eye on the tangle of destruction that would line the right-of-way through Leipzig, Jena and Fulda, Frankfurt and Darmstadt, all the way to Heidelberg.

Disappointment grew as the train moved south from Frankfurt. There were fewer and fewer signs of destruction. But for the occasional uniforms at the stations they rolled through, there were almost no signs of war at all. *Bucolic* was the word that came to her. But Rita was unprepared for what she saw as the train began to glide along the River Neckar. First the green of the ivy, overhanging ancient stone walls down to the very tracks, then the lush hills rolling away across the river to the north. Along the river there came into view a storybook stone bridge of arches and towers. It held her eye until she saw the vast castle looming up through the windows on the other side of the train. Nothing had prepared Rita for Heidelberg in the early morning sun, its stone warmed into a molten glow. The beauty of this place was yet another mystery in a world in which nothing was distributed in accordance with reason or justice or merit or desert. *How,* she wondered, *could there be such a place on the same continent with the Warsaw ghetto?*

Rita glanced at her instructions once more, pulled her case off the baggage rack, and left the compartment. She was the first one out of the carriage when it came to a halt. Surrendering her ticket at the barrier, she walked out of the station and into the dreamworld that she had glimpsed from the train.

She boarded a tram. Settling herself at the window, Rita could watch the passing scene as it wended its way through the streets to the river. The vagrant thought that a Jewess had no right to use the tram at all passed through her mind, but at this moment, the regulation didn't seem to apply to her. A small chink in her identity.

Perhaps she was on the way to becoming Margarita Trushenko, *echt-Deutsch*—a real German.

A brace of round white towers framed the bridge at each end. Past one set the tram crossed the slowly moving river and then turned east along its bank on the Neuenheimer Landstrasse. Above the two- and three-story buildings at the river's edge, all painted a gleaming white, villas climbed the forested hillside. Rita turned to watch the castle come into view again on the far side. Along the footpath following the river just below street level, women were pushing prams, couples strolled casually, old men sunned themselves on benches. Retaining walls bounded each of the streets leading up from the river into the wooded hill. On each there was a painted arrow with the word *Philosophenweg*—philosopher's trail— written across it.

The tram came to its last stop. *"Bitte, Mein Herr,"* she said to the tram driver, "can you direct me to Schlangenweg?"

"It's that narrow little path going up the hill, back about fifty meters."

And now she was climbing up a steep cobbled lane, with high, honey-colored sandstone walls overhung by ivy. The path twisted up from the river so that the main road was no longer visible. Rita suddenly felt she was moving through a labyrinth, trudging higher and higher with nothing but high wall on either side and no outlet before her or behind her. Then she began to see steps, and just to their right a gate. Here she was, at the back entrance to number 48 Werrgasse. She had been warned not to use the front entrance, but to climb up this way. Rita dropped her case, opened the gate with both hands, and stepped in.

There she found a girl of about nine pummeling a smaller boy, already muddy at the knees and forearms, while two other children watched, laughing. Seeing her the older child turned to the house and shouted, "The new *Ostie* is here." The fighting stopped, and the chorus went up, "*Ostie, Ostie, Ostie.*" Even among the youngest, a strain of derision rose in every repetition of the word, until at last an adult came to the back door to quell them.

"Children, she is no *Ostie.* This girl is almost an Aryan, she is *Volks-Deutsche.* There is a big difference."

The woman was of middle height but running to fat, round-faced, blonder than Rita, with much darker, fiercely plucked eyebrows, wide open green eyes, too much lipstick, a heavy gold chain worn above a crocheted dress in light blue. There were several rings on each hand, a bracelet on one wrist, and a watch on the other. Even at a distance, Rita could make out the swastika pin over her heart.

"Come this way." She led the way in, followed by the four children who had been playing outside. She continued speaking all the while. "The children are a bit confused. The last girl was an *Ostarbeiter*, blue patch and all. I found her through the *NS*-Frauenschaft." This was the Nazi Women's League. "I had to send her back. Not strong enough, and she took sick as well. Frankly, I suspected she might be a Jewess. But I had no proof." By now they had entered a parlor, and the lady of the house turned around. "Let us formally introduce ourselves." She cleared her throat. *"Heil Hitler,"* the arm raised toward the ceiling. "I am Frau Lempke, and you are . . . ?"

There was no alternative. "Heil Hitler. I am Margarita Trushenko."

"Your papers, please. Can't be too careful."

Rita pulled them from her purse and handed them over. Frau Lempke pulled on a pair of spectacles and examined them. It was clear to Rita, who had watched her papers examined many times before, that this woman did not really know what she was looking for or even at. Good.

"All correct. Now, let's meet my brood."

CHAPTER TWENTY-NINE

These are my three oldest, my Rhine maidens, Flossie, Gunde, and Brone. Flossie is nine." Here Frau Lempke was interrupted by the child who repeated her mother's greeting, "*Heil Hitler*," at a pitch so loud it suggested the child was disturbed or unable to control her voice. She was wearing a *Jungmädel* BDM badge, which she pushed forward with one hand as she saluted. Rita was required to repeat the salute. The other two curtsied slightly when introduced. They were seven and six. "The big boy here is Horst. He is five." The big boy was still in diapers. Not yet trained evidently. "The babies are napping in the nursery." She clapped her hands twice, and the children scattered. *Babies? Lempke had said nothing of babies.*

"Please sit down. I'll explain your duties and take you on a tour of the house." The duties were well beyond the time and the endurance of any single person. Frau Lempke proved, however, oblivious to housework herself and had no idea of how difficult and time-consuming these duties were. There were ten rooms—six with drapes and rugs to dust and beat—and a coal furnace to stoke, which also produced the dust to be beaten from the rugs and which heated the water for washing three sets of diapers. In the kitchen meals were to be prepared in accordance with the Reich's guidelines on food waste by following the *Reichseierkarte*—the coupon book named after the egg consumption it restricted.

A kitchen garden supplemented the ration book's allowances, but it needed to be weeded, watered, and protected from vermin. There was a small orchard of a dozen trees, whose fruit was to be canned and preserved against winter shortages to come. "It may take many more years to defeat the Russians, Rita. I will call you Rita. Fräulein Trushenko is too formal. You may call me Frau L for short."

Back to the list of duties: there were shirts to iron when Herr L was at home—something that no longer held so much mystery for Rita—and the rest of the family's laundry to be done, in the cellar laundry tub, equipped with the latest in modern hand-wringers, Frau L eagerly observed. "You'll see it when you go down to your room in the cellar."

The tour took them to the second floor. There was a nursery, a library of matched but apparently unread books, all bound in rococo, a sewing room showing as much dust from lack of use as the library, and a master bedroom, whose unmade double bed accused Rita of skipping work she had not yet started. Back downstairs they came into the large kitchen, with an indoor hand pump and wood-fired stove. Finally they reached the cellar stairs, down which Frau L pointed without actually deigning to descend.

"Please begin when you have unpacked, Rita. Lunch at one o'clock. There is an *NS*-Frauenschaft wartime cookbook to follow." *NS*, Rita understood, was *National Socialism*, the polite form for *Nazi*.

Rita lit the kerosene lamp at the top of the stairs and carried it down into the dark cellar. The first things to be seen were the laundry sinks and the promised clothes wringer, the coal furnace, with scuttle and coal bin, and beyond it, a door. Rita pushed the door open to reveal a sparsely furnished, windowless room: bed against the wall next to the furnace, a deal bureau with many more drawers than she needed—none of them sliding smoothly—a small table on which to put the kerosene lamp, and a wooden chair. Underneath the bed, which like the one upstairs had been left unmade, Rita found a chamber pot. She pulled it out from beneath the mattress and saw a piece of paper folded in half. This she opened and began reading. It was in good Polish:

To my successor:

Frau L never comes down here and couldn't bring herself ever to touch a chamber pot, so I am sure this note will reach you undisturbed. Some tips that may help you survive longer than I did.

Steal! It is the only way to survive. Steal the best pieces of meat or veg from the beastly soup you have to make them every day. Eat every scrap from their plates; don't let them see any fruit that has fallen from the trees. Eat immediately. When you go to the market, you can always scarf some of the edibles before you get home. But don't cut any corners on the diapers. You will have to stay up with a baby suffering from diaper rash. Frau L will never get out of bed for them.

Watch out for Flossie. She spies and tells her mother everything she sees, and she lies when she doesn't catch you out. If she sees you leaving the house without your OST badge on, she'll tell her mother.

You can keep warm in the winter when Lempke is away. The frau likes it warm and doesn't understand how much coal you use or the price. It's not rationed to party members.
Good luck!

This woman was evidently no simple Ostie farm girl. Probably Frau L's suspicions were correct. But she must have been on the strict *Ostarbeiter* ration. Would they put a *Volks-Deutsche* on it?

Rita lit a cigarette and burned the note in the ashtray. It was the last time she would be able to sit down and smoke till after midnight that evening. Looking at the ashes made her realize she had to write to Dani. She had bought one postcard on the journey in order to write. Now she took it from her bag and dashed off a line for the censors:

Having a wonderful time; wish you were here. Send news to me at this address.
Love, R.

No reply ever came. A week later she summoned up the courage to write to Magda Halle. Back came a postcard, also written with the German censors in mind:

Danielle Nowiki left on holiday the week after you did. Visiting the sights of Warsaw.
Cheers,
Magda Halle

By the time she received the card, Rita had found a routine. Actually keeping this house clean was impossible for one person, or three for that matter. Everywhere you had to cut corners that any good housekeeper might notice. For example, you could make a lot of noise beating rugs without really putting your back into it. Reversing sheets instead of changing them went unnoticed by Frau L. No one ran their fingers along the wainscoting looking for dust. Stealing food while cooking was easy, and if you *Heil Hitler*-ed

Flossie often enough, she would get tired of the game and leave you alone in the kitchen. The hard jobs were hauling *Lebensmittel*—food, often from the farmers' markets across the river—in a child's wagon, every day or so, up the steep Schlangenweg; repeatedly washing the ammonia out of the diapers without bleach or even much laundry powder—an item in short supply even for the party elite, she discovered; and the endless canning, which began in the autumn when the fruit started to fall from the trees. Not a peach or apple or plum was to be lost to scavenging squirrels or field mice. Nor could fallen fruit easily be diverted to the housemaid's belly, for the children had been enlisted as orchard sentries. Boiling jars, stewing fruit, pickling vegetables, sealing lids, and putting them up in the kitchen cold larder made it easy for Frau L to keep count and tell when one was missing. She kept a small notebook with the count continually updated to be sure.

⁓

Frau L was a patriot, having had six children for the *Führer* in nine years. Five children entitled her family to a significant quantity of milk daily and an egg a week for each child. The sixth earned double rations. But it was up to Frau L how to best deploy these scarce commodities in the interests of the Reich.

The lady of the house frequently entertained neighbors. "Rita, tea with milk in the parlor, *sofort*."

"A word, please, Frau L."

"What is it? Can't you see I have guests?" she hissed at Rita, standing at the parlor door.

Rita whispered, "We only have half a liter of milk left, and the children have not had supper yet."

"Do as you are told." Frau L turned and rejoined her guests.

❦

Some days later, into the kitchen strode the lady of the house. "Rita, the children want their eggs poached this morning."

"There are none left, ma'am."

"There were two yesterday. Have you been stealing?" High dudgeon spread across Frau Lempke's face.

How was Rita to remind her she had ordered up an omelet for herself the day before? "You were indisposed and needed the eggs yesterday, remember, Frau L?"

"Ah yes. The children will just have to soldier along then." She turned and left the kitchen.

❦

A governess came in four days a week to school the older children, and there was still a wet nurse for the infant twins, eighteen months old. Rita saw the two women come and go. Neither had any interest in engaging the servant in conversation. The former was a corker of a Nazi, and the latter was an uneducated local girl. Rita occasionally wished she had been left alone with the children, if only to cure them of Jew baiting as a form of play. In this house the greatest fear was that a Yid from the Nazi cartoons might be lurking under your bed, ready to carry you off to the east.

One day in early June, Rita was in the back garden folding away the last of the linen, watching the shadows rise across the castle above the Neckar. One after another the facets of wall, gallery, crenellated tower, keep, and clock tower were cast first in gold and then in purple, until at last the whole became an indistinct romantic mass in the deepening gloom. Frau L had come to the back steps of the house and noticed both the splendid scene and her maid's appreciation of it, something characteristic only of a refined person.

"Rita." Frau L startled the other woman. *What now?* Rita thought. *Have I forgotten something?* She began going over her mental list of chores. Instead, she heard, "Come in and have a cup of tea with me in the kitchen."

Rita made the tea, with a bit of milk, while Frau L opened the conversation. "It's so nice to have a refined person in the house. Tell me, your German is so excellent. You must have spoken it from birth."

"My *mutti* had two German grandmothers, and her mother spoke German." Rita was improvising. She knew the story had to be consistent. "She spoke to me in German from birth, when everyone else was speaking Polish."

"What became of her?"

"Oh, the Russians sent her and the rest of the family to Siberia when they occupied eastern Poland. They thought I was just a barmaid at the hotel, so they left me alone when they took it over."

"The Jews must have run riot when the Bolsheviks occupied."

Tread carefully, Rita. "Actually, there were very few Jews in our town."

"Have you ever seen those horrible *Ostjuden*? The ones in the newsreels—swarthy, fleshy noses, loud ties and zoot suits, like blacks? Or the ones with long beards and wide hats, coats hanging to the floor?" Frau L was now disturbing herself with her own word pictures. She shivered.

"I saw some of the religious ones in Warsaw once when I went there before the war. Were there no Jews here in Heidelberg?" There, she'd done just what she had promised herself she wouldn't do: ask a subversive question. Why couldn't she keep her mouth shut?

"Oh, yes. But they were all professors, doctors, lawyers. You couldn't tell them from anyone else. In fact, that was the trouble.

And they took all the best posts in the university. There was no room for a German. Anyway, they all went to America years ago."

Frau Lempke hesitated. She had a reason for this conversation, and it wasn't to tease out Rita's biography. Frau L obviously wanted to ask Rita something, but could hardly bear to do so. *What*, wondered Rita, *could it be?*

Finally, courage mustered, the lady of the house began again. "Rita, I am terribly afraid for the children. If we lose the war . . . I mean, if the Russians get here . . . they are already in Poland . . ." Rita was not going to interrupt or discourage this line of thought. "I mean, you have lived under them. What was it like? What will happen? What should I do?"

Now Rita understood. It wasn't the children, it wasn't the fatherland, it wasn't the party or the Führer that she worried about. It was rank terror at the prospect of sexual violence—rape—at the hands of a Soviet soldier from Mongolia. This was Frau Lempke's nightmare.

How to reply? What did this woman want to hear? Could Rita frighten her without bearing any cost? Provocation had already gotten her into trouble before, in Warsaw, and then in Berlin. Better to appeal to the kind of woman Frau L aspired to be.

"Frau L, you will of course think first of the children, and you must be prepared for the worst." She paused to let Frau L contemplate the unnamed worst, for herself. "You cannot let your beloved ones fall into the hands of Mongols. Such beautiful children must be protected from these monsters at all costs." Rita subsided.

Frau Lempke was nodding in sorrowful acceptance of this sage advice. "Perhaps I can get advice from the *NS-Frauenschaft*."

"A good idea, Frau L!"

A few days later, hearing about the Allied landings in Normandy, Frau Lempke could now console herself that this part of the Reich might end up occupied by British and American soldiers, not the Asiatic hoards of the Soviet Army. The *angst* of Russian occupation receded, inspired now by the hope that her *Führer* would find a way to combine with the western Allies to stop the Russians at the Polish border. It was clearly not beyond his political genius. Frau Lempke speculated on this aloud more than once. Would she chide Rita for needlessly frightening her?

In mid-July Frau L's worst fears resurfaced. The Russians were still moving west briskly. By the beginning of August, they had already occupied all of Poland to the Vistula and were poised to take Warsaw. But then the Allied advance from Normandy slowed. One morning, cleaning in the upstairs bath, Rita found that a glass vial of seven cyanide pills had appeared in the medicine chest. Was this the formal advice Frau L had received? Then the Russians' advance stopped at the Vistula. Had the Germans found a defensive barrier after all?

∽

In the early fall, lectures began again at the university. Though her workday was 6:00 a.m. to 11:00 p.m., Rita had been given Thursday afternoons and evenings off. She needed badly to escape the house, or even these few hours would have been forfeit. With no money to speak of and no interest in German films or the *Deutsche Wochenschau* newsreels, she was at a loss about where to go. She wondered, *Would I go unnoticed in a lecture theater?* They would probably be filled mainly with women, the wounded, and those otherwise unfit for war. But the lectures would be free, warmed by many bodies sitting close together, and if large enough, they would be anonymous. Most of all, she hoped, the university might be a relief from the pervasive monotone of National Socialism. Rita couldn't know that Heidelberg was the most Nazified of the German universities.

Thinking about what lectures to follow, Rita realized that now what she wanted most of all to understand better was science—in fact, biology. She needed to know whether anyone in the zoology faculty read Darwin the way she did. Her first free Thursday afternoon found Rita searching for a rear seat in Foundations of Biological Systematics. The lecturer entered. The audience stood. Raising his hand, palm to the sky in the manner of the *Führer*, the lecturer shouted, *"Heil Hitler."* The audience responded, repeating the greeting as one. *So much*, Rita thought, *for disinterested science*.

The lecturer looked around the hall. He removed his glasses and cleaned them. "My name is Gerhard Heberer. I am professor of general biology and anthropology at the University of Jena, and I am an *Untersturmführer* in the SS. The faculty of biology here has given me the honor of offering a series of lectures on evolution and race."

Heberer now looked down and began to read aloud. His account of evolution bore no resemblance to what Rita had read, over and over, in the same books he was citing. Heberer said nothing about variation, chance, extinction. But he did have a great deal to say about progress, racial purity, and mongrelization. As he read, Heberer would add to or remove slides from a projector, pushing them from one side to the other, illustrating racial differences and Aryan superiority—skulls, femurs, and pelvises of a variety of primates, a chart of the volumes of crania, dimensions of foreheads, chins, and noses, along with average heights and ratios of arms to body. All this he delivered with off-color innuendo about African and Semitic races. Heberer came to a peroration urging German youth to be worthy of their superiority to other creatures.

Rita left the lecture theater thinking, *So much for science at this university*. She still had time for another lecture before returning to the Lempke house.

❦

Unterscharführer Otto Schulke stood at the doors of the zoology hall. He should have savored his good fortune. A few years in the prewar Wehrmacht, mustered out of an artillery battery with deafness from stupidly standing too near a howitzer barrel. His eagerness as a *Hitler Jugend* and his father's service in the Mannheim *Ordpolizei*—the municipal police—had been enough to land him a plainclothes job in the depleted Heidelberg Gestapo soon after the war had become serious in the summer of 1941. A decent salary, a long black leather coat, a Luger under his arm, the authority to ask impertinent questions—it should have been enough for him.

But the sources of his resentment were multiple, and they easily swamped any recognition of his good fortune. Otto Schulke was not a happy policeman. He didn't look the part of a cop—too round-faced, and he didn't need to shave more than once a week, no matter how often he tried. He was too chubby; even rationing couldn't dissipate the baby fat. And he was too fastidious for police work—always washing his hands and paring back the cuticles of his nails. He couldn't help himself. Assignment to internal security in the university district was deeply rankling. All those women who smirked at him, wounded veterans who couldn't be intimidated, and the shirkers who had found a way to be excused service. They were the worst—enemies of the state. The least any of them deserved was a little inconvenience. He was not above imposing it.

"Papers!" Schulke stood at the central door of the zoology building, making his demand. He had ordered the two side doors locked so everyone had to undergo his personal scrutiny on their way out. He could hear the mutterings along the queue, now stretching back up the stairs to the lecture theater, as students fumbled for their identity cards. "Miss my next lecture . . ." "Last tram home . . ."

"Nothing left in the shops for supper." Schulke's satisfaction began to well up. If he had had the word "cossetted," he would have used it. Harassing these wastrels was the least he could do for the *Führer.*

But now there was something more interesting before him than just another professor's child eyeing him with class hatred and intellectuals' contempt. The girl was visibly frightened. Her hand trembled as she proffered the *Ausweis,* eyes cast down, poor—threadbare coat, bad shoes. He noticed these things. He had been a poor boy once himself. And she was patient, no pulling back the card, no sarcasm in her voice, no resentment at all. Schulke looked from her face to her card and back. They matched. Then he looked again and saw the Warsaw endorsement, then the Krakow police registration. He looked up. *"Volks-Deutsche?"*

Rita nodded.

"What were you doing in there?" He looked up the stairs to the lecture hall. "Trying to stay warm?" She nodded. *Why,* he asked himself, *did I have to help her? Answering his own question; I'll never make a good policeman.* "Never seen an *Ostie* at the uni before. What were you doing up there?"

"As you said, sir. Just passing the time." Rita was obsequious.

Schulke took out a notebook. This time he was going to be a smart cop. Laboriously he inscribed Rita's particulars, as the students behind her grew more voluble in their annoyance. "Address?" Rita mumbled the number on the Schlangenweg. He handed her back her card and jerked his head toward the exit.

Now what? Rita walked out the door, down the stairs, wondering whether the *kontrolle*—the identity check—was something to worry about. *What is the least suspicious thing I can do? Just do what you were going to do anyway.* She headed for the philosophy faculty.

CHAPTER THIRTY

Rita watched the young man who had quietly entered from the lecturer's entrance in the well of the hall. As he did so, the students began arranging themselves on the edge of their seats, ready to spring forward in a unison of salute to victory, *Sieg Heil*. The lecturer, however, raised his hands to forestall them and began. "Dear students of the university, my name is Eugen Fricker, docent in philosophy. It is now fully ten years since the address made to us by the then rector of Freiburg University, Martin Heidegger, on the great challenge that lay before us in uniting the university to the new German spirit of National Socialism, whose torch is carried by our *Führer*, Adolf Hitler." Now, aroused by fervor repressed, all rose in unison, raising their arms in obligatory expressions of unity. Rita joined in, almost laughing at the comedy of her raised arm and shriek.

Fricker now looked down at his notes and began to read. At first Rita listened, recalling the abstractions she had become familiar with in the faraway philosophy library at Krakow. But as Fricker droned on, turning pages, it became harder and harder to concentrate on the sounds wafting up from the podium. From the rustling of papers and murmurs, it was evident that the sounds had evidently lost their interest, if not their meaning, for most of the students around her. Once or twice a particularly ardent student— or was he an ardent Nazi—sitting a few rows below Rita turned to his right and left, demanding quiet and respect in a stage whisper. Rita decided to try to concentrate, to make something of it. But Fricker's monotone was hypnotic. She could not prevent her eyelids from falling again and again. A half-dozen times, her chin hit her chest, and she woke with a start. Once the young woman sitting beside her stepped on Rita's foot, and she awoke to find Fricker glaring directly at her, or so it seemed for a moment. Surreptitiously she looked at her watch—fifteen minutes left, twelve . . . five.

Turning over the last page of his notes, Fricker looked around the lecture hall and gave his final peroration. "Rector Heidegger recognized that it was the destiny of the German *Volk* to return philosophy to the true path, from which the Greeks strayed, from the error the Jews used to trick European civilization. It is our *Führer* and the party of National Socialism that have taken hold of the fate of our true being, our soul, our *Dasein*." The lecturer's voice was growing louder with each phrase. "He has mobilized philosophy itself to destroy the twin enemies of being—Bolshevism to the east, the materialist plutocracy to the west." Now Fricker subsided, rhetorically spent, almost in imitation of the *Führer*'s fatigue at the culmination of a speech. He let his head hang so that his broad forehead glistened in the lights focused on the podium. The audience rose up in unison, finally freed from mere philosophy by the invocation of their world historical duty to triumph over Germany's enemies. Once more shouts of "*Heil Hitler*" filled the lecture theater. Then the students began to file out.

Leaving the university Rita felt she needed to wash her thoughts clean of the muddy verbiage she had been sprayed with. So, as she walked back across the bridge, she let herself be distracted by the dappled fish scales of sunlight—silver, gold, purple—that blinked up at her from the Neckar as the afternoon sun set. Rita was fairly gliding as she moved up the Schlangenweg and opened the gate to the back garden. Quietly she entered the kitchen. There, evidently awaiting her return, was Frau Lempke, tapping her foot in a caricature of impatience.

"Fräulein Trushenko, what were you doing at the university today?" The tone was peremptory, and without waiting for an answer, she continued, "I have had a visit from the local Gestapo, thank you very much! Never a spot of trouble in all my life, and now . . ." Frau Lempke was momentarily lost in her own chagrin.

Rita worked hard to look innocent. "Have I done something wrong, Frau L? I only meant to improve myself a little." Alarm bells were going off in her head, but she needed to stay calm.

"An officer came to confirm your name, work permit, and address. That's all. But it was so shaming, to be called upon by the police, as if one were a criminal." The woman literally shivered with embarrassment, reliving the call. "Well, I told him what he had to know." She looked at Rita as sternly as she could. "Now, you tell me why the daughter of a hotelkeeper from the east, an *Ostarbeiter,* is skulking about the institutions of higher education, putting on airs and graces, playing at things well above her station." She continued tapping her foot even as she paused. "Or perhaps you are not what you say you are after all. Perhaps you are one of those jumped-up, cultivated, Europeanized Jewesses, masquerading as a Gentile, but finally unable to cloak your true identity as a cosmopolitan?"

Rita was taken aback at Frau Lempke's erudition—*cosmopolitan,* indeed. One of the alternatives frightened her, but the other might be a lifeline. She could throw herself on the good lady's mercy

and plead the desire to rise from her station and profit by exposure to true German culture, perhaps by invoking Nazi philosophy.
What was a little more abnegation after so many years of it?

"You are right, Frau Lempke . . . I had no right to be there. But
I was not taking up space that an *Echt-Deutsche*—a real German—
could have used. The lecture halls are half empty with so many
young heroes at the front. But I do aspire to the civilizing influence
of German culture." She paused to gauge the reaction. At least she
was not yet being interrupted. "I was at a lecture on the thought
of the important national Socialist philosopher Martin Heidegger,
who gave the great lecture here at Heidelberg at the beginning of
the Third Reich, calling students to the *Führer's* service."

Evidently Heidegger was a name beyond Frau Lempke's ken,
for her brow furrowed. At last she found the name she was searching
for and, now knowing that she had caught Rita out, replied with
hauteur, "The philosopher of the party is named Rosenberg, Alfred
Rosenberg."

"Please, Frau Lempke, if only you had heard the lecturer
explaining how the *Führer's* thought and Germany's greatness were
stolen from them two thousand years ago in the misunderstandings
of the Judaizing Greeks Plato and Aristotle."

"So, you were at a lecture on the philosophy of National
Socialism? I suppose there can be no harm in that for a *Volks-
Deutsche*." Rita was back from the danger of being an *Ostie* to the
good graces of incipient German womanhood. She breathed an
inward sigh. Frau Lempke was, however, not yet satisfied. "But,
Rita, how can a girl, even a part-German girl, with no studies, no
gymnasium, no *Abitur* from the state school examiners, understand
lectures on philosophy?"

"I never had any call to mention it, but for a while, I took some
instruction from the sisters at a local Catholic gymnasium in my
hometown. But then the Depression hurt my father's business so

much he withdrew me and I had to go to work. Of course, I did not understand a great deal of what I heard today, Frau Lempke. I was hoping to be able to ask you about it. I thought what I could not grasp, you would be able to help me understand."

"Perhaps. But it's a bit too late tonight. Good night, Fräulein Trushenko."

What Rita really needed to know was how much trouble she was in. But that was the last thing she could ask Frau L.

∾

Untersturmführer Schulke was still working. For a long time, he simply sat and thought about the details he had learned from the very cooperative *Hausfrau* he had interrogated over two cups of tea and a plate of children's cookies. Exactly when had her little housemaid arrived, and exactly from where? How long had she worked for the good woman's husband in Poland, and where? They had even spent a few minutes in the girl's cellar room, taking note of the few documents and letters in the drawer by her bed. The lady of the house admitted her own suspicions about the maid. She and the plainclothes policeman enjoyed every moment of their brief appearance in a detective thriller.

When Otto got back to the office, the *Kriminalsekretär*—the duty officer—in charge that night had smirked at his zeal. "Catch a spy, Schulke?" Poor Otto was the butt of a certain amount of raillery in the local unit—a little too much *Heil Hitler*-ing, and not much to show for his police work. He made no response, but bent over his typewriter.

Three times he had to rip the paper and carbons out of the typewriter. The first time he had filled out half the form before realizing that he had put the carbon paper in the wrong way. The second time, he had torn the onionskin trying to erase the spelling errors his thick fingertips and erratic education had combined to commit. Finally, though, he had found his stride. Telexes to Berlin, to Krakow, to the Warsaw *Gestapo* records, now withdrawn to a town in Silesia, requesting information on Rita Trushenko: registration records, employment history, police reports, known associates. Schulke managed to find a place in the flimsy for every bit of data he had managed to bring away from his meeting with Frau Lempke.

By the time he'd finished, everyone had left the office, including his boss and the teletypist. That was a break, Schulke realized. The *Kriminalsekretär* might have demanded to see his message and denied it priority: no time to waste tracking down the past of a domestic servant from Poland. Then the teletypist would have had to ask the boss whether it should go out, and she'd follow his orders. With everyone gone, he could just leave it on the top of her out-tray to be sent the next morning.

By the time the first replies began to come back, five months later, Otto Schulke had almost forgotten about the entire matter.

CHAPTER THIRTY-ONE

One day in early November, Flossie, the nine-year-old, thrust her head around the kitchen door. "Rita. There is a beggar woman around the back of the house asking for you."

Shaking the dishwater from her hands and reaching for a rag to dry them, Rita wondered what this could all be about. A silly prank by the older children, a ruse to get her out of the kitchen so they could steal a jar of preserves? Someone selling vegetables from an allotment? She stepped outside, and there before her was indeed a woman in a torn coat, with dark hair matted by the mud, which had also spattered her coat, gaunt of face, her face furrowed and scabbed in places, carrying a small brown package tied with strands of broken, unraveling string. Beggar was exactly the right description.

The woman looked up, tried to smile, and in a hoarse whisper said, "At last I have found you, sister."

It was Dani. Again! This time a real wraith, but a living one. Rita rushed to her and found that instead of hugging her, she was suddenly supporting her friend's—no, her lover's—weight, preventing her from falling to the ground. They turned, and Rita half-led, half-carried Dani inside to a chair in the kitchen.

First Rita needed to short-circuit intrusive questions from Flossie and prevent the wrong messages being carried to Frau Lempke. Thankfully the lady of the house was out. Rita had perhaps an hour to figure out how to deal with Dani's arrival. She turned to Flossie. "My dear, this is my sister-in-law Dani, who has finally escaped from the Bolsheviks and come to Germany. As you can see, she has had quite an ordeal getting here. But she is finally safe among her fellow Germans." And then, as an afterthought, *"Heil Hitler."* Flossie nodded. "Please be sure and tell your mother as soon as she gets home. Meanwhile, I will take my sister to the cellar, and she can clean up a bit."

When the child was gone, Dani looked up. "Bad penny I am. Forever turning up at your doorstep threatening to ruin everything." They both smiled.

"What do you need first—food, a cup of tea, sleep, a bath, a doctor?"

"All of them. First a cup of tea, then a bath, then some clean bandages for a wound." She winced and put her hand to her right side. Rita winced with her. Then she rose and put on the kettle.

"Tell me everything. I knew you went to Warsaw after I left Krakow. Magda Halle sent me a postcard."

"You were right."

"About what?"

"About everything." Dani broke down.

It wasn't the moment to ask what she meant. Rita took the kettle off the hob and helped her friend down the stairs.

Lying on Rita's bed, Dani looked up at Rita and patted the mattress. "I'm too agitated, too excited to sleep right away, Rita. I want to tell you everything anyway. So, sit by me." She began.

A week after Rita left Krakow at the end of April, Dani had quietly slipped out of the apartment and disappeared, taking her few belongings and, of course, her new *Kennkarte*. Magda had been right: Dani had gone looking for the Home Army. She found it intolerable to remain sheltered from the reality of the war by the protection of Nazis, even if they were only *MussNazis*. She was going to make her life count for something, even if doing so required her to put an end to it. Arriving in Warsaw, this time with a solid identity, she found a room in Praga and began to frequent bars, cafés, pool halls, workers' clubs of the prewar trades-union movement. Surely, she thought, these were the places in which she would find the resistance, the underground, the parts of the Home Army that she could join.

With a real *Kennkarte,* Dani felt, if not invulnerable, at least willing to take risks. By now the German army and even the Waffen-SS were busy holding back the Russians surging across the Polish border. They were too preoccupied to spend a great deal of time trolling Warsaw for Jews. Besides, the ghetto had been cleared, burned, and razed. Even extortionists—the *szmalcowniks*—had become edgy. They were being picked off by underground elements. No one could tell whether it was Home Army or the remnants of ghetto resistance or the internecine struggle over scarcity—fewer and fewer Jews with any money left at all to prey on and eventually sell out to the Germans. The Gestapo was as ruthless as ever, but its first priority was a line of retreat back to the Reich, and the Polish Blue Police now knew exactly which way the tide was running.

Dani found work in one of the cafés near the bridges across the Vistula, on the city side, away from Praga. But try as she might, she could not make contact with the Home Army resistance. Surely they were there, in the cafés and the workers' restaurants, the police, the brothels. Late one night in June, she found herself alone in the café where she worked, closing up. The last customer was still nursing a beer at the *Zinc* as Dani tried to send him a signal to go, ostentatiously lifting the chairs and turning them over on the tables preparatory to mopping the floor. "What's the rush, sister? Have one with me." The man pushed a coin across the bar and pointed to the beer tap.

"Since you asked nicely." Dani came back around the bar, pulled herself a pint, and glided down the bar till she was facing him. "Pretty quiet tonight," she volunteered. "Even the streets . . . hardly a German patrol all night."

"Before the storm," he replied. She looked at him quizzically. He offered, "The Home Army is laying low, just waiting for the Russians to get a little closer. Then all hell will break lose."

Was this her chance finally to make contact? Or was it a provocation? Why would anyone raise the matter so openly? She had been looking for a way into the resistance for too long not to risk a direct approach. "Is that so? How can a woman help?"

"Sorry, sister, no Jews." He put up his hands to wave away her protest. "Don't bother denying it or showing me your documents. It's in your voice. You can fool a German but not a Pole. I'm not going to turn you in or shake you down. But don't expect me to put you on to the resistance." The man moved back from the bar, drew himself up, and delivered himself of a little speech. "The Home Army is a patriotic expression of Polish national identity." Dani thought, *I am watching a propaganda poster come to life from the past, from one of the old right-wing groups—ONRA, the National Radical Camp, the National Democrats, or the Green Ribbon League.* It was as if the war had never happened. "We are not going to let a lot of emancipated Yids worm their way into our fight. We'll have enough trouble with all the Yids running the Red Army when it gets here." With that he rose and walked out of the café.

So, five years of occupation by a common enemy had not yet reconciled Jew and non-Jew in Poland. Was there anything left of the Jewish Resistance Organization—the *ZOB*—that had organized the uprising in the ghetto? Even if there were, it would be harder to find than the Home Army. Courting all the danger she dared, Dani wandered the ruins of the ghetto, haunted the precincts of the remaining prison for those few Jews still left in Warsaw, searching for some sign of their existence. But she was exciting no interest from anyone at all. Even German sentries were no longer much interested in checking *Kennkarten*.

There was nothing Dani could do but keep trying. There had to be some part of the Home Army that would take her on. But by the end of July, she was ready to give up her quest. Then everything changed. Suddenly, on July 27, *Generalgouvernement* posters went up on walls all over town, announcing a requisition of 100,000 citizens to prepare entrenchments, ditches, tank obstacles for the Wehrmacht. This was a signal to everyone to get off the streets. It was also a signal to the Home Army. Four days later the battle for the city began to rage. The Poles inside Warsaw had committed themselves to liberating their capital before the Russians arrived. And the Russians across the river were happy to let them try. They knew it wouldn't work.

Suddenly Dani found herself in a war zone. With Russian forces waiting and watching just across the Vistula, Warsaw continued to be one for the next two months.

"What did you do from August to October? How did anyone survive?"

"That's when I finally got my chance to become part of the Home Army."

"You fought?"

"I was more of a human booby trap." Dani shuddered and went on, "When the fighting first started, people just stayed inside, away from windows. But then as it became more intense and the Germans began shelling buildings, we had to move into basements.

At the end we were living in sewers, nothing to eat or drink. That's when I got my 'chance.'" She almost laughed through the sobs that welled up. "I was in a basement with a unit of the Home Army. They brought me to the commander. He had been told I wanted to help. It turned out there might be something I could do and they'd share their food and water with me."

"What was it?" Rita almost didn't want to know.

"Be a whore, be their whore, service their troops. How did the officer put it? 'Build morale.' Find a corner of the basement and open a one-woman brothel!" She stopped for a moment. "I just turned and started to walk away. I wanted the food. I was dying of thirst. But I couldn't believe what he was saying. Anyway, he grabbed me and turned me around. He was smiling, and I could actually hear him say to himself something like, 'Well, it was worth a try.' Then he said, 'All right, there is something else you can do. It's much more dangerous, but it will help.' He sent me through the sewers out behind the fighting to where German units were billeted. They used me as a decoy, as bait in the ruins, to waylay German soldiers, boys on patrol, so they could kill them and take their equipment and weapons."

Rita gasped. "You were willing to do that?"

"I had no idea what I was getting into until it was too late . . . Rita, it was horrible, maybe worse than being their kept woman. I would sit out at twilight trying to look innocent enough not to be a threat, but sluttish enough to give a Wehrmacht soldier or even an entire patrol an idea. I wouldn't resist, but I would insist we go somewhere 'private.' When we did, the Home Army soldiers would quietly garotte the soldier, take his helmet, rifle, ammunition, medical kit, anything . . . and not just that. In fact, that's not what they really wanted. They'd strip the body, take the rations, the cigarettes, his watch, the money, read his letters, deface his family pictures, and sometimes if they were really drunk, they'd mutilate the body . . . I couldn't watch. The only thing that kept them from attacking me is that they needed me to continue their game."

"I don't know how you could have done it. Though at least, I suppose, you were fighting."

"Fighting? Was it fighting or was it robbery and murder? I told myself I was doing it to survive. Rita, I got a good look in the eye of every one of those German soldiers. Kids—seventeen, eighteen, twenty at the most. They'd even talk to me on the way to where I was taking them . . . tell me it would be their first time, or talk about where they were from, how scared they were. Then, just as I opened my coat and pulled them onto me, the wire would cut through their necks . . . I was killing innocents."

"How long did this go on?"

"We must have been there for five or six days. By the time the German unit began to notice their losses, there were a dozen bodies stacked up and rotting. The smell would have given us away if it hadn't been for the fact that everything smelled that way in the ruins . . . Anyway, we finally retreated back through the sewers. And that was pretty much the end."

"How did you get out?"

"Well, the Russians were on the other side of the Vistula, just watching the Germans destroy the entire city and almost everyone in it. At the end, people were moving out of the sewers toward the Vistula, driven by the fighting, the fires, thirst. The night I got to the river, the few boats were already overloaded. Once they started across, the Wehrmacht began firing flares, illuminating the whole bank. Their artillery simply sank every boat in the river. Then the Germans began firing into the crowd on the bank. That's when I got hit." Dani lifted her dirty blouse to reveal a bandaged wound around her ribs, yellowing around a fading red mark on her right side, in the flesh below the rib cage.

"Let me help you off with these clothes." Rita began unbuttoning the blouse from the back. "We'll wash them . . . or maybe burn them and find you others. How badly hurt are you?"

"The bullet was probably from a pistol. It was not big, and it went clean through my side without touching any organ, I think. Anyway, here I am, and it's healing. But when it happened, I must have lost consciousness, because when I awoke I was already bandaged and in a group of people still on the German side of the river at daybreak. It was early in October, maybe the first or second—I never knew. We decided to surrender and walked into the German lines with a white flag.

"They made us join a much longer column of people leaving the city under Wehrmacht guard. The march ended up at Pruszków railway station. People said we were going to a labor camp from there. But I knew what that really meant. There were thousands of people, all kinds—Home Army soldiers, civilians from all over Warsaw. I still had my papers and tried to show them to the sentries. But whenever I did, someone would yell out Jewess or Yid or something. Anyway, once my wound stopped bleeding, I knew I had to get away. After a few days in this assembly area, they put us on a passenger train—seats and windows, not even a cattle car. We must have had high priority for extermination. Anyway, I could tell we were headed toward Krakow and probably the extermination camp at Auschwitz. When the train had begun moving and most people were asleep, I jumped."

"With your wound?"

"I was too frightened even to notice. I didn't have a choice. Something was forcing me to try to survive, no matter what I wanted. That's how it felt. When I jumped the fall knocked me out again. It was the second time I woke up surprised to find someone taking care of me. Why are people like that, just as willing to save a stranger as kill one?" Rita thought she knew. But it wasn't the moment to explain. "This time it was a peasant woman near Tomaszów Mazowiecki." It was a large town halfway between Warsaw and Krakow. "There I was, in a bed in her house. It was more like a hut attached to a barn. She told me a Catholic priest had brought me in, calling me a hero of the Warsaw uprising. It must have been the wound in my side. She kept me fed for three days. Then her husband showed up and said I had to be a runaway Jew. Next day she made me leave. But she gave me a little food—half a loaf of bread and some shriveled apples. By that time the wound in my side was bleeding again and looked like it might have become infected."

Dani stopped for a moment. Rita handed her the only nightshirt she had. Sliding it on, Dani pulled the blankets down and slowly lowered herself onto Rita's bed. Then she took up her narrative again. "I had to get the wound treated properly. So I walked into Tomaszow and went to the hospital. I didn't say much, but when they saw it was a gunshot wound, they assumed I was Home Army and had been in the fighting in Warsaw. So I got it cleaned and properly bandaged. The antiseptic they had was excruciating. But then the questions started—what's your name, where are you from, how did you get here? After a while I could see the look on the nurses' faces: she's dangerous; get rid of her. It wasn't that I might have been a Home Army member resisting the Germans. No. I heard one say to the other, *She sounds like a Yid.*

"So I just got up and walked out. Wandered around town till I couldn't stand up. Fell asleep on a park bench. At dawn I was awoken by a German soldier poking me with his rifle. I raised my hands, showed him my *Kennkarte*. He made me follow him, but at least he stopped pointing his gun at me. We ended up at a public bathhouse where a lot of Polish women were being deloused. After that we were put on a train to Katowice, headed for forced labor in Germany.

"When we got to Katowice, I finally caught a break. They took us off the train and told us to wait in the station for another one that night that would take us to Germany. I could already hear the whisperings among the other women about me. I knew I'd have to run for it at some point. So I walked off the platform and out into the street. There, in front of me, was a soup kitchen for refugees—*Volks-Deutsche,* from the east, escaping to the Reich. There and then I became one of them. I had a good *Ausweis,* that *Kennkarte.* They were all Germans, not a Pole among them to question my looks, accent, or anything else about me. In the mob of refugees, I was safe, just another homeless German seeking shelter in the Reich. They fed us without a lot of questions. We slept in a warehouse near the station that had been requisitioned for refugees. Trouble was, I was fast asleep by the time the train I was supposed to be on left. The next morning I was interviewed, showed them my papers, and told them I had a sister in Heidelberg. They gave me a pass as far as Breslau and told me to report to the relocation office there." Dani stopped for a sip of water.

"As we got closer and closer to Germany, there were more and more document checks, three before the train even got into Breslau. I jumped off as it slowed down for the main station. The wound opened up again. I circled back to the station entrance, found another refugee soup kitchen, had a meal, and then hid myself till nightfall. I found a line of freight wagons loading a crowd of *Volks-Deutsche* for Poznan and got on with them. In Poznan I hid in the toilets. There was a moment when I looked around and saw this grimy hag staring at me. I was frightened till I realized I was looking at myself in the mirror!" Rita couldn't help smiling at the image.

"It took ten days, hiding in bombed buildings, sleeping in doss houses, spending hour after hour in washrooms, avoiding ticket barriers, identity checks, blending into refugee crowds in Cottbus, Braunschweig, Hanover . . . and finally Frankfurt. Sometimes the trains went in the wrong direction. The farther west we got, the more they had to stop while bomb damage was cleared. But finally I am here." Dani closed her eyes.

Rita was left with one question: what had Dani meant at the beginning of her narrative when she had said, "You were right . . . right about everything"?

CHAPTER THIRTY-TWO

This woman is your sister?"

Rita nodded. "Sister-in-law, actually. Wife of the brother who was taken by the Russians."

"Well, she can't stay here."

"I know, Frau L. I will find her another place *sofort*—immediately." With that the matter was closed, and the lady of the house left the kitchen.

Dani had been listening. She turned to Rita. "She asked no questions. She didn't need to see any documents. But she looked like she didn't believe you. I think she is going to turn us in."

"No. She's much more afraid of losing a decent housemaid."

"What about Herr Lempke? When he gets back, he'll recognize me, and that will be the end."

"Stop worrying. He is almost always in Berlin. We hardly ever see him. We'll get you a job before he comes back. Besides, he knows they are losing the war. Lempke is too smart to get his hands any dirtier than they are already by actually turning someone in to the Gestapo. Just you wait till he tells me he knew I was a Jew all along and was protecting me!"

∽

Mannheim was twenty kilometers away and had been bombed so badly it had become a rubble field. Few domestic servants wanted to work there. It was not hard to find Dani a place with an elderly widow whose expectations about servants were not high. The flat was small, and the maid's room was adjacent to the mistress's bedroom. It was not an arrangement that invited callers. So Rita left off going to lectures at the university on Thursday afternoons, and the two women began to explore what was left of bombed-out Mannheim. Within a month they were well acquainted with every café left standing in the town.

Twilight, December 14, 1944. A low winter sun, obstructed by little more than a few broken building walls, glinted through the taped window glass of a café and revealed every wrinkle in the yellowing wallpaper. The empty chairs cast long shadows across the chessboard tile work of the floor. Dani and Rita had been nursing cups of *Ersatzkaffee* for the better part of an hour, murmuring about the distant past and wondering aloud about the unforeseeable future.

"When you first got here, Dani, and told me what had happened, you said I had been right, right about everything. Now for weeks I have been trying to get you to explain, but you always change the subject. What was that all about? Was there something you were wrong about, something those weeks in Warsaw and your escape made you recognize or realize?"

Dani smiled. "You know, seeing the world straight doesn't make you smarter or better. It might just make you worse and more complacent about things."

"What are you talking about?"

"It's the argument you and I have been having since 1942 back in Karpatyn. You have never been willing to try to make sense of things, to figure what they mean for us, or for anyone really. To you this whole war, and everything that led up to it, along with all the tragedies that it has produced, don't add up to anything. It's just— how did you used to put it—blind variations in an environment that changes so rapidly that yesterday's survivors are tomorrow's victims. I always thought that you were wrong. Events had meaning for what came after them, people's individual choices made a difference at least for themselves, there are reasons for what happens. Well, I was wrong. There you are. That's what you were right about."

"So, what changed your mind?"

"The Germans, the Soviets, the Poles . . . August to October. I lived it. I saw how the process worked itself out. Anyone looking for a moral to the story, for the unfolding of a meaning behind the war, is going to have to conclude that history just aims at killing people, killing hope, freedom, and human progress." Dani paused and thought. "But that is so perverse a thought, you're better off concluding that history doesn't mean a thing. What's the line? It's just sound and fury."

Rita nodded, but Dani was going on. "Here's another thing you were right about. Even when something looks like it's a force for good, the way the Home Army must have looked to those hoping for Polish independence, on the inside it's just another group of creatures preyed upon by parasites. I don't mean the commanders were, or the Germans they fought, or the Russians. People aren't the parasites. It's the ideas that infect people and spread from them to others . . . and destroy each one. But not before the parasite has the chance to spread further. Ideas spread like the germs of a disease. Like the deadliest diseases, they die out because they kill their hosts before they can jump to new ones. That's what happened to so much of the Home Army, even those murdering thugs I was with, killing off Germans one by one. They weren't garotte-artists before, and if any of them survived, they aren't now. People think they are agents, really making choices . . . but we're all just victims, even those whose victims we have been."

"You seem to have my theory down better than I do." Rita smiled. "Of course it isn't really mine. Did you know Freddy Kaltenbrunner in the Karpatyn ghetto?"

"The old boy who gave you those books? No, I never met him. That was a long time ago."

"It wasn't so long ago. Everything was really hopeless then. Now it's beginning to be tempting to think we might even survive." Rita looked at Dani. "The Germans are going to lose the war. In a year or maybe less, we'll be free. What will you do?" She moved her hand onto the open palm of Dani's hand. Rita knew her own answer to this question, and she needed Dani to know her answer as well.

"Stay with you, I think. We'll find some place together, yes?"

"Dani, I want that. But first I've got to know whether my son is still alive somewhere in Poland. Until I know about Stefan for sure one way or the other, nothing else will be possible."

"So, you'll go back to Poland?" Rita nodded. Dani sighed audibly. "I am glad. I have to go back too. I was afraid you wouldn't want to. I need to know if anyone is left of my family. Maybe it'll end the nightmares." The two women fell silent. "Let's walk," said Dani.

"Right." Rita brightened, and together they left the café.

It was now dark, and the derelict streets leading from the town center were completely deserted. They began walking arm in arm, in a manner long common among European women. To Rita and Dani, it meant something different.

The evening was cold enough for snow, and soon their arms were stretched around each other's waists, pulling their bodies closer. Beneath the thin coats, their thighs moved together, and then simultaneously Rita and Dani found themselves thrusting hips against each other. It broke the somber spell that had loomed over them. They also knew they would not be together again for another week. Rita began looking around to see if there was anyone on the street behind them. Meanwhile Dani squinted into the darkness of the bombed-out buildings for a little shelter, perhaps an overhanging upper floor. Finding a relatively protected alcove with a splintered door, she pulled Rita inside. Both laughed in anticipation of pleasure, mutual embarrassment at remnants of personal modesty, and the thrill of making love in a bombed-out ruin. By the time their mouths found each other, neither woman was any longer cold, and the thin coats were unbelted and open to their exploring hands.

As she began to move her face away from Dani's, Rita thought there would not be time or space enough to give Dani what she wanted to give. The cold air, the broken gravel scraping at her knee, the fatigue of the posture Dani had to adopt to give Rita access—discomfort was apt to break through their passion and move their feelings back inside their bodies. But still Rita was going to take her lover as far as she could. Dani pulled her skirt up and loosened her underwear. She was evidently going to follow as far as Rita would lead.

Dani began to open her legs while holding herself with an arm against a collapsed wall. She could feel Rita's tongue on her labia, searching up and down. She was quickly becoming wet as Rita caressed with a tongue and probed with a finger. Then her shoe moved a stone, a piece of mortar, perhaps a loosened brick, which tumbled over a ledge and down into a pit, carrying flotsam with it that thudded with a dull report and what even seemed to the women to be an echo. Suddenly they heard a voice and then another.

"What was that?" It was a man.

Then another male voice. "Seemed to come from that direction." The light of an electric torch played across the open doorway beside them and back to the rear wall.

"Probably just a couple of alley cats."

The sound of the footfalls came closer. When the light trapped them, Rita was still rising off her knees, and Dani was balancing on one foot as she pulled her underwear up the other leg.

In the dark space of the bombed-out ruin, two darker shapes loomed. Then the voice. "You are both under arrest for public indecency," followed by the snapping of a holster clasp. It was a noise they both recognized. "*Ausweis, sofort*—immediately." Rita opened a purse while Dani withdrew her identity card from the pocket of her coat. One of the two lights continued to shine in their faces, while the other played across the documents. Then they heard one of the two men emit what sounded like a growl of satisfaction, followed by the sound of metal against metal as he pulled handcuffs from his leather coat.

Twenty minutes later Rita and Dani were still cuffed together, side by side, at Otto Schulke's desk in the Heidelberg Gestapo headquarters. He was seated facing them, leafing through a folder of onionskin sheets, carbon copies, telex messages with edges torn from the teletypewriter, scribbled case notes. And Schulke was smiling.

Neither woman had said anything. Each could feel the other trembling through the handcuffs. Strangely, the young Gestapo creature before them had said nothing either, nothing beyond the telephone call he had placed as they listened. "Herr *Sturmscharführer*, please come immediately. I have apprehended two persons committing a serious disorder, and one is implicated in crimes against the state. They are also almost certainly Jews." After a silence, he concluded, "*Heil Hitler*," and put down the receiver. Now Rita recognized him—the Gestapo officer who questioned her at the university the previous spring. How much was in his file? Suddenly she became frightened, not just for herself and Dani, but for the terrible secret she had been carrying since her escape from Karpatyn two and a half years before. The secret of the code, a secret she had finally come to know had to be true as the war unfolded, that had assured her through everything that there would be a victory worth surviving for. Could they have connected her with Erich, and him with the code? Would anything they did force her to reveal it? Was it something she could bargain away? How could saving her life be worth destroying so much? Through the handcuffs that held them together, Dani could feel Rita's trembling increase.

At one o'clock in the morning, the *Sturmscharführer* arrived, hung a hat on the hat rack, and slowly removed the obligatory leather coat to reveal a rumpled shirt, no collar attached, and a pair of nonuniform trousers held up by military suspenders. He was a man in his midforties, unshaven, with a face lined by a lifetime's experience as a policeman. He sat down at another desk. "All right, Schulke, what's this about?"

"Richtman and I caught these two in a sexually incriminating state tonight in Mannheim."

Rita and Dani could see a look of irritation spread over the older man's face. The words were forming there: This *was the reason I am called back to the office in the middle of the night, to deal with a couple of lesbians?* Before he could spit out the words, Schulke went on, "I was readying to arrest one of them anyway. Rita Trushenko, certainly an alias—anti-Nazi agitation, complicity in the July conspiracy against the *Führer*, suspicion of false identity, theft in Warsaw, flight from the *Generalgouvernement* . . . probably a Jew. The other one is certainly a Jewess, and her name surfaced in the reports on the first one—"

"Where did you get all this, Schulke?" His boss seemed impressed.

"Well, sir." He pointed at Rita. "I found the blonde at the university last spring and started tracing her back . . . all the way to Poland. She or someone who matches her description was reported in Berlin last winter for defaming the Wehrmacht. In Krakow she was employed in the same office as a blood relative of one of the July 20 *Führer*-assassination conspirators on the Army General Staff. A woman named Magda Halle. Before that, I have reason to think she may have been reported by her employer in Warsaw for theft and suspicion of communist labor agitation." Rita was staggered by the ability of the German bureaucracy to marshal such detail about a nobody while the entire nation was crumbling around it. "And that's not all, sir. She meets the description of someone the RSHA—Reich Security Main Headquarters—has been after for two years with the absolutely highest priority." Schulke read out from a flimsy. "Report immediately to *Generalmajor* Friedrich von Richter, Wehrmacht *Abwehr*, if and when apprehended."

"Very impressive, Schulke, but—"

The *Kriminalsekretär* was unable to staunch his subordinate's enthusiastic report: "Now we have found her *in flagrante delicto* with another woman. And this woman carries the identity papers of another acquaintance of the woman implicated in the attempted assassination of the *Führer*. Dani Nowiki, worked with the Halle woman, left the employ of the Reich Tax Inspectorate in Krakow without leave, now turns up here six months later with the first suspect and is her lover apparently." Schulke slapped the file of papers on the *Sturmscharführer's* desk, smiling in triumph. He had finally vindicated himself.

Now the enormity of what was about to happen became clear to Rita. They knew. It was the *Abwehr*—the intelligence department of the German General Staff—that wanted her. That could mean only one thing. Somehow the Germans had learned that she held a secret. She would never have the strength to resist interrogation and torture, to deny what Erich had told her and had warned her could cost not just her life but the Allies the war. Why had he done so? Merely to give her a reason to survive? At the risk of the Germans winning the war? She began to look around her. Was there something she could use quickly to put an end to herself? A window to jump from, the edge of a desk to strike her head on, a letter opener upright in a pencil dish she could impale herself upon? Could she hang herself in the toilet? Anything. But she was handcuffed behind the chair to Dani.

"Very good police work, Schulke. Patient, thorough, all watertight. I am sure you have finally managed to track down some serious enemies of the Reich, at least a couple of Jewesses in hiding." The *Sturmscharführer* stopped, leaned back in his chair, lit a cigarette, drew in a breath, and blew a series of smoke rings, each perfectly shaped and replaced by another as it dissipated. After an appreciative glance at the paperwork before him, he turned to his subordinate. "Now, unlock those handcuffs and let the nice young ladies go home."

"What?"

It was said with too much defiance from an *Unterstrumführer* to let it pass unnoticed. "That's an order, *Unterstrumführer*. *Sofort*— immediately. And don't ever use that tone with me, even after the surrender."

Schulke could not respond. He could do nothing but sputter.

"Yes, that's what I said . . . after the surrender . . . to the *Amis*." The *Sturmscharführer* looked at him, realizing that the stupid man just couldn't understand his situation. If he had, he would never have carried this pointless little exercise so far. "Unlock the ladies and sit down; there's a good fellow." Wordlessly, Schulke pulled a key from his waistcoat, walked around the two women's chairs, took off the handcuffs, and returned to his desk, where he slumped into the chair.

"Let me explain, *Unterstrumführer*. The *Amis* are at the Siegfried Line, a hundred kilometers from here." Calling them *Amis* made the Americans sound almost like friends. "With any luck the war will be over in a few weeks. When it's over, we'll be the lucky ones—alive, in one piece, and occupied by the Allies—not the Ivans. About the only thing you and I can do now to lose our particular war is to go around making difficulties for nice young Jewish girls." Schulke still didn't get it. "Look, when the Americans get here, people who went out of their way to give the Jews a hard time are going to pay. The people who took their property are going to come in for a beating too. But people who were just following orders—policemen, for example—well, what choice did we have? The *Amis* will understand that. Besides, they'll need us to keep things running smoothly, just like we are going to need them to eat next winter.

"If, right up to the last minute, you make it your business to ship Jews off to some extermination camp that probably won't even be working anymore when they get there, well, it won't be very easy for the *Amis* to overlook that kind of zeal. Understand, *Untersturmführer?*" He turned to Rita and Dani. "You girls just go home. In fact, I'm going to drive you home. Wouldn't do to be caught after curfew."

As the *Kriminalsekretär* drove them away from the station in a *Grosser Mercedes*, Rita couldn't suppress a swelling feeling of vindication. It was, after all, perfectly clear. The idea that Erich had inoculated her mind with, that had kept her alive for so long, had in the suddenly changed environment of the police station become fatal to her. But then she had been spared by another Darwinian struggle. The bacillus of Nazism was losing the struggle for survival against other parasites in the German mind. It wasn't kindness or scruple or opportunism she had to thank for the comfortable ride she was getting back to the Lempkes. It was something that had recently taken hold of this man's mind, something that had displaced what had been there, running his life, for the previous twelve years or so. Something different from Nazism, better in the current circumstances at exploiting his own personal desire for survival, another trait imposed on him by Mother Nature. All that, plus a certain amount of random chance. She was going to survive to be liberated.

~

Three days later, and liberation did not seem so palpable a thought after all. The *Grossdeutscher Rundfunk* was full of the great breakthrough battle in the Ardennes, on the border with Belgium. At last, the *Führer*'s masterstroke that would divide the *Amis* and the Limeys from the Bolsheviks, bring the war in the west to a standstill, and allow Germany to mass all its strength in the east. Was the complaisant *Sturmscharführer* going to change his mind and send Schulke after Rita and Dani after all?

Frau Lempke kept the radio on all day long, listening for bulletins. Rita was required to maintain a joyful countenance as she went about her work, being called hourly into the parlor to join the family in listening to news of the advance. How could this surprise have overtaken the Allies? Perhaps they didn't have the German codes after all. Perhaps someone like Rita had known and betrayed them. If so, could the Germans bring the Allies to a standstill in the west? *Perhaps*, Rita thought. But nothing could any longer stop the Soviet onslaught. After a week with no news of any German victories in the east, the same thought must have begun to occur to Frau Lempke.

One afternoon before Christmas, she turned to Rita. "What if the *Amis* stop before they reach the Reich and the Russians sweep all the way to the Rhine? What then? Have they thought about that in Berlin?"

Rita had never been asked to respond to a geopolitical question before. Silence seemed the safest response. The lack of reassurance made Frau L more loquacious. "I thought about your warning. I have purchased poison—cyanide pills—for the children." She omitted herself, though Rita knew there were enough pills for the children and their mother.

Rita felt the urge to be provocative. "Do you have enough for yourself? Can you spare one for the housemaid?"

"I have thought about it. I cannot take the easy way out. If there is any chance, the *Führer* will need more Germans. I am still young enough to have more children. So I won't be needing mine. Therefore I have an extra dose I offer you."

"Thank you." Rita added a quiet, "*Heil Hitler*."

❧

Once the Allies had rolled back the last German offensive to the Siegfried Line at the German border, Frau Lempke began thinking harder about how to cope with the coming western occupation. Barrels were procured, brought up the Schlangenweg by Rita, filled carefully by Frau L with silver, china, her Dresden figurines, crystal, and damask, then carried out to the back garden, there to be buried. Rita made it her business to misremember the exact location of each hole she dug and to scrupulously record the misinformation in Frau L's little copybook.

In late March, the day after she finished her excavations, the entire family found itself for the first time visiting Rita in the cellar. Apparently, low-level Allied air strikes had set off the air-raid alarms in Heidelberg, almost for the first time in the war. The scream of engines approached and then began to rattle windowpanes. Frau Lempke would not stand on ceremony. She brought her entire brood down for a visit to the cellar. Soon Rita was asked to go up in the kitchen so that there would be enough room for Frau L and the children in the only room without a window in the house. Rita found herself standing alone in the kitchen reflecting on the irony that, after five years of war and almost four years of German bestiality, she was about to be killed by the American Air Force. As the sound died away, she began to see what looked at first like large white snowflakes flitting through the air. Suddenly she realized they were too large for snowflakes. Some caught a tree limb, but most landed across the back garden. Yet they did not melt in the warm sun or in the wet puddles. They were handbills.

Stepping out the back door, Rita could see writing on the papers. In roman script but German language, the pieces of paper called upon civilians in Mannheim to evacuate the city or remain in bomb shelters, basements, or other protected areas. Evidently the leaflet bombers had missed their target, twenty kilometers to the west. Now the children came out of the house and, led by Flossie, began picking up the leaflets and carrying them into the kitchen to burn. Frau L stood before the door. "Did you get every last one, children?"

∽

The next afternoon Dani arrived at the back door. Rita was unsurprised to see her. "The old lady I work for has left town. She forced me to clear out before she locked up her flat. Everyone in Mannheim is getting out."

"We saw the leaflets. They dropped some here."

"There's a *Volks-Sturm*—people's storm unit—and what's left of a *Hitler Jungend* brigade defending the city. The *Bürgermeister* tried to surrender the town, but they won't allow it. There'll be street-to-street fighting in the ruins. When I left I could see civilians with rifles hiding in wait. It's going to be like Warsaw."

"You can stay here, at least for a few days. Go on downstairs. I'll deal with Frau Lempke." Just then the parlor bell rang on the kitchen wall.

Rita went upstairs and found the front door open. There was Herr Lempke, whom she had not seen more than twice since she had arrived from Krakow, carrying bags from a government *Opel* into the house. She walked down the front steps, took a valise from his hand, and brought it up to the front door. He nodded at her, and she followed him into the parlor, where he took off his hat and coat and handed them to her.

Frau Lempke was standing at the bellpull. "Ah, Rita. Bring Herr Lempke a pot of tea."

"With milk, madam?"

"If there is any."

By the time she returned with the tea, the Lempkes were in heated discussion. Rita stretched out the process of preparing, pouring, and serving the tea. She needed to hear what Lempke had to say. She also had to prepare him for the surprise of seeing the kitchen maid he had last seen in Krakow.

Lempke was talking. "No. I am not going to any Bavarian redoubt, and that's flat."

"But if Reich Minister Frank ordered you to, you have no choice."

"What do you mean, I have no choice? They can order, but they can no longer enforce their orders. They couldn't even get me through the lines out of Berlin. I had to figure my own way out, traveling with filthy refugees in hard-class carriages. It took three days to get here. Coming out of Berlin, we were strafed by Russian aircraft and bombed by the RAF every night."

"But you can't desert. They are hanging deserters on lampposts in Mannheim, not fifteen kilometers from here."

"I'm not in the Wehrmacht. They can't hang me for deserting it."

Frau Lempke stood, trembling. "But this is the time to stand with the *Führer*."

"I am sorry, my dear. I was never a fanatic." The word hung in the air between them. It seemed to Rita that Lempke had stopped just short of saying "a fanatic like you." "Now that the war is lost, we need to start thinking about how to survive. Continuing to follow orders from the Reichsministerium für Finanzen is not the way to do that."

"We cannot lose, you defeatist!" she hissed. "What about the Vengeance rockets, the secret weapons? The *Führer* will bring our enemies down with us."

He ignored this remark and continued to try to put her in touch with reality. "I brought some papers that will help the *Amis* figure out the government finances. I am going to use them to get on the right side of the occupation that is coming."

"But you are a party member, Heinrich. You swore a personal oath to the *Führer*."

Lempke grimaced. "Yes, just like all those officers who tried to kill him last July." He stopped and reconsidered. "You aren't worried the Americans will lock me up? Look, the *Amis* and the British won't have a choice. They will have to make use of all the *MussNazis*, and even some of the real ones, to keep the country running." He turned to address Rita. "You've listened to enough of this, Fräulein Trushenko. Go back to the kitchen."

Perhaps telling Lempke about Dani could wait a day.

ᴄ᷍ᴐ

But there wasn't another day to wait. The next day Rita's war was over.

PART VI

AFTERWARD

CHAPTER THIRTY-THREE

It was time to become Tadeusz Sommermann again, alas. In Spain Gil Romero had set him free. But now, here in Moscow, with the war about to end, Gil Romero was a death sentence. The only chance of reprieve was to turn himself back into Tadeusz Sommermann.

The death sentence to be passed on Gil Romero had many counts: he was a foreigner, he was a doctor, he spoke too many languages, he was an intellectual, he had opinions he could not suppress, he had been in Spain, where he was bound to have met Trotskyites or even to have been one himself. That he had violated the law against abortion, that he had taken bribes in gold, that he had lied about his identity—these were not the most serious problems he faced. His real problems were ones he shared with literally a million others in the Union of Soviet Socialist Republics. Each of them had one or more mark of cosmopolitanism likely to attract the attention of the NKVD.

That Gil had compromising information about figures in the Spanish Party might put him at risk, but he didn't think so. Enrique Lister had ended up a general in the Red Army and had long ceased feeling vulnerable enough to send Gil anything more to hide away on his behalf. In fact, the second time they had seen each other, at a dacha party in the summer of '44, Lister had looked right through him and walked past without any sign of recognition. That was fine with Gil.

But Gil was in danger. How great a danger had been made clear by his famous writer friend Ehrenberg. When they met for the last time, it was a few days after the Soviet army had crashed through the thin line of German resistance on the Vistula. Everyone in Moscow knew the Soviet pause before Warsaw in the summer of 1944 was purely tactical. Stalin had even refused the Americans and the Brits the right to land planes dropping supplies to the Home Army in Warsaw. The Germans had done his work, disposing of any hope of noncommunist Poland. All this Gil and Ehrenberg saw clearly. Now, in November, with the Home Army crushed by the Germans, there was no reason to hold back. There was every reason to push through the rest of Poland and take as many German towns and cities as possible before the western Allies got there.

"I'm going back to the front, Gil," Ehrenberg said. "Soon."

"Why? Haven't you seen enough killing?" Gil wasn't really surprised. He knew Ehrenberg enjoyed the action and the limelight, and didn't mind the discomfort and risk.

"I have been hearing things about German atrocities. I have got to find out for myself, and tell the world if it's true. I've also got to get out of Moscow. In fact, that's why I'm glad I ran into you." Ran into Gil? Ehrenberg had insisted on a meeting, and in an open park, at that. He had obviously been worried about something. There was no question of this being a casual meeting. "Gil, take my advice. Get out. I saw their terror campaign before the war. Once it's over and they feel confident again, they are going to start asking questions about educated people, tracing proletarian provenance all the way back to your grandmother's calluses. Foreigners will be suspect.

Lucky you're not a Polish Jew. The Georgian mafia really has its long knives out for them."

"But why, Ilya?"

"It's true believers, and capable ones, they fear the most. All those 'wreckers' in the '30s—the engineers, the agronomists—they were guilty only of being too ambitious for the success of the revolution. They were dangerous. It's mediocrity and thuggishness that rules here, I fear. Get out. You have a passport, right?" Gil nodded. "They never took it? Good. Use it, please."

∿

Ehrenberg was too well connected not to take seriously. By January a temporary government for Soviet-occupied Poland had been set up in Lublin. Gil realized they would need politically reliable people, real Polish nationals. Physicians with *bona fide* Polish papers would be safe and cared for.

∿

Gil was sitting in the Maternity Hospital director's office, not at the desk, but facing the director across a low table between two leather armchairs. "So, you want to have some time off, Romero? Well, you deserve it. Three years now at Number 6 with no break except for that duty in the Crimea. Hardly a picnic, eh? How much time do you want?"

"Can I be spared for two weeks?"

"Take a month, Romero. Where are you thinking of going?"

"South, perhaps back to the Crimea or Odessa. Someplace on the Black Sea with a bit of sun, fresh vegetables. Someplace far from the war zones."

"I'll have some furlough documents drawn up. You don't want to travel without authorization these days. And you won't get any rail tickets without documents."

"Very kind of you, Comrade Director." Gil rose, and they shook hands.

It would be tricky. He would be able to make it to Kiev without much trouble. After all, that was the route to the Black Sea. But then he'd have to start moving west toward the front. He would need to find exactly the right moment to bury Gil Romero and recover Tadeusz Sommermann. He could only hope that the closer he got to Poland, the more disorganized and fluid things would be. Pulling out the valise he had carried since leaving Lvov, his hand felt the seam for his Sommermann papers. Then he packed a civilian suit, his personal gear, and the sack of a dozen gold coins he'd collected—medals for services rendered to military morale. He decided to start out wearing the uniform they'd given him for duty herding the Tartars out of their homelands. It gave him the temporary military rank of major. He deserved it, after all. He'd been a major at the beginning of the war and served loyally.

Moscow to Kiev. A long ride, but at least his documents got him a seat in first class—officers' territory, with access to the restaurant carriage. The express didn't stop often, but as the train slowed through stations, he could see groups of German prisoners of war working on the roadbed or clearing ruins. It was January, but many were in the remains of summer uniforms, stuffed with old newspapers, hatless, with rags wrapped around holes in their jackboots, if they had any boots at all. One morning at Bryansk, he saw a Russian on a platform toss his cigarette butt on the tracks, and three Germans scrambled for it. The sight sent a thrill through him. *Yes*, he thought, *we've done it. We've beaten them!* The feeling was so strong, so clean, so invigorating, he had to experience it again.

Getting off the train at Kiev, Gil handed his case to a porter. It wasn't heavy, but the porter would cost almost nothing, and it did not befit an officer—a major—to carry his own luggage. He walked down the platform. On each side was a long single file of German prisoners—no officers, no noncommissioned officers, just ragged, bedraggled, unshaven, dirty, prematurely aged men with vacant eyes and chins fallen to their stoved-in chests. Gil drew a breath, expanded his chest, forced his shoulders back, and straightened his spine to give him maximum height. Then he quickened his step into a military stride and walked down the quay, every inch the victorious Soviet officer. Every few steps he raised his arm in a mock salute and announced in impeccable German, *Wir danken dem Führer*! The phrase that had echoed through the thousand-year Reich—We thank the Führer. But the disheveled, hungry, threadbare conscripts on each line were too fatigued, too dispirited, too numbed by what had already been months of retribution even to look up and take in this little indignity. Gil, however, didn't notice. He enjoyed himself right to the stairway at the end of the quay.

❧

The train had been nothing but soldiers—replacements heading toward the front, moving with high priority to the replacement depots in Lvov. There would be no chance to become a Polish civilian yet. Perhaps none when he alighted. Lvov, he was certain, was to be Ukrainian and Soviet forever. In the war it had become Lemberg; now it would be L'viv, a thoroughly Ukrainian city.

In the great hall of the railway station, he could still see the word Lemberg bleeding through the whitewash of the walls beneath the now aggressive Cyrillic lettering. He walked out onto the open square and immediately knew where he was. He looked down one avenue toward the hospital and down another toward the building where his flat had been. Lvov, Lemberg, L'viv—it was almost untouched by war. He knew with equal immediacy that he couldn't remain here, not if he was to become Tadeusz Sommermann again. He turned back to the station and began to stand in the line of officers queuing for space on the next train west, to their units, to the front and the Germans. It was early, and the desk was not manned. But the line was already long. It grew longer behind him.

Once the queue began moving forward, Gil consulted his mental map of what was once Poland but henceforth would be the Ukraine. He needed to get as far west of this new eastern border of Poland as he could. Briefly he considered a detour south and east 150 kilometers to Karpatyn. *Why?* he asked himself. Not his parents. They had been deported by the Russians and couldn't have survived in Kazakhstan or beyond the Urals. Rita? If she was alive, she was not there. And the chances she was alive were so slim, he would not allow himself to fold her into his future, even in his imagination. So, west, not south. He had to move west as far and as fast as he could. He came to the head of the line. The word "Gleiwitz" entered his head. Between the wars it was the last town in Poland or the first town in Germany, depending on whether you were a Pole or a German. It had taken a League of Nations plebiscite to decide the question. It was on the German side of town that Hitler had staged the pretext—a mock attack on a radio station by Germans dressed in Polish uniforms—that began the war.

Gil put down his identity card and travel permit.

The officer looked up at Gil's medical uniform. "Where to, Doc?"

"Gleiwitz." He tried to say it with a combination of authority and as an offhand matter of fact.

"Gleiwitz, Doc?" The officer was skeptical. "All the frontline units went through there more than a week ago. No field hospitals or evacuation hospitals there. Besides, you're not attached, according to these documents."

"It's a little delicate, sir." The man at the desk was a captain. Technically Gil outranked him. But a little respect might smooth Gil's way. So, "sir, you see . . ." He lowered his voice. "You've seen all the women in the forces, more and more of them, even at the front, drivers, clerks, little friends for the officers. Well, not all of their medical needs are the result of war wounds. You understand." The officer nodded, beginning both to be uncomfortable and to lose interest in this matter. Gil went on a little further; it was remarkable how little men wanted to know about women's complaints. "I have been asked to establish a branch of Moscow Maternity Hospital number 6 at Gleiwitz for . . . well . . ." He stopped.

The captain pulled a rubber stamp off a rack, inked it, and pressed it down on the bottom of Gil's travel document. He then picked up a pen, wrote out his authorization, and scrawled a signature. He jerked his head toward the platforms. "Next."

Some distance away, waiting on the same line, Urs Guildenstern noticed Tadeusz Sommermann get his travel orders.

&

Gil was sitting in the station officer's canteen, waiting for his train, nursing a small tumbler of vodka, when he saw Urs enter. Urs was looking straight at him. Retreat and escape was impossible, as was any pretense that they did not know each other. Urs came over, pulled out the chair opposite, and said, "May I?" while peremptorily taking a seat. He looked at Gil visibly tensing before him. "Don't worry. I bear you no malice any longer. The personal problems of three people aren't very important after six years of this war. What came between us happened a long time ago. I am not going to turn you in to the NKVD just because you are impersonating a Spanish doctor." He lit a cigarette.

Why not? Gil thought. *Mainly because you want nothing to do with the secret police yourself. Doesn't matter how innocent you are, once you put your boot on that tar slick, you can't get unstuck.* "How did you find out?"

"Rank. I'm a colonel; the transport officer is a captain." He didn't need to say more. "So, you survived the war."

"It's not over yet, Urs. We both still have a chance to become heroes."

"How did you do it, Tadeusz?"

Answering this question might be difficult. He was tempted to tell the story, to show how cleverly he had done it. But if he was going to cover his tracks, he couldn't afford to tell anyone. The story he would fabricate had to be hard to check, and it had to be plausible. "Same way you did." He looked at Urs's rank and service pin. "Medical Corps."

"Then you learned a lot of medicine they never taught us in medical school." Urs looked down at his hands, obviously contemplating the surgeries he'd done, over and over. "Where did you serve?"

Tadeusz had to improvise. "Don Army, Stalingrad Front." If he was going to cover his tracks, why not do it impressively? "It was tough. For six weeks we lived on vodka and American powdered eggs." At least that part was true. He had lived on vodka and eggs. But the six weeks in question had been passed in Moscow. "Then I helped move a lot of fascist sympathizers out of the Crimea in '44."

"We heard about that in the Medical Service. Forty thousand died of exposure and malnutrition out of about 200,000 during the move."

"Hard to work up sympathy for people who fought alongside the Nazis. There was a whole Tartar Legion fighting with the Waffen-SS."

"I don't know. They never got anything from Soviet power before the war. The way they thought about it, the enemy of my enemy is my friend, I suppose. It was the women and children, mainly, who suffered in the relocation."

This kind of talk is not going to preserve Urs's life very long in Stalin's Russia, Gil thought. "Fascists need to learn a lesson." He waited for a rejoinder. There was none. "How about your war?"

"I was on the Leningrad Front. They would have killed for powered eggs in Leningrad." He changed the subject. "I was still in Karpatyn when the Soviets took your mother and father away in '40. Were you able to trace them?" Tadeusz shook his head. It would have been dangerous and pointless too. In fact, this was the first hard news he'd ever heard about their fates.

"How about your family, Urs?" He wanted badly to ask about Rita, but wasn't going to risk provoking the cuckold.

"Everyone is gone. Murdered by the Germans. I passed through Karpatyn last month. They've set up a local information bureau. My mother was killed, and my father was sent to Belzec extermination camp pretty early. The whole ghetto was liquidated and burned. No one survived. That's what I was told, anyway." Urs wasn't going to mention Rita. "All killed. Including my boy."

"You had a child . . . with Rita?" Gil blurted out. Urs nodded. "I am very sorry about all of your loss, Urs—your parents, your son . . . Rita."

"Actually I have remarried—a Russian girl I met in Moscow— and we have a boy."

"Congratulations. So, you had confirmation that Rita died, then?"

"Nothing specific. But a woman alone, with a small child. There was no chance." Urs seemed little affected by this, though.

"You're right."

"Look, Tadeusz, we both started out from the same place, and five years later, we're both still alive and not even scratched, when everyone else from back there is dead. Do you ever wonder why? Doesn't it bother you? I can't sleep nights thinking about it."

Surviving didn't really bother Gil. And he knew perfectly well why he had survived. It hadn't been luck. It was foresight, being smart enough to always see which way the tide was running, being unconflicted enough always to seize the main chance, not scrupling the means when the end was worth it. He had deserved to survive. It would be nice to crow about it, but it also seemed the best way to tempt fate. Gil said nothing.

Urs rose. He looked down at Gil from his great height. "Oh well, I should have known better than to ask you what it all adds up to."

Gil rose, trying to lessen the distance he needed to look up. "What do you mean by that?" Every fiber of his being was straining to stop himself from saying what he really thought: *Urs, you fool, you didn't deserve to survive. If only you'd succeeded in your suicide back in '38, I would have had Rita, and she might have survived with me. Instead, she's dead, and you've come out of the great patriotic war a colonel.*

But Urs replied, "All I meant is that there's no point asking questions like these of someone who never thinks how he affects other people's lives." He looked at his watch. "My unit is headed for Katowice. I better get back to it." He turned and walked away without offering a hand or making a farewell.

Did Gil have to worry their paths might cross again? There was little he could do about the matter, so he turned his mind to other things.

 ❧

Gil wasn't the only one attracted by the geography of Gleiwitz. The town had swollen with refugees—Germans, Poles, many from the former Polish provinces now permanently annexed to the Ukraine. He had found lodgings quickly enough by wearing his uniform. The trick was how and when to stop wearing it. Pulling Tadeusz Sommermann from the bottom of a valise, where he had been for seven years, Gil registered him with the local refugee information office and gave the names of his family members when they asked whom he wanted to be reunited with. This would build up a record. If Urs was right about the extirpation of their families and acquaintances in Karpatyn, there wouldn't be anyone left to challenge a story, no matter how improbable, about survival in hiding, fighting with partisans—communist, not Home Army. Documents in hand he went to the Municipal Police to register himself, and to the local authorities to renew his Polish identity cards.

Then he—Tadeusz—set about looking for work as a doctor. This was a little more difficult, as the only documents he had from Marseille bore the forged name Gil Romero. He would have to send to Marseille for new copies with the real name. Nonetheless, the need for medical staff was too great for hospitals to stand on ceremony, and Tadeusz obviously knew what he was doing. Within days he had become a locum at two different clinics.

Almost from the first, nothing felt right to Tadeusz Sommermann. Daily he felt the need to be Guillermo Romero—for the nurses, for his patients, for their families. He needed to be the debonair, exotic romantic with the Catalan name and flair. Instead, he was Tadeusz Sommermann, a perfectly competent physician, but a Jew in *Judenrein* Poland. After six years of Nazi occupation, people were no longer proud of their feelings against Jews, but they still carried them. No matter their surprise at meeting a Jew who had survived, his Jewishness produced a chill, then disquiet about his diagnosis, prognosis, and treatment, none of which could be hidden. Orderlies brought the casual anti-Semitism of the streets into the wards. Nurses did not respond to his informality or his willingness to listen, to consult them, in the ways they had warmed to Gil Romero. Doctors would not go beyond the exchange of pertinent patient information. Tadeusz wasn't really their colleague. He was a wraith, a throwback, an oddity, a reminder of indifference, of complicity, and worse. He was someone they had to work with—because of the war, because of the Soviets, because of their guilt—but not because they wanted to. Life with Tadeusz Sommermann was not going to be easy for anyone, including Tadeusz himself.

CHAPTER THIRTY-FOUR

The morning of March 30, 1945, Rita came down the Schlangenweg onto the Neuenheimer Landstrasse, which ran along the north side of the Neckar. She was on her way to find some milk for the children. Looking up toward the bridge, she saw two loose lines of men in green uniforms, some with short khaki jackets and all with green helmets nothing like the German ones. Their walk was gangling, and they did not have the smartness or the relentless pace she associated with German soldiers. They were carrying weapons in a variety of ways—some across their shoulders, slung behind them, some even in their hands parallel to the ground. Across their waists there were a variety of pouches, pockets, and tools that seemed to move up and down as they walked. Nothing was tied down neatly, as with German infantry. She stood there and waited. Between them a small open vehicle with a flat bonnet, looking nothing like a Kubelwagen, came into view, approached her, and stopped. It had a white star in a dashed circle on its hood. At last Rita knew what she was looking at: Americans—"*Amis,*" the Germans called them, as if they were distant cousins. *Amis,* who would treat Germans better than the vengeful Brits.

She would learn to call the vehicle a jeep—it was almost her first word of English. An officer jumped out and asked, in halting German, "How far along to the next bridge?" He was her age, but grimy, unshaven, with hooded eyes, a single white bar on the front of his helmet. He held a clear celluloid map case, but no weapon besides a pistol.

"I don't know. I have never been past this point on the river. I am not a native." Suddenly she realized she was being forthcoming. Telling someone something true about herself, instead of hiding the truth.

"Can we find someone who does know?" His German was basic, without the declensions, she found herself noticing.

"Yes. Please follow me." Rita led the officer up the Schlangenweg.

"Where are you from, if not here?" he asked as they mounted the step path. The officer had not taken out a weapon.

It was then, as they trudged upward, that the realization of deliverance reached her. She turned back. Tears welled into her eyes. She threw herself on this strange American one step behind her on the steep pathway. "At last! I am free, I am released, alive. I love you." She gulped. The German words had come out unbidden.

He pulled her hands from around his neck, but he smiled. "Free, released? And already in love with me?" He had understood every word. "Were you a prisoner?" His German wasn't as limited as she thought.

"I love you because you have come. And yes, I am—I was—a prisoner." Would he understand the past tense? She turned back up the path, but now walking beside the officer. "I'm a Pole, a Jew, in Germany on false identity, working for a Nazi family."

"Is that where you are taking me? To some Nazis up this path? Should I call my platoon? Do I need a weapon?"

"I don't think so. Only watch out for the nine-year-old girl and her mother. The rest are harmless, and the husband's a tax collector, not a zealot for Hitler." They reached the back gate. Rita held it open.

As they walked into the kitchen, Rita called down to the cellar. "Dani, come up quickly." A moment later Dani was there. Instantly she understood how suddenly everything had changed.

"You are an American?" Dani said it in English. She spoke English! How could Rita have known her for so long without knowing this?

The officer addressed her. "Yes, ma'am. I'm Lieutenant Shaw." He looked to Rita inquiringly. "Her?"

"She's Jewish, like me, Lieutenant. False identity. Like me, from Poland, hiding in plain sight."

He nodded. "Maybe you can help me. Come along." Then he walked through the kitchen and into the dining room, followed by the two women.

The family was assembled and eating breakfast. All stood as they stared at the intruder. He began in German, "I am Lieutenant Shaw, 44th Division, US Army. Consider yourselves under military authority in a war zone. I will ask some questions. Any failure to provide accurate answers will be considered a violation of the regulations of the occupation authority." It sounded like a memorized script. Lieutenant Shaw turned to Dani and spoke English. "My German may not be up to this. If the answers sound wrong, you'll tell me?" She nodded. Meanwhile, Lempke had begun to study Dani's face. After a moment, a flash of recognition crossed his eyes.

Shaw began to fire questions at the Germans: about the locations of nearby bridges, German facilities. But between questions and answers, an exchange began between Lempke and his wife in rapid colloquial German. Lieutenant Shaw looked at Dani. "What was that about?"

"Sir, the wife told him not to answer, and he told her to shut up, they were at your mercy now." She smiled. Lempke now began to answer Shaw's questions in a German he could understand. After a few moments, Lieutenant Shaw turned to leave. Dani followed him out the door, and Rita rushed after them both.

Dani was speaking in English. When she saw Rita was behind her, she began to translate what she had said. "Are you just going to leave us with this Nazi family, sir? What should we do?"

"Ah, yes. Good question." He thought for a moment, then took out a piece of paper and a pencil. He switched to German. "Here is my name and unit. We are going to bivouac down the Neckar about two kilometers, between here and the bridge they told us about. There's a military police unit there too. If they give you any *flak*—that's a German word, do you know it?—just come down to my unit and ask for me. As for them"—he pointed toward the room where the family was still gathered—"I wouldn't feel any need to take orders anymore. You might even want to give some." Lieutenant Shaw turned and walked out of the house.

A moment later Herr Lempke made his way into the kitchen. "Ah, Dani. What a pleasant surprise. I am so glad to see you. I was worried from the moment you left us in Krakow."

Dani was venomous. "In Krakow you didn't know I existed. Now the war is over, and you have lost; it's too late to be solicitous."

"My dear, I knew you and Rita were Jewish girls in hiding from the start. That's why I took you in, to protect you." He turned to Rita. "Well, Rita, now the war is over, at least for us. Where will you go; what will you do? You may, of course, stay here, under the same terms, if you wish." He smiled slightly, whether at his cleverness or his generosity she couldn't say.

Rita had been waiting for this little address and now she spoke. "Thank you, Herr Lempke. I will stay, and so will Dani. But not as your servants. We are moving into one of the rooms upstairs. You and Frau Lempke will have to move two of the children out of their room and into yours. I won't be working for you any further. I will be your guest, as will be Dani. If we are not treated properly, Lieutenant Shaw of the 44th US Division will learn of it."

Frau Lempke had been listening. She was growing redder and redder, and finally burst out to her husband, "This little Jewess cannot talk to you like that, Heinrich. Call the labor office immediately. Call the Gestapo, or they'll run away." She walked over to Rita and demanded, "Go get your papers and give them to me!"

Rita looked Frau Lempke up and down. Then she raised her right hand, slapped the woman across the face, back and forth, and left the room.

As she left, Herr Lempke was remonstrating. "Dear, you don't understand. The war is lost. If we don't curry the favor of these young women, they will make life difficult for us with the occupation."

～

An hour later the two women were lying across the slightly too small children's beds in a bright room on the second floor of the villa overlooking the Neckar, smoking cigarettes from one of Herr Lempke's silver cigarette boxes. Their few possessions had already displaced the children's toys and clothes.

From the bed Rita was staring out the window at the Heidelberg castle across the Neckar, a sight she had almost never had time to contemplate from a second-story window of the villa. She turned to Dani. "You know, when I met that *Ami* officer, I said to him, 'I am free, I am released, I am alive. I love you.' What must he have thought?"

Dani smiled. "But what are we free to do? Now that we have been released, what do we do? Where do we go? What do we want now that we have our lives back?"

"The first thing you are going to do now that you're free is teach me English, Dani. I am going to need it. And you, with your English—the *Amis* are going to need you."

Dani wasn't listening. There was an overwhelming lassitude in her, a feeling of total emptiness, as if all the air had rushed out of her, leaving a complete vacuum. She barely had a will to speak. Quietly she began, "Why was I allowed to survive? There is no reason at all." She stubbed the cigarette out in an ashtray. "Rita, I can't accept that. I feel like dying, along with everyone else. Starting over, walking away from what has happened . . . I'm too tired, I don't have the will for it. What can I do?" Rita came over to her bed and held Dani for a long time.

That night as they climbed into the soft warm beds, Dani asked the question she already knew the answer to: "Will you really go back to look for Stefan? Is that for sure?" Her friend nodded. "I'll go back too, with you." At least it was something to do.

◊

Two days later, in the late afternoon, Flossie came up to the women's bedroom. "The *Ami* officer wants to speak to the woman who knows English." Dani followed her down the stairs. Lieutenant Shaw had turned up at the Lempkes' villa.

A few minutes later, Dani returned. "There was another officer with Shaw. He only spoke English. He asked me to come and work for the *Amis*. He said they will pay US dollars and give me American rations, including real coffee. I told him I'd do it if they took you too. I told him you were learning English."

"What do they want us to do?" Rita was suspicious. They both knew the use to which Wehrmacht units put local women in occupied territories.

Dani understood. "No, no. Nothing like that. It's all right. The other officer was a Christian chaplain. He said they have a facility, a club for soldiers, and they need hostesses who can give information, serve snacks—not drink, Rita!—and maybe help them not feel lonely." Another grimace from Rita. "No, he promised, it's not like that."

"Real coffee?" Rita had already accepted in her mind. "When does he want us to start?"

Dani switched to English, and Rita tried to follow, "Tomorrow, at the train station café in town."

～

Fitted with rather snug but clean khaki officers' jackets and forage caps, both sporting the insignia USO, Dani and Rita began working at the counter of an enlisted men's club across from the Heidelberg railway station the next day. A Negro cook, the very first black man either had ever seen, taught them how to deep-fry doughnuts and how to make coffee the way American soldiers liked it—definitely an acquired taste for two women who had not had a cup of espresso for five years.

American soldiers were completely unlike German ones. Not nearly as formal or polite, far friendlier, and much more willing to share candy bars, cigarettes, chewing gum, cans of Spam, rolls of toilet paper, bags of cotton balls, without any expectation of a *quid pro quo*. They didn't always stand when an officer entered, or even always salute. One told Rita it was completely unnecessary when not wearing a hat. Their uniforms differed from one to another, and they sometimes didn't stay in uniform. Shoes were unshined, ties askew when worn at all. These soldiers treated the USO club as a refuge from the war and from their officers, who rarely ventured in. They wanted to dance when the radio played a big-band tune. But it was not the sort of dancing Dani and Rita had ever learned or even seen in films. The women tried to jitterbug, but at first it made them dizzy, and the steps were too complex and too athletic. The soldiers tried to teach the steps slowly, even demonstrating with one another. It might have worked if the chaplain—the only officer Dani and Rita ever saw much of—had not discouraged the practice.

Another thing the chaplain discouraged was the vernacular English they were rapidly learning from the troops. Dani had begun assiduously teaching Rita English. But her grasp of American slang was weak, while her knowledge of Army abbreviations and acronyms was understandably nonexistent. These they both learned at the same pace, along with oaths, curses, and obscenities, which they began to use in exactly the way the enlisted men of the 44th Division did, but without the benefit of knowing what the words meant.

One morning, upon hearing their language the chaplain asked, "Ladies, do you know what SNAFU and FUBAR mean?"

"Yes, captain," Dani volunteered. "One means when something has gone wrong; the other means broken, not working, screwed up."

"Screwed up? Who taught you that word?" He frowned and left the club.

∾

In early May, when the Nazis finally capitulated to the western Allies and to the Soviets, Dani and Rita were still living at the Lempkes'. The lady of the house had not reconciled to the new order. But Herr Lempke had continued to cultivate the fiction that he had been protecting the two women since their earliest days in Krakow.

A day after the capitulation, Lempke came into the parlor in the evening and announced to the two women, "I have just learned that Magda Halle is still alive."

"What happened to her?" They had not dared to ask, but the surprise in Lempke's tone prompted their curiosity.

"Well, they came to arrest her soon after the July 20 plot against Hitler. Seems her cousin was part of the Wehrmacht staff unit that tried it, and they were rounding up anyone with links to them."

"But she worked with you for two years. Why didn't they arrest you too?"

"Oh, they came back and questioned me after they took her. They seemed to think she was providing *Ausweise* for fugitives right under our . . . under their noses. She was sent to Buchenwald, but she has survived." He smiled.

"But you didn't know anything about that either, yes?" Dani was sarcastic.

"I'm glad she never told me about the plot or the papers she got for people in hiding. It would have been dangerous for me to know about it." Lempke had for some time been convincing himself that he was just an innocent bystander for the twelve years of the *Dritte Reich*. "We certainly did not know anything about the atrocities committed by . . . others. Rita, Dani, you know we never so much as saw a uniform in the Krakow office, let alone Gestapo or SS."

He withdrew a piece of paper from the inside pocket of his gray double-breasted suit coat, unfolded it, and took out a fountain pen, whose cap he screwed off. "Rita, I have prepared a statement I would be grateful if you would sign."

"Oh yes? Please read it." Rita sounded polite.

"'This is to affirm that I, Margarita Trushenko, was employed first in Krakow, as housekeeper to the Office of the Tax Inspectorate, and then in Heidelberg, Germany, as housemaid in the home of Heinrich Lempke from February 1943 to March 1945. During this time I was paid the prevailing wage, provided with room and board, treated correctly, respectfully, and my identity as a Jew and an opponent of the German Reich was protected by Herr Lempke.'"

"I regret that I cannot sign this statement, *Mein Herr*. To begin with, that is not my name. I am Rita Feuerstahl."

∾

"Hey, Rita, Chaplain wants to see you and Dani over in his office right away." It was the chaplain's clerk-typist, standing at the door of the USO. "Say, got a doughnut you can spare?"

They straightened their uniforms, gave the corporal a doughnut, and followed him out of the canteen.

"Ladies." He spoke only in English, hoping they would understand. "I have found much more suitable and much more important work for both of you. We are dealing with a flood of refugees moving across Europe now that the war is over. The US government has set up an office to manage reunification of families, food and shelter for former slave-labor victims, concentration camp inmates, everyone who suffered under the Nazis. Anyway, they need people who speak the languages, who will be trusted by victims, and who understand what they have gone through. It's an important job, and all over Germany, the chaplain corps are looking for people who can do it. I think you two would be perfect. So, if you want, I'll cut orders to get you up to Frankfurt to join this project. It's called UNRRA—United Nations Relief and Rehabilitation Agency." He looked from Dani to Rita. "What do you think?"

CHAPTER THIRTY-FIVE

Within a week Dani and Rita were in Frankfurt, out of USO fatigues. Instead, there were UNRRA uniforms. They were nice, but Rita and Dani wore them only rarely. It was important to dress like a civilian in the work they now began to do. Refugees were allergic to uniforms.

With German, Polish, some Russian, more Yiddish, and newly acquired English at their disposal, both were almost immediately put to work in the Tracing Office, the information desk dealing with inquiries from across Germany about family reunification. The officer in charge, a burly Canadian, Major Thompson, told them they were the first European women they had been able to find suitable for this work. Suitable, Rita and Dani eventually decided, meant nothing more than that they were not so victimized by the war that the work would overwhelm them.

The Tracing Office was the epicenter of almost every town in the former Reich. Every DP—displaced persons—camp in central Europe had one too. In the first weeks after the Nazi surrender, camps operated by UNRRA were swamped with former slave laborers. In Frankfurt many were from Speer's underground rocket-works in the Harz Mountains. Though skeletal, these people were stronger than survivors from concentration and extermination camps.

Rita and Dani were assigned to Salzheim, a camp near Frankfurt-Hochst, a western suburb. The buildings were not much better than German prison barracks, but there was food, shelter, clothing, and medical attention. Arriving refugees had more urgent wants, however. They came with names—dozens, scores, and sometimes a hundred names of family members, people about whom they sought information. Their information had to be distributed to every part of occupied Germany. The resulting lists were constantly updated and exchanged, continually consulted, checked, rechecked, corrected, and cross-indexed. Even as they added to their lists, Rita and Dani became so familiar with them they could produce names from memory.

Many of the refugees were *Osties—Ostarbeiter*, forced into the factories, construction works, synthetic oil plants, and armaments factories of Krupp, Thyseen, and I. G. Farben. They were Ukrainians, Russians—Soviets who had served the Germans willingly enough when they were winning and now were fearful about the prospects of repatriation to the east. There were even *Volks-Deutsche* from the Baltic countries—Latvia, Lithuania, Estonia—taken into Soviet citizenship at the beginning of the war by Stalin with Hitler's compliance, then "liberated" by the Nazis, and at last evacuated by their German governors as the Russians moved west. And, of course, there were the Jews, from the extermination camps, from slave labor, from hiding all over Germany and Poland.

The first thing Rita noticed about Jewish refugees, especially about the younger ones, was their self-identification. They were Polish, Lithuanian, Yugoslavian, Rumanian, Hungarian, even Austrian—a citizenship that had not existed since 1938. But rarely would they admit to being Jewish. Until, that is, she let it be known she was Jewish herself. Then everything would change: demeanor would become more animated and demands more aggressive. And they would begin talking about their experiences. They had to tell her, and she had to listen. And for the same reason. She was the first apparently unscarred, healthy, visibly normal Jew they had met.

For all her personal terror of the ghetto, slave labor, false identity, and extortionists, Rita soon realized that compared to almost everyone in these camps, her war had been . . . what? How to describe it? She kept searching for the right word. She had no right to compare it to theirs. Mostly it had been a harrowing ordeal, but not much more than that. It had been punctuated by terror, fraught with risk, and included periods of harsh deprivation and much personal loss. But most of these people had experienced all this along with years of unremitting torture, bestial sadism, dehumanizing degradation, obligatory self-abnegation, starvation, epidemic sickness, the ever-present extermination machine . . . Rita had been confronted with it only intermittently—in the ghettos of Karpatyn and Warsaw. These were glimpses of their reality. What the survivors of the camps had lived through would have been more than enough to have made her throw herself against an electrified fence, cross over a trip wire into a killing zone, provoke a guard into killing her quickly. There was no particular value to surviving such a life. She knew it beyond the shadow of a doubt.

Rita's work settled into days of standing at a counter, responding to requests from DPs, filling out records of new arrivals, updating lists, and collating information. Sometimes she would have to make her way through the camp to deliver news—more often bad than good—to a resident. Walking along the muddy lanes between rough one-story pine shacks with tarpaper roofs, communal kitchens, and rather foul-smelling latrines, Rita would have to remind herself of the conditions their occupants had only lately known. She was continually surprised when people smiled and waved. She would find young children amusing themselves with makeshift toys, or pass groups of older children gathered around someone teaching. Women were already tending garden allotments. There were people continually moving into and out of the camp. Surely they would become restless and dissatisfied. *But not yet*, she thought, *not yet*.

Late in June, a still emaciated young man arrived at Rita's desk for registration.

"Name, please, and place of origin." Her words were automatic.

"Kurtzbaum, Moritz, Gorlice, Poland."

Rita reeled. This was her home, and this was a name she vaguely knew. She looked up but was unable to place the face. Never mind, it had been nine years since Rita had married and left the town, nine years during which a child could grow to adulthood and an adult could become a ghost, an apparition before her. She put down her pen. "Did you know the Feuerstahl family?"

"Of course." He brightened at the question. "When I was little, they lived across the street. That was before the war. Once the ghetto was established, we were in the same house with them." He stopped, then went on in a darker tone. "We were taken in the same *Aktion*."

Rita didn't know what to do first—identify herself or ask the question she dreaded an answer to: what about Stefan? Was he with them? *Go slowly*, she said to herself. *Establish the provenance of your question so he will have a reason to remember something he should want to forget.* "My name is Feuerstahl, Rita. I am their daughter."

"I'm sorry. I don't remember you."

Rita was not listening. Her eyes were burning into his. "Now this is very important. Was there a baby, a child about two years old or so, with my parents when you were taken?"

"No. It was just the two old folks and my family."

"Are you sure? Really certain?"

The young man became grave. "It was the worst moment of my life. I can tell you every detail." His voice rose. "There was no child!"

Rita wanted to exult. But she couldn't. "Sorry. Let's get back to you . . ." She picked up her pen.

"Was it your child?" His anger had been replaced by sympathy. She nodded. "You should be glad then. We were all loaded onto cattle wagons for Auschwitz directly from the *Aktion*. I'm sorry, but your parents were selected immediately."

Suddenly Rita had the image. She would not allow herself to dwell on it for a moment. Not now. Perhaps later. "And you? What happened to you?"

"I was sixteen. They took my parents and my younger sister. They put me on the fire brigade for Canada—that's what we called the storage depot in Birkenau where they kept all the stuff they took off the people they gassed. Then they moved me around to some of the other camps. Then I was a cook for a while. That saved my life . . ." He looked down at his hands, all bones and protruding veins. "Fattened me up." He laughed. "Then we marched for months back to Germany last winter."

"So, anyone to trace?"

"I had some cousins in Nowy Sacz."

❧

"I'm going back to Poland as soon as I can." It was the first thing Rita said to Dani that evening. Working at separate desks in different barracks, they had not seen each other all day. Before Dani could ask, she explained what she had learned. "There is a chance, you see? He may still be alive somewhere."

Dani did not even pause to digest the news. She pulled a battered suitcase out from beneath her cot and unbelted it.

∾

"Don't do it, Rita." Thompson, the camp administrator, was considering the matter the next morning. "No passports, and anyway, the borders are closed between Germany and Czechoslovakia. No idea what the situation is at the Czech-Polish border. I'd wait till things get normalized more. Besides, we need you here."

Both women shook their heads. Dani spoke. "The longer we wait, the colder the trail gets."

"We? Are you both going?"

"I never found out exactly what happened to my parents or . . . my brother." Dani didn't have a brother. Rita supposed the lie was just something Dani had contrived to add to her urgency.

"Look, I'll rough out some official-looking documents—authorizations, identities—on official letterhead. At least I can get you accommodation in Munich and Regensburg and travel authority for the railways. You'll have to go through Regensburg to slip into Czechoslovakia. It's the shortest path to Poland. I'll give you the name of someone who can help on the Czech side."

"How do you know anyone?" Rita was surprised at the offer and the local knowledge.

"Some of the Canadians have been helping refugees make their way to Palestine through Czecho'. I'll trust you not to mention anything to the Brits."

∾

Karlsruhe, Stuttgart, Augsburg, Munich—every station was seething with the flotsam of European humanity, climbing over one another on platforms, sleeping rough or waiting wordlessly for space on the roof of a train. Like so many ant colonies sending out and receiving foraging parties, from each station packed lines of refugees fanned out and funneled in. At each there was a UNRRA desk ready to help Dani and Rita, who pulled such rank as the uniforms they now wore could provide. At Regensburg they showed Major Thompson's counterpart his letter of authorization. When the officer saw the name, he brightened.

"We need to get across the Czech border. Can you help?"

"Not too many people going that way, ladies. Most of the traffic is moving the other way, into the American zone. It's not just Czechs, either. Mainly Poles, Ukrainians, Bulgarians, Romanians. A lot of them don't seem to make it across at all. Passport checks by the Soviet frontier guards. Where are you headed?"

"Katowice, in Poland, Major."

"I hope you're planning on a one-way journey, ladies." The women were silent, so the officer continued, "Look, are you girls Jewish? Because if you are, there are people in Prague who can help. There's an office there set up by the Joint."

Rita and Dani asked the one-word question simultaneously: "Joint?"

"The old American JDC. They're supporting surviving Jews and trying to move those who want to go to Palestine." But JDC meant nothing more to Rita or Dani than the word "Joint." He tried again. "JDC—Joint Distribution Committee. Don't know why it's called 'Joint,' but they probably have field agents in Poland too. Here's their address in Prague. Now let's see about a truck to Elsarn; that's the last town this side of the Czech border."

❧

At midnight they were following a farmer down a dry two-track lane through rising summer wheat, pale in the half moon. The track wound into a copse of trees, and then they found themselves creeping through the knee-high stalks in a newly cultivated field until they reached the first trees of what was a thick woods.

Following the farmer they clambered over a wall made from five hundred years of stones laboriously dislodged and moved to the edge of the field. He stopped. "You're in Czecho now. There's your path into Zelezna. You'll have to hitch a ride into Smolov, but there are lots of farmers that'll take a couple of girls like you." He held out his hand for payment. Dani reached into her haversack and handed him a carton of Camel cigarettes. Best currency there was in circulation.

◦◦

Prague was far beyond the writ of the UNRRA. It had been occupied by Russian forces, though most of the units were already preparing to pull back to Poland. But the Joint—the JDC—was clearly visible in the main waiting room of Prague Central Station. The desk could have been mistaken for a UNRRA operation: lines of inquirers, Joint workers passing among them, others behind the desk collating lists, checking for names, organizing housing, transport, documents. Rita and Dani held back. They knew from experience that these workers wouldn't give any priority to a couple of well-fed, healthy-looking, cleanly clothed women.

When the woman at the desk finally had a moment, she spoke. "We can put you up for a day, girls. It will be cramped. Tickets to Brno are possible, but you probably won't have any seats. From there anywhere in Poland won't be too hard to reach. There are even seats going there." She looked at Rita. "Are you really Jewish?"

"Yes, why do you ask?"

"You both look pretty healthy." She looked at Rita. "But it's the Bavarian peasant braids pinned up the side of your head, I guess. Probably saved your life. With your German it was a great disguise."

Then she confided what she'd really been thinking. "Not a very popular look these days in Prague."

Getting to Katowice was as easy as expected. The Joint office in the train station was not hard to find either. Now they were supplicants, like a thousand others on line, and they waited their turns. Finally Rita found herself standing at the counter. Her form was in her hand, filled out: maiden name, Feuerstahl, married name, Guildenstern—it had been five years since she had written it or even thought of herself as Guildenstern. No need for Trushenko on the form at all. How strange. Birthplace: Gorlice, Last Polish residence: Karpatyn. She pushed the form across the counter, and now suddenly she knew how the others had felt, many hundreds, perhaps even a few thousand people, who had stood expectantly across from her in the Frankfurt UNRRA office. They would watch as she moved a finger or a pencil down one list after another, moving from clipboard to clipboard, looking up occasionally to see a face hoping against hope. Nine times out of ten, she would disappoint them with, "Sorry, no one by that name on our lists." Now it was her turn to feel the emptiness of being a castaway, a sole survivor, tossed by the currents in a sea of hollowed-out faces washing up at tracing desks all over Europe. The woman behind the desk had a "United Kingdom" shoulder flash on her sleeve. "You speak English?" Rita nodded but drew Dani forward. "We've been working for the UNRRA for three months."

"Sorry. Nothing under Feuerstahl. Very unusual name. Let's see about Guildenstern. Another uncommon name. Makes things easier." The woman went back to her first list. She smiled and looked at Rita with a rare look of pleasure. "Well, this is unusual." She didn't appear to recognize the conflicted look that began crossing

Rita's face as she conveyed the information. "Guildenstern, Urs, Karpatyn, Colonel, Medical Corps, Northern Army Group, Soviet Forces, stationed Third Evacuation Hospital." And now her voice rose so that coworkers and supplicants on line turned their heads. "Current location: Katowice, Poland. You're practically on top of him. Your husband?"

Rita nodded. The woman lowered her voice. "But this is strange. The file says 'seeks information about parents presumed dead' . . . but nothing about 'spouse.' I am going to check the files in the cross-index." She turned away from the desk and moved toward a back room. A few minutes later, she returned to the desk, frowning. Rita had remained mute the entire time. "Coincidence. Can't be who you are looking for. Or else it's a cock-up in the files. We've an entry back there for a Guildenstern that lists a wife, Karla, citizenship USSR, child, Saul, born Moscow, 1944." She looked up at Rita, ready to ask more questions. The woman stopped when she saw the look in Rita's face. It was literally a blank. Rita stood her ground, mulling over the information, testing out the emotions it elicited in her, inwardly standing back and observing how the news sat with her. Then she moved back from the desk a few paces, still thinking things through.

Now it was Dani's, or rather Dani Cohen's turn. The Karpatyn lists were still in the Joint officer's hands. "Let's see, lots of Cohens here. Michael and Deena? Both taken to Belzec. But then we also have a Michael Cohen, from Karpatyn, registered at the 'Joint' field station in Rzeszow, daughter Dani. Is that you?"

"Could be my father. Must be my father! Rzeszow—where is that, please?" Dani asked anxiously.

"It's the last town in Poland before you get to Lvov, L'viv now, on the other side of the Soviet border. There were a lot of Home Army forces fighting there, first against the Germans, then against the Russians. Shall we send word, or do you want to go? Getting there would be pretty tricky for a woman."

"Why?"

"A lot of Soviet soldiers between here and there. They haven't seen a woman looking like you in a few years, and their officers aren't much interested in discipline anymore. Probably not much sympathy for Polish Jews among the local peasants. And no direct rail service yet. I'd stay here, and we can send word. If it's your father, we can probably get him transport here."

Dani gulped. "Yes, please. Right away."

"Where are you two staying?" the woman asked, looking at their information forms.

"We just arrived from Prague," Rita said. "We were working in the Frankfurt UNRRA office"—Rita looked around—"doing this."

"I guess you better stay with the Joint staff. We have a billet across the street from the station."

"Thanks. One more thing." Rita bit a lip and continued, "I'd better look up this Colonel Guildenstern. He's probably a relative of my husband's."

She looked back at Rita and down to her clipboard. "Third Soviet Evacuation Hospital, center of town. I'll get someone to take you."

◦⌇

Rita had to wait twenty minutes or so while they tracked down Lieutenant Colonel Guildenstern. It gave her time to go over several different conversations. Most of all she wanted to avoid falseness in the initial exchange. She wondered whether there was any chance the tone of the meeting could be businesslike. After all, they were adults, and neither should have to explain himself or herself to the other. Yet the prospect was fraught with potential for recrimination, she knew. Her complaints would be obvious. But so would his, especially when it came to Stefan. And he would be right, she thought. Her action had sacrificed their child.

Standing at the flaps of the large field tent—lend-lease and marked with the now familiar white star in a broken circle of the US Army—where the evacuation hospital's administrative unit was housed, she saw him at a distance, still too tall and too thin, picking his way awkwardly through the muddied truck ruts, slipping and grabbing hold of parked vehicles, taking salutes with a slightly flustered motion of a right hand to his cap. It was clear that three and a half years had not produced a military officer. *So much the better*, she thought. He climbed with some relief onto the duckboard five meters from the tent, pulled his tunic down below his Sam Browne belt, and pulled off his forage cap. Seeing Rita, he could not help breaking into a smile. Her immobile face quickly melted his smile away. He came in, and they took two seats at a desk, facing each other in the shadow of the ill-lit tent.

She spoke first. "Almost four years."

"Three years, eleven months, three weeks, and one day."

Had he just made the calculation, or had he been keeping count all this time? She knew the answer.

CHAPTER THIRTY-SIX

So, you survived," he stated.

Was this observation a reflection of his surprise, disappointment, or just the potential for complication he now faced?

All she could say without showing anger was, "As you can see."

"I had no idea . . . how?"

"Blind luck, inefficiency, indifference, and a little help from people who had no reason to help. Never mind. I am here." She remembered how glad she had been to be rid of him there on that platform in Karpatyn that day in late June 1941. It would be the very falseness she wanted most to avoid were she to now recriminate him for desertion. Yet the temptation briefly overcame her. "Were you really so sure I hadn't survived, or weren't you very interested in whether I had?"

"What do you mean, Rita? That's very hard."

"Your inquiry sheet at the Joint office . . . it was just your parents' fate you were interested in, not mine, not even Stefan's. And unless their records are wrong, you have married some woman in Russia and had a child. All that without much of an inquiry about whether your wife or child were still living . . . that's what I mean." It was all exactly what she had promised herself she wouldn't do. Rita raised both her hands. She was about to apologize and try starting over when Urs's unemotional demeanor broke down completely.

"How dare you say such things to me. You who traduced me before the war and sent my child away so that you could survive during the war."

That she was guilty of adultery did not trouble her, but the apparent obviousness of her guilt in Stefan's death overwhelmed her. Rita began to sob.

This Urs hadn't intended either. He handed her a handkerchief.

She took it for a conciliatory gesture and began to explain. "It wasn't like that. Gorlice was not ghettoized, people were not suffering, there was food, no *Aktions*. No transports to the extermination camps. All that was happening in Karpatyn. I thought he'd be safe."

"I understand." He seemed sincere.

"But Urs, he never got to Gorlice. Stefan was taken by a woman, a courier for the Home Army. When my parents were sent to Auschwitz, there was no baby with them. I was told by someone who was with my parents when they were taken and who somehow survived the camp."

"Stefan couldn't have lived, Rita." Urs was moved by her explanation but unwilling to accept even the possibility that Stefan had somehow survived.

"I don't know. But that's why I came back, to try to find him. I looked for him in the Warsaw ghetto just before the uprising there. They had no record. Who knows? He might be in a convent or with Polish people somewhere."

"No." Urs was shaking his head.

"What do you mean, no?"

"The new government at Lublin has secured lists from all the churches, the convents and the Catholic orphanages, underground organizations, tax registries, of the names of children kept or hidden during the war. They are to be returned to their parents if still living.

There is no child of the name Stefan Guildenstern on any of these lists. Since I got here, I've been kept informed regularly of additions to the register."

Rita sighed. "I see. Well, congratulations on your marriage. I don't think we need to go through a divorce. Our marriage was dissolved by the war. I will never make any claim based on it." What she really thought was that the marriage was dissolved long before that, but there was no point in being provocative. "Urs, your child has every moral right to legitimacy. Don't give our past together another thought."

"That is very generous. Still, I'd like to explain." Rita shook her head as if to say, no need, but he continued. "Karla is a girl I met in Moscow in '43, after we heard that the Karpatyn ghetto had been . . . liquidated and everyone sent to Belzec. Anyway, she became pregnant, and I had to marry her. She was willing to have an abortion, but it was illegal."

"Illegal?" Rita observed. "But you could have done it without risk, no?"

"No, I wouldn't, I couldn't. I won't break the law or the Hippocratic oath. I was never built like your—" He sought the right word: *friend, lover, partner in adultery*? Finally he just settled on the name. "Like Gil Romero."

"What do you mean?"

"He spent most of the war in Moscow performing abortions for hard currency and gold." The contempt was evident.

"How do you know?"

"My wife gave birth to our son in Moscow Maternity Hospital Number 6. Romero had been working there for two years when she was admitted. He was away when my wife delivered. But everyone in the hospital, at least all the doctors, knew he was performing abortions for hard currency."

"He wasn't caught?"

"No one understood why he wasn't. So many people knew, somebody must have talked to NKVD or even just the Moscow militia police. It wouldn't have been safe to know a thing like that without telling the authorities. He must have had important protection. That is what the doctors thought."

"Is he still there?" Rita surprised herself by voicing the question.

"Don't you know?" She looked at him blankly. "He's probably not forty kilometers down the road from here. In Gliewitz. I saw him a month ago in Kiev, and that's where he was headed."

∾

That night, without finding Dani at the Joint offices, Rita left for the east. She had to be as sure as she could that there was no trace of Stefan before thinking about the rest of her life. She spent an hour between trains at Krakow, wandering through the old university section again. But all her memories of the '30s were now obliterated. The war, the German occupation, the ghettos, the drudgery of Lempke's offices, the constant threat to her and to Dani—her lover, her partner *contra mundum*—these were what she remembered now. Not her life before the war.

She started in Nowy Sacz, where there was a tracing office. She lodged the standard inquiry form about her parents and Stefan. As expected, parents transported to Auschwitz in 1942. No record of a child taken at the same time. The Germans had been methodical. The records were probably complete.

On the third day out of Katowice, Rita was walking the streets of her birthplace. Gorlice was a town already rebuilding itself, as if after a whirlwind. There were new sheds—not really houses—now rising on the burned-out street where her family's home had been located. But along the street where she had grown up, there was not a name or face she could recognize. Those houses she could recognize were occupied by new residents.

Rita presented herself at the local constabulary. It was obvious that no one was much interested in the recent past or immediate future of Jews formerly living in Gorlice. The sole officer on duty was preoccupied or indifferent to everything except the cigarettes he was rolling, one after another, almost perfectly.

"Sorry, miss, all inquires have to be made in Nowy Sacz, local district seat." The policeman turned back to cigarette papers and loose tobacco.

"Can you tell me anything about the Home Army hereabouts?"

That got the man's attention, and not in the way she had hoped. "Excuse me, comrade." He was looking right through her. "We know nothing about terrorist fascist organizations here. This is a police station. You want to go to State Security. That's Nowy Sacz too."

"Terrorism? I don't understand." Rita stood her ground. "I need to find out about a woman courier for the Home Army who operated in this area in 1942." Then she added, "This woman couldn't have been a fascist; she was fighting the Nazis."

"Home Army, terrorist organization, miss. Still out there in the hills, fighting the legitimate government. I advise you not to ask further, or I may have to inform the security organs about this inquiry."

"I'm sorry. I have been out of the country for many years. Can you just explain about the Home Army being a fascist terrorist organization?"

Looking at Rita now, the officer turned avuncular. "Well, my dear, all I know is that last winter they attacked the provisional government's prison at the Castle in Rzeszow, trying to rescue Home Army thugs arrested for resisting our Soviet allies. The scum were caught, and they're in prison now. Enough said." Rzeszow, she recalled, was the town they had been told Dani's father was to be found in.

"Thank you, sir."

"Piece of advice, sister. You're such a pretty girl. I don't want to see you in the slammer. Don't make a lot of inquiries in Nowy Sacz. Jews, Home Army . . . well, the state organs of security don't welcome questions about them."

Back to the tracing desk in Nowy Sacz, the district capital. The middle-aged Polish woman behind the desk had nothing new for Rita. She had not expected anything. "I have one more question. Is there a convent, orphanage, or children's home here in Nowy Sacz or in the district?"

"No. Unfortunately." The woman, evidently a devout Catholic, launched into a historical lecture. "Not enough wealthy Catholic families to support a convent. Just the Dominican sisters' school. All closed now. Never were enough unmarriageable girls to need a convent. A lot of the money hereabouts was Jewish, and most of the Christians were Ukrainian. The few girls who had a calling went to Krakow . . ."

Rita was not listening anymore. Suddenly she wanted to be cured of the need to seek out Stefan. After the last three years, she finally had no emotional energy left for further struggle, danger, disappointment. He was dead and that was that, she told herself with finality, and began to search around in her thoughts for ways of making the conclusion stick.

No more Urs, no more Stefan. Just Dani. The three thoughts repeated themselves in a sequence whose rhythm matched the clicking of the wheels as they slid over the gaps in the rails. The train carrying her west, back to Katowice, was much fuller. Everywhere it was the same, the asymmetry of many going west and few going east. Everyone understood why. Rita hurried out of Katowice station eager to find Dani and tell her that she had finished trying to resurrect the dead and was ready to get on with their life together.

She arrived in the dormitory room of the Joint residence where they had been provided with beds. There at the back, sitting on her bed, she saw Dani facing two others—men sitting on the opposite bed. The older was a burly figure, with graying curly hair above a well-lined and leathery face. Despite age, the man was strong, his shirtsleeves taut around arm muscles. There was a younger man next to him, tanned, fit, darkly attractive, almost handsome. As Rita approached, Dani said in a voice loud enough for Rita to hear, "There she is now." She stood up from the bed. "Rita, this is my father, Michael . . ." She paused, obviously flustered. "And my fiancé, Paul Bernays." As she said the words, she reached out for Rita's right hand and squeezed it very hard. Rita recognized the meaning of the gesture, but she was reeling from the news.

She forced a smile. "But, Dani, you never told me you were engaged. In all these months and years . . ." Rita had no idea how to continue, what to say, where to steer the conversation now.

The young man decided to help. "Yes, well, she had no reason to think either of us were still alive. Tell her how we managed it, Michael."

Neither man appeared to notice Rita's distress. The older man cleared his throat. "It was the last roll call Leideritz ordered in the Karpatyn ghetto. I wouldn't be separated from Eve."

Dani volunteered, "My mother."

"Paul and I were able to escape out of one of the last Belzec cattle cars. One guy in the car had somehow gotten bolt cutters past the guards. He cut the lock on the sliding door as the train slowed for a bend. Twenty of us jumped and ran for it. They stopped the train to try to round us up, but the guy with the bolt cutters knew where he was going in those woods. We followed him. We traveled at night for a week or so to the Pripet Marshes north of Belzec. Impenetrable to German trucks or tanks, and full of partisans."

The shock of Dani's fiancé was now replaced by Rita's realization of who it was this man was talking about. "The man with the bolt cutters, who led you to the Pripet Marshes and the partisans. Did you ever learn his name?"

"Oh yeah. We lived with him for another year. Strange bird. People respected him, but no one got close. Or at least no decent person. His name was Erich Klein. He was a *feygele,* a queer, a nancy boy."

Paul added, "One tough guy, but a homo. Lived with another guy in a bunker for almost the entire time we were together."

"What happened to him?" Rita demanded to know, looking from each of the men to the other.

Paul volunteered. "He was killed in a fight with the Wehrmacht. Probably killed, along with his . . . buddy. No one was willing to go out for their bodies after the firefight. So we can't be absolutely sure. There were some pretty violent Russians among the partisans with us. They didn't like *golubye*—queers—any more than we did, and they didn't mind acting on their likes and dislikes. So he might even have got it in the back during that skirmish."

Michael Cohen now interrupted, asking with a hint of suspicion, "Did you know him?"

Rita was not going to dissimulate for a moment. "Yes. We were close friends in Karpatyn. In fact, he rented a room from me, and then we shared space in the ghetto. He saved my life. He was a wonderful *man*."

Neither man knew how to respond to this proud assertion. Michael finally said, "Well, I am sorry if he was a friend of yours, but he was a degenerate . . ."

Rita was too tired and too bitter to deal with this attitude. She simply rose and walked out of the room. Out on the street, she was stopping to light a cigarette when Dani caught up with her.

"Why didn't you tell me you had a fiancé, that you were going to be married?" Rita accused.

"Why didn't you tell me you were living with a homo in Karpatyn?" Dani responded.

"What? Are you going to take a high moral tone about men after being my lover for two years?" Dani was silent, so Rita continued, "You never told me anything about a fiancé, or even so much as a male friend."

"You never asked, and I had every reason to think he was dead."

Rita decided to cut this argument off. "Look, Dani, I have satisfied myself that Stefan is dead. I can't stay in Poland. When can we head back west?"

Dani took a breath. "I'm not . . . I can't go back. I'm staying." She began to cry, seeking Rita's shoulder, but Rita held her away, glaring into her face.

"I've been gone three, maybe four days. What's happened? Is it that boy upstairs? Your father's disapproval?"

"No, no . . . he doesn't know about you, about us."

"What? Didn't you tell him about the last two years?"

"I can't talk with my father, with any man, with anyone at all about . . . about that." Rita thought, *You can't even say "us." Instead, what we had has turned into what we did—"that."* Dani was still talking. "You heard them upstairs."

"Yes." Rita realized she would have been equally unwilling to talk about what she had done with Dani to them or anyone. "I understand, Dani. You don't have to say anything to them. But you're coming, aren't you? Back to Frankfurt?"

Dani shook her head. "No. I can't. I am going to stay. I'll try to make a life with Paul."

"But . . . I love you." As she said it, Rita asked herself whether she believed it, whether it was true. They had never said these things to each other, even in the moments their bodies had responded to each other's touch. What reticence could have come between their bodies to stop them saying it? Now as she said the words, Rita knew they were true.

But Dani shook her head again. "It was the war, Rita. It was the fear, the loss, the abandonment we suffered. It was the need for a little pleasure in a world with none of it. It wasn't really love, the kind you can build lives from."

Now Rita understood. "It's not guilt, it's shame that's driving you away from me. You never felt guilty about lying in my arms, not for a moment. You did love me. You still do. It's what other people will say, the shame they'll extract from you, that is too much for you to bear."

Now Dani burst out, "Yes! It's too much after all this. I just can't keep living a secret anymore—with another woman, under another false identity. It would be a constant reminder of the horror. I can't keep fighting against . . . everything. There's a real life with Paul, with my father. With you, we'd spend our lives pretending we were something we aren't."

It came to Rita: Dani couldn't deal with her love for Rita because she suddenly had a family again. Rita had the luxury of being alone. There was no one to shame her. And she wasn't really the kind of person who could be moved to shame by what others thought anyway. She had known this all the way back to when the bullyboys called her a whore for sitting on the ghetto benches in the lecture theater at the law fac' in Krakow.

Rita pulled Dani toward her, even as her thoughts were pushing Dani away. She knew that there was no reasoning with emotion, no inducement that could convert feelings. There was nothing to do but accept their reality and walk away. She might hope for a change in Dani later, but for now, there was nothing to do but cut her own losses. Rita thought she understood people well enough now not to delude herself about what moved them and what didn't. And then these analytical thoughts were replaced by her own emotions—disdain and anger. "Very well. I understand. Good-bye." She stood back and took a long pull at the cigarette in her hand, as though she were trying to draw a breath from it. Then Rita walked away, trying to control the turmoil inside her, trying both for the sake of her appearance to Dani and for the sake of her own mental balance. To finally lose the hope of Stefan without being able to find oblivion in love was so much to carry. All she wanted now was to sleep, alone, in a room by herself.

If she was going back to Frankfurt, the Polish zlotys in her pocket wouldn't be of much use. She decided to spend them on a hotel room all to herself.

❧

Late the next afternoon, kitted out in her UNRRA uniform, Rita was crossing the street from the Joint hostel to the Katowice railway station when an American jeep with a Red Army insignia pulled up beside her. Out from under the canvas top, an officer's cap emerged. She heard the word, "Rita." It was Urs. He called again, "Rita." She stopped, putting down her bag. "Please get in, Rita. I have been waiting for you to get back for the last few days."

"I just got in last night. What do you want?"

"I want to take you somewhere." Rita waited. "Not far. Forty kilometers . . . Gleiwitz, if you must know." Now she understood.

CHAPTER THIRTY-SEVEN

Urs stopped in front of the Polyclinic door. "Go in and ask for Tadeusz. He knows you're coming. I'll be in the café." He pointed across the street.

"How does he know I'm coming?"

"I told him I'd bring you."

"Pretty sure of yourself, aren't you?"

"Sorry. What I told him was that I would try."

Rita thought, *Well, you didn't have to try very hard.* She had been thinking things through all the way across the rutted roads as mud splattered into the jeep, finding its way between the metal and the canvas top and sides. She recognized that she was worried about how she looked. She couldn't deny the hints of arousal she was feeling. Was it the hard seats and the jostling vehicle? Or was it memories of languid afternoons long ago? Was she so variable in her sexual attractions? *I suppose I am*, she thought with feelings of candor and satisfaction. *Think back to Erich . . . You might have loved him, and let him slake his appetites without possessiveness.*

The real question wasn't whether she could have with a man what she had with Dani. She understood herself well enough to know that she could. The real question was whether she wanted to start again with someone else, so soon, with a man or a woman? And if so, was this the right person? Could there be real . . . compatibility, chemistry, partnership, love, between this man and Rita? Once, in what seemed another world, she had thought so. *Well,* she said to herself, *these questions will soon sort themselves out, thanks to Urs of all people.*

She walked into the clinic and asked for Dr. Sommermann.

"Appointment?"

Rita thought briefly. "I suppose so."

"What name?" The nurse looked up at her, holding the receiver.

Good question, she thought. Feuerstahl, Guildenstern, Trushenko? "Just tell him it's Rita, please."

❧

At least the chemistry was there. She could feel it grow even as he walked down the hall toward her, grinning, then smiling, finally laughing with delight. It was infectious, and despite the admonitions of caution she had imposed on herself, she too began to smile, rather sheepishly.

"You are alive! You are here!" He repeated it three times. But he didn't reach out to touch her, as though fearing she would dissolve, disappear, evaporate, evanesce.

"So are you." She said it quietly. Finally she reached out, and their hands met.

"How did you make it?" Was he asking or exclaiming?

"Same as you, I think. A great deal of chance and not much foresight."

He turned to the receptionist. "I'm finished for the day, Nurse." He took off the white coat and pulled a suit jacket from the closet at the desk. Turning to Rita he said, "There's a café across the street."

"Urs is there, waiting to take me back to Katowice."

"Should we tell him to wait?"

"No." Her emphatic reply surprised both of them.

❧

She and Tadeusz were two hours in the café, getting slightly drunk on Romanian wine, telling each other a few half-truths, several three-quarter truths, but only a few complete truths about their respective trajectories through the years since 1938.

It was dark long before they noticed. Tadeusz looked up at the gloom. "Dinner?"

"Can we get a good meal anywhere in Gleiwitz?"

"Only at my place," he replied. She agreed with alacrity.

They walked arm in arm. Rita searched her feelings as they did so. *I did this last with Dani, when she was still Dani to the world. Does it feel as natural now? Yes. I don't understand it, but I can live with it.*

"I'd like to make you a Barcelona paella, but I just ran out of saffron." Rita missed his joke, and Tadeusz decided that explaining it would be a mistake. "I got a half dozen real eggs from a grateful patient yesterday. I am going to make you a Spanish treat, a tortilla de patatas."

❧

Dinner over, Rita offered Tadeusz an American cigarette. He lit hers and then his. Both leaned back, exhaling smoke through their nostrils. Watching Rita do this aroused Tadeusz. Remembering their afternoons eight years ago, Rita immediately realized its effect on him.

"Rita, will you marry me?"

Before she could answer, he came around behind her and bent over, his lips reaching hers as she turned her head up. He slid his hands from her shoulders to her breasts and felt the nipples harden through her khaki uniform shirt as she deftly unbuttoned it. At the same time she rose, pirouetting to face him. They began tearing their clothes off.

"So, we'll get married and live happily ever after." He stopped for a moment, but not to hear her answer. "Not here, not in Poland, and not as Mr. and Mrs. Tadeusz Sommermann." He had not noticed that his proposal had been left unanswered.

"You have it all worked out?"

"No. I have only filled in a few of the blanks. It's up to you to fill in all the others. We'll live where you want, so long as it isn't Poland. You don't want to stay here, do you?" Rita shook her head. "And I don't want to be Tadeusz Sommermann. I want to be Guillermo Romero. I'll go anywhere I can become him again."

Later they made love again, with infinite slowness, teasing and tempting, each bringing the other to the brink again and again, before finally spilling over the precipice together, punctuated by spasms from her, modulated by long moans from him. Then he collapsed on top of her. It was the way they had done it once, before the world had gone to war. Each quietly rejoiced in the reality that they had been able to do it still.

In the haze of smoke rising from two more cigarettes, they lay next to each other staring up at a ceiling, watching headlamps occasionally play across it. He spoke first. "Rita Romero. Has a nice ring to it, no?"

"Gil"—she was already calling him that, and he liked it—"I think I prefer my own name, Feuerstahl, Rita Feuerstahl, no matter what happens."

He didn't seem to notice the possibilities the statement implied, or if he did, he had decided not to respond to the provocation. "Shall I tell you how I managed to survive?" Gil was expecting a warm invitation to begin a romantic narrative that would occasion expressions of surprise, admiration, even enjoyment, and in the end satisfaction. But his words hung in the silence.

Finally Rita responded. "Not now, Gil. I think I know why you and I survived. That's enough."

Months later, working backward, Rita was sure her twins had been conceived that night in Gleiwitz.

∾

The next morning, in two uniforms—UNRRA and Soviet Army Medical Corps—they left for Brno. It cost Gil a nice Swiss watch to get them both there in comfort, and another one to cross the Czech border at Bratislava. A few weeks later, Rita was working at the tracing desk in the Salzburg railway station, and Gil was the medical officer for six displaced person camps in the American zone of upper Austria. And they were living in the loveliest apartment in the city, requisitioned by the US Army from a Nazi family.

∾

August 1947. Mirabelle Gardens, Salzburg, Austria. One could sit there all day, looking up at the castle under the hard blue Alpine sky. Rita listened to the fine white gravel crunch as people strolled, dogs scampered, and small children trudged, pushing the small stones ahead, their open-toed sandals making wakes behind. Late every afternoon she would bring her twins, pull each from the pram, and allow them to crawl, toddle, and begin to walk along the low hedges in the grassy rectangles that surrounded the fountain.

Rita sat at a distance rather greater than a young mother might have. The boys were not her first, and she knew toddlers were not fragile. A woman approached. "May I?" She pointed to the space next to Rita's. Rita nodded without really looking up, and she sat down.

The woman took a book from her bag and laid it on her lap. It was Polish. Rita looked more closely at the cover. *Lord Tadeusz*, the epic poem Dani had been reading that first day they met at the Terakowski works in 1942.

The woman opened the volume at a place marked by a ribbon and began to read.

As she held a page down, Rita noticed her finger ends. No nails, none at all. It was too late to dissimulate her look of discomfort when the woman happened to glance at Rita. The woman flushed slightly and closed her fists, hiding the nailless finger ends.

Rita addressed her in Polish. "I know that book."

The woman smiled. "It meant a lot to me in the war."

"Me too."

Now Rita looked up from her fingernails to her face. She was about thirty-five, thin, tall, with short, prematurely gray hair. So short it had to have been completely cut off and recently regrown. Delousing? Rita speculated to herself. The face was lined by experience, and there was a scar across the forehead. *This woman's war was worse than mine.* There also was something else about her. Her mouth seemed slightly tilted to the right. A stroke, a birth trauma?

The woman closed her book and began to speak. "The Germans took them—the fingernails." She opened up her hands again and contemplated the fingers.

"That's what I thought."

"I was in the Polish Home Army. They caught me. I wouldn't talk. They took one fingernail each day. Then they let me go."

"Very brave."

"Not really. If I had confessed, they surely would have killed me." She glanced toward the boy coming up the path toward them, who seemed to be about seven. "And then, he would have had no one." Rita looked at the woman's left hand. No ring.

The child had approached and was patiently waiting to speak. "*Mutti*, my sailboat." The woman reached into the bag beside her and handed the child his toy. "Here you are, Stefan."

"Thank you." The child kissed the woman, went off to the pool in the middle of the garden, and launched his craft.

There was no doubt. You don't forget your own child's face, and it doesn't change that much from almost three to seven. And then it all came back to her. The courier—the woman to whom Rita had handed over her son. The tilted mouth, the beautiful nails. The nails that had been pulled out, one by one. Rita's feeling of admiration for the woman was instantly replaced by gratitude. Keeping Stefan, protecting him, raising him, had cost this woman so much. The boy before her was fine-looking and evidently happy. How could Rita ever repay her for what she had done at such expense to herself? The love this woman must have lavished on a child who was not hers. Rita could never pay this debt, but she would have to try. She began thinking how. But the ideas of recompense were flooded away by the urgency that the boy know Rita was his mother. Then came the need to shout his name, search his face for recognition, rush to the sailing pool, sweep him into her arms.

The woman hadn't noticed the sudden joy in Rita's face. She had closed her book and begun surveying the toddlers a few meters away. Then she spoke. "My name is Francis . . . Sajac. My friends call me Frania." She offered her hand and smiled. "Making acquaintance on a park bench used to be frowned upon before the war. But it's a different world, isn't it?"

Before she realized what she was doing, Rita had taken her hand and returned the smile. "I'm Rita Feuerstahl. Pleased to make your acquaintance." But she was just mouthing the words, her thoughts absorbed by all the wonderful complications of recovering her son.

He would have to learn that he wasn't Stefan Sajac after all. She would have to tell Urs. There wasn't much he would do, far to the east, with a new family, on the wrong side of a border no one could easily cross. What about Gil? He wasn't Stefan's father, had never even seen the boy. Would he be a problem? It didn't matter. But what about this woman Stefan had just called *Mutti*? She had to remain part of his life—and Rita's.

She looked at the woman, whose glance had turned to Stefan circling the fountain to tend his sailboat. Then she thought, *This woman, smiling with love for her child, has no way of knowing what she is about to lose.* How would Rita assuage her for the loss she was going to suffer? How could Rita keep her as part of Stefan's life?

Her new friend interrupted these thoughts. "I'm from Radom. What part of Poland do you hail from?"

How should Rita reply? She had only to mention the town she had sent Stefan from or the town she had sent him to. The coincidence would unravel in a few more questions, and Stefan would be hers again.

Suddenly she realized she could not let that happen. He could not share the joy she was feeling. For Stefan the reunion would first be confusion, and then bereavement for the only protection and love he could really remember. He had been torn from his mother once already. And it was Rita who had done it. She would not take Stefan from his mother a second time. Then she felt again the pain of that loss, sending him away in the hope he would survive. She couldn't inflict such pain on the woman who had sacrificed herself to save Stefan.

Rita repeated the woman's question, "Where am I from?"

Then she knew what she had to say. "I'm from Krakow." Gesturing toward her twins playing on the manicured grass, she continued, "Those are my boys. I hope they grow up to be as polite as your son."

ABOUT THE AUTHOR

Photo © 2011 Jim Wallace

Alex Rosenberg has written many books about philosophy and science, including the widely reviewed *Atheist's Guide to Reality*. He teaches at Duke University. *The Girl from Krakow* is his first novel. He and his twin brother were born in Salzburg, Austria, in 1946.